C000088504

Pam Charles was born in Leeds. She had twenty years in the insurance industry before she had her second child and was diagnosed with Ménières Syndrome. In 2008 she went back to study at Leeds Metropolitan University and graduated in 2011 with a 1st class honours degree. Shortly after, she started to write again. In 2013 she set up her own company and her book was accepted for publication.

She has two boys; her eldest is in the Sheffield Eagles Scholarship programme. She is a huge Liverpool FC fan (long story), a season ticket holder at Leeds Rhinos and a self-confessed petrol head.

Beyond the Past

Pam Charles

Beyond the Past

Vanguard Press

VANGUARD PAPERBACK

© Copyright 2014
Pam Charles

The right of Pam Charles to be identified as author of
this work has been asserted by her in accordance with the
Copyright, Designs and Patents Act 1988.

All Rights Reserved

No reproduction, copy or transmission of this publication
may be made without written permission.
No paragraph of this publication may be reproduced,
copied or transmitted save with the written permission of the publisher, or in
accordance with the provisions
of the Copyright Act 1956 (as amended).

Any person who commits any unauthorised act in relation to
this publication may be liable to criminal
prosecution and civil claims for damages.

A CIP catalogue record for this title is
available from the British Library.

ISBN 978-1-84386-789-0

Vanguard Press is an imprint of
Pegasus Elliot MacKenzie Publishers Ltd.
www.pegasuspublishers.com

First Published in 2014

Vanguard Press
Sheraton House Castle Park
Cambridge England

Printed & Bound in Great Britain

To my darling boys, Wesley and Lucas – your dreams can be fulfilled through hard work, determination and self-belief. Reach for the stars and you will always shine. Love always from a very lucky Mummy.

This book is dedicated to anyone who dares to have a go!

I also dedicate this book to the families of the victims of Hillsborough – your strength and determination is a shining light for all of us to follow. God Bless JFT96.

Acknowledgements

Mum and Dad – always there to help and pick me up. Thank you will never be enough.

Lisa Wightman – my Big Sister. Your input was so important to me. My harshest critic – I knew you would be brutally honest but true. Thank you for all your support and enthusiasm. Get ready to resume your editing services.

State of Mind Charity – a fabulous charity, looking after the mental health and well-being of the Rugby League community and beyond. Keep up your inspiring work.

Part One

Why Us?

1

Just past the Halifax junction on the M62, Mark Smith noticed a car tailing him. It had been there for about three miles. After recent events, he changed lanes a few times, the car followed. Annie sensed his anxiety and watched him cautiously looking through his mirror. Suddenly the car overtook them and lingered at their side. Mark looked across to see the driver but the tinted windows prevented any identification. He slowed down, the car slowed down. The cat and mouse antics went on for a couple of miles.

"Annie! Ed! Keep your wits about you. Annie ring Harry and let him know. When I slow down see if one of you can get the registration number," Mark instructed.

Annie's heart was pounding but she was more concerned she had one of her precious boys with them. Ed wasn't at all fazed. He was watching Mark intensely. Mark braked suddenly and the car skidded to the left. It was enough for Ed to take a note of the registration number. However, the car slowed down and pulled in front of them. Mark was forced to brake hard to avoid a collision.

Annie Swift's life flashed before her eyes. She'd not had an easy life; her first marriage was violent and the only good thing to come out of it all was her eldest son, Matt. Oh God! Matt she thought. He was on the verge of re-signing a contract to play Rugby League for his home town, the club she had supported as a child with her grandpa. She didn't want her life to end now! Her mum and dad needed her, her boys needed her and most of all she'd finally met someone she could grow old with, who loved her unconditionally and made her happy at last. Life had been cruel but it was worth the heartache to have such beautiful boys and now a new partner. She had come through so much and was finally in a good place in her life. It was inconceivable it could end now.

"Shit!" Mark shouted as he swerved out to the middle lane. As he tried to overtake the car, it too increased its speed. Then, without warning the pursuer swerved into the middle lane, again Mark's defensive driving avoided contact but this was getting really scary.

Annie was shouting down the phone to DCI Harry Fisher.

Ed turned to Mark. "Mark keep calm you are doing great. I think we should try and get off the motorway at the next exit."

Annie interrupted, "Harry suggested that too. I am going to put the phone on loudspeaker so we can tell him what's happening."

Just as she said this, Mark managed to manoeuvre past the car. He was an ex professional rugby player, not a racing driver! He put his foot down and was doing ninety-five mph when the car came right up behind him. There was no getting away from it. Mark was shaking but was trying his best to get them out of trouble.

"The next junction, junction twenty-four, is coming up. I'm going to let him pass us and then slip off the motorway."

DCI Fisher's voice bellowed, "Mark, listen to me, do not do anything stupid! Stay within the law, we will be there shortly. The motorway police are three minutes away and the helicopter five. Stay calm but do not, I repeat do not speed." Mark realised it was stupid trying to outrun the car. The shaking subsided a little as he reduced his speed to seventy. The car overtook him again but this time re-joined his lane and slammed on again in front of him. Annie and Ed screamed and Annie lifted her hands to her face.

Mark swerved again and braked but it was not enough. The passenger side front wing clipped the rear of the car in front. It spun the BMW out of control and into the central reservation. The airbags activated.

For what seemed an eternity the three of them said nothing. Annie could hear the faint sirens of the emergency vehicles. The searing pain from her leg was unbearable.

"Mum! Mum you okay?" She recognised Ed's voice.

She tried to speak but the words wouldn't come out. She nodded but wasn't sure if her head actually moved. The pain was taking over, it was so, so intense. She could hear Ed and Mark's voice and a strange distant voice calling her name, she recognised it was Harry but couldn't understand why he was there. She passed out.

Ed and Mark walked out of the mangled mess and sat in an ambulance close by. Both shocked, Ed had a small cut on his left cheek and on his hand where a splinter of glass had hit him. It seemed a very strange situation to him. He was sitting calmly in an ambulance whilst the scene outside was pandemonium. None of it seemed real. It resembled a scene from a Bruce Willis blockbuster.

Panicking Ed stood up, hitting his head on the roof of the ambulance and shouted, "MUM, Mum I have to get to her." Mark grabbed his arm and beckoned him to sit down.

"Ed we can't do anything, leave it to the professionals mate. They know what they are doing." Mark was trying to stay calm for Ed's sake but inside he was erupting like a volcano. He wanted to hold her; please God please let her be all right, he thought, tears welling in his eyes.

Ed held his arm. They stayed together watching the carnage. The cutting equipment grinded on the car's frame and made them both cringe. They watched intently as Annie was released from the vehicle. She was now talking and semi-coherent. Mark and Ed came out of the ambulance to greet her on the stretcher. She had a drip in her arm, and blood all down her face from a gash on the bridge of her nose, she whispered, "I'm fine," to both Mark and Ed who now had tears rolling down their faces. The paramedic told them she had a suspected broken leg, concussion and bruising from the airbag but they weren't listening. As they lifted her into the ambulance, a familiar face emerged from the flashing lights.

"Mark, she is going to be okay," Harry said. "The same can't be said for your car. I will come to the hospital shortly and see you all. Take care of each other."

Huddersfield Royal Infirmary was not a place any of them liked, especially Annie as the last time she visited was to say goodbye to her beloved grandpa. The buildings were old and resembled blocks of flats built in the 1960s. Inside the paint was peeling from the walls in spite of recent refurbishment.

Mark was impatient with the nurse and considered any time spent on him was wasted. He had a couple of bruises on his face and sore ribs. All he wanted to do was be with Annie.

Ed was pretty much the same, but he found amusement in telling the nurses he was a professional rugby player and enjoyed their fussing over him. They told him the cuts were superficial and he laughed that they wouldn't spoil his good looks.

Finally Mark and Ed were free to see Annie. She was being treated in the next cubicle but the doctor was with her when they arrived. They paced up and down until he emerged from behind the curtain.

"Mrs Swift has concussion and a broken leg," the doctor declared. Ed thought, tell me something we don't know but he didn't say it. The doctor continued, "We are going to send her for a CT scan and an X-ray. She will be staying with us this evening and we may need to operate on her leg depending upon the extent of the damage. You can see her now if you like."

If we like, Mark thought as they raced like school children behind the curtain. Annie smiled back at them but her facial injuries made them both stop in their tracks. Ed hugged his mum; he wanted to hug her tightly but was afraid of adding to her pain. Mark stood back and let mother and son have some time together. Ed was sobbing into his mum's chest.

"Ed it's okay, I, we are all fine. We will sort this. Come on baby you will be okay, it's just a shock."

Ed lifted his head up and wiped his face on his sleeve. "But Mum I don't know what we would do if we lost you. You are everything to me and Matt and if we'd have lost you." He laid back onto her chest. Annie looked at Mark; tears were running down his cheeks too.

Annie soothingly rubbed her son's head and gestured for Mark to come towards her. With her other hand she held Mark's hand too.

"You're a right pair you two aren't you, I'm the one laid here waiting in this crappy place for people to prod and poke me and you two go to pieces. I will be fine, you will just have to run round after me for a bit that's all."

Mark squeezed her hand, which made her grimace. She was concealing the fact that her whole body hurt from her head to the tips of her toes.

Ed composed himself. "I'll do anything, Mum, anything. I am coming home from London after this season, I want to be near you, Matt and Mark." She hugged him and suggested he went to call Matt. As Ed walked out of the cubicle, Annie stroked Mark's hand and said, "Look at me Mark. You haven't looked me in the face since you came in." It was true Mark had not looked at her; he was ashamed that he had not protected her. He wished it were him lying there instead of her.

Mark's eyes welled as he spoke. "I am so so so sorry Annie. This is all my fault. I am bad news and look at my beautiful, beautiful angel lying here."

Annie was firm. "Mark, listen to me. This is not your doing. This is mad, nothing you have brought on. We need to get it sorted; this is more sinister than we thought. I am scared someone could get killed, we could have got killed but it's not your fault. In fact I believe you saved our lives. Your driving was great Mark, great."

Just as she finished, Harry walked in. The shock on his face was self-explanatory as Mark and Ed had had the same look when they first saw Annie.

Harry cleared his throat. "I need statements from you but not tonight. The car you hit was abandoned by the time we got there." The disappointment was clearly visible on his face.

He continued, "We are going to leave a policeman here with you tonight Annie. What are you intending on doing?" he said turning to Mark.

Without hesitation Mark confirmed, "Ed and I will be staying here. We have already discussed it and we are not leaving without Annie."

"I have sent a car for Matt to come here too." He paused. "This is now an attempted murder case."

Annie and Mark looked at each other. This was no longer just a few notes and strange happenings. This had taken a turn for the worse, much worse.

"I will be back in the morning for your statements. Look after each other." Harry smiled and left.

It seemed hours until the doctor re-emerged even though it had only been half an hour. "Right Mrs Swift, I am sending you down for your CT scan now."

"Can I go with her please?" Mark asked.

Shaking his head the doctor said, "I'm afraid not, you can go with her for the X-ray but not the scan. I'll show you to the relatives' room and you can come back to see Mrs Swift when she returns."

"Annie, please call me Annie," Annie interrupted.

The doctor raised a faint smirk and continued, "You can come back to sit with Annie when she returns."

The curtain burst open and Matt, Annie's eldest son, ran through throwing himself at his mum. They hugged and both cried.

Annie reassured her son, "I am fine Matt honestly."

Matt got up and moved towards Mark. "My God Mark, you okay too?" He hugged him tightly. It was an adoring hug, which took Mark completely by surprise. He felt sure he would come in and smack him in the mouth; after all it was because of him they were in there.

Annie was wheeled out for the CT scan. The boys moved into the relatives' room, adjoining the ward. It was going to be a very long night. Matt and Ed went to find some refreshments and left Mark on his own.

Mark sat staring at the pale blue wall. The room was bright but cool and had a sense of grief in its walls. What had just happened tonight? He remembered the car but just couldn't remember how they had come to rest in the central reservation. He shut his eyes but could only see the flashing blue lights and Annie; oh Annie's blood-soaked face. He cupped his hands around his face and wept uncontrollably. He heard the door open but didn't care. His baby was hurt and his past had caused all this. He shouldn't have tracked her down.

"Mark." He heard a voice and looked up. "Mark, where is she?" Andrea, Annie's mum wept.

"They have taken her for a CT scan," he said wiping his eyes.

Annie's father, Charles sat down at the side of him and Andrea at the other side. Andrea held Mark's hand. "The police have told us what happened, you are all safe now thank God." She squeezed his hand.

Mark looked up at her and at Charles. They had both been crying. What had he done? These beautiful people adored Annie and he had caused all this pain. He started crying again. Andrea just held him. Matt and Ed returned with the drinks.

Matt, shocked at Mark's state said, "What's happened, what?"

Andrea replied, "Nothing more love, your mum is okay."

Ed stood behind Mark and laid his hands on his shoulders. "Come on mate, we can all work this out together."

Over the next few hours, Mark and Ed filled Matt, Andrea and Charles in with the whole story. Mark was convinced they would hate him but to his surprise they did not. On the contrary they wanted to help, not just Annie but him too. He loved this family they were so supportive and positive. It's a shame his family had not been the same.

The doctor interrupted the discussion. "Annie's CT scan is clear. If you want to see her you can. She will be going for the X-ray shortly. If you could keep the noise down and say two to the bed at a time." They all nodded.

They agreed Andrea and Charles would go first. Mark was going to accompany Annie to the X-ray and Ed and Matt would go and see her when Grannie and Gramps had finished. Andrea and Charles fussed over Annie and made her feel exhausted. When they returned to the relatives' room, Matt and Ed ran in to see their mum. She looked a lot better with her clean face. The nurse came in once or twice to calm the laughter down until it was time for Annie's X-ray.

The porter wheeled her down to the department with Mark tagging along, not letting go of Annie's hand once. It was confirmed that Annie had broken her left leg but thankfully didn't need surgery. By 3 a.m. she had her plaster cast on. Mark slept in the chair beside her bed and the boys and grandparents occupied the relatives' room.

*

2

Days before the incident...

Annie couldn't help but smile. It had been a lovely evening, one she hadn't expected. Her experience of dates, although limited, was dull and boring but this one had been different. Climbing into the taxi, she shouted, "Ninety-six Pembroke Place, please." She sank into the back seat and slipped into deep thought. In reality she had only ever had two men in her life and one fling but they had left her mentally and physically scarred. She wondered why this one felt different even after only two glorious evenings. Her instinct told her she could trust Mark but she'd been wrong before.

"That will be seventeen ninety-five, Miss." The taxi driver broke Annie's thoughts. She grappled around for her purse, paid and exited the car. The gate was bolted when she tried to push it open, almost dislocating her shoulder. Smiling to herself she unlatched the lock. Stepping inside she couldn't help but turn and scour the street, she felt sure she was being watched. The paranoia continued inside the house. Annie quickly drew the curtains and lit the open fire. The house was a semi-detached and too big now the boys had grown up and moved on but it was her home. She spent most of her time in the bright airy kitchen. At one end was the range oven she had longed for and now only used once or twice a year for cooking and at the other a farmhouse kitchen table that held so many happy memories she felt loathed to part with it. Instead it had become her makeshift office. During the summer months sunlight beamed through the large double glazed windows and in winter the warmth from the range provided a homely feel the rest of the house sadly lacked. From time to time the house would be once again filled with laughter and childish behaviour but for now the boys were pursuing their own lives.

Nights out with colleagues and friends were great but coming home to an empty house didn't always suit Annie. At forty-seven it seemed to take her weeks to recover from one night out! After a drink of tea and flicking through the forty-plus channels, Annie retired.

Annie had barely reached over the threshold when she was bombarded with questions.

"So come on, how was last night? Did you see Mark again? What happened? Did he come home?" demanded Lucy as Annie walked into the café at the college. Simultaneously Annie's phone chimed twice in quick succession notifying her of two text messages.

Annie looked at Lucy, a twenty-five-year-old slight build girl, with long blonde hair and so full of life. She was a good companion when things were tough even though she was incredibly naïve. "Let me grab a coffee and we'll sit over there in the corner. I'll tell you the boring details…" Annie added. "It was only the second time I have seen him so don't expect too much." She smiled, walked over to the counter and ordered two skinny lattes. Once she had her fix within her grasp, she turned towards Lucy to find another colleague had joined them. John, a senior lecturer at the college, insisted on letting everyone know he was the longest serving member of staff. He was in his fifties, silver hair and well maintained. His wife had died eight months previous. Since her death, Annie and he had spent a number of hours talking about their lives. Annie was very fond of John and considered him a good friend yet her colleagues felt he had more than friendship on his agenda.

Annie joined her two colleagues, hidden in a corner near the window, both eager to hear of her escapades the night before. The September sun was beaming through the window, reflecting off the metal tables. Annie was particularly cagey, as she did not really know what to say. Yes, she had enjoyed Mark's company but she couldn't really admit to her friends, let alone herself that she was deeply attracted to him after just two evenings.

"So come on I can't wait any longer, I would have texted you last night but I didn't know whether he would have been there with you." Lucy was beyond excited; she was like a child waiting for Christmas. Although this childish anticipation was endearing to Annie it wound John up.

"Oh Lucy it's not that big a deal," he moaned.

Lucy cross with his tone, "Well it is to me. I'd love to see my best friend in a happy and loving relationship; God knows she deserves it after all she has been through."

John reacted angrily to the accusation that he did not share Lucy's desire for Annie to be happy and snapped, "And I suppose I don't want her to be happy."

Annie interjected, waving her hands in the air, "Guys, hi I'm here."

There was an awkward silence before Annie spoke again. "Last night was great. I really enjoyed being treated like a lady. He has this sophistication about him that I can't put into words but he is lovely, down to earth and nice." Annie paused to think of last night and how Mark had behaved. The perfect gentleman.

They had met at 7.30 p.m. at the Crowne Plaza Hotel. Lucy had warned Annie the previous day not to meet at a hotel, it might give off the wrong signals – Annie smiled wryly thinking it wasn't such a bad idea! Mark was waiting outside the hotel and they had walked to the local pub just around the corner. Annie remembered being really nervous but her fears were dispelled when they had sat down in the corner with their drinks. Mark had ordered a bottle of Cabernet Sauvignon and two glasses. At first, there was an awkward silence between each sip of wine but as the wine flowed, the conversation loosened. During the silent moments, Annie had the opportunity to study her companion. Mark, a former rugby player, was tall and well built. He had thick brown hair, greying around his ears and the most striking blue eyes. It was obvious he had still maintained his fitness after retirement. Apart from the battle scars of a broken nose he had a fresh clean look. Annie suspected he was in his early forties but it was hard to gauge from his looks.

"ANNIE!" shouted Lucy. Annie jumped and so did the other occupants of the café. "Jeez you're not telling us it was a 'good' night and he was 'nice' when you sit there in a deep trance with a smile on your face. SPILL the beans now!" she demanded, leaning over the table towards Annie.

Annie, startled out of her daydream, looked at her watch. "Guys it's ten a.m. I should be in class now." Getting up, Annie turned to Lucy. "I'll catch up with you at lunchtime." With that she glided out of the café.

The morning's lessons were torture for Annie – two first year lessons full of freshers, keen to start their new ICT courses. Annie was glad she had spent hours preparing work and lessons. Students were given their tasks. She pretended to be busy but her mind wandered. Lunchtime took an eternity to arrive. Annie dismissed her final morning class and suddenly remembered the unread text messages from the morning. Fumbling around in her handbag, she finally located her phone – there were three unread messages. Eager to find out the details, Annie closed the lecture room door and sat down on the first available seat. The first message was from Matthew, her eldest son, checking up to see if his mum had survived the night out. Matt wasn't yet aware it had been a date, there was no point raising suspicions until Annie was sure something was to come of it. The second message was from Mark, oh my God from Mark she thought. Suddenly she remembered exchanging mobile numbers with him as they left the pub to say goodnight. With trepidation she opened the text and read it out loud. *Hi, really enjoyed last night. Would love to see you again as soon as possible, tonight if you're free? Let me know, I have a meeting in Manchester at 3pm but can be back for 5. M x.* Annie read the message over and over again. Finally she closed the message and read the third message which was a reminder from her mum that they were having lunch on Monday, Annie's half day.

"Shit!" Annie exclaimed. She had completely forgotten her promise of lunch with Lucy. Annie gathered her belongings and ran to the café where she found Lucy sitting at the same table as this morning, this time alone.

"I am so so sorry," Annie said whilst throwing her coat and bag onto the chair. "I was catching up on a few things when…"

Lucy shaking her head said, "It's okay Annie, I don't mind being stood up," and they both laughed.

"I am glad we are alone this time Lucy. I wanted to tell you everything this morning but I don't think John approves of me dating or looking for my soul mate at my time of life."

Lucy mocking, "At your time of life, oh Annie, don't you know he fancies the pants off you and he's jealous?"

"Nonsense," interrupted Annie. "Anyway about last night… Mark was a perfect gentleman. He met me at the door of the hotel and we went to the West Riding Pub around the corner. Nothing flashy, just nice wine in a quiet quaint pub. It was lovely… he is lovely."

Lucy stared straight into Annie's face. "Oh Annie you really do like him don't you? I have not seen you this distracted before. Just be careful Annie but if he is the one go for it!"

Annie smiled but didn't really have anything to say. "Oh God, what is wrong with me?" she said as she grappled around in her bag. "He sent me a text message and I've forgotten to reply." Annie read the message out to Lucy who beamed with pleasure.

"Meet him tonight," she said hastily. "Don't mess him around Annie, give him a chance."

Lucy knew Annie had a tendency to dither when it came to decent men and that the longer she logically thought about things, the more likely it was for Annie to talk herself out of it or worse she would start to doubt who he was.

"There," Annie declared, "done it. I am meeting him tonight." Before the sentence had been completed, a reply had been received confirming the rendezvous time and place.

The girls chatted over lunch and Annie departed to her afternoon lessons with a very light heart. At 4.30 p.m. she left the college and returned home, once again feeling sure she was being watched as she entered the garden gate.

3

Although September was drawing to a close, it was a beautiful evening with a warm southerly breeze, still summer clothing weather. Annie had settled on a three quarter length print dress, which had seen a revival that summer, covered only by a white crotched shawl her mum had made her.

Mark was waiting, once again on the front walkway of the hotel. He was dressed in smart black jeans and a semi tight short-sleeved shirt that emphasised his well-built physique. He opened the taxi door for Annie to alight and placed his hand on her back giving her a loving kiss on her cheek. She felt sure she had gasped a little.

Still holding her in his grasp, Mark whispered, "Have you eaten? I'd like to take you to one of my favourite pubs tonight."

Annie replied, "No I haven't eaten and that would be lovely."

"Then we need to go by car as it is just on the outskirts of the city." A little wary, Annie complied and Mark led her to his car, a navy blue BMW M3 convertible. They headed south of the city. Annie again had the opportunity to survey her suitor. She never had him down as flashy and was surprised at the car. Mark interrupted Annie's daydreams.

"So this pub is owned by one of my friends, someone I used to play rugby with. He is a bit rough around the edges but a good mate. I hope," he paused to check the traffic then continued, "you don't mind me introducing you to some of my friends but I have to confess I really like you."

Annie blushed. He continued, "I am sorry Annie I didn't mean to embarrass you. I just thought it would be great to go somewhere where we can continue chatting."

Annie apologetically said, "Mark I just wasn't expecting what you said. I am more than happy to meet your friends and I really want to spend as much time as I can with you…" There, she thought, I've said it. He now knew her interest. With that, he slowly lifted his hand and placed it on Annie's leg. They looked at each other, smiled and Annie returned the gesture by placing her hand on his.

The pub was situated close to the river and as they pulled up to the car park, Annie was delighted to see the evening sun reflecting over the rippling water. She got out of the car and couldn't help but stand for a moment to take in the peaceful still of the September evening. Her trance was broken when Mark gently placed his arms around her shoulders and kissed the back of her neck. Annie clasped her arms around him.

Mark whispered in her ear, "I told you it was beautiful… Annie I wanted to share it with you." With that he kissed her ear once more before slowly turning her to him. He kissed her again on the lips and Annie offered no resistance. Annie felt she was walking on air as he led her into the bar.

"Now then Mark," said a portly, bald man from behind the bar. "How are you big man? Err. This must be your latest conquest…" It was obvious this last remark both hurt and embarrassed Mark. Annie was taken aback and suddenly felt she had been thrown into yet another situation where she was going to be left hurt and wounded. Garry grabbed Annie and gave her a big squeeze.

"Oh Garry, you're such an idiot. This is Annie." Mark glanced at Annie who was clearly mortified at being the latest conquest.

Garry went on, "I've saved the table by the window for you." He led the couple to the back of the room. The building looked like an old mill that had been converted. The bare stone walls were littered with Rugby League memorabilia, including pictures of Mark in his playing days. Annie tried to maintain interest in Garry but couldn't help but glance at all the framed shirts and photographs. The rear of the bar was beautifully lit partly from the setting sun and the large amount of conservatory type windows servicing it. To Annie's delight the table overlooked the gently rippling water.

Mark pulled the chair out and signalled for Annie to sit down. He sat opposite and looked straight into her eyes.

"Don't take Garry too seriously; he's an old rugby mate."

Annie interrupted, "So I'm your latest conquest?"

"No Annie. I have had two serious women in my life."

"So how many not serious?" Annie interjected.

Mark smiled but blushed. "I think you have completely the wrong impression of me. I have not seen anyone for the last ten years, well actually twelve but who's counting! I admit I have had dates but nothing that has led to even the third date," he laughed.

Annie smiled too. "So there's hope for me then," she added.

Mark stood up to pour the wine into the glasses. As he did, he leant over Annie's shoulder and gently whispered, "There is more than hope."

He placed the bottle in the middle of the table and sat back down.

An awkward silence was interrupted by Garry who plonked himself in the chair next to Annie.

"I will leave you alone shortly but I just want to say I was only joking when you walked in. Mark is a sound guy and if you are half as lovely as he says you are, you will be well suited. I do hope you can make this sorry bastard happy again." Garry left the table.

Annie and Mark watched him leave the room, then looked at each other and laughed. That one moment seemed to break the ice between them and the conversation flowed all night. Mark told Annie he had been married but it had ended in a very messy and nasty divorce. He explained his wife was insanely jealous and insecure. With his career in its prime, she used to be paranoid about losing him on drunken nights away with the lads. She never understood how much Mark actually loved her and according to his account, he would never have cheated on her especially as he doted on his daughter. In the end the paranoia drove them apart. They divorced and he was banished to spending every other weekend with his daughter. Sophie was at University now in Manchester and that was where he had been that afternoon. His face beamed with pride.

It struck Annie how honest he appeared to be and how he wasn't afraid to show he was upset. It was an endearing quality she loved. Annie was thankful they had spent the evening talking about Mark's past, if she unleashed her terrible past he would run a mile in the opposite direction.

Mark continued his story during coffee. He had won the Rugby League title twice, once with Garry.

"Shall we set off back now?" Mark suggested. Annie nodded.

They bid goodnight to Garry who scuttled around the bar and landed a huge kiss on Annie's cheek. "Be seeing you," he said. He turned to Mark and warned, "You better keep hold of this one." They hugged.

Mark reached out for Annie's hand and led her to the back of his car. He pulled her close and tenderly kissed her, squeezing her gently. Annie obliged and really did not want him to let go. Only the flash of another set of headlights made the couple retreat to the car.

Mark started the engine, put the gear into reverse then stopped.

He put the handbrake on and leant over to place his hand over Annie's right cheek, he whispered, "Thank you," and with that his lips caressed hers. Annie sighed, closed her eyes and sank against the leather interior of the car. His warm tongue slowly moved around her mouth. She had never been kissed with such fervour or passion but yet tender. She held her hands around his tight muscles feeling very safe and secure. When Mark tried to sit upright, Annie did not want to let him go. He looked straight into her eyes but moved back over to the driver's side.

For what seemed an eternity neither moved nor spoke.

"I'll drive you home," he said as he reversed the vehicle out.

Not much was said during the journey home. They both glanced every now and then at each other but neither could really find the words.

Annie directed Mark to her house. They arrived outside. Mark leant over to kiss Annie but before he could she said, "Would you like to come in?"

There was no hesitation when Mark replied, "Yes I would love to and I promise not to bend your ear about my sorry past."

Annie grabbed his hand. "That's how we get to know each other."

Getting out of the car, Annie was determined it would be coffee, chat and then the night would be over. She repeated this to herself as she unlocked the door and put on the kettle. She was reaching up for the coffee cups when Mark came up behind her and reached over her for the cups. Once he had placed the cups on the side his hands were drawn to her waist. Her hair was tied up and her bare neck was too inviting not to be kissed. Mark kissed her and she felt her legs buckle. She wriggled round to face him, found her body consumed by his and sank into him with such ease. He held her tight. His hands roamed up and down her back whilst he kissed her slowly over her neck and lips. Annie kicked her shoes off and shrank by a further three inches.

The couple broke apart when the kettle reached boiling point. Annie, full of excitement and passion, hurriedly made the coffees and led Mark into the living room. They sat close together on the sofa but stared into the fire drinking their coffee. Annie could not stand the suspense any longer; she put her cup on the table, took Mark's cup off him and placed it next to hers. She knelt on the sofa next to Mark and kissed him on the lips. He reciprocated and pulled her across his lap.

Mark whispered in her ear, "Take me to bed please." Getting up, she held her hand out to Mark and he obliged, stood up and they walked upstairs holding hands.

Both were like teenagers on their first date and had longed for this from the first time they had seen each other at the Rugby League benefit dinner. Annie was there representing one of the sponsors and Mark had been the guest speaker recalling his antics as Great Britain and Wigan star. They had briefly talked at the end of the evening but nothing more. Mark had gone to great lengths to track Annie down although Annie was not quite sure how he had and at this point in time she didn't really care.

Annie led Mark into her bedroom. She whispered, "I must warn you I am not very good at this."

Mark kissed her on the lips and slowly unzipped her dress, which fell to the floor. He led her to the bed and they stumbled onto it never letting their grasp loosen. He slipped his shoes off whilst Annie undid his shirt buttons to reveal his tight and well-formed torso. She couldn't help but run her hands across his smooth skin. As she did Mark shuddered a little but he never stopped kissing her. Slowly Mark fumbled with her bra cursing, as he couldn't open it fluently. They giggled.

Resuming their composure, Mark pulled Annie close to him, both their bodies now entangled and warm. She could feel his manhood through his jeans trying to burst out. Slowly, she ran her hands down his massive thighs. She moved her hand over to the right and brushed his erect piece. It was his turn to let out a sigh of pleasure. Annie struggled to undo his button and unzipped his jeans. Soon they were both naked. Annie caressed his manhood whilst he lovingly played with her breasts. His touch was slight but very effective and not at all like a clumsy teenager. Annie felt his fingers slowly move down her body and he rubbed her wet lips. It wasn't long before Annie could not take much more; she had not been intimate in such a long time. Sensing this, Mark slowly inserted himself inside her. She let out a gasp then enjoyed every moment of his well-formed body inside and out until they both reached their peak and he slumped at her side. Both lay holding each other.

*

Judging by the alarm going off at 7 a.m. they must have fallen asleep. Annie reached over Mark to turn the alarm off. She kissed his ear whilst rubbing her warm hands along his side and upper thigh. Her breasts rubbed his back. She repeated this motion a few times then reached over and rubbed her hands on his inner thigh. With that, Mark was aroused and he turned and placed his hand onto Annie's face and kissed her with such passion it took her breath away. Annie climbed onto him kissing his face, his chest and moving down to his groin. He moaned with satisfaction. Annie played with him and teased him until she took his full length into her mouth. It was warm and hard and thick but she loved every minute of it. So did Mark, he was writhing when suddenly he burst with pleasure. She clambered up to him, kissed him on the cheek and returned to her position at his side. A few moments passed, then Mark spoke, "Good morning!" she returned the words with a smile and they kissed.

*

Saturday mornings were always good but this was especially pleasing. The dull house seemed alive again and as Annie made the coffee she daydreamed of last night's and this morning's events. Daydream soon turned to worry as she thought she had given herself too early. What if he gets bored? What if that's all he wanted? What if he turns out to be like the others?

"Shall we go out today?" Mark announced entering the room fresh from his shower. Annie jumped as he kissed her on the cheek and grabbed the cup of coffee off the side. Thankfully Annie's paranoia subsided.

"Yes I would love to go out," she replied. "Where would you like to go?"

"Well," Mark said, "do you fancy a drive over to Widnes, they are playing Wigan this afternoon? We can grab something to eat."

Mark was unaware of the full extent of Annie's ties with Rugby League and she had not yet told him that her eldest son played for Leeds. Without hesitation, Annie moved towards Mark and put her arms around him. "Yes I'll go to Widnes with you today if you will come to the Leeds and Castleford game tomorrow with me."

Mark looked extremely confused but hugged her all the same. Annie looked up into his eyes and realising his confusion explained, "Rugby League is one of my passions. I'm not just a fundraiser and trustee of the charity; my eldest son plays for Leeds." He put his cup down and held her tight for what seemed to be an eternity.

He rested his head on hers and sighed, "How lucky am I, finding someone so special who shares my love of rugby?" He squeezed her, then released her and walked into the hall.

"We going now?" she shouted after him.

"No," Mark picked up his car keys from the table in the hall, "I have my rugby shirt in my gym bag in the car." He sprinted out to the car whilst Annie watched him from the lounge window.

He returned with his Wigan shirt, promptly changed and said, "Come on then let's get going." They laughed.

4

The drive over the M62 was usually slow and painful. It was an incredibly windy and cold day with a very low autumn sun, a complete contrast to the previous evening. The car was all over the place. Still it was a perfect time for Annie to observe Mark a little more. He had the most delightful blue eyes that were highlighted by his blemish free smooth skin and clear complexion. His broken nose made him look rugged but still handsome. She couldn't determine how old he was. Annie recalled him playing for Great Britain but was ashamed that she did not know his playing statistics but then why would she, she thought. She only knew her son's because he had asked her to be his manager when he signed his first professional contract at sixteen.

Mark looked across at her staring and smiled back. Annie returned the smile and rested her hand on his lap. Mark rubbed her hand and spoke, "You all right? You seemed to be in your own little world then. Do you have any regrets from last night?"

Annie defended herself. "Absolutely not! I loved every minute of it. I was just admiring your looks, you really look after yourself." He laughed out loud. If only she knew, he thought.

"In reality I don't really look after myself, I use the gym but that's out of habit rather than routine."

Mark repaid the compliment. "Look at you, you look amazing and you were unbelievable last night. But all night, not just in bed. I love your company Annie and I can't believe how easy it is for me to talk to you." He stopped abruptly to slow down in the traffic that had built up in front of him.

He continued, "I find it hard to believe that someone like you is living all alone. You are bubbly, clever and so full of life."

"Yes but old and worn down," Annie interrupted. She looked down at her hands.

Mark asked softly but firmly, "Why do you put yourself down so much? You are not old, look at you, you are..." he stopped. Annie looked at Mark to investigate why he had paused mid-sentence. It was his turn to be deep in thought;

he was paying particular attention to a car behind him that had been mimicking all his moves since they had left Annie's house. He couldn't decide whether it was just a coincidence or he was being paranoid.

Annie enquired, "Why are we stopping?"

"Because I would rather show you how gorgeous you are." He indicated left pulling into the services. He got out of the car and approached the passenger door. He opened it. "Come here," he said holding his hand out for Annie to grasp. She complied and stood at the side of him. She looked so small now, no heels just Ugg boots and he towered over her. His torso in front of her eyes, begging her to grab hold of it.

The car that had been following them pulled in to the car park and slowed down at the side of them. Mark tried to look inside but it sped off. He asked Annie if she knew who it was but neither of them did. They didn't think any more of it and carried on. They kissed and he held her.

"Annie," he said, "you are extremely special and I am so glad we met. The more time I spend with you, the more time I want to be with you." She hugged him tightly. Annie really didn't know what to say. Should she say she felt the same or just not say anything at all. The truth was she was falling head over heels but she'd been there before and it had all gone wrong. Instead she looked into Mark's blue eyes and returned his declaration with, "I feel the same way Mark but I don't want us to rush into it and find we later regret it."

"Well maybe we can now talk about your past and I can put your fears to rest once and for all," Mark replied.

"Erm you might run in the opposite direction," Annie remarked.

Mark replied, "I doubt that very much." He escorted her back to her seat.

They continued their journey across the Pennines and reached Select Security Stadium about an hour before kick-off. As a former player he parked in the Officials and Members car park. Annie was used to driving around the streets to find somewhere to park her car and was impressed with the welcomed change.

"Hi Mark," the car park steward shouted as they got out of the car. This amused Annie as she hadn't thought of Mark being well known or famous, to her he was just Mark – the man she fancied like crazy and had mad passionate sex with last night, oh and this morning. She giggled.

Mark wanting to share her amusement asked, "What you giggling at?"

Annie replied, "Nothing it's okay."

He accepted this and put his arm around her as they walked together across the car park. They entered the stadium by the main entrance. The stadium was a relatively new building and had replaced the old shed, Naughton Park. Unfortunately on the few occasions Annie had been, the atmosphere was not as intense as at the old stadium. The main entrance was carpeted in black, emblazoned with a Viking's head. The hospitality suite was packed with people, some in suits but others wearing their club colours with pride. Annie loved the passion of Rugby League both on and off the pitch. Even though there was rivalry between fans it was not bitter and nasty like in football. Banter was rife but the majority of fans knew it was a family game and many had been brought up on the terraces of their beloved clubs. Annie had started going to the Leeds matches with her grandpa from the age of six. He used to sit her on the wall of the old East Stand and she watched young players in the academy becoming well known popular stars of the first team.

Annie loved the sport but at first was reluctant to let her precious boys play it. She relented and Matt was now on his way to becoming one of the stars. Ed, her youngest son was part of the academy at London. His father had moved to London so it was not really an option for Annie to move too although had Ed have wanted her to she would have given up everything and moved.

Her two sons were complete opposites. Both were home birds when they were younger but her determination to raise them as independently as possibly had paid off. They were a great credit to her both receiving accolades from their respective coaches for their skills and temperament, on and off the pitch. "What would you like to drink love?" Mark asked.

Annie replied, "I will have a glass of red wine please. It's not often I don't drive myself to a rugby match. I will come with you."

They walked over to the bar and stood brushing against each other. Annie spoke first. "It's great coming to a neutral match, there's no pressure as a fan. I can just enjoy the game."

Mark scoffed. "It's okay for you then!" It had never crossed Annie's mind that he didn't support Leeds.

"Sorry I just assumed you were a Leeds fan living in Leeds," she scoffed.

"Ha-ha," he replied. "Wigan through and through."

Annie retorted, "A pie eater then, that's why you're always at the gym." Mark gave her a playful dig whilst the man next to Annie couldn't help but laugh at her remark.

He joined the conversation. "Watch it love you're on dodgy ground 'ere. Mark was one of our best players in 'is time."

Annie blushed then repeated, "… in his time, ha-ha." Again Mark gave her a dig in her side and she let out a little shriek.

"Not sure I want you to have this after that comment," he laughed teasing her with the glass of wine.

"Err it's a very brave or stupid man that comes between me and my wine."

The man at the bar joined in once more. "Spoken like a true Yorkshire lass." All three laughed and Mark shook the man's hand as they moved on.

They settled for a small, quiet spot in the room. Annie was pleased since they were able to stand close by each other with their arms brushing.

"So what's your prediction for the score then?" Mark enquired.

Annie thought for a minute then smiled. "Twenty-four eighteen to Widnes."

Mark placed his pint on the vacant table at the side of them and grabbed Annie causing her to spill a little wine on her hand. Being a Yorkshire lass, she licked the spillage off. Mark found this highly amusing. He took her glass from her and placed it with his. Annie could feel a warming inside her as he drew her close to his well-formed body and held the back of her neck as he kissed her tenderly. As they reappeared from their embrace, Mark surveyed the room. Annie noticed his mood changed almost instantly and his complexion turned white.

He whispered in her ear, "Let's find our seats."

Mark ushered Annie out of the room and they sat in their cold damp seats overlooking the new artificial pitch. Annie was impressed with how real it actually looked.

She held Mark's hand and snuggled up to him to try and deflect the biting wind.

She asked, "What happened in there, Mark?"

"I am sorry I treated you badly but my ex-wife was in there. What is she doing here? Why won't she just leave me alone?" Annie had never seen Mark vexed. She held his hand tighter and said, "Mark you didn't treat me badly, you just startled me. She probably knew you would be here today."

Mark deep in thought muttered, "Yep you're probably right. Can we talk about this later? I don't want to think about her, I want to think about you and me." He kissed her forehead and they sat linking arms until the players emerged from the tunnel when they stood up to salute them.

They settled back down tightly together to watch the match only interrupted by the occasional 'Hi Mark' or 'can we have your autograph please?' After the interruptions subsided they both became absorbed in the game, shouting and cheering at every opportunity. The first half was very close with only two points separating the teams, in Widnes's favour. This caused much amusement for Annie who ribbed Mark through the half-time break.

Mark was asked again to sign another autograph. Annie giggled. Mark turned to her, "Right you! That's twice today you have giggled at my expense, what is so funny?"

Annie smiled and looked directly into Mark's eyes. "I had not thought of you as famous until the steward in the car park spoke to you, people asking for autographs. To me you are just my Mark." She giggled, "But in the car park I thought to myself he is just my Mark the one I made mad passionate love to last night and this morning." She laughed and blushed. Mark wrapped his body around her and hugged her.

"So I'm *your* Mark then?" he laughed.

The second half started. Both were over animated in their support even if it was for opposite teams. At the final whistle the score was Wigan 26, Widnes 20. Mark left a happy man and scorned at Annie, "Ha you're not always right then. Mind you, you can't know much about rugby if you're a Leeds fan." Annie didn't rise to the bait other than laughing and pretending to kick him on the shins.

"Hope you don't mind but we'll give the post-match drinks a miss," Mark advised.

Annie replied, "I don't usually enjoy such luxury anyway. Besides I was hoping to have you to myself and I promise I won't ask you for your autograph." With that she ran to the car so he could not retaliate.

The journey back across the Pennines was sublime. Both gave their versions of the game. Mark was very impressed with Annie's knowledge of the game; clearly her experience of the game was not restricted to a general spectator.

Mark's curiosity got the better of him. "How did you become so knowledgeable? It's clearly not just from watching the Whinos, I mean Rhinos." Annie reached over and slapped his thigh.

"Do that again," he dared and she did. He laughed; he loved the physical contact.

Annie recalled, "When Matt asked if he could play rugby I flatly refused. I was persuaded by my grandpa to let him have a go. He took to it like he'd never been out of the sport. I then became involved in junior rugby, first as a mum then a fundraiser and eventually a coach. I gave up coaching when Ed my youngest joined the London academy, eight months ago."

A wave of insecurity suddenly overwhelmed Mark. He realised he knew very little of his new playmate. Nevertheless he knew she was the one.

Mark replied, "Annie Swift you are so full of surprises. I want to know all about your life. You fascinate me."

"I can assure you I am not that interesting and some of it will make your hair turn grey. You may also want to run to the other end of the earth." Annie fell silent, she wanted to blurt everything out to Mark but he was driving. She wanted to protect them both from her troubled past.

Mark broke the silence. "That is twice now you have said that. I am not going anywhere unless you want me to. I have only just found you, we have so much to explore. For once I feel alive, free with an equal."

Changing the subject, Mark suggested, "I know I promised you dinner but how about we get a takeaway and take it back to mine. You don't have to it is just an idea."

"No Mark I would love to come to yours." She reassuringly rubbed his leg.

"Chinese?" he enquired. She nodded. "I am not assuming anything but would you like to call at yours and get some things?"

Annie looked at Mark and couldn't resist a sly dig. "You think I'm that easy?"

Mark embarrassingly remarked, "No, no it was just an idea. I'm sorry if I've offended you."

"Mark you haven't, I am just pulling your leg. I would have been really upset if you didn't ask me." Mark for once felt he had met his kindred spirit.

*

Annie floated into the garden with Mark following close behind. Unlocking the door she said, "Won't be a minute," as she bound up the stairs. Mark entered the living room. He observed it was a sparsely furnished room with a small black and white sofa and a coffee table in front of the fire. His eyes were drawn to a cabinet in the alcove holding a display of fine trophies and medals. On closer inspection these had been awarded to Matt and Ed but also to Annie for Coach of the Year and Fundraiser of the Year. Mark felt a wave of pride run through his veins. "She is unbelievable," he muttered.

In the second alcove there was a display cabinet, which very strangely housed an array of Formula One replica cars and memorabilia.

"So you have found my other passion," Annie said skipping into the room.

"Yes I suppose I have," Mark replied.

Annie scuttled around the room picking up objects and throwing them into a holdall.

"I'm sorry but I'll have to bring some work with me," she sighed. "I haven't prepared my lectures for next week because a gorgeous hunk of a guy distracted me."

"You'll have to introduce me to him some time." Mark's quick response resulted in Annie jumping on the sofa and leaping into Mark's arms. They kissed.

"I will just close the blinds in the kitchen then you can lead me astray even further," Annie said brushing past Mark and tapping his bottom as she left.

The kitchen was warm but a little messy. They had left in such a rush that morning that coffee cups were in the sink. Oh sod it Annie thought. Just as she leant over to grab the string of the blind she screamed.

Mark came running in. "What the hell?"

"Oh Mark, there was someone standing there in the garden." Mark looked over her quivering shoulder but there was nothing there. He reached up and closed the blind.

"Come on, let's get out of here." Mark led her to the back door. Annie only let go of him to lock the door. Both pensively walked out of the garden looking over their shoulders but there was no one there. When Annie got in the car she locked the door.

For a moment both of them sat there breathing heavily. Mark came to his senses, started the car and pulled away from the house. After two miles, Annie with wet eyes turned to Mark.

"There was someone there, I know there was."

Mark felt her pain. "I know love. I know I believe you. Let's go straight to mine and I'll order in."

Annie had never felt a problem at the house until recently. Each time she had come home she felt sure someone was watching her. She shared this with Mark. He listened but did not say anything. He did not want to alarm her but it looked as though it was happening all over again.

5

Still visibly shaken, they completed the short journey across North Leeds to Mark's home. It wasn't a home, it was a mansion! Annie could not believe the size of it. The house was amazing. Mark opened the gates remotely to reveal a long winding, dimly lit driveway.

"You live here alone?" she asked.

"Yes I do but didn't always. My daughter spent every other weekend here when she was growing up. I was going to sell it but she is attached to it especially the tree house at the bottom of the garden." He pointed at the quaint weather beaten little house in the oak tree to their left.

At the end of the driveway, there was a magnificent south-facing detached house, boasting two patio doors and an archway over the front door. To the left was a double garage with white doors. The roof of them was surrounded by a small fence and patio furniture stacked up in the corner of it. My boys would have loved it here, thought Annie especially the makeshift set of rugby sticks at the bottom of the drive.

As they approached the garage, the door automatically started to open. Mark reversed the BMW in. Annie could see there was a door at the back of the garage that led straight into the house. Good, she thought having to escape going outside again on the dark dreary night.

Mark climbed out of the car to greet Annie at the door.

The garage led into a small utility room with a huge hallway on the left and the kitchen on the right. Annie kicked off her Ugg boots in the doorway next to her holdall. The house was spotlessly clean and everything had its place except the rugby boots and walking boots thrown under the hall table. Annie remembered chastising her two boys for doing exactly the same thing. Her kitchen and living room would fit into his hallway! She was lost for words.

He switched the alarm system to standby and said, "Make yourself at home love. I will get the menu and the wine and we can decide what to have."

Grabbing the bottle of wine and two glasses Mark led Annie into the sitting room. A 50-inch 3D television imposed itself in one corner of the room. The leather sofas were comfortable and Annie sank into one of them as she sat down. Mark drew the curtains.

Annie smiled and commented sarcastically, "I'd have thought they would be remotely controlled too." Mark smiled.

They chose their meals although Annie was still feeling a little sick from her earlier encounter. Whilst Mark rang in the order, Annie could not resist playfully kissing his ears, which made Mark stutter and redden. He ended the call and grabbed Annie wrestling her onto her back on the sofa. She laughed so much she could not catch her breath. Just as she was begging him to stop, Mark turned the tickle into a loving embrace. He held her so tenderly. He wanted her to know he would keep her from harm.

Annie jumped up when an alarm started ringing.

Mark reassured her. "It's okay baby it's only the intercom on the gate."

Intercom on the gate! This is a different world from that of the college lecturer. Mark left the room. Annie sat up, straightened her hair and casually knelt on one end of the sofa. Mark seemed to have been gone ages. When he returned he was empty handed, no takeaway. Annie looked at him perplexed but could see from the look on his face all was not well.

"What's the matter Mark?" Annie said. Mark sat down next to her and took a large gulp of wine.

He took Annie by the hand, turned and faced her and explained, "I have something I think I need to tell you. No one answered at the intercom when I tried but I could sense someone was there."

Annie was confused. Her heart started to beat faster. "It was probably kids."

Shaking his head he continued. "About twenty years ago, I got to know a fan. She seemed really nice and interested in rugby." Mark could see the worry on Annie's face. Reassuringly he gripped her hand tighter. "Our friendship on my part was totally innocent, I swear to you nothing happened or ever entered into my head to happen. Anyway when I asked her to back off she became aggressive and threatened to kill my family and me. She accused me of raping her and it got really out of hand. Once the police had investigated the matter, they sectioned her under the Mental Health Act. I told you my divorce to my ex-wife was bad, she couldn't hack it, she believed I could have an affair." There was a long pause.

"Why are you telling me this now?" Annie was very confused; her mind was racing at 200 mph.

Mark justified his outburst. "I just get nervous when strange things happen like tonight and I wanted to be honest with you. I don't think it has anything to do with the visitor at your house tonight and what's just happened but you need to know. Annie I would hate for anything to come between us. I know we haven't known each other long but I want us to have the chance to really make a go of this."

Annie was hunched up in the corner of the sofa cradling her glass of wine. Unsure what to make of it or what to say she just stared into the glass.

"Annie say something please," Mark begged.

Annie finally found some words. "I don't know what to say Mark. You obviously have doubts whether this girl is back on the prowl else you would have not mentioned it now. I don't understand how she would know about us yet, God I don't fully know about us yet! I think we are probably being paranoid because of our pasts and like you I don't want either of our histories to stop us now."

With that, not another word was said on the subject. On Annie's part she didn't want to spoil the day by delving into her past and Mark was inclined to feed her piecemeal as the past was something that he had no desire to relive.

The intercom alarm sounded again, both looked at each other laughed and ran together to the system controller. Mark pressed the button warily. A voice at the end shouted, "Order for Smith!" Mark pressed the access control and went to the front door. Annie found her way to the kitchen and looked for cutlery and plates. She had placed them on the side before Mark re-entered.

He suggested, "Come on let's take it into the room and sit on the floor by the table. We can put an old Grand Final on and pick it apart. No doubt you can analyse it a lot better than I can." With that he gathered the plates and gave her a cheeky slap on the bottom.

They placed the food and plates on the coffee table. Mark threw the cushions from the sofa into one area. He selected a DVD and sat down on one of the cushions. Annie had perched herself at the far end of the cushions. Mark motioned for her to move closer and she certainly was not going to say no.

The food was fabulous and welcomed, although Annie could not eat the whole meal. Feeling bloated and stuffed she laid her head in Mark's lap as they watched the Leeds v St Helens Grand Final again. Annie had seen this about twenty times with the boys but never tired of it. She looked up to Mark who was not even watching the television but looking down at her. She asked, "Why if you hate Leeds did you put this one on?"

Mark stroked her cheek. "Because my dear I had a feeling you would love this one."

Annie got up to her knees, turned to face Mark and rubbed her hands along his smooth, unblemished cheeks. She kissed him. He reciprocated. His tongue ran a marathon in her mouth. She loved it and was on fire inside. She couldn't help herself and sat astride his lap, she could feel his warm body through his and her clothes. Mark placed his hands on her bottom cheeks and slowly squeezed as she kissed him, her tongue becoming entwined with his. He broke free and nipped her ear with his teeth. She squealed but all the same enjoyed it. He squeezed her cheeks tighter drawing her closer to him. She could feel he was hard and eager to please and she continued to tease him through his jeans. Losing patience, Mark grabbed her top and ripped it over her head, showing her tight, large breasts. He reached in and released her breast, kissing it tenderly and slipping her nipple into his mouth. Annie rose in ecstasy but sat back on his growing bulge. No longer being able to resist his body, Annie unbuttoned his shirt whilst he looked on with admiration. His stare did not falter even when she leant forward and kissed him on the lips moving slowly down to his wonderfully defined chest. She continued to kiss his heavenly body whilst undoing his jeans, releasing his wonderful piece into her hands. She took a glance up; Mark now had his head back with his eyes shut. She raised her head and kissed his neck under his chin. As she did she slipped him inside her. She felt it deep inside as she rode him. Mark accepted the pleasure, his body completely empowered by her. He clenched her buttocks as she moved rhythmically. Mark moved his left hand up her back and round to her breast. He caressed it and couldn't help but bite the nipple. Annie gave out a pleasurable cry. Sex had never been this intense before. He could not bear being without her, he had never felt like this before nor had he experienced such pleasure as they came together.

Annie rested for a while on his bare, warm body.

"Let's go to bed Annie," Mark whispered in her ear. "I want you to fall asleep in my arms." She didn't need much persuasion. Either Mark was very clean and tidy, for a man, or he had run in and tidied up before she joined him. He was already in the bed and had turned down the covers ready for her entry.

Mark was warm and inviting and Annie sank into his body. They laid in silence together until they fell asleep.

6

Sunday morning was dreary and wet. Annie woke wondering where she was at first. She reached out but Mark had already vacated the bed. More's the pity she thought. Annie lay there listening for any sounds but nothing. You could judge the actual time of day by listening to the volume of traffic outside her house but not here, it was so peaceful.

Her thoughts turned to the day ahead; she was going to see her baby play rugby just like the old days but on a much bigger stage. Annie habitually brought her phone to bed with her. She reached out and pulled it out of its case. It was eight-thirty. Matt would be up already going through his match day rituals including his lucky red pants. She smiled whilst texting him good luck and reminded him of the extra ticket she required for the match and the Bar. Mark re-entered with two coffees, toast and the Sunday paper.

"I could really get used to this Mark," Annie remarked.

"Funnily enough I was thinking the same when I was making the breakfast." He placed the tray on the end of the bed, kissed Annie and resumed to fuss over her. She lay with her knees up resting the newspaper on them whilst he lay with his coffee cup in one hand, his other propping up his head staring at Annie. He observed and loved the way she read the paper and tutted and hated some of the articles that had been written. He laughed at how she turned to the sports page first and how she sat further upright when she found an article of interest. Annie caught Mark staring at her out of the corner of her eye but she didn't mind, in fact she loved his attentiveness. When the coffee and toast was finished Mark placed the tray on the floor and resumed his position as admirer. After five minutes, Annie could sense he was getting bored and before she could remedy this, Mark swiped the paper from in front of her. "You've read it enough now. It's my turn."

"I don't think so," she said snatching it back, only his and her grip resulted in the page tearing in two. Mark gathered up the whole paper, threw it on the floor and jumped on her. She playfully squealed. His weight was squashing her but there was no way she was going to object. He looked her straight in the eyes, opened his mouth but nothing came out. Annie mouthed what and he just smiled warmly.

"I can't remember ever being this happy," he admitted.

She lifted her arms and held his face directly above hers. "Neither can I."

"We better get sorted out for the Whinos, I mean Rhinos match then," Mark changed the subject. Annie brought her knee up against his groin.

"Careful," he laughed. "You're only doing yourself out of fun. I have run a nice bath for us. So Mrs, get in the bathroom so I can scrub your mucky body." The latter was said in a pirate accent that made Annie laugh.

Mark's bathroom was more like the Harrogate Turkish bath. The bath was a hot tub situated in the corner of the room. Candles had been lit around the tub and the blinds were drawn closed. Both of them climbed in next to each other. Annie could not resist but splash the bubbles in Mark's face. Rubbing his eyes, he blurted, "How childish," whilst grabbing her and ducking her into the hot water. She came up coughing and spluttered, "You sod, you wait you've just declared war." They were like two kids having fun in the summer paddling pool. Mark gestured for Annie to sit between his legs and he gently rubbed her neck and body. This was heaven. They reversed roles and this time Annie delighted greatly in getting hold of Mark's bulging body. She loved his defined lines and as she rubbed his neck she thought of how long she had longed for such a loving relationship. This is what she had hoped for from her past two relationships but they had been disasters.

Mark seemed to know instinctively Annie was delving into the past. He asked, "Annie I assume you have been married before?"

She rubbed his head with the sponge and kissed his shoulder.

"If I must," she replied. He found her leg under the water and gave it a squeeze. "I was married once and it was a disaster." Pausing to draw a deep breath, she continued, "I met my first husband at school. We married when we left school and had Matt when I was twenty-three. When Matt was born we were happy. We had some good times and I thought it was for life. My mum and dad had their reservations as they had seen him advancing on some of my friends but I was completely blind to it. Until I left him of course when everyone knew of his indiscretions but me!" She paused to fill the sponge with water then released it across his chest.

Continuing, her voice broke a little. "I didn't see it coming. I thought we were blissfully happy but then things started to change, he started to change. He would be home late or he'd come home in a blazing mood spoiling for a fight. At that time I worked full time in a very demanding sales job. He lost his job through stealing and reverted to being self-employed. I was the main breadwinner but would have been happy for that to be reversed. Anyway one day he came home to tell me he had lost his wallet that contained our holiday money, all £800 of it. I went ballistic. That was for our first holiday with Matt. I believed him and felt sorry for him until a friend informed me he had seen him at the casino the night before. Weeks passed and money started disappearing. I knew then he had a problem. I broached the subject but he was defensive and became aggressive and violent. I was scared not for me but for Matt." She drew a very deep breath.

"If it's upsetting stop now," Mark said.

Her eyes welled. "No it's fine, you told me about your past." He held her shoulders as she continued the story. "One night he came home and I knew he'd been with another woman. He had lipstick on his ear and shirt. I tried to speak to him but he didn't want to know. Matt woke early the next morning and his father was already downstairs. We both got dressed and went downstairs together. I didn't speak but Phil was spoiling for a fight. He locked Matt in the living room and wouldn't let me pass. I could hear him screaming and I begged and begged but he wouldn't let me in." Tears were now rolling down into the bathtub. Mark squeezed her arms but she signalled she wanted to go on. "He grabbed me by the throat, told me I was the worst wife and mother in the world, that I would spend the rest of my life with him or alone. He… he… err raped me." Annie couldn't stop sobbing. It was over twenty years but still it was deep and raw. She looked at Mark who had a single tear running down his cheek. He consumed her into his chest. She sobbed but wanted to finish the story. "Luckily Matt had cried himself to sleep. I… erm… waited until Phil left for work, I packed our bags and left everything behind. I lost everything, my beautiful home, my 'ideal' marriage, everything. The worst thing was no one believed me including members of my family. I hit rock bottom and the only part of my life that stopped me from ending it all was Matt."

Mark was crying with her. He sobbed, "I'm sorry, I'm sorry it happened but I am so sorry for asking you to relive it. You honestly think I am going to run a mile after what you have told me?"

He pulled her away from his chest. "You are brave and clever and I love you all the more for being so honest." She slumped back into his arms.

"Come on let's get ready. I'm sure your wonderful son would like to see his fantastic Mum." Mark kissed her and climbed out of the bath. He passed her a towel and as she got out, he wrapped her up in it very tightly, wanting to protect her.

Annie was exhausted and she'd only been up a couple of hours. The next couple of hours were whiled away getting ready. Not much was said. Annie was too weary, embarrassed and ashamed of her past and Mark was too upset to say anything constructive. He was not prepared for such horrific truths.

They left the house at lunchtime to head to the ground. It was only four miles away but they were going to grab some lunch before the three o'clock kick off. A couple of turns from the house, Mark seemed twitchy and kept looking in his rear-view mirror.

"What's up Mark?" queried Annie.

"Don't look back but the car that's two cars back was the one that followed us into the motorway services yesterday."

Resisting the temptation to look back Annie tried to view it through the door mirrors but to no avail.

She asked, "Can you make out the registration number?"

"No," he said, "but I might just pull in and see if it passes. I'll wait 'til we are on Wetherby Road, it's straight and no room for it to turn off."

The anxiety was palpable. Keeping to his word, Mark pulled into the lay-by. The car sped past. Mark managed to get the number plate and Annie looked at the driver.

"It was hard to tell whether it was a man or a woman because of the tinted windows," she admitted. Mark was more successful and had the number plate NW68 STH.

"I think we should report it to the police Mark." Annie was quite adamant. Mark agreed. "Yes but not today, tomorrow I'll go to the station. Today it's about Matt and you."

They hugged and kissed then continued on their journey. It wasn't long before they had reached Headingley but Mark drove straight past heading towards Kirkstall – food was calling to him.

"Thought you might like to go to Nandos with me before the match."

Annie nodded as it beat sitting in the stand trying to catch a glimpse of her son. At Nandos, both ordered Diet Cokes in the hope of redeeming their calorie intake of the night before. Annie texted Matt to let him know where she was and she received the customary 'kk' answer, which meant 'I'm busy okay'. She smiled.

They both ordered the medium strength chicken. Annie had hardly dared look into Mark's eyes since the confession in the bathtub this morning. Mark was so conscious of this and whilst he didn't want to labour the point before Matt's game, he wanted to let her know she had his full support and he was definitely not going anywhere.

"You know Annie we all have a past. I am shocked and hurt at what you had to endure but I am going nowhere nor would I ever do anything to hurt you." Annie looked up. She reached across the table and held his hands.

Sighing she replied, "I know that Mark, I really do. I have to confess that I am falling for you and would hate for it to be over now." She looked down at their combined hands.

"Look at me Annie, please look at me." She looked directly into his eyes. "I have fallen for you too; I love you. This weekend has been the best of my life. For the first time I know what I want and it's you. I want you! I want to hold you, fix you, make you safe, fight with you and yes make love to you!" At that precise moment the waiter served on the table. His crimson face concentrated on placing the food on the table not daring to make eye contact with either of them. He left the table to the sound of sniggering from his customers.

"Oh Mark you have some quality comedy timing," Annie declared, releasing his hands so they could both eat.

The food was good, the company even better. Both chatted and laughed with each other. The time was ticking on and they had to get to the game and park. It was a great ground with an unmistakable atmosphere but parking in the surrounding streets was horrendous. Annie didn't enquire where Mark was going to park as she assumed he was familiar with the streets.

Surprise, surprise Mark knew the parking steward and parked in the official car park next to the South Stand. Annie left the car shaking her head. Mark knew what she was thinking and remarked, "Well what can I say, I am known everywhere." They joined hands and walked around to the St Michaels Lane end. The tickets were collected from the ticket office where Matt had left them.

"Good afternoon Mrs Swift, let's hope Matt has a good 'un," said the steward as they left the counter.

Mark bumped into Annie's shoulder. "See, this is your territory now." They both laughed.

The ground was heaving. The Castleford and Leeds faithful never missed a decent derby. As local rivalry went, this was one of the biggest derbies.

"MUM!" About a dozen women turned their heads including Annie. "Ed! What you doing here? Oh my God it's so great to see you." They embraced as if he was five again. "When did you get here, how long you here for?"

"Calm down," Ed said laughing. "I have a couple of days, due back Tuesday. I stayed at Matt's last night and no, before you say it, we were not on the PS3 till four o'clock. It was two!" he laughed just like his mum.

"Very funny cheeky! Ed this is Mark. Mark and I are… Err… friends." Annie blushed and looked at Mark who was amused by the spectacle in front of him.

"Mum I know he's more than a friend from the embarrassed look on your face. Pleased to meet you Mark." Ed held his hand out to Mark. Mark, like everyone else who encountered Ed, took an immediate liking to him. He shared his mother's pale complexion and had the same impish bright blue eyes.

"Are you sitting with us?" Annie asked with renewed excitement. They compared tickets and yes they were all sitting together. Ed grabbed Annie's arm. "Sorry to be the one to tell you this but Dad's here and sitting near us too."

Annie reassured Ed. "It's okay love. I am fine with it." Annie turned to Mark whose face was like thunder. He was livid.

"Mark and I will just have a wander and we'll meet you round there." Annie kissed Ed again much to his disgust and they parted company.

Mark burst as soon as Ed left. "How the fuck can you expect me to sit with that sick bastard?"

Quick to allay his fears, Annie explained, "Mark, Paul is Ed's dad not Matt's. He was my second relationship." Mark felt about three inches tall and reprimanded himself for jumping to the wrong conclusions.

"Paul and I stayed friends for Ed and Matt's sake. He was okay just a Mummy's boy who wanted me at his beck and call. I gave up everything for him and turned into his mother! I left with the boys. I am sorry I didn't get chance to complete my life story." Mark held his finger against her lip, removed it and kissed her. Annie's knees buckled but Mark had tight hold of her, he wasn't letting her go.

They walked hand in hand to their seat.

Annie heard, "Annie?" She turned and John from work was fast approaching. "Hi John how are you?" Annie enquired.

"I am good thanks. You must be Mark." John's tone was a little off in Annie's eyes.

She returned, "Yes this is Mark, I'll see you tomorrow at work. Have a good game."

"You were a bit off with him," Mark commented.

"I helped him out when his wife died of cancer but now he thinks he can run my life and comment on everything I do. I want to keep him at arm's length as he appears to have an affection for me, so my friends tell me."

They took to their seats. Ed was eagerly awaiting his mum's company. Paul sat at the far side of him, raised an eyebrow as Annie acknowledged him but nothing else.

"By the way," Annie leant to whisper to Mark, "I was really turned on when you swore at me."

Mark shook his head and laughed at her. "You are unbelievable," he chuckled.

"I know but that's why you love me," she said confidently. Mark shuffled up to her and held her tight.

Annie turned to Ed. "Where are you staying tonight?"

"At Matt's, if that's okay with you. We are going out after the game, well after the Bar." Ed hugged his mum. Annie was happy the boys had their own lives and were making good progress but loved to see them and spend time with them. They were inseparable which is what she wanted more than anything after spending a life embroiled in bitter sibling rivalry.

Mark was in awe of Annie's relationship with her boy. They were as thick as thieves. He was close to his daughter but nowhere near the same level. They laughed, joked and were totally at ease with each other.

Annie stood up. "I'm just going to nip to the loo before the game starts." As she tried to get past Mark he trapped her within his legs. She laughed. "Save it for later," she said playfully.

His reply was equally suggestive. "Been looking forward to it since this morning." She bent over and brushed her breasts against his chest. He had to conceal his excitement with his coat.

*

When Annie returned to her seat, Ed and Mark were in deep conversation. I hope Ed isn't driving him nuts, she thought as he did have a tendency to talk too much, a trait that he picked up from his father. Just in time, Annie returned to see the team come out onto the field and the place erupted. Mark observed Annie as she joined in with the chanting and singing. He was amused how she did not hold back and knew all the words. Then she copped eye of her son Matt, number thirteen, loose forward and she beamed with pride. Ed shouted some abuse to him, which was not well received by other members of the crowd until they realised it was from his own family members.

Mark leant over to Annie and said, "You should be immensely proud, they are both a real credit to you." She looked up at Mark and nodded with tears in her eyes. He kissed her forehead and smiled.

The game started and Annie resumed her seat, every now and then kissing her grandpa's scarf she held in her hands. Mark surveyed Annie's family carefully. He was not struck on her ex-partner. Whilst Annie was adorably positive and encouraging, he seemed to dwell on the negatives and constantly shouted profanities when there was a lost ball or Matt wasn't in the position he felt he should have been in. Annie glared at him a few times and Ed laid a hand on her arm as much to say 'you know what he's like'. She subsided and concentrated on Matt. He had a fabulous game. Two tries, four goals and a drop goal to add insult to injury. It was no surprise he was named Man of the Match. Mark was quite envious, if only he had had that amount of talent he thought.

Mark escorted Annie, followed by Ed and his dad to pitch side. After completing the obligatory interview, Matt jogged over to his mum, gave her a huge kiss and picked her up off her feet. Mark realised the close relationship was not exclusive to Ed but ran deep within her maternal family.

Matt leant over the wall with his hand out. "You must be Mark, and I am very pleased to meet you."

They shook hands; Annie was so proud both boys had been so polite. "I'll see you in the bar after the game." He high-fived Ed and jogged into the changing rooms.

The extended party made their way out of the North Stand, past the club shop and into the bar.

"Boy this brings back memories Ed," Annie said turning to Ed.

"Yes Mum, many a post-match we spent in 'ere gettin' autographs. You said for me but secretly they were for you." Mark and Ed let out childish laughs. Annie smiled. Her boys were together with her new man and they seemed to hit it off, that's all she asked for.

Annie turned to Ed. "I'm meeting Grannie for lunch at the college tomorrow at one o'clock if you want to join us, you and Matt could meet us there."

Ed loved his grannie; they had such a special relationship. "We went to see her today. She gave us both twenty quid and she's already invited us." Ed stuck his tongue out.

Annie replied, "Oi you're not too old for a crack. Good, you two can buy us lunch then, sorted!"

Paul added, "You can buy us a drink now!"

Before Ed could wind his dad up, Mark interjected, "No the drinks are definitely on me."

"Hi Annie, good to see you," said a deep voice at the entrance. The tall overweight man leaned over and kissed Annie on the cheek.

"I'm great Keith, how are you and Penny?"

"Good, good. Your lad did you proud, he did us all proud. We miss having you around here Annie. You always brightened the dullest of days," Keith said smiling.

"Aw thanks Keith I miss you all too."

Ed turned to Mark and whispered, "You better get used to this mate, my mum has a wider fan base than we do and she's not playing." Annie caught the comment and clipped Ed over the back of the head. Mark winced for him.

They climbed the flight of stairs up to the bar. Nothing much had changed since those days when Annie brought the boys in. She wound her way through the ever-increasing crowd to the players' family area in the top left-hand side of the room. Throwing her stuff on the settee, she turned to Mark. "I'll help you with the drinks." Paul was his true sulky self and didn't want to accept a drink from Mark grunting he wasn't thirsty. Annie and Ed's look to each other said it all.

"He's a charming bloke," Mark said walking away from the seated area.

"He is Ed's dad. He wasn't always that miserable, it started about five years into our relationship. Miserable git lost his sense of humour. Always maintained it was my fault, I didn't pay him enough attention. Apparently I was too busy with the boys to care about him." Annie scorned, "He left as soon as Ed turned ten. Good job Ed was so level-headed, I thought he might have gone off the rails but he was great, took it in his stride and him and Matt took on the role as my protectors."

By now they were leaning on the bar waiting to be served. Mark leaned into Annie nearly sending her flying into the man next to her. After apologising, Annie turned to Mark giggling, "What you do that for, bully?"

Mark ruffled her hair. "You my dear are a wonderful mum, look at the way you are with them, and it's great. They really look up to you." It was true Annie did have an exceptionally close relationship with both her boys. She was immensely proud of that.

"I am jealous of it," Mark mocked as he pushed her again. Thankfully Mark was only joking as Annie had had a lifetime of jealousy and trouble.

After Matt had signed autographs, posed for photographs and made his Man of the Match speech, he was finally reunited with his mother. He bent over, kissed her and then sat on the arm of the sofa close by her. Mark was perched on the other side with Ed. Paul sat opposite.

Mark, handing Matt a bottle of beer, spoke first. "Well done Matt, great game today. You were exceptional out there."

Paul snorted. Everyone looked at him but no one more than Annie. She was sick of his miserable ways already.

Matt retaliated, "If you don't like the way I played, go home. My two bosses (Matt meant his coach and his mum!) were happy with my performance." Matt and Paul stared at each other.

Paul finally opened his mouth. "I just thought on a couple of occasions you made the wrong decisions but you'll learn as you play more."

Mark observed the uneasy silence that followed. How could he do that? The kid was only twenty-three. He had played out of his skin and showed an immense amount of courage and experience beyond his years. He turned to Annie and could see she was deeply hurt and saw her squeeze Matt's hand. Ed stood up and shook his brother's hand. Paul sensing he had said the wrong thing, left without another word.

As Matt looked at Annie he said, "I know he's jealous but that's no excuse Mum. I'm gonna stop getting him a ticket."

Ed agreed with Matt and said, "Don't let him get to you Mum; he knows what buttons to press to get a reaction out of you. He can see how happy you are, don't let him spoil it."

The boys decided to mingle which was a welcome relief for both Annie and Mark. Mark felt especially awkward but spoke first.

"Boy! Aren't you glad you never married him?" He went on, "Annie!" She was staring into space. "Annie the boys are right. Forget it now, it's done. It's been an amazing weekend and he or anyone is not going to spoil it for us." Returning from her trance she nodded, gulped a mouthful of wine and gripped Mark's knee.

About an hour later, the boys returned. "Right we're off! PS3 calls," Ed announced.

Matt looked concerned. "You all right Mum? You going home now?" Annie had not honestly thought of what she was going to do that evening. The truth was she didn't want to go home to an empty house and not be comforted by Mark's warm body but it was work tomorrow and she had to prepare her lectures.

Annie answered, "Yes I have to get ready for work unfortunately."

Mark offered, "Can we give you boys a lift. My car is in the car park."

The boys, eager to see what toy Mark had, accepted his offer. As they left, Annie and Mark walked hand in hand. The boys sauntered behind giggling like naughty school children up to no good. The night was cold but dry. By the time they reached the car, Annie was shivering. Both boys stopped at the side of the car but could not control their laughter. Matt told Ed to be quiet but that made him even worse.

Ed couldn't help himself. "Mum, I thought you mocked BMW drivers for being egotistical maniacs who loved themselves!"

Annie smiled and went to grab hold of Ed but he dodged her grip and ran around the car. In hot pursuit she followed him. He was nimble on his feet but she was no slouch.

Mark and Matt watched on in amusement goading Annie to get him and thrash him.

Matt turned to Mark and in a softly spoken voice said, "Mark, I have never seen Mum this relaxed and happy. She obviously likes you a lot 'cos she's let her guard down. Whatever you do, please treat her kindly. All my mum has ever asked for is respect, love and honesty. She thinks of everyone else before herself. Ed and I would love nothing more than for her to be happy and with a fella who loves the bones of her like we do."

Annie, returning with Ed in an arm lock, interrupted the conversation. Mark was hysterical with laughter.

"Ed let that be a lesson to you, she might be old but she's still got it."

Annie looked at Matt and replied, "Do you want some as well? I'm not old I'm mature!"

Mark joined in, "You call chasing a professional rugby player around a car park mature?" He could not believe what he had just witnessed but he was in awe of her and her passion for life.

"Right I'm knackered now. Let's get these two monkeys home," Annie said, climbing into the passenger seat. Ed and Matt clambered into the back. As Mark set off he noticed a piece of paper under the windscreen wiper. He completed the short journey to Matt's flat and as Annie was fussing and giving the boys their goodnight kisses, Mark reached over to the note. It read, 'I'm watching you both!' That was it. Not to worry Annie, he slipped the note in his pocket and continued the journey to Annie's home.

Back at the house, Mark grabbed Annie's holdall from the boot and escorted Annie back in. He scoured the surrounding area looking for clues of the note's author. The street was deserted save the next-door neighbour's tabby cat. Mark agonised whether to tell Annie about the note but he remembered Matt's words, 'respect, love and honesty'. If he told her she would be worried, if he didn't he wasn't being honest. He opted for the latter as nothing was going to stop him from fulfilling the boys' wishes and his too for that matter.

They were in the kitchen making coffee when Mark slid his hand on Annie's that was resting on the table top. She looked at him. "I have something I need to show you," he said sullenly.

In good spirits she laughed, "I've seen it all weekend but don't mind if I do!"

Mark looked disapprovingly at her, not because of the content but the timing. He declared, "I found this on the windscreen of the car in the car park." He handed her the note. She read it and read it again. The colour drained from her perfect face. He knew it was not good. She calmly placed the offending paper onto the table and lunged at Mark, grabbing him with both hands.

"Why us? Who is doing this?" she cried. Mark shook his head but couldn't speak as to see her so upset killed him inside.

"I'm sorry I had to tell you, I didn't want to keep it from you." He reached down and lifted Annie's head to look at him. "I will sort this. I will go to the police tomorrow and report it, the person in the garden, the intercom at home, the car and that." He pointed in disgust at the note.

"I want to come with you," Annie said. "After lunch tomorrow. Come to lunch with me, my mum and the boys but I don't want them to get wind of this, you understand." He nodded and kissed her on the forehead.

"Mark please stay tonight." Annie was desperate for company. She really couldn't bear to part with him tonight.

"Of course I will. If it's okay with you I'm going to run a bath, you can scrub my back if you want."

He ran out before she could react but Annie shouted, "I might scratch it!"

"Oh promises, promises!" Mark shouted.

The bathroom was small with just a standard sized bath in it. The décor reflected Annie's incredibly good taste. Mark climbed into the hot water and lay down. It was so quiet. He reflected on the weekend's events and was bursting with excitement; he had finally found someone who loved him the way he was. He didn't have to change; he didn't have to miss his rugby matches. Moreover his new companion was not only beautiful she was adorable and funny and oh such fabulous company.

"What you smirking at?" Annie entered the room naked just sporting two glasses of red wine. She climbed into the water, which was an incredible squash. She intimately placed herself between Mark's substantial thighs and drank from her glass. It was amazing how comfortable they had become with each other in such a short space of time. Mark had been so self-conscious he wouldn't strip off. When he told Annie this she laughed so loud. "How can you say that, look at you? I want to strip you naked and run my fingers all over your body when I am with you. It's such a fine specimen." She kissed his arm that was laid across her breasts.

How he can be so self-conscious, she thought. She was the one that had lost four stone since leaving Paul. She sagged in places she ought not to. Mark whispered, whilst kissing her neck, "You too have reservations about your body don't you?"

"Yes," she replied.

"Well you don't have to, I love every bit of you inside and out."

It's a good job she was laid in the bath otherwise she may have lost the use of her jelly legs. She felt her body temperature rising rubbing Mark's silky skin whilst he dabbed her shoulders with soap and water, occasionally not being able to resist a quick kiss on her neck.

After bathing they retired for the evening, both falling asleep instantly in each other's arms, only waking to the sound of the alarm clock.

7

"Oh, please tell me it's not Monday morning and that was not the alarm?" Mark's croaky morning voice came from under the covers.

"Well I could tell you but I'd be lying and as I am a good virtuous girl, I cannot lie to you!" Mark pulled Annie under the covers with him. She tried to resist but he was too strong for her.

He tucked her body under his and declared, "You're not going anywhere until I have my wicked way with you!" He tickled her as she tried to get out of his grasp.

"I'm going to be late and it will be your fault," she gurgled as she was released from his arms, "but hold that thought for this evening."

Mark, disappointed, rose from the bed. Annie felt guilty for refusing his advances but remedied the disappointment by sitting astride Mark at breakfast, kissing him. Mark soon forgave her. They left at the same time but in separate cars. Annie consoled herself knowing she would be reunited with her new playmate at one o'clock, although she was concerned what her mum's reaction would be when Mark turned up.

Annie had been lecturing for five years, attaining the college job shortly after graduating with a PhD at Leeds University. The business faculty she was part of had seen some changes of late and she was thankful she had survived the recent jobs cull. This was the first morning in the five years she felt unprepared. Entering the staff car park, she mused over two lectures this morning. Thankfully Monday was a half-day so she didn't have much blagging to do. Parking up she glanced over and saw Lucy racing over to the car.

"So you was with him all weekend then?" she blurted out finding it hard to conceal her excitement. Annie got out of the car and gathered her bags.

"How do you know?" Annie was slightly annoyed that her news had reached Lucy before she had the opportunity to say anything.

"John rang me last night to tell me how you were cosy-ing up at the rugby match," Lucy explained.

Annie could feel the anger rising in her body but resisted showing it. The last thing she wanted was Lucy tittle-tattling with John behind her back. Annie declared, "Yes I was with Mark all weekend. We had dinner Friday and sex,

Saturday sex then rugby match, then sex. Sunday bath together, rugby and bed TOGETHER!" Annie left Lucy open mouthed digesting her words.

Lucy soon caught up with Annie; walking along-side her, she said, "So you like him then."

Annie looked at Lucy and they both burst out laughing linking arms. God do I! Annie recalled she had had sex more times over one weekend than in the last five years!

"The sex was great Lucy but it was more than that – we connect far deeper than I have with anyone else I have ever met." Both chatted away walking across to the campus. They decided to avoid the café just in case John was in there.

Annie had been given a small lecture room on the ground floor. It held approximately thirty students. It was serviced by natural light from one Georgian styled window. At the front there was a desk, a lectern and a computer. Annie was still trying to master the advancement in technology even though her degree was in computing. She excused her ignorance by reminding everyone it was in strategic management of IT systems, that was her excuse and she was sticking to it!

Annie checked her watch to find she had five minutes before the lecture started although the students had started to wander in. Whilst she knew it was against college policy for tutors to display their mobile phones, she couldn't help herself. Had he texted her? Yes there was a text from Mark. All giddy she opened the inbox and the message read *'missing you M x'*. Her heart fluttered and quickly she typed in *'me too, looking forward to holding that fabulous body later A x'*. As quick as a flash a reply was received *'only holding me, I will be doing more than that to you hehe Mx'*. Unable to resist, she replied, *'If you are a good boy I may give you a BJ Ax'*. That was it. She had to put the phone away.

"Right," Annie barked as the students filed in. "Please sign the register. Today we are going to try something different. There is a question on the board. Decide if you agree or disagree with it. The 'agrees' move to the left of the room and the 'disagrees' to the right." She pointed in either direction. Annie was improvising due to her lack of preparation. "You have twenty minutes to work together to debate your reasoning. Choose a spokesperson. This is a debate similar to the House of Commons but preferably more maturely undertaken without the sniping and pathetic name calling." The crowd was amused by her ramblings.

Twenty minutes soon passed and Annie was aware she had to take control. Instead she appointed a speaker. Tony fancied himself as a bit of an entrepreneur and looked down on women; it was Annie's perfect opportunity to give him a platform in which to make himself look more stupid than normal.

The debate went really well, the students remarked on their enjoyment as they left the lecture theatre. Annie was feeling really proud of herself and the next lecture was a walk in the park. She was to sit and observe one of the Teaching Assistants giving a lecture. It was part of the college's CPD programme. Just enough time to check her mobile thought Annie. She fumbled in her bag. The message was clear. *'I got the impression you didn't want me to be a good boy! Either way I am missing you like crazy, roll on 1 o'clock Mxxxxxx.'* Annie just had enough time to send lots of kisses back.

This was torture for Annie. She longed to be with Mark but had to concentrate and grade her colleague, who was mighty boring. She couldn't help but notice some of the students yawning, which made her smile. Monday was always the worst day to lecture; students were recovering from their wild weekend frolics. Annie knew for once, how they felt.

Finally, after what seemed an eternity, the lecture was over. She stepped forward and gave a glowing recount of the lecture just dropping gentle hints of how to spice up his monotone voice. Eager to learn, her colleague listened intently and nodded enthusiastically.

Annie practically skipped all the way to the café. She waved through the window and was delighted to see Ed, Matt and their grannie colluding at the table but no Mark. She couldn't help but feel a little disappointed but that soon dispersed when her sons started telling tales to their Gran.

"Grannie you should see them, it's so sweet," mocked Ed. Annie sat there and took the mocking in good humour.

"Stand by Grannie, here comes…" Matt laughed.

Annie turned around eagerly and walking towards her was her hunk of a man carrying a massive bouquet of flowers.

"Sorry I am late and sorry for being corny!" Mark looked at the two giggling boys assuming the mocking was for his benefit. Annie cottoned on to his thoughts and stood up. Taking the flowers, she kissed Mark on the lips and said, "Don't worry about these two, they've been showing off to Grannie."

Mark sat next to Matt, nodded at him and leant over. "You must be Annie's mum?"

"Oh I am, I'm Andrea." She smiled so warmly he knew immediately where Annie got her inner strength and love. Matt, Ed and Mark went to look what was on offer at lunch.

Andrea smiled and said to her daughter, "He seems nice. Just be careful you know… don't jump in too fast." Annie acknowledged her mum's words but couldn't help think it was a bit late for the pep talk.

Annie was quiet over lunch. The boys were showing off and having a good banter with Mark. Her mum was watching Mark's every move and interaction with her grandsons. Annie's thoughts were on the evening that lay ahead. She just wanted to get Mark to herself; how selfish she felt.

"You all right love?" Mark asked. Annie nodded and smiled. He planted a kiss on her lips.

The boys immediately piped up in unison, "Aww how lovely, Grannie buy a hat!" The party laughed.

"So cheeky. When you going back down to London?" Annie turned to Ed.

Ed's response was suitably sarcastic. "Can't you wait to get rid of me?"

"Haha, very funny. I want to know if I will see you again before you go." Annie hated him leaving; she worried so much about him in London.

Mark joined the conversation. "Well I have an idea. Your mum and I have something we need to do this afternoon." Matt and Ed raised their eyebrows and nudged each other. Smiling Mark continued, "No but that would be great. We have something to take care of. When we've finished we can pick you up and you can come to mine for tea, if that's okay with you Annie?"

She beamed, knowing the boys would love Mark's place. "Yes that would be great."

They bid the boys and her mum goodbye and headed to the car park. Andrea was taking her two grandsons shopping then home.

Mark spoke first. "Shall we go to my local police station? Do you want to leave your car at mine?" Annie agreed.

She followed Mark up his driveway and parked the car outside his garage. Her car did not look out of place at all. She exchanged positions and joined Mark in his BMW. They drove to the police station neither sure how to make a complaint.

"I have been thinking," Annie said finally. "Do you think we are over reacting? It's only a couple of strange things that could have just been kids." After much debate they both agreed they were being paranoid.

"Before we pick the boys up, let's go for a walk," Mark suggested.

They parked up by the long meandering river in Wetherby. The paths were laden with ducks and geese. They managed to negotiate around them without losing grip on each other. They stopped at the side of the river. Mark stood behind Annie who was leaning on the safety barrier. The wind blowing through their hair, both their faces displayed a look of total contentment. The perfect picture of tranquillity and happiness.

They could have stayed there all afternoon but remembering their promise, well Mark's promise to the boys, they strolled back to the car. Annie accosted Mark at the driver's side of the car, closed her eyes and started to kiss him. He happily complied and soon they were emerged in each other again. Letting go was torture but necessary. As they drove away, Mark shuffled in his seat; Annie leant over and rubbed her hand along his jeans, yes she had done it to him again!

*

Annie watched with eager anticipation for her sons' reactions as they approached the house gates. It was hilarious, for the first time they were both lost for words, even Ed! Matt, ever protective of his mother, could not help but wonder how Mark managed a place this size on his former Rugby League's wages. It was a fair assumption as it was a well-known fact the pay was very modest in comparison to footballers' wages.

Mark parked the car in front of the door and they entered through the main entrance instead of the trade man's entrance Annie had used on her first night there. Annie kicked her shoes off which the boys found highly amusing. She remarked, "What has gotten into you two?" Ed leant on his mum. "We are just happy for you and Mark."

Matt nodded in agreement but Mark sensed Matt was a little wary of this union.

"Drinks anyone?" Mark enquired. Once watered, he gave them all a guided tour of the house. The bathroom and master bedroom drew particular attention from the boys especially when Mark blushed showing them in.

Back downstairs, he showed them the kitchen and the dining room. Then led them away from the garage entrance to an area Annie had not seen before. At the end of the corridor there were large double doors hiding a well-stocked gym including a sauna. The boys yelped with delight and started looking around the equipment.

Matt couldn't help himself. "Mark how come you can afford this house and all this stuff? Sorry and forgive me for being so rude, but I wouldn't have imagined this the home of a former rugby player."

"Matthew Swift!" Annie shouted. "How rude of you. I would expect something like that from your brother but not you."

"Thanks a lot Mum." Ed was offended.

"I'm sorry Mum but I have to ask. I don't want to upset either of you... it just seems strange."

Mark interrupted. "Matt it is perfectly okay to ask. I understand you want to protect your mum. She is an amazing woman. This house was paid for from some compensation I received from a Sunday newspaper that printed a load of lies about me. I invested it in the house so that my daughter had a future."

Annie was so embarrassed and threw a dirty look at Matt. Mark, seeing this, pulled on Annie's arm and drew her into him. "Annie it's fine, honestly."

Turning to Ed and Matt, Mark made a statement. "I want the both of you to understand one thing. I love your mum very much. I know it's crazy that we haven't known each other long, but I know I have never felt this way before and can categorically say I have never met anyone like this lady. I promise you I won't intentionally hurt her. Now you are to treat this house as your home. The room at the end is the lounge. In there you will find a TV and PS3 – set FIFA up for three of us please. I just want a minute with your mum." The boys hurried out of the gym heading straight for the lounge competing to be the first one there.

Mark whispered, "I would have got round to telling you anyway. Matt just made it easier. Annie, I do love you and if the boys weren't here now I would show you how much." He squeezed her whole body so she could hardly breathe. "Now it's my turn to put them in their places." Mark bounded off to play with the boys.

Annie stayed in the gym looking around all the equipment. She took herself to the patio doors and stared out of the window at the leaves changing colour on the trees. Autumn was her favourite time of year.

She could hear the banter between the three of them and it took her back to when the boys were young. On entering the room Mark looked at her and smiled. Mischievously Annie pretended to stand in front of the television and received abuse from all angles. She laughed.

After tea they resumed their tournament. Annie perched at Mark's side and watched the three of them interact.

She asked Ed, "What time is your train in the morning love?"

Ed in between playing and cursing at the missed shot replied, "Ten thirty at Leeds station."

Matt was training in the morning so Mark had already volunteered to pick up Ed and drop him at the station. He then informed them he was heading over to Manchester to see his daughter; Wednesday he had interviews all day providing his opinion on the up and coming places and impending Grand Final. Thursday he was in Salford for the Super League Show. Annie was impressed with how busy he was, envisaging he spent most of his days in the gym.

Mark spoke to the boys. "I don't know why I'm doing the interviews your mum should be. She knows far more than me." Turning to Annie he continued, "Maybe when you have some time off you can join me."

She ran her fingers through his hair and said, "I'd love to."

At 10.30 they all decided to call it a day. Annie decided to drive the boys home then return home to her house. She had a full day at work the next day and wanted to plan some of the lectures this time.

On leaving, Matt turned to Mark. "It's been great and thank you for being so open and understanding."

Mark shook his head. "Honestly it's fine – respect and honesty." Matt winked at Mark as he departed.

"Ring me when you get home please," Mark shouted. Annie agreed she would and off they went. Mark locked the door and was not ashamed to admit the house felt cold and lonely. He didn't like it at all; he wanted to pick up the phone and beg them to come back. He decided against it, as he did not want Annie to feel he was becoming overpowering.

"Night Mum." Matt kissed Annie on the cheek.

"Night Mum." Ed repeated the action. "I will ring you when I get home. Love you."

With that they were gone. Annie hated being alone now she had found Mark. She thought she'd get home and ring him there. Completing the fifteen-minute journey, she parked the car and walked to the house, closed the door and bolted it. Was there anyone out there? She wandered around the house putting the lights on and drawing the curtains except the kitchen blind which was too high for her to reach without a chair.

She sat on the bottom step and dialled Mark's number. "I'm home," she said. She was relieved to hear his voice. Sensing her anxiety, he enquired what was wrong. She explained her paranoia that she felt someone was watching her. He reassured her it was probably her imagination.

He asked, "Can I call round tomorrow when I get back from Manchester? I'll be home about seven o'clock." Annie agreed and knew that would give her a couple of hours after work to sort the house out. They said goodnight.

The bed was unbelievably bare without her. Mark lay there wishing she was at his side. He thought it ridiculous how he had fallen for her in such a short space of time. Oh but he adored everything about her. He smiled as he recalled the day's events, the boys' prankish behaviour, her reprimanding them but then her loving ways, so concerned for their and his welfare. She was such a warm-loving person and he missed her. He drifted off to sleep.

8

The sound of the alarm made Annie jump out of her sleep. Her head was pounding and she was reluctant to step out of the warm duvet. Out of habit, she picked up her mobile phone from the side of the cabinet; there were three unread messages. Blurry eyed, she opened the first from Ed. It read, *'Love you Mum, come down to London soon xxx'.* The second was from Mark. *'Hope you are okay this morning, up already heading to the gym. Will pick Ed up and take him to the station. Be at yours about 7 love u M xxx.'* This lifted her spirits. The next message curiously unnamed next to it just a number. Annie jumped out of bed when she read its contents. *'You have been warned. Stay away from Mark. He's trouble.'*

Her heart started racing, she could barely stop her hands from shaking as she looked through her call list for Mark's number.

"It's me," she said, her voice quivering as Mark answered.

"Annie what's up? Annie?" She found it hard at first to form any words but breaking her silence she explained what had happened.

"Stay there," he said, "I'm coming over."

Annie replied, "No I have work today."

Mark persuaded her this was more important than work and encouraged her to throw a 'sickie', which she reluctantly complied with. She showered and dressed going over in her mind whom it could be. Her thoughts turned to Paul, her ex or to John. She concluded it couldn't possibly be anyone Mark had crossed; they wouldn't know her details. Her trial ended with the sound of the doorbell ringing. She bounced down the stairs, looked through the glass panel and was relieved to see Mark standing there.

Mark crossed the threshold holding out his hand for the offending text. He kissed Annie and led her into the living room on the couch where they sat studying the contents of the message and the number. Neither knew the number. Mark pressed a number of buttons, put the phone on loudspeaker and dialled. Surprise, surprise it went onto the network answering service.

He turned to Annie. "Did you ring work?" She nodded.

Mark announced, "Right, we'll get Ed off to London, we'll go to Manchester and then go to the police station." Annie studied the concerned look on his face.

She was a little angry that he felt the need to come in and take over. "No," she replied, "I am going into work later. I am not going to change my whole day because of this."

"Yes you are!" He was so adamant, she half admired it and was half gutted by it. She knew he was right and didn't really want to be on her own but she felt wounded Mark presumed she couldn't take care of herself.

*

"Not a word to Ed about this," Annie warned Mark as they pulled up outside Matt's flat.

"I do believe you're sulking," Mark jested digging in her ribs as she sat looking so fresh and beautiful. At first she didn't even look at him choosing to stare at her feet but then she couldn't hold the laughter in any longer. Annie reached over and slapped his thigh. They were back on track!

The journey to the station was only ten minutes but trying to hide the truth from Ed was easier said than done especially when he knew his mum should have been working.

He studied them both for a little while before curiosity got the better of him. "Mum, why aren't you at work? And why are you two so quiet?"

Mark answered on Annie's behalf, which irritated her again. "Your mum's coming to Manchester with me today to see Sophie my daughter."

Annie was cross. "Oooo Mum you naughty girl, throwing a sickie." Ed couldn't help making fun, he was a loveable rogue.

Annie barked, "I am not throwing a sickie. I have a day off in lieu and thought I would see you off."

She looked out of the passenger window to try to prevent herself from bursting into tears. It wasn't like her to let things get to her but this was new territory. She'd met a wonderful man but just as she thought she was going to be happy beyond her wildest dreams, a spanner had been thrown in the works. The story of her life!

The rest of the short journey was in silence. When they pulled up at the train station, Annie was the first one out. Ed joined her and she slipped £100 into his coat pocket. He thanked her and hugged his mum with great affection. He knew there was something wrong when the return hug was tight and she lingered not wanting to let him go.

"Mum," he whispered, "you're squashing me. I will be home again soon or why don't you and Mark come down to London to see me. I'll take you to Hamleys." She let go and smiled. Making no promises she bid him farewell and slumped back into the car. Before Mark could ask if she was all right, she was dialling Matt's number. It went to the answering machine, which she knew really, as he would be training. She just wanted to hear his voice. She left a message and hung up.

Mark really didn't know what to say. He didn't understand why she was so angry with him. Did she think he was making the threats? He knew it was possible that a number of psychos from his past could be stalking them but how did they get Annie's personal phone number? He thought it best not to discuss it any further until Annie had got her head round it and could at least look at him again.

Annie broke the silence as they were approaching Birch services. "Can we stop please? I need a drink!"

Mark nodded and pulled over to the left-hand lane ready to exit the motorway. Pulling up in the car park, Annie turned to Mark and placed her hand tenderly on his cheek. "I'm sorry. I am not used to complying with someone else's orders."

Mark joined his hand with hers and brought them down to his mouth, kissing her fingers. "I'm sorry too. I shouldn't have taken over and assumed you wanted me there. I was a jerk." He continued as Annie shook her head, "I was Annie. I am so scared that you are going to be taken from me."

Mark allayed her fears. "No not that I think any harm is going to come but that you are going to leave me."

Annie withdrawing her hand from him replied, "I don't want you to get hurt either but these messages are starting to freak me out. It's always the case in my life that when someone fantastic comes along, trouble invariably follows. I can't just be happy."

Mark answered, "You can and we will. We will get through this. This will pass. We will be together. Now come on, I need a coffee."

Mark's words were warm and her mood lightened as they walked hand in hand into the service area. She looked up at him and laid her head on his arm. He soothingly ran his hand over her face and kissed her on the forehead.

*

All caffeined out, they both left the services with smiles on their faces. The cloud had lifted from above them and they walked like two school children swinging their entwined hands between them. The rest of the journey was lighter. Annie had managed to speak to Matt who had finished training and Ed had texted her from the train to tell her how much he loved her. Life was sweet again and looking on the bright side, feeling a little guilty for letting work down, she looked over to her companion and relished spending the rest of the day with him.

As they approached Salford, Annie glanced in the mirror. "No it can't be," she said out loud. "What was the registration number of that car Mark?"

Mark replied, "I can't remember off the top of my head, it's on a piece of paper in my wallet, here." Mark passed his wallet to Annie. She opened it to find a photograph on the inside of a beautiful blonde girl with amazing crystal blue eyes. She assumed it was Sophie. Returning to the matter in hand she scrambled through his wad of cash and cards. The paper was there. She read it out: "NW68 STH," as she scoured through the rear-view mirror.

"Mark it's there again, three cars back!" Mark confirmed it was there but again the tinted windows prevented them from securing the identity of the driver. Mark put his foot down but knew he was running out of motorway to shake off the chaser. Junction eighteen was fast approaching. Mark stayed in the middle lane until the last moment then dived off the junction. The pursuing car had no choice but to remain on the motorway. Once off the motorway, both occupants looked at each other and knew it was definitely time to seek professional help. This was ridiculous. He was a retired rugby player and she was a college lecturer, a beautiful clever and very sexy one but all the same Mark could not find an explanation why this was happening to them.

Thankfully, the rest of the journey was uneventful. Annie's hand only lifted from Mark's thigh when he had to change gear. He had been right in them staying together today. Her nerves were on edge and she doubted whether she could cope with all this alone. It reminded her of her marriage break up when she was constantly pursued and harassed by her ex-husband. The lengths he went to, to prevent her from carrying on with her life were truly terrifying. She was confident this was not his work; he had disappeared two years after she left, neither her nor Matt had heard from him since. She half expected him to crawl out of the woodwork when Matt achieved his first professional contract – both Matt and she had been prepared but had not relished the idea. It never happened. She decided that she would tell Mark all her sordid past that night. It was best it came from her and was out in the open, in case this was her doing.

"We are here love," Mark said as he squeezed her hand. The halls of residence were nothing like those she remembered. Fallowfield was known as "student village" and a short walk from the university. It was a complex that had lots of halls of residence located together and conveniently close to the Manchester nightlife. Mark led Annie into Linton House, a small old building that smelt musty and felt cold. They walked up two flights of stairs and Mark finally knocked on a green door. The young lady on the wallet photograph opened the door with childish excitement. She was taken aback that her dad had brought a companion with him. As they walked through the hall, Sophie asked, "Is this Annie then Dad?"

Mark nodded. Sophie continued, "Hi Annie I'm Sophie. Please excuse the mess, my flatmate is a slob and if I'd have known Dad was bringing a visitor I would have tidied up!" she said glaring at her dad's imposition.

"It's all right Sophie; I was a student once and now lecture students. My two boys are the untidiest people you could meet."

Sophie laughed and hugged her dad. "You brought me anything?" she said, trying to peek into the bag Mark was carrying.

"I might have," he teased. She took the bag from him that included two new tops, a couple of CDs and some groceries including her favourite tipple, vodka.

"I'm sure she only wants me to visit so I bring things for her," Mark smiled as he filled the kettle with water, "and look, I even have to make my own drink."

Annie smiled. She didn't feel that Sophie warmed to her as much as her boys had warmed to Mark but she understood that Sophie had not had to share her father in a long while.

Mark asked Sophie, "Do you fancy getting dressed and going to lunch? I thought we'd go to Sam Platts." Annie loved Sam Platts but today it would be a little quieter. She recalled when the boys were little, they would go there just before the Grand Finals and soak up the atmosphere of the fans from all different clubs chanting and singing together. Only in Rugby League, she thought.

Sophie scuttled off to get ready. Mark made the drinks and both of them settled down facing each other at the table. It was a pokey place, the kitchen diner quite dull with not much natural light. They sipped their drinks but Mark couldn't help himself. He could not sit opposite Annie without reaching out his hand. She mirrored him and they sat there.

"Sam Platts eh? Our paths must have crossed so many times in the past without us even knowing. We spent hours before each Grand Final in Sam Platts. It became a superstition as the only time we lost was the year we didn't go in," Annie said.

Mark smiled at her. For once he just wanted to listen to her, her enthusiasm and zest for life was so infectious. Why couldn't their paths have crossed years ago, all those wasted years they had both suffered to get where they were now. The thought saddened Mark to think why both of them had had such hard lives – had they deserved it or brought it on themselves? Sophie returned fully clothed and ready to go.

It was approximately five miles from Sophie's to Sam Platts. Annie and Sophie exchanged pleasantries during the short journey. Mark and Annie knew Sophie was trying to survey her dad's new playmate; she was suspicious of her and made no attempt to hide it. After the events of the morning, Annie was tiring of her cross-examination. Mark could sense this as he led them both upstairs to the bar. Annie chose a window seat overlooking the quay watching the university rowing team practising their strokes in the water, doing their best to avoid vexing the swans that really didn't want to share their water.

Annie looked over to the bar. Mark and Sophie were deep in conversation, well more of a telling off by her father. When they joined Annie at the table, she knew Sophie had been reprimanded for her incessant questioning and sarcasm. Mark sat opposite Annie and pulled his chair in. He strategically placed his knee so that it was touching her. She responded by wrapping her foot around his ankle and smiled. The remainder of the lunch was very pleasant. Annie had ordered a light lunch commenting on the lack of exercise over the weekend coupled with the indulgent meals. Mark squeezed her leg with his and she knew what he was thinking. The exercise had been there just a different type that certainly wasn't disciplined, more's the pity, she thought.

Mark spoke. "You can use the gym when we get back. I'll make you sweat." Annie looked at Sophie and they both burst out laughing.

Sophie scoffed. "Dad! Leave your dirty thoughts at home, young impressionable girl present!"

Mark blushed, he could always be relied on to drop clangers but they were always priceless ones. They chatted about Sophie's studies, the grand final and the impending play-offs. Mark insisted on settling the bill much to Annie's annoyance but she did not want to pursue her independent morals again.

As they drove back to Linton House, Sophie asked, "I have a music recital next Monday evening in the City Campus. Will you both come?" Annie felt this was a breakthrough. They agreed to attend and Annie put the details into her phone so that a reminder would ensure they did not forget especially with everything going on.

Mark and Annie watched Sophie bounce into the halls of residence. As she opened the door, she turned and blew a kiss. Mark reversed the car and said, "You'll have to excuse my daughter's inquisitive mind but she doesn't know when to give it a rest."

"A bit like Ed," Annie replied. They both laughed. It had been a pleasant afternoon, the September sun was low but when in the direct sunlight it was warm. They took a leisurely drive back to Leeds both not really wanting to reach their destination of the local police station but it had to be done.

Pulling up outside the police station left a sinking feeling in both their stomachs. They knew they would have to go through every sordid detail of their past, neither quite sure how the other one would take it and whether their newly formed alliance would last.

9

"Are you sure we should be doing this?" Annie said nervously as they walked across the car park. Mark was confused by her hesitation.

Annie qualified her stance. "I mean we haven't discussed all of our pasts and things might have to be said that could put you off me."

Mark was stunned. He found it hard to find the words to come back at such a daunting prospect. "What can be worse than you have told me already?"

She hugged him and stammered, "Lots."

Mark replied decisively, "However hard this gets for either of us we have to promise we will see it through. Promise me, Annie." He looked straight into her eyes, his determination for an answer palpable.

"I promise," she said as she opened the door.

"This is DS Charlie Dunne and I am DCI Harry Fisher. Please come this way." The greying gentleman led the couple into an interview room. Charlie Dunne, the smaller but plumper of the two closed the door and switched on the lights.

"I understand from the desk sergeant that you want to make a complaint? Don't be alarmed but we will be recording the information in case we need to use it later. Give us a few minutes to set up. Would either of you like a drink?" the DCI said whilst fiddling about with the tape recorder situated on the desk between the policemen and the couple. Annie thought in this day and age you'd think they'd use newer technology.

Both Annie and Mark turned down the offer of a drink opting to get on with it. They both shared the desire of getting out of there as quickly as possible. Mark gave his account of the note, the black car and Annie confirmed his account and added the text message and today's further run in with the car. Every now and then the officers would glance at each other raising their eyebrows. Annie couldn't help but think they didn't believe them especially as when they finished their accounts, they sounded so absurd. Both Mark and Annie left the room and were escorted back to the front desk.

DCI Fisher turned to Mark and said, "Do you think this has anything to do with your previous problems with that fan?" Mark shrugged his shoulders hoping it wasn't.

"We'll be in touch. We will check her whereabouts now just to eliminate her. In the meantime if there is anything else, my mobile number is on this card. As a precaution we recommend you get a security expert to your house – you still live in that divine detached property?" Mark nodded, wanting the ground to swallow him up. He could feel Annie's glare piercing the back of his neck.

Annie joined in, "We don't live together. I live off Street Lane," as if wanting to wound Mark for not telling her about the 'fan'. The DCI should have known that. He had just listened to her version of events!

The DCI looked at Mark and then Annie. "Until we eliminate her from our enquiries I would suggest you remain vigilant and try not to be alone for too long. It may be useful if you don't live alone."

Walking out Annie was adamant she was not losing any more of her independence. No way was she moving in with Mark until she was ready and it would be on her terms. She stomped back to the car. "Who the hell does he think he is?" she shouted.

"Shhh," said Mark. "He'll hear you. Annie he is only doing his job."

Annie retaliated, "Doing his job. Instead of telling me how to live my life, maybe he should be out there looking for who is doing this to us."

She slammed the car door. Mark joined her and continued, "Please don't be mad at me. I don't want any of this. I just wanted to meet someone beautiful, kind and loving to share precious times with." He took his frustration out on the gearbox as he tried to find reverse.

"Where we going?" he snapped, leaving the car park, his tyres screeching.

She didn't mean to take it out on him. It wasn't his or her fault. They had got together in all innocence both knowing each would have a past.

"Mine please," she finally said lowering the tone of her voice.

They didn't speak the whole journey, both of them in their own worlds going through things over and over again. Neither knew what would stop this, well they did but there was no way breaking up was an option, not at this stage anyway.

Mark pulled up outside her house. She got out and he stayed there staring straight ahead of him. He was hurt and annoyed not just at the way she had lashed out at him but at the thought that the mad cow was after him again.

Annie bent down into the car. "You coming in? It will take me about an hour to pack the things that I need." Mark was so shocked; he'd resigned himself to dropping her off and not seeing her again. He hadn't even realised her car was parked in his drive. She added, "Come on you can put those muscles to good use."

"Aye aye Captain." Mark saluted at Annie following her into the house.

Annie had decided the best thing was to look after each other and stand united. There was a chance of someone driving a wedge between them if they lived apart, besides recalling the DCI's words, this could fizzle out and be over in a couple of days. She grabbed the large suitcase and holdall from under the bed whilst Mark looked on feeling totally helpless. She threw the holdall at him and suggested he started to fill it with the books she needed for work.

The phone rang. She jumped and cagily retrieved it from her jean's pocket. "It's Matt." They both sighed with relief.

"Hi love. Yes I did want to speak to you to let you know Ed got the train okay and I'm going to stay at Mark's for a couple of days... Yes I'm at the house at the moment. See you in five then." She hung up and looked at Mark who was busy studying her books. "He's calling in now. We have to tell him. He needs to know."

"Okay whatever you think is best." Mark knew Matt was level-headed but wasn't sure he would understand what was going on; no one in their right mind would.

After filling the suitcase with clothes and toiletries, Mark and Annie made their way downstairs to collect the laptop and paperwork. The doorbell rang and Mark answered the door. Matt came in, kissed his mum and moved straight into the kitchen, opening the fridge door. Annie laughed; this was a habit both her sons had not grown out of.

"So why the rush?" came the voice out of the fridge.

"Sit down Matt," Annie said. Holding his hand she recounted the recent events. Matt tried to interrupt a few times but Annie continued regardless. After hearing all, Matt turned to Mark. "Take care of my mum. Make sure no harm comes to her or I swear there'll be trouble." Matt thought once more before saying, "What you doing with this place?"

"I thought you might like to move in for now, give up that pokey flat. You could ask one of your team-mates to move in with you. I'd rather it not be left empty," Annie suggested without thinking of the consequences of potentially putting her offspring at risk. Neither her nor Mark thought it possible that this crazed person would direct their attentions at anyone but them.

"I'll have a word with Mick and Ben and see if they want to. I know they are sharing digs with rats at the moment." He looked at his watch. "I have to go I have a personal appearance in Pudsey tonight. I still have my key somewhere. I will move in tomorrow. Will you call after work?" Annie agreed she would call on her way home from work. She kissed Matt goodbye and locked the back door not before she did a quick scan of the street.

Time was pressing on. Mark was standing by the sink when she returned to the room, his head and shoulders down, looking as if he had the weight of the world on his shoulders. She walked up behind and wrapped her arms around his waist for as far as they could go. Her head rested in the middle of his back. His breathing was erratic. She let go and forced him to face her. Tears were rolling down his face. She kissed them as they fell. Hugging him, it was his turn to lay his head on her shoulder.

"I'm sorry Annie, I'm so sorry," he sobbed. "If I'd have thought I would have brought you misery I wouldn't have tried to track you down." She squeezed him hardly making an impression on his body. Her arms stretched up and held both his wet cheeks.

"You didn't, the idiot that's doing this is. I want to be with you Mark. We can get through this together. We just have to be united and have faith." Again Annie demonstrated her inner strength that she swore she did not have but she had it in abundance.

He wiped his face on his sleeve and, placing one hand on her back the other on her neck, he kissed her. The kiss was different somehow. It was sensitive and loving not with force or vigour. Annie's knees started to go weak again. He moved his arm from her back to round the back of her knees. Mark scooped her into his arms. Carrying her upstairs, he never stopped kissing her. In the throes of another passionate encounter they forgot all about the stressful day and were lost together in a demonstration of lust for each other.

It was dark when they reappeared from the bedroom. Just a few more things to pack then they could be off. Annie drew all the curtains and left some lights on. Her suitcases were piled next to the door in the hallway where they had left them. Mark was in the lounge flicking through the TV channels. Annie had thought about taking her F1 cars and trophies but she didn't know how long she would be away. Matt would look after them. The letterbox rattled behind them. Mark threw the remote down and went to discover a scrap of paper on the floor; it read: "You're finished!" in the same handwriting as the first note. He unlocked the door and gave chase. He ran barefooted down the street but there was no one about. He returned to the house, gave Annie the note and sat on the bottom step to catch his breath.

"Let's get out of here," he said breathless. Annie could not agree with him more. They loaded both cars with stuff, locked the door. When they arrived, Annie moved her car. Both cars fitted in the garage and the door came down. Safe at last they both thought.

After unloading the car, Mark moved some of his clothes out of the bedroom into a spare room. Annie replaced them with her clothes.

"While you do that," he said, "I'm going to ring the police station and let them know about the next note." He tapped Annie on the bottom as he left the room.

Annie looked around the large bedroom. It was so tastefully decorated in cream and chocolate with a seating area located in the large bay window. There was a door in the corner of the room that she had not noticed before. Inquisitively she opened it up to find a beautiful balcony with breakfast area. Looking around she surmised this was above the garage and she imagined herself sitting there on a summer's morning drinking coffee and reading her Kindle.

Mark walked in behind her. "So you have found my hiding place then?" he smiled, kissing her on the back of her neck. "This is where we can drink coffee in the summer if we are still together." He squeezed his arms around her shoulders.

Breaking free to resume putting her clothes away, Annie asked, "What did the DCI say?"

"He is coming to see us tomorrow night about eight. I thought that would give you time to see Matt and come home to papa." He was perched on the end of the bed. She jumped forward and pushed him flat on the bed. She tried to get off but he held her down. She was balanced on his torso and mouthed I love you. He kissed her then let her go. He got up and disappeared out of the room.

Ten minutes passed before he re-entered the bedroom. Annie had just closed the wardrobe door, she saw his reflection in the glass door and burst out laughing. He was standing in the doorway wearing nothing but a shower cap and carrying a bottle of champagne and two flutes. He winked and turned around; she followed him skipping to catch up and struck him with her palm on his bare backside. He squealed like a pig. He had spent the last ten minutes preparing the hot tub, candles were lit all the way round and soft music was playing in the background. The bathroom was filled with the smell of camomile; steam rose from the tub. Mark balanced the glasses and bottle on the side of the tub. He turned to Annie and started undressing her. When she tried to assist, he slapped her hand. "Allow me," he whispered in her ear and she loved every minute of his hands touching her body.

Annie got into the water first, boy it was hot. She winced and sat down just in time for Mark to splash bubbles everywhere when his body hit the water. He poured the champagne out and passed Annie a glass. She smiled and leant forward to whip the shower cap off his head and throw it to the floor.

She shook her head. "You nutter!" she declared.

"Yeah but I hope I'm your nutter." He ducked himself under the water and came up with a face full of suds, she laughed so loud. She pulled him towards her, rubbed the bubbles from his face and declared, "Yes you are mine."

Mark slipped to the side of Annie and they laid there in silence sipping the champagne. Both had the same thoughts. They could get used to this. Mark put his glass down and shuffled around so he was in front of Annie laying his head between her breasts looking up at her with puppy dog eyes. She tried to pretend not to be interested but it was short lived. They rubbed noses together.

Mark, resting his hands on her thighs said, "We can get through this together. It's going to get worse before it gets better but I'll do everything to stop this."

Annie believed him but asked, "What did the police mean by 'fan'?" Mark sighed slid under the water and re-emerged at Annie's side. "When I was playing I met a fan."

"You mean you had one fan! Wow," Annie laughed.

Mark screwed his face up and continued. "I told you about her when we were at Garry's place." Annie remembered the story but looked confused.

"I didn't tell you the whole story." Guilty of being selective with the truth, Mark continued, "I said she had befriended me. It was more than that; she became obsessed with me. Wherever I went she was there. I tried to let her down gently and when that didn't work I was really abrupt and direct. I took advice from the club's solicitors and they arranged an injunction to stop her from coming to the training ground, the club and my home. The injunction only made it worse… it got much much worse." Mark paused reliving the events in his head. "We think she killed our dog, he was found poisoned in the woods. My life was made hell, my car was vandalised four times but the last straw came when she accused me of raping her. Annie it was the worst time of my life. Young rugby star portrayed as some kind of sex pest. I was accused for doing nothing. My wife didn't even believe me, and she left with Sophie to her mum's. We lived in Wigan at the time and all my family was plagued and hounded by the press."

Annie could not get her head around this; she thought she'd been unlucky! "How did you prove your innocence?" Annie asked.

"Thankfully the club believed in me and the solicitors they used were outstanding. Her story had so many holes in it. It went to trial but I was found not guilty. She was assessed under the Mental Health Act and sectioned for schizophrenia." Mark spared Annie the gory details; he really did not want to scare the living daylights out of her nor did he want to relive the details.

"I kept a scrapbook of the newspaper clippings for Sophie just in case it was ever raised again."

Annie stroked his head. "So the copper thinks she may have been released?" Correcting her, Mark said, "No Annie he is just checking that's all. Tomorrow I will ask the security company to come round and service the alarm. I don't want to live in Fort Knox but I do have someone very precious to protect."

"Aww love you too," Annie said.

Mark laughed. "I'm more terrified of what your boys would do to me if anything happened to…" before he could answer Annie pushed his head under the water. Mark had not expected this and resurfaced coughing. Playfully he went back under the water and pulled Annie's leg first under with him. They re-emerged in the middle of the tub and kissed each other.

"Come on you shrivelled prune, let's get you out," Annie said as she started to climb out. He lay down and watched her covering her beautiful body with his bathrobe. He thought he must have done something right to have found such a warm and tender person. When he finally got out of the bath Annie was right he did look like a prune. He walked into the bedroom with a towel around him only to find she was asleep on the bed. The day had exhausted her. It had all been too much for her. He grabbed a pair of shorts, turned all the lights off and climbed into bed behind Annie. He couldn't resist putting his arms around her waist and lying with his head resting on hers.

10

Annie's alarm sounded at 6 a.m. She awoke to find Mark fast asleep at the side of her. She had showered and dressed before he'd even stirred. Annie heard him coming down the stairs; she popped her head out of the kitchen. "Morning sleeping beauty."

He yawned and smiled. "Morning." He kissed her as she handed him a cup of coffee.

"I'm going to have to set off shortly. I need to go in early and mop up any problems from yesterday." She gulped her coffee down whilst putting on her shoes. Mark admired her look this morning. Smart black skirt, white blouse, black cardigan and a very sophisticated black and silver scarf. "You look gorgeous, better with no clothes though," Mark commented under his breath.

She smiled. "I love it when you talk dirty to me and just for you, I have stockings on."

He winced with pleasure.

Mark now knew how he was going to pass the hours between interviews today. He had a very sly wry smile on his face. Annie knew he was up to no good. She gestured for him to push the dining room chair out a little. As he complied she sat on his knee. "Now see if you can stay out of trouble while I'm at work. You can get yourself into all sorts of trouble with me tonight. I'm thinking early to bed but little sleep." With that tease, Annie got up, gathered her things and was out the door.

Suited and booted Mark left the house at ten to arrive at the Leeds Metropol Hotel for eleven. The first interview was scheduled for twelve then every half hour 'til two thirty p.m. He reflected how good his life was, especially now. After the interviews, he planned to visit the supermarket for a special tea and get some keys cut. He then remembered he needed to call the security company. Fearing he might forget later, he rang the number on the hands free. The helpful voice asked what service he required. He explained, in not too much detail, that he wanted a free security survey including the possibility of CCTV. There, the engineer was booked for four o'clock, he thought.

Annie could hear movement in her office. Nervously she twisted the door handle and entered. "Jeez John you scared me!"

John looking sheepish explained. "I wasn't sure if we would see you today so I was looking for your planning and preparation file." Suspiciously he shifted away from her desk and stuttered, "So how are you today? You wasn't at home last night, I called to see you."

Alarmed at this statement, Annie went on the defensive. "I stayed at Mark's. He looked after me."

Noting her tone of voice, John left with nothing more to say. Annie too had a number of tasks to complete this morning and taking an A4 piece of paper she started making a list:

Weds	*Lectures – prepare on Adam Smith's theory of free enterprise – level 4*
Thurs am	*Lectures – prepare on European economic policy during WW2 – level 5*
	Mark assignments
Research	*MS articles*
	Don't forget call at the house to see Matt.

Annie surveyed the list and wondered how she was going to get it all done in one day. Research was her speciality yet it had never entered into her head to look into Mark's past. She could do it discreetly and secretly so he would never know she had been delving into his past. Yet she felt incredibly guilty – how could she ask for honesty when she was searching about him behind his back? She didn't even know how old he was for God's sake!

The phone bleeped, another text message from Mark. *'Arrived at the Metropol shame you're not here. They have some wonderful beds, could just imagine you naked across one inviting me to join you Mxx.'* She loved him, there was no doubt. *'I would rather be there being naughty with you than stuck in this office on my own. Mind you it would be nice if you was perched on the desk right in front of me with your…'* she left it at that.

Right Annie, she thought, you better get your work head on and try to complete at least one task. She put on her music in the background and set to work. She did not stop working until twelve o'clock when Lucy popped her head around the door to collect her for lunch.

"Have you got much done?" Lucy asked. Annie nodded. She was tackling a huge question in her conscience. Should she tell Lucy everything or keep it to herself? She could certainly do with a confidante at this moment in time but she wasn't sure whether that should be a work colleague. After much consideration she opted to use Matt has her confidante. She did decide to drip feed selective information to her over lunch.

After selecting and paying for their lunch, Lucy and Annie sat down. Annie spoke first. "I've moved into Mark's."

Lucy spat her coffee all over the table. "You didn't waste any time did you!" was her reply whilst she wiped the table clean.

Annie leant forward over the table and whispered, "There are things happening Lucy that I can't explain to you right now." She paused fearing she would say too much. "You have to trust me on this. Things are great between Mark and I but there is someone trying to cause trouble. We don't know who yet but we will." Annie regretted saying the words as soon as they came out but it was said.

Biting into her sandwich Lucy said, with her mouth full, "Well as long as you both know what you are doing." Changing the subject Lucy said, "I can't wait 'til half term, I am fed up already."

Annie agreed. "We've been back a couple of weeks and I'm sick of this place."

As they finished their sandwiches John joined them at the table. He looked haggard and windswept. He was carrying some papers that were all curled up at each corner.

"Assignments to mark?" Annie enquired smirking.

John vexed with her mickey-taking snapped back, "No actually. I thought you'd be interested in these." He thrust the papers across the table at Annie.

She briefly read the headline: 'Rugby Star's underage sex'. Red-faced she grappled with the papers ready to explode. "How dare you?" she said. "Who the hell do you think you are prying into my business?" She stood up and the table rocked.

John stood too. "Well someone has to tell you the truth because HE isn't!"

Something snapped inside, Annie had never felt such anger. "You stupid sad man. These stories were untrue. He received compensation after suing the papers."

John was purple in the face. He realised he had not scored vital points but alienated the woman he loved. He turned and scuttled out of the café with twenty or so pairs of eyes glaring at him. Whilst Annie was fuming at the lies and confrontation, Lucy was having a good look at the materials John had obtained. Shaking her head every now and then.

"It's all lies." Annie defended her man. "Lucy it's all lies. We have been getting hate mail and being followed that's why I have moved in with Mark. The police think this nutter," Annie pointed at the photograph in the paper, "this nutter may have been released."

Lucy was too immature to take it all in at once. Her response was inevitable. "God Annie you always pick 'em! What you gonna do, you can't stay with him."

Annie was reddening again. "I can and will be staying with him. We will get to the bottom of all this. I am going back to my office. I'm going to cancel my lecture this afternoon and go home."

Annie left. She emailed the Senior Administrator and said due to unforeseen circumstances she would have to leave now and would not be returning today. She advised she would email in the morning if she wasn't going to be in. Annie locked her office day and stomped down the corridor.

Her phone bleeped. It was a message from Mark. *Just finished, running a few errands then will be home. See you when you get back from meeting Matt Mxx.'* She rang him.

"Hi." His voice beamed with happiness.

"Hi," she replied in not such a happy tone. "I am leaving work early. John has printed all the past newspaper articles off concerning you and threw them at me at lunch. He was mortified that I knew about it all. I swear if I stay I will do something I will regret."

Mark knew she was furious and suggested she met him at the supermarket. She agreed.

Mark was waiting in his car. He greeted her with a loving kiss and a hug. She had calmed down during the journey.

Mark mused, "Well this is a first, shopping together – a right proper couple now," he joked. She dug her elbow into his ribs as they walked to the entrance. Walking around the store, they exchanged stories of each other's morning. Mark advised her, the security guys were coming round at four o'clock. It was quarter past three when they left the supermarket. Annie decided to go straight to her house to wait for Matt while Mark had the pleasure of putting the shopping away and waiting for the security company.

*

Ben was unloading his things from his car when Annie arrived at the house. Ben and Mick were doing their best to trip each other up in childish pranks. "Hi Mrs S," Ben said as he heaved boxes into the house. Matt came out of the living room to hug his mum and asked, "Mark not with you?"

Annie replied, "No he is back at home." Matt smiled, even if she would not admit it he knew his mum was smitten and he predicted she would remain at the mansion and not return to her humble abode.

Matt continued, "I spoke to Ed last night. He told me I had to keep an eye on you, he suspected something was up but didn't know what." Matt looked straight into his mum's eyes. She was hiding something, he knew it. Sitting down at the dining room table, she beckoned Matt to join her. She told him everything and showed him the newspaper clippings John had found. He surveyed the information and asked, "Is he worth it Mum?"

"I think so," was her reply. "No he is Matt, I have fallen for him but not in a way I have ever fallen before. He is so warm and gentle, attentive and thoughtful. I don't want to lose him over our pasts. Let's face it my past hasn't been a walk in the park."

Matt reached out and held his mum's hand and said, "Hang on in there then. I will let Ed know about all this. Mark seems a decent guy and I have a strong feeling he is trustworthy. If it's okay with you and Mark, I'll come over to the house tomorrow night and we can have a chat without these idiots interrupting us." Annie's phone rang and as if by instinct, it was Ed. He was jovial as ever and couldn't wait to burst out that he'd been picked to play in the first team against York City Knights. Annie squealed with delight. The game was on Sunday at York and he'd ordered tickets already.

"Mum I've got tickets for you, Mark and Matt. I hope you don't mind but I'm gonna try to avoid telling Dad, he'll just criticise me…" Out of the mouth of babes, Annie thought, only they weren't babies any more. She reassured him it was up to him and said goodnight. Matt shouted he would ring his little brother later.

Time was ticking on and Annie really wanted to be there when the security firm called round. She also wanted to prepare herself for the visit from the police. She kissed Matt and drove home. That was a strange thought to her – home. She wasn't quite sure whether to call it home.

Mark was outside in the garden when she pulled up the drive. He was talking to the security guy, his arms animated. He was standing in a white Adidas T-shirt, Bermuda shorts and flip-flops. Annie felt a weird sensation run through her body as she looked at him. He was a picture, his bulging muscles peeking through the white T-shirt. She pulled her car into the garage and was met by Mark.

"How was your day dear?" he said mockingly. "Come here while I kiss you all over." Annie ran around the car. "Mark we have a guest," nodding towards the security guy who was standing, watching.

"I have serviced your alarm and written out a plan for the extra sensors and vipers for the windows. We have ordered the four CCTV cameras and the camera access control panel for the front gate. Someone will be back on Friday to fit them." He bid them goodbye and left.

"How much is all that going to cost?" Annie said as she walked into the kitchen, kicking her shoes under the table.

Mark grabbed her from behind. "A small price for our safety and sanity." He kissed the back of her bare neck, fumbling his hands all over her body. She gasped as he brushed her breasts. He spun her round and kissed her passionately. His tongue dancing round hers, she could hardly catch her breath. He stripped her scarf and cardigan off letting them slip to the floor. Annie, instantly turned on, slipped her hands under his T-shirt. She scratched up and down his back and he groaned in her ear. He moved their bodies towards the table and threw all the papers off onto the floor. Annie climbed up on the edge of the table. Mark pressed up against her; she could feel him, hard against her. Annie reached into his shorts and started caressing him. Mark stood back a little to let her play. She slipped off the table and knelt before him, inserting him into her mouth. He fell against the wall. Perfect, it was perfect. He enjoyed every minute of her lips, how she teased him with her tongue. He picked her up under her arms and as he lifted her on the table, rubbing his hands on the top of her lacy stockings, he inserted himself into her. She writhed with pleasure, both their bodies jerking and moving against the wood until both screamed in delight. He slumped on her in a heap.

Moving slowly from her, he said, "We had better sort out some tea pronto and get ready for the coppers coming." He kissed her bare inner thigh. They showered individually and then whilst Annie was clearing up the mess their little escapade had caused, Mark made tea. Homemade risotto. He plated it up and they opted to eat in the lounge whilst watching the television. They sat side by side eating and chatting, winding each other up with little jibes.

After tea, they cleaned up and Annie lay in Mark's lap on the sofa enjoying each other's company. The intercom sounded and they knew it was time to be invaded by the police. Mark released the gate and turned to Annie. "Let's get this over with and play nice!" She laughed and playfully flicked his ear.

Annie left Mark at the door to greet the police; she went to make coffee. Coffee done, she returned to the room to find the conversation had started without her. She poured the coffee and knelt on the sofa next to Mark, making sure there was no air between them. Mark responded with a smile and put his arm around her shoulders. He updated Annie. "I was just telling DCI Fisher about the improved security we are having installed."

Annie studied DCI Fisher as he drank his coffee. He was a tall man, her guess was 6' 5" possibly. He must have been in his mid-fifties and very trim. DS Dunne on the other hand was a portly man with rosy cheeks, a bit of a cross between Danny DeVito and Columbo. This thought made her smile.

DCI Fisher continued. "Please call me Harry. I have had a look at the past case and can see some similarities. My officers are still trying to locate the offender but she changed her name after she was released. We are doing our best to find out where she is now. Can you think of anyone else that would want to hurt either of you in this way?" There was a silence but both shook their heads. In all honesty both could list about half a dozen people each that were capable of this but neither wanted to contemplate it.

"I need you both to think very carefully of anyone else. It is really important we establish possible motives. This could be the work of a mischief maker or something a lot more sinister and I am really hoping it's not the latter."

DS Dunne joined in. "Mrs Swift, has the security been improved at your place?"

Annie explained, "I have moved in here since the last note. We thought it best to take your advice and stay together."

"So who is in your house then?"

This question bemused Annie and she enquired, "How do you know someone is in my house?"

Harry took over. "We sent a patrol car around to make sure you were okay. We noticed there were three young lads."

Annie interrupted. "Yes my son and two of his mates. They are professional rugby players."

Harry fell silent for a moment; Mark suspected he was looking for the right words without causing too much alarm. He finally said, "We noticed you don't have a burglar alarm at the premises. Might I suggest you consider having one installed? You can't be too careful at the moment." Annie's heart fluttered in a panic. She'd not thought Matt or Ed would be in any danger. Mark sensed her anxiety and whispered in her ear he would sort it. She nodded in disbelief. Was this really happening? Had she really put her sons at risk? She had spent her whole life protecting them.

The conversation continued but Annie was not listening. She was in a state of panic and wanted to get to her boys. Please be safe, she thought.

"Until we can locate the previous offender I want you both not to go anywhere alone. Always have someone with you and if you have to, ONLY if you have to go alone, you MUST ring each other every hour. Mark you will be familiar with this protocol from your previous dealings." Harry continued, "Please put each other's phone numbers in your phone as ICE, Annie – In Case of Emergency."

Annie angrily interrupted. "I know what ICE is, both my sons had ICE numbers in their phones."

Harry, very apologetically said, "Forgive me I get into work mode and am a bit of an arse sometimes." Annie thought, only sometimes!

"Now, if you don't have any more questions, we'll leave you to enjoy your evening together. We will get to the bottom of this. If there are any more suspicious incidents, however small please ring me." The officers bid them good night and Mark accompanied them to the door.

Annie shouted, "What about the car?" Mark and the officers stopped. Mark had forgotten all about the car. They both got the impression both officers wanted to avoid the subject. Sheepishly, DCI Fisher replied, "The good news is we have traced it... err... the bad news is it was hired from Manchester airport to a Ms Louisa Smith." Mark leant on the doorframe, shocked at the news.

"Who?" Annie was confused.

"My ex-wife!" Mark declared.

DCI Fisher interrupted. "We have spoken to her and she denies it. She even provided proof she was out of the country that day. She said she was with one of her clients." Louisa was a sales rep for a medical research company. He continued, "We are still looking into it, it's too early to make any assumptions. We are hoping to pick the car up on CCTV which could identify this person. The car has not been returned yet."

Annie's mind was racing at 200 mph. Was his ex-wife involved in this? Was Sophie aware of all of this? She didn't even notice the men leave the room.

When Mark returned to the room, Annie was already on the phone to Matt telling him what the police had said. The call ended abruptly as Matt was on the doorstep. She had forgotten he agreed to call over.

"Hi Mum." Matt bent over to kiss his mum who remained on the sofa. Mark fetched two bottles of beer and a glass of red wine; as he passed the latter to Annie he said, "Thought you might need this." Annie smiled.

They spent the next two or so hours going over everything with Matt. For his age he was worldly wise and didn't suffer fools. He was a better judge of character than his mother.

After hearing all the evidence, Matt turned to Mark and asked, "Do you think it's the same crazed fan?"

Mark nodded but wasn't really sure. Matt realised it was a half nod but knew not to pursue it as Mark was trying to protect his mother.

Matt spoke again. "Look guys you have done the right thing by following the police advice." He looked at Mark. "I know Mark you wouldn't do anything to hurt her and any fool can see how much you mean to each other."

"Mum... Mark, Ed and I will do everything we can to protect you but you are going to lose some of your independence until the police solve this." Matt knew how much Annie's independence meant to her.

She defended herself. "To be truthful I would rather know we were all safe. I am not convinced yet that this is Mark's past creeping up or mine and I am scared, really, really scared." Annie couldn't help it she burst into uncontrollable sobs. Matt and Mark both tried to console her.

She sobbed, "Why can't we just be left alone to get on with our lives? I just want our life back. We were just getting to know each other and having a great time. Now we have this to spoil it all."

Mark interjected, "Only if we let it." He gripped her arm accidentally pinching her skin.

"Mark's right Mum, don't let them spoil it. Take this as the opportunity to spend loads of time together and get to know each other."

They were right, Annie thought and hugged them both. Mark turned to Matt. "Why don't you stay here tonight? The lads are back at the house."

Matt agreed. "Get the beers in then Mark." Mark laughed as Annie clipped Matt's ear.

The remainder of the evening was spent chatting about rugby. Mark told tales of when he was a hooker at Wigan and then for Great Britain. Annie wasn't sure whether she wanted to hear what her son might get up to in the future. Annie was shattered but the boys wanted to continue their stories.

She kissed them both goodnight and as she left the room she turned to Mark and declared, "I'm not going to work tomorrow, can't face another day with him, not 'til I get my head around it all, so if it's okay with you I'll come to Salford." She went to bed.

The beer continued to flow and before long they were playing Rugby League on the PS3. Matt texted Ed to join them online. He received a sarky message back. *'Oh yeah you cosy up to our new Daddy.'*

Mark smiled, he loved the male company but not as much as Annie's though. They chatted over their turtle beaches. Ed, shouting as he always did when on the headphones, "Mum told you I'm playing against York City Knights on Sunday. Made the first team man!" Mark pretended he knew. He didn't want Ed to know she had forgotten and he didn't want him to know why she had forgotten.

Mark teased Ed. "You're no longer the bench warmer then!" Ed scoffed and cursed at Matt.

"You got training tomorrow?" Mark asked Matt.

"Nah I am over in Salford for the press release for the Grand Final."

Mark looked at Matt. "So am I, and your mum too now."

Matt nodded. "I know. Can I hitch a lift with you guys, shame to spend my money on petrol?" Mark and Matt laughed.

Mark admitted to Matt how much his mum meant to him and reassured him he would do everything to sort the problem out. At 2.45 a.m. they said goodbye to Ed and retired.

11

"Do you think there will be somewhere I can plug my laptop in?" Annie asked Mark as she got herself ready. "I take it we are going to the new BBC studios in Salford?"

Mark kissed her neck. "You are right we are. I'll take you to lunch at the Lowry. It's lovely. Matt will be joining us." Annie's face lit up. It was going to be a great day, she thought.

Matt arrived in the kitchen in the clothes from the night before. His mother gave him a disapproving look and he defended himself. "It's okay, we are calling at the house before we go."

Mark opened the passenger side door for Annie and kissed her as she climbed in. He loved the way she boarded, sat sideways and slid round – a proper lady. He shut the door wondering what a beautiful lady saw in a rough, uneducated, retired sportsman. Annie rang her boss who was not impressed by her absence. Annie felt like a naughty schoolgirl reprimanded by her head teacher when she had finished.

During the journey, Matt studied the two lovebirds. He couldn't help but admire what they had. He had longed for the love of his life but was always sceptical when a stunning girl made advances on him – he was concerned they wanted the fame rather than him and he was not really good-looking enough for a stunner. That was his opinion of himself. His precious mum had now, hopefully, found someone she could grow old with. She deserved it! So many sacrifices for Ed and him. Sure they could lavish her in presents and their love but it was not the same as sharing intimacy with that special one. Oh God, Matt thought, that was a disgusting thought, thinking of Mark doing it with his mum.

Mark and Annie chatted about the Grand Final, which teams they thought would be there. They argued over their own allegiances and Matt interrupted and reminded them he was in the car and his very own team was still in with a shout. Both parties agreed if Matt got there they would support him whole-heartedly.

The journey flew by and they managed to be early. The security guard directed Mark where to park. The new BBC building was very impressive. It was glass-fronted and in the modern, light reception area there were white sofas scattered around. Mark and Matt were met with some questions, by the presenters and researchers, when they arrived together. All the questions were deflected and ignored. Matt met up with his coach and Chief Executive. Mark's interview was scheduled first and by 10.30 he had finished. Matt's interview was at 11.30. Annie and Mark agreed to go for a wander then return in time to have lunch with him.

Annie and Mark left the building and decided to leave the car in the car park. Linking arms, they walked along to the trading estate close by. Mark started the conversation. "Not bad for a day's pay."

Annie was soaking up the cool September air. "Yeah not bad! It will probably take me months to earn what you earn in a day!"

Mark placed his arm around her shoulders. "You are brilliant at what you do and are far cleverer than me," he said.

The shops were the usual retail park shops – furniture and electrical shops. They mused around, Mark scouring through televisions and Annie looking at notebooks and digital cameras. He noticed her interest in one particular camera and made a mental note of it, knowing it was one other present he could lavish her with.

"We better set off back," Annie said looking at her watch. As they exited the store through the double doors, the black car that had plagued the pair was parked in the car park with its engine running.

"Phone the police," Mark shouted as he set off running towards the car. He reached it and banged on the door. His heart pumped out of his chest but he was so full of anger he did not stop to think. He had hold of the door handle when the car accelerated and pulled off. Mark fell to the floor banging his head on the kerb.

"MARK!" Annie shouted running across the car park. "NO! NO!" she screamed. Seeing the commotion, the security guard ran out and over to Mark. He was sitting on the kerb when Annie reached him. She slumped to the floor and threw her arms around him. She shouted at him, "Don't ever, ever do that again you stupid man!" A man in jeans, T-shirt and body armour said in a strong Mancunian accent, "You should listen to your Mrs. I have radioed the information in and there will be cars looking for it now. Did you know who it was?"

"No!" Mark said gingerly getting to his feet. "That's what I was trying to find out." Mark explained the full episode to the detective. Annie passed DCI Fisher's card to him and asked him to speak directly to him. An ambulance arrived but Mark refused treatment – he wanted to go back to get Matt home safely.

The detective dropped them back at the BBC centre. Annie walked into the foyer first and found Matt was pacing up and down. "Where the hell have you been? I've been worried sick."

He stopped when he saw Mark's head and the ashen colour of his cheeks. They explained what had happened and suggested they drove back to Leeds and had lunch there. Mark wanted to leave the building before any nosey reporter got wind of the episode.

"Annie, can you drive please?" Mark asked. "I'm feeling a bit dizzy and sick."

"Yes of course but I think we should go to casualty first and get you checked out properly."

Mark reassured her, "I'm fine Annie, just a bit shook up. I'm too old to be the chivalrous knight, looking after his princess."

Annie reached up and kissed his lips and said, "Come on Rambo let's get you home."

Annie was terrified of driving his pride and joy. Matt and Mark ribbed her until they got on to the motorway. They soon shut up when she knocked it down to third gear and put her foot down on the accelerator.

"Okay Michael Schumacher, you've made your point," Matt said as he straightened himself up on the back seat.

Annie looked at Mark who had his eyes closed. She shouted, "MARK!"

He jumped and looked at her and she apologised. "I'm sorry just please don't go to sleep yet."

Mark yawned and turned to speak to Matt. "If anything strange happens at your house, please contact me or Mum straight away. I'll give you my mobile, give it to Ed too. I'll also give you Fisher's number." Mark didn't want to admit it but today had scared him.

Matt responded, "I'll put them in my phone now."

Mark nodded and said, "Are you playing Friday night?" Matt nodded.

"If your mum agrees, why don't you come back to mine, I mean ours, after the game and stay the weekend," Mark suggested.

Annie's phone rang. Mark reached into her bag and Lucy's name was displayed on the screen.

"Answer it please," said Annie.

"Hi Lucy it's Mark, Annie is just driving… Yes I'll ask her to call you, yes… yes… I promise… bye."

Mark turned to Annie. "She needs you to call her urgently, something to do with work and John. It seemed urgent." Annie rolled her eyes. They agreed to have a coffee at Hartshead Moor services so she could return the call.

"You go in, I'll just make this call," Annie said switching off the engine.

"NO!" Matt and Mark said in unison. She got out of the car and linked arms with her lover and son. The boys went to the counter for the drinks and she found a table.

"Hi Lucy it's me," she said. "What's up?"

"Slow down Lucy and start from the beginning." What Annie was hearing was beyond comprehension. She sat and listened with her mouth wide open. Her chest and cheeks were becoming hot and very red. Eventually she said, "Okay Lucy thank you for the warning. I will see if they get in touch with me. Yes it's a bit of a nerve when this is the only time off I've had in five years."

Lucy was speaking and Annie just listened. Then she interrupted. "Oh Lucy how could you, I told you that in confidence, you silly girl." Silence again, Annie then said, "Thanks, I will, I will ring you if I hear anything. You'll have to come and see me if they do…" She hung up.

Matt and Mark had already approached the table and were sat bearing fearful expressions. Annie put her head in her hands and said in a muffled voice, "You will never believe what has happened now?"

Fearing the worst Mark and Matt asked, "What?" again in unison.

Annie lifted her head up from her hands, drew a deep breath and started, "John has been to the Faculty Dean and shown her the newspaper clippings. He has told her that I have spent the last few days living the high-life at your mansion and there is nothing wrong with me. On top of that Lucy had told him about the recent scares." Justifying confiding in her, Annie continued, "I didn't give her details just a basic outline. Anyway the upshot of it is: the faculty board are meeting this evening to decide whether I should be suspended on full pay until this is sorted out as in their words 'they don't want any bad publicity for the faculty'."

Matt, knowing what her job meant to his mum said, "They can't do that, can they?"

"Apparently so but I'll get in touch with my union rep in the morning. It's okay guys it will sort itself out."

Mark could sense the frustration and disappointment in her voice. Yet another stab in her heart. He cuddled her and said, "We'll get a solicitor to meet with the faculty." Annie looked up at him, his head now bruising, was a purply-blue colour.

"Do you know my love, what will be, will be? You could have been seriously injured today. My job is not as important as keeping you and you (pointing at Matt) and Ed safe. Now drink your drinks 'cos I want to go home."

Matt decided to go straight to his house. He wanted to catch up with Ed and had an early training session in the morning. Leaving the car, he turned and smiled. "See you Friday at the game. Look after each other."

Annie shouted from the car, "Give our love to Ed. Matt." He turned around again. "Ring me after training tomorrow please." He nodded and disappeared. Annie drove home and was glad to be in the house and away from prying eyes.

Mark put the kettle on. "I'm going to run the bath Mark if that's okay." He turned the kettle off and without a word joined their hands and led her upstairs.

Mark sat on the side of the bed and could hear Annie running the water. She returned to the bedroom with his bathrobe on. God she looked so sexy, he thought. She had cotton wool and a bowl of water to bathe his head. He winced like a little boy and she scoffed at him for doing it. She put the water down and started to undo his shirt. He just sat there partly out of pleasure partly from exhaustion. She unbuttoned his jeans, he stood up and they fell to the floor. Annie led him by the hand to the bathroom, the robe slipping onto the floor as she climbed into the water.

Mark gingerly joined her and Annie sensing his pain, moved over and kissed his forehead. "Ouch!" he said.

"You wuss," was her reply. She laughed, "It was a bit like when Murray Walker asked Nigel Mansell if the bump on his head hurt as he poked it with his finger."

Mark replied, "I need looking after, I need to feel better."

Annie retorted, "Like we need an excuse." She grabbed his arm and swung round onto his lap, the water splashing everywhere. She thrust her tongue into his mouth and ran her fingers through his hair. He moaned with pleasure as he reached under the water and ran his fingers through her pubic hair. She opened her legs and led his hand in and gasped on his shoulder. "Oooo that's good," she whispered in his ear and he pressed a little harder. She fumbled around under the water and drew his piece in between her thighs. Mark closed his eyes and held Annie really tightly; he didn't want her to slip off him like a bar of soap. She sat on him and he easily slipped inside. As she gyrated and moved, Mark kissed her breasts. He drew her nipple into his mouth and she screamed out in pleasure. Mark placed his arms around her and twisted them both around until he was on top. Biting her neck and chest he made passionate love to her, forgetting about the pain in his head. Annie pulled his head to her mouth, she licked his ear and he liked that, showing it by thrusting harder. Annie whispered, "I'm coming," with that he ejaculated.

After a couple of minutes he turned his head and admitted, "That's my first time in a hot tub. It was, you were fantastic. I really love you Annie."

Catching her breath she replied, "I love you too Mark. You are without doubt, the best man I have ever met." She leapt onto his knee and looked him straight in the eye. "Not just the sex, but by God it's the best I've ever had but you are loving and caring. I am not losing you, if we get bored of each other, then fair enough but I want you and need you."

He kissed her, a long smouldering kiss and then replied, "Annie I feel exactly the same way. I didn't think it was possible to fall in love with someone when you had just met them but I am head over heels. I want to spend all my life with you." They kissed again but decided it was time to get out of the bath. They could hear the intercom bleeping. Mark looked out of his bedroom window and could see a car parked in the gateway. He recognised the tall man standing at the side of the car. Mark ran downstairs and released the gate. The DCI entered the hallway as Annie walked down the stairs drying her hair with a towel.

"Good evening Annie," he said while Mark led their guest into the living room. The DCI sat down and started, "I won't keep you long. DS Lister contacted me from the Greater Manchester Police and filled me in to what happened. You should have gone to casualty Mark, that looks nasty," pointing to Mark's head. He continued, "I don't think I need to tell you how dangerous it is to take this matter into your own hands."

Annie interrupted him. "Harry I think Mark knows that now. Are you any closer to finding the driver?"

Harry shook his head. "We have found the car, it was abandoned in Wyke just off the M606 near Bradford. We are carrying out a forensic examination." He wanted to remain positive. "This person will trip themselves up, I promise you and we will be there when they do." Harry suggested providing a police officer as escort but Annie and Mark declined as they felt it would draw even more attention to themselves. Annie explained the situation with her work. Harry said if she needed him to speak to the Board, he would be happy to do it.

After Fisher left, Annie and Mark cuddled up on the sofa. Annie suggested, "So far the police haven't really provided any help." Mark admitted she was right but added, "At least we know they are there." He hugged and kissed her. "Let's go to bed I'm knackered."

They both lay in bed, staring at the ceiling. Annie rolled around to face Mark and noticed something glistening on his face. A tear ran down his cheek. She got up and lay at the side of him with her head on his chest. "Mark none of this is your doing."

He squeezed her but then mumbled, "Yes but today I couldn't defend you. I tried but I'm an old man now."

Annie lifted her head and stared at him. "You're an old sexy, fantastic lover," and she smiled. His heart melted. "Now stop feeling sorry for yourself and show me how much you love me. I want you to be very, very naughty. Give it me NOW!" she demanded.

They made love again. On catching her breath, Annie looked at the ceiling and suggested, "I am getting used to being treated like a princess I thought I might go and get the rest of my stuff on Saturday."

Mark jumped up and turned to her. "You kidding?"

She shook her head. He squeezed her so tightly she couldn't breathe. He let go, looked at her, "Are you sure?"

"Never been so sure about something in my whole life. I'm not selling my house yet. Matt can use it. If we don't work out then fair enough but today has convinced me life is way too short and you and I have already wasted a lot of time when we didn't know each other."

They lay in each other's arms, both floating on clouds. Yes it was definitely the right thing to do. Annie's final words were, "Mum and Dad should come over on Sunday after Ed's game."

Mark nodded but was too blissfully happy to say anything.

Very sleepily, Mark said, "Tomorrow the alarm company will be here."

"Well," Annie said, "I have Fridays off so I am at your beck and call." They cuddled each other.

12

Annie woke up at 5.30 a.m., she could not sleep. Mark was fast asleep and she slithered out of bed so not to wake him. She hoped she would remember the alarm code when she reached the panel. Thankfully she had otherwise the police would have turned up like something out of Beverley Hills Cop.

Annie unpacked her laptop and placed it on the kitchen table. She switched it on and made a cup of tea whilst waiting for it to boot up. This seemed very strange. She knew where the cups were but couldn't find the tea at first and then the milk. She started to have a major attack of self-doubt and thought 'what am I doing here? I don't know this man, not really. He could be doing all this to me and I wouldn't know any different. I don't know his birthday, his favourite colour, what his dislikes are… this is crazy, definitely crazy'. As she found the milk in the fridge in the utility room, she continued with her thoughts. '… but he is fantastic and thoughtful. The sex, oh my God the sex – snap out of it Annie this is your future and your kids' safety. You need to do some research, check him out. Stop it Annie, Stop it!' Her imagination was running away with her and she always did just this when something good happened. She talked herself out of things and she was determined whatever the outcome she was going to make it work with Mark. For once her instincts told her he was right for her and this time she was going to trust them.

She logged into her work portal to find twenty or so emails. She sifted through them and two stuck out the most, one from Lucy and one from the Dean. Lucy's email was asking Annie to get in touch but it was sent before they had spoken. With trepidation, Annie opened the Dean's email, all it said was:

'Annie I am really sorry to hear you are unwell at the moment. I hope you are taking care of yourself. Please could you attend a meeting in my office on Monday at 10am? I need to discuss a matter with you that has been brought to my attention.

If you are not well enough just let me know in the morning. I really do hope you feel better by then, we all miss you.

Best wishes

Elspeth'

Annie was surprised at the tone of the email. It was friendly and warm. She had psyched herself up to a big fight. Annie formulated an equally friendly reply advising she would be returning Monday and enquired what the subject matter of the meeting was. She already knew but thought they didn't know that. She waited for a response.

Mark surfaced at 7 a.m. He joined her in the kitchen and kissed her head. Annie could not believe the size of the lump on his head nor the bruising that had come out.

"Are you sure you want to be on TV today?" she asked. Mark nodded, she pointed to the screen and he leant over her, she could feel his breath on her cheek as he studied the email in detail.

Mark kissed her neck, he whispered, "It's only just turned seven, we don't have to be out 'til later, come back to bed." Annie did not need asking twice.

As they lay in bed, Mark asked Annie, "Were you serious last night… about moving in?"

Stroking his chest she answered, "Absolutely. Are you having second thoughts?"

Mark without hesitation, "Absolutely not, no way. I think we should announce it after Ed's game on Sunday but I don't want to take away his thunder on such a big day for him."

"I would rather we told them before Sunday. Matt and Ed can be told today and I think after what happened in Salford we should ask my mum and dad back for tea after Ed's game. What about your parents?"

Mark looked into her eyes. "I can't tell them. They haven't spoken to me since I divorced Louisa." Annie's heart sank, as she could not have coped these years without her parents. Mark continued, "They believed Louisa and helped her out financially when she told me I'd thrown her out. I didn't, she left but she was always a brilliant manipulator." Mark fell silent.

Annie thought, me and my big mouth and said, "Mark I am so, so sorry. You have had a lot to contend with, haven't you?"

He nodded and replied, "But now I have you and we have years to dwell on our horrible pasts. Today is about the future and us. I am so happy you want to move in. Now come here."

Annie resigned to the fact that she knew very little about Mark but it just felt right and natural. They were both old enough to know what they were letting themselves in for.

He pulled her towards him. His tongue once again danced around hers, both bodies increasing in temperature as they became one. It was different this time, more tender and slow. Still passionate and fabulous but both of them knew it was for keeps; they made love slowly both studying each other's faces carefully. Annie felt very deep love for this man. She knew it had never been like this before and this lovemaking was something she had never experienced before. When he came inside her and she came shortly after, she wanted to cry. It was beautiful and surreal. As Mark separated from her, he whispered, "I love you Ms Swift."

After having lain there an hour, Mark got up first. They showered together giggling and fumbling each other. They got dressed in the bedroom together, then raced like two children to see who would be the first one to the bottom of the stairs. Annie won. Both their routines had changed forever in more ways than one. Now it was time to learn about each other's pasts and understand why they both carried deep battle scars.

*

The gate alarm sounded at just before ten to reveal the security company had arrived to install the new equipment. Annie laid on the sofa in the living room flicking through the channels. She could never understand the attraction of daytime television. Mark popped his head around the door to advise her of their latest intrusion. He smiled, "So glad you feel at home," and then shut the door behind him.

It was true Annie did feel at home but also felt very guilty at being laid in front of the box when she knew there must have been things to do around the house. She decided to stop being lazy and walked into the kitchen to boil the kettle for the workers' drinks. She jumped as she walked out of the room, "What you doing here?" She turned to Carl who was carrying in some ladders.

Carl as jolly as ever, "I'd have thought that was bloody obvious!"

Shit, Annie thought, it had not crossed her mind that the company Paul used to work for would be fitting the equipment.

Carl put the ladders down and picked Annie up. "How are you my lovely? Oh I haven't seen you for ages. You are still as gorgeous as ever."

He spun her round like a little girl just as Mark entered the hallway. Annie explained to Mark that Carl used to work with Paul. Carl's two kids had played rugby at the same club as theirs and the two families had spent loads of summers going on holiday. Annie walked over and nestled under Mark's arm. "Carl this is Mark, I live here now." Her face beamed with pride.

Carl was shocked. "That's great Annie. Shame you couldn't work it out with Paul though. Chris and I would have loved to have seen you all again."

"Well you're welcome here anytime you like," Mark said. The jealousy had waned once he realised Carl was not an old flame.

Carl replied, "That's very kind of you Mr Smith. I followed your rugby career with interest, you are one of my lad's heroes." Mark blushed and Annie giggled.

"Well come on then let's have some coffee and we can catch up. You have all day to work." Mark directed them into the kitchen.

*

Carl was older than Annie, he was close to retirement and Chris, his wife, was about three years younger than him. Over coffee they recalled their holidays to France camping, mocked Paul's foul mood on a morning and laughed about the time when Chris and Annie got so drunk they passed out in the loungers under the stars. Mark just listened and laughed. He loved the way Annie was so animated and her face lit up when she was talking. If only he had been the one with her on the adventures.

"Well, it's been great catching up but I have lots of work to do," Carl said as he stood up.

"I mean it Carl, you should bring Chris and the boys round to see us," Mark said.

"Thanks Mark, that means a lot to us. We will definitely arrange something but now I need to put some graft in." Annie hugged him but remained at the table finishing her second coffee, staring into space but smiling to herself as she reminisced. Mark showed Carl around then re-joined Annie at the table. He leant at the side of her looking down smiling at her. His hand stroked across her face. She cocked her head to one side to trap his hand against her chin.

"Annie, I think we should go away next weekend. Both of us could do with a break. I've looked at the fixtures and Matt is playing Friday at home. Ed, if selected will be playing at home at the Stoop on the Sunday. What if we watch Matt's game, drive down to London, spend Saturday on our own in London, then Sunday at Ed's game. We can drive back Sunday night. Matt can come with us, he can stay at Ed's or I'll book him a room and we can stay in a hotel in London. What do you think?"

Annie looked up at Mark, stood up and pressed her body against him. "I think you are wonderful." She kissed his lips. "That would be a brilliant weekend but you have to promise me one thing…"

Mark looked into Annie's eyes. "What?"

Annie smirked. "No Rambo antics!"

Mark grabbed at Annie but she was too quick, she escaped his grasp and ran into the hall. Mark chased her into the living room where they both fell onto the sofa in fits of laughter. They regained composure when they saw Carl was up the ladder laughing at them.

"Come on," Mark said and grabbed Annie by the hand. He led her upstairs.

"Mark we can't, Carl's here." Mark laughed.

"Get your mind out of the gutter girl. I am taking you to my office so we can arrange our travel."

"I didn't know you had an office." Annie smiled at Mark.

At the top of the stairs they turned right. Mark's office was a converted bedroom. It was pristine like the rest of the house. The furniture was walnut like. A large bookcase that ran the full length of the sidewall dominated the room. Under the window there was a large desk overlooking the garden.

"Mark it's beautiful in here. Look at the view." Mark was bent over getting his notebook out of the bottom drawer. Annie could not resist, slapping his bottom. Mark stuck it out a little further encouraging her to hit it again. She laughed.

Mark sat in the large leather chair and signalled for Annie to sit on his knee. She immediately obliged and kissed his cheek whilst he switched the computer on. Annie could not help herself. She started kissing him and running her hands over his thighs. He kissed her back but pulled away. "Behave you naughty girl. We need to book something for next week."

Annie tutted. "Spoil sport!" she said as she continued to molest him.

He spun the chair sideways and grabbed her, returning the kiss and the grope. He could not help himself; he was so attracted to her and the slightest interest from her, sent him wild.

They both stopped when Annie's mobile rang in her pocket. It was Lucy.

"Hi Lucy… yes I got an email calling me into a meeting on Monday at ten a.m… I know but it was very friendly… yes I will be in Monday. Why don't you come to tea Monday night…?" Annie looked at Mark with a nod and Mark gave an approving nod back.

"Okay, yeah that'll be great. See you Monday love." Annie hung up.

"She's coming on Monday. She is going to take Monday afternoon off to come home with me at lunchtime."

Mark replied, "Well that's a shame 'cos I had plans for me and thee on your half day… it involved the hot tub; bed and…" before he could finish Annie kissed him. He tried to speak but her tongue was in the way, not that he minded. When they finally agreed to put their frolicking on hold, they started looking for hotel rooms. Annie was used to the Premier Inn but Mark wanted to impress her. He wanted something special. In the end Annie relented. The weekend had been Mark's idea. They booked the Cavendish Hotel in London between Pall Mall and Regent Street.

"I think we should just tell the boys our plans. The less people that know the better." Annie agreed with Mark. She was so excited.

"Mark," Mark turned to look at Annie, "would you mind if I use this as my office too? I love the view from here and the room is fabulous."

Mark pulled Annie close to his chest and rubbed his nose on hers. "Annie this is your home now too. This is our office not mine. It will be fun trying to work in this position every day."

Annie kissed his nose and laid her head on his shoulder. This was all too surreal for her. She felt sure she would wake up and realise none of it was real.

For the rest of the day, they pottered around the house. They had sat in the living room reading, throwing cushions at each other. Carl finished work at four o'clock and they exchanged telephone numbers.

"Right," Mark said as he shut the door, "it's time for us to get ready to see Matt play. Tomorrow we need to move all your stuff. Shit, did I need to hire a van?"

Annie laughed, "No not yet. The furniture is staying for Matt and his friends. I have my cars, trophies, photos, clothes and a few other things."

"Like I said I should have hired a van!" Mark dodged Annie as she tried to grab him. He ran upstairs with her in hot pursuit. He hid in the bedroom cupboard. Annie burst through the bedroom door but couldn't find him. She noticed the cupboard door was slightly ajar and knew where he was. She left him there and went into the bathroom for a shower. Mark was laid on the bed when she came in with the towel around her.

"I knew you were in there," Annie said pointing to the cupboard. She jumped on the bed at the side of Mark and rested her arm on his torso.

Mark rubbed her leg. "I know you did, you were mean and left me in there." As he said this he leant over and kissed her wet leg. Annie closed her eyes. He continued kissing her moving up her leg to her inner thigh. She shuffled around and lay on the bed. Mark unwrapped the towel and made slow perfect love to her.

*

Match time! Annie thought as she rushed out of the house with her scarf in her hand. Mark locked the door and jumped into the car smiling at Annie. "I have a good feeling about tonight. Matt is going to be awesome."

Annie smiled and gripped her grandpa's scarf. Friday evening on the M62 was a complete nightmare yet it was an uneventful journey for once. They parked up at the John Smith's Stadium and walked across to the main entrance. Mark and Annie showed their passes and were directed into the bar.

"Mark, Mark Smith?" a grey-haired man shouted across from the table. Mark turned, grinned and held his hand out.

"Oh my God Harry, how are you? I haven't seen you in years. I thought you'd gone back to Australia when you retired." Annie guessed they used to play together. Mark explained they had been team-mates at Wigan and shared digs when they first joined.

Harry continued his story. "I did go back home but I am over here working at the moment. I am a talent scout for St George Illawarra."

"That's fantastic Harry. I hope you aren't gonna pinch any of our young 'uns tonight. Sorry Harry, let me introduce you to my partner... this is Annie." Annie stepped forward but in all honesty was quite happy to stand back and listen to the two men. She was fascinated.

Annie kissed Harry on the cheek. "Very pleased to meet you."

"Mark you've done well for yourself." Harry had a very slight Australian twang. He was shorter than Mark but that was probably the stoop he had developed. He seemed much older than Mark.

Mark got the drinks from the bar and they sat together in the corner. Annie saw out of the corner of her eye that a tall, handsome man was approaching them from her left. It was Billy, Matt's coach. She stood up. "Hi Billy is everything okay?"

He gestured for Annie to sit down and he sat down at the side of her.

"Everything is fine Annie, great in fact. I just wanted to say as Matt's manager, the club would like to arrange for you to come in and discuss Matt's contract sometime next week. I know it's still got eighteen months to run but the Board want to start negotiations now." Billy realised Annie was not with family and turned to her. "Annie I'm sorry. How unprofessional of me to mention this in front of your guests."

"Billy it's fine. This is Mark, my partner and this is Harry, who used to play with Mark at Wigan." Billy stood up and politely shook their hands.

He turned to Annie. "Annie I didn't realise you were keeping with legends." He smiled and turned to Mark. "Watch out Mark she is a mean negotiator, don't get into an argument with her."

Annie said, "Billy, you know me. My boy's future is more important than anything. Besides, if I recall it was you that was mean." Billy shook his head.

"No one can be mean to you Annie. I have to go and get the team ready but please call me early next week." He stood up shook Mark and Harry's hands and kissed Annie.

Harry leant over to Mark. "I am confused..."

Mark explained to Harry who Annie was. Harry's eyes lit up. "Ahh, Matthew Swift, very talented young man. I wouldn't mind having a chat with you both too." Harry handed Annie a business card and said, "I won't bother you tonight but call me next week. Even if nothing comes of it I would love to meet Matthew. Mark you come too, we can catch up. Now if you could excuse me I need to mingle a bit." With a kiss for Annie and a hug for Mark, Harry pottered off into the crowd.

Annie sat back in the chair. "Wow what a night already."

Mark leant over her and whispered, "You shouldn't be surprised at the interest in Matt. He is a very clever lad." He put his hand on her knee. "I don't need to be at the meeting next week."

Annie shook her head. "Yes you can come and see me in full flight. It's great when the fat cats think I am easy meat until I leave them in shreds." She laughed.

Mark was in no doubt at all that she would chew them up and spit them out. With that thought, they finished their drinks and moved out onto the terraces. It was a cold night and they could see the heat coming off the players' bodies like mist. Matt looked up and saw his mum and Mark. He concentrated on his warm up knowing they were both safe.

"Annie." It was Marcus, Matt's 'big' boss.

Annie stood up and shook his hand. "Hi Marcus, how are you?"

"I'm good thanks. Looking forward to our meeting next week, I am sure it will be lively." He smiled and turned to Mark. "Hi Mark, you're looking well."

"Hi Marcus. Thanks. You're not looking bad yourself." Mark used to play against Marcus.

They sat in their seats and Mark put his arm around the back of Annie's chair, he whispered, "He's a bit of a wanker." Annie laughed and dug him in his ribs.

"He is paying Matt's wages. I want him to give him a massive pay rise."

Mark laughed, "Ooh what commission you on?"

He was joking of course but Annie whispered back, "Enough for me to keep you in the lifestyle you are accustomed to."

He squeezed her. Suddenly she jumped up out of her seat and started shouting – the teams were back on the pitch. The game was pretty one-sided in the first half. Leeds led eighteen nil at half-time. Matt had set two tries up and scored all three goals.

Mark returning from the chuck van with two coffees said, "He's having a great game again Annie. Mind you I've not seen him have a bad one yet."

Annie smiled. She was immensely proud of Matt and Ed. They had worked so hard and sacrificed a lot for the game they had loved. Both had been budding footballers too, playing for academy sides from the age of six. However, they had fallen in love with rugby.

"I am really pleased for him Mark, he's worked so hard," Annie replied, sipping the hot coffee which was a welcome respite from the cold air.

"Annie, what would you do if St George wanted him?" Mark asked. It had already crossed her mind that he might one day play in Australia or New Zealand. If it wasn't for Ed she would jump on the plane too but she would never make the heartbreaking decision of leaving one over the other unless they wanted it.

"I don't know – let Matt decide. If he wanted to go to Australia he would. Look at the bright side, we can go out there and see him," Annie joked. Mark knew it would tear her apart if Matt or Ed went to Australia. She loved her boys and wanted them close but also knew how important it was for them to live their own lives.

Knowing she was struggling with the image of Australia in her mind, Mark kissed her cheek. She smiled. The teams reappeared for a second half that appeared just as one-sided. The final score was 38 nil. It was an awesome result for Leeds and resulted in them being one game nearer to Old Trafford. It put both Mark and Annie in buoyant moods.

Waiting in the bar seemed to be forever for Mark and Annie but Matt entered to rapturous applause. He was being patted on the back and had his hand shaken. Mark looked at Annie who was beaming with pride with tears rolling down her cheeks. He cuddled her and called her a softie. Matt ran over to his mum and picked her up in a really warm embrace. Mark could see they were both very emotional.

"I really enjoyed that, Mum, it was brilliant," Matt said whilst taking a drink of the beer. "Billy wants me to go back to the stadium on the bus so can you follow us and pick me up from there." Annie nodded but still could not speak.

Matt turned to Mark. "What did you think Mark?" Mark shook Matt's hand again. "Matt you and the team were awesome. I wish I'd have had the talent you have."

Annie could see the approval meant a lot to Matt. Matt hugged her again, drank his beer quickly and ran off to catch the club coach.

As Annie and Mark were leaving, Harry caught their attention. "Annie, Matthew was brilliant tonight. Please do ring me early next week, we need to talk." Annie nodded and as she turned round she caught a glimpse of Marcus staring at them. Cunning as ever, Annie made a point of agreeing to call Harry so that Marcus overheard her.

When she told Mark he laughed. "I am really going to enjoy watching you crushing their balls next week."

Annie linked arms with Mark. "I don't know what you mean, Mark. I am a mere woman in a man's sport." She fluttered her eyelids at him and made him laugh hysterically.

Matt climbed into the car and hardly spoke on the way home. Annie knew the signs. He was coming down from a massive high and needed time to take it all in.

Mark looked at Matt through his rear-view mirror. "You okay Matt?"

Matt knew Mark would know how he was feeling. "Yeah I'm okay. It's just…"

"I know kid," interrupted Mark.

When they arrived in the garage, Annie woke Matt up. Mark walked through to the kitchen shouting, "Who's for a drink then?" They all shouted at once. "Anyone hungry?"

"No thanks I ate at the club," Matt said, "but I'll thrash you at FIFA if you want."

Mark looked at Annie. "That's all right," she said, "I just want to chill now."

They took their drinks into the living room. Matt texted Ed and he joined their FIFA game.

"It's becoming a habit this bro, you being round at Mark's," Ed teased.

"Ed you're only jealous, you'd be here if you played for a Yorkshire club," Matt retaliated. Annie laughed and suggested they played nice.

Annie decided to leave the boys to it and went to bed. She read for a while but must have dozed off. She awoke when she heard the boys coming to bed. They must have had a few more beers and were laughing and giggling as they staggered upstairs.

Mark leant over and kissed Annie's lips. He stood up and started undressing. Mark put his arm around the back of her neck. She nestled into his chest and kissed his torso tenderly. He kissed her forehead and softly spoke. "Thank you for coming into my life. I love you Annie and your boys are a chip off the old block."

Annie replied, "Less of the old, old man!" They squeezed each other and kissed each other goodnight.

13

Annie was in the kitchen cooking bacon when Matt came downstairs. He leant on the doorframe,

"Morning Mum," he said as he scratched his head.

"Morning love, you sleep okay?" she asked as she kissed him.

"Actually I did. I need a lift to the training ground this morning for the post match. Then I'm free for the rest of the day. If you and Mark fancy it I think we should go out to Harrogate for lunch and do some shopping."

Before Annie could answer Mark bounded past Matt and said, "I'll take you to the training ground while your mum goes and pa…" Mark stopped himself just in time. He had forgotten Annie and he had not yet told Matt she was moving in permanently.

Annie explained to Matt. "We can go through to Harrogate later but first I have something to tell you. Mark and I, no I have decided I am going to move the rest of my stuff here and live with Mark." Matt looked at his mum then at Mark who was beaming like a Cheshire cat.

"Mum, Mark that's great. I pray it works out for both of you. From what I have seen you are made for each other." He got up from the table, hugged his mum and whispered; "You so deserve this Mum." He walked over to Mark, shook his hand and whispered, "Look after her." Mark nodded. Matt walked towards the door. "I need to be off shortly." He turned around again and added, "This means more FIFA tournaments." They all laughed out loud.

Mark and Matt left together in Mark's BMW and Annie left to go start packing everything up. She rang Ed on the mobile. She realised she had got him out of bed. "Ed I have something to tell you."

"You're pregnant," he replied.

"Ed you nutter," she laughed. "No but I'm moving in with Mark." There was a silence at the other end of the phone.

"Ed, ED are you there?" Annie shouted.

"No need to shout, yes I am. I was joking. I am made up for you both Mum. After the game tomorrow, I've been given leave 'til Tuesday. Can I stay at Mark's, I mean yours and Mark's?"

"Of course you can. You only want to stay to play with his games," Annie said.

"Busted!" Ed replied. They said their goodbyes. She was looking forward to seeing him make his first team debut tomorrow.

The next conversation was with her mum. Annie decided it was best not to blurt out the news over the phone. "Hi Mum."

"Hi love how are you?"

"I'm great Mum. You and Dad still coming to Ed's game tomorrow?"

"Wouldn't miss it for the world. We watched Matt's game last night. I was crying at the end."

"So was I Mum."

"Tomorrow after the game, Mark has asked us all back to his house. Would you and Dad come please?"

"Of course we will. Your dad is eager to meet him."

"Is that a good eager or bad eager?" Annie asked. They both laughed. Knowing how protective her dad was, Mark would be in for the third degree. They finished their conversation just as Annie pulled up outside her house.

The house was empty as all the boys were at the training ground. She really didn't know where to start. Annie decided to work from the top down and started in her bedroom. It was typical of the boys disappearing just when she needed help. She started emptying her wardrobe and the family photographs were the first to be packed. She systematically moved between rooms kicking Ben's clothes out of the way. She left a lot of the towels, sheets and everything for Matt to use.

She had piled the boxes high in the hallway. The living room and kitchen were next but she decided to take a break and make a drink. The coffee was a welcome relief and she stared out of the window day dreaming of the boys playing rugby in the garden when they were younger. How things had changed. She would spend hours watching them and avoiding conversation with Paul. Now she could not stop talking to Mark, oh and kissing – boy she had never been kissed and touched so much but it wasn't annoying and overbearing. It was loving, heart-felt and passionate. Her thoughts were interrupted with the clatter of the letterbox. She walked out into the hall to find the postman had been. Amongst the bills was a letter postmarked Leeds. She opened it. It was a small postcard inside with the words inscribed: "YOU WILL PAY!" She threw the letter to the floor. In a blind panic she was not sure what to do. She searched around for her mobile and rang Mark. He didn't answer. Oh God, what was she to do? She rang DCI Fisher. He answered.

"Harry it's Annie Swift. I'm at my home packing and have received a letter. I can't get hold of Mark and need someone here now." She sat on the steps with the phone in her hand. Just as she began to dial Mark again, she heard him walking down the path with Matt.

Mark hugged Annie whilst passing the note to Matt. DCI Fisher came running through the gate. The party moved into the living room. Harry spoke first. "Look this letter being sent here means the perpetrator doesn't necessarily know you have moved to Mark's address."

Annie interrupted, "I was here today to move the rest of my stuff." She sniffed. "I was supposed to be moving in permanently." Harry took the note away. Matt spoke first. "Let's get all this stuff packed and over to Mark's, I mean yours and Mark's. We can talk about the rest of it at home or in Harrogate."

The boys loaded the boxes into the cars, using Matt's car too. Matt gathered a few things he needed to stay over. Annie finished packing then they set off in convoy to Annie's new home.

*

"Can we put these boxes in one of the spare rooms for now? I will unpack them later," Annie asked Mark who was carrying in three boxes at a time. Annie really could not bring herself to start sifting through belongings.

"We can put them at the back of the gym," he suggested.

It did not take three of them long to store the boxes. Mark made some drinks and they sat in the lounge.

Matt spoke first. "I am not convinced this is someone from Mark's side. All the incidents have occurred either at your house, Mum, or when you were together. I am guessing it could be one of your crackpot family or friends."

Annie looked at Mark then Matt. "I was thinking the same Matt. It seems very odd but I don't know who."

Mark was the only one who thought lightning was striking twice over his affairs. He had not had any serious girlfriends since his marriage had broken down. Now from the moment he found Annie, there had been trouble.

He admitted, "I don't agree with you. I really think this is the past repeating itself. I am so sorry you have all been dragged into this."

There was an awkward silence, broken by Matt jumping to his feet. "Come on you two, I didn't accept your invite to stay tonight for us to be miserable. I say we go through to Harrogate, have some tea and then come back and play old fashioned Monopoly – you do have a Monopoly board Mark?"

Mark laughed. "I think we do. God I have not played it for years. You're on!"

Whilst Matt and Annie got ready, Mark went into the loft. He found the games and sure enough the Monopoly was there along with lots of old games. Coming down the loft stairs, he met Annie at the bottom. She hugged and kissed him. "Wow there are so many rooms to the place that I didn't know existed."

"I know but we can explore when we find homes for all your stuff. Annie?" She turned and faced Mark. "I promise you we will sort all this out and when we do we are going to have a perfect life together. I am going to make you feel so special."

Holding on to his waist she whispered, "You already do."

*

Annie received a text from Ed letting her know they were travelling to York on the coach.

"So where do you two fancy eating?" Matt enquired.

"I don't mind," Annie replied.

Mark pondered for a little while then answered, "Well I don't know about you two but I fancy good old-fashioned pub grub and a nice pint."

That was agreed. Shopping followed by a decent pub dinner. Harrogate was one of Annie's favourite places along with Knaresborough. She had spent a lot of time in both. It was still her ambition to retire over to Knaresborough. She shared this thought with Mark and his answer was he would be prepared to sell the house and move if it meant she was happy and they were together. Annie squeezed his leg.

Matt studied the body language and interaction between his mum and Mark; they were so relaxed. He had never seen his mum this happy. She was not a miserable person, not like Paul, but she had been serious and had bordered on depression when he and Ed were younger. Matt knew she had had a tough life but felt she had sheltered them from most of the truth. It was very strange for him to step aside and let Mark take over as her protector. Matt had always protected Annie and felt that Mark was the ideal candidate to assume that role.

They shopped for three hours, which was more than enough for Annie and Mark. It was starting to get overcast and dull. They piled into a small pub on Princes Street. Annie found a table close to the open fire. Mark came back from the bar with Matt.

"You didn't tell me that a St George Illawarra guy was at the game on Friday," Matt said.

Mark interrupted, "Sorry Annie I was just talking about when I played and Harry was mentioned. I didn't mean to put my foot in it."

Annie, swallowing her wine shook her head. "You haven't Mark I just haven't got round to telling you. Sorry Matt. Billy also came to see me and asked if we could meet next week to discuss your contract."

"But I've got eighteen months left yet," Matt said.

"I know but they want to talk about an extension now."

Matt picked up his pint, "I'll drink to that," and smiled.

Mark said, "Cheers Matt. You do deserve a great contract. From what I have seen you're a cracking player and should make the England squad. The Four Nations in November would be a good stage for you."

"Yep let's hope so but there's plenty of other players to fill the shirts so I won't hold my breath. It would be great if I could tie up a new contract though."

Annie asked directly, "Would you be interested in playing in the NRL?"

Matt surprisingly shook his head. "No not yet. Yes I would like to spend some time out there but not now. Leeds is my home and I love the club and the lads. But never say never. Besides if I went my manager would have to come with me."

Annie and Mark looked at each other and said in unison, "Sign up now then," and laughed.

This was great Annie thought but she missed Ed being there. Mark must have read her mind. "Shame Ed's not here." Annie rubbed Mark's arm affectionately.

Matt shook his head. "No we can all get a word in now," and smiled.

The food was fabulous and conversation continued about rugby. Not once did they mention the other business. The atmosphere was relaxed and fun. Annie settled the bill whilst Mark was at the toilet much to his annoyance. He slapped her bottom as she walked past him.

The weather had turned drizzly and damp. Fog was rolling in from the north. Mark and Annie walked arm in arm with Matt at the other side of Mark chatting away. They could see a piece of paper flapping around on the car windscreen. Mark and Annie's heart sank, not again! Matt ran over to the car and plucked the wet paper off the windscreen. He started laughing and passed the paper to Mark. It was a flyer for happy hour at the Stick and Twist. Mark hugged Annie and laughed.

Before returning home they stopped at the supermarket for some food for tomorrow night. Matt scoffed that Mark and Annie were buying the best stuff to impress his grannie and grandpa.

"I can't believe you're buying champagne, it'll be wasted on Grannie and Mum," Matt said.

Mark replied, "I know Matt but it's a big deal tomorrow for me. I want everything to be perfect for this lady." Mark rested his chin on the top of Annie's head. Annie was oblivious to the conversation.

"Mum, what you staring at now?" Matt asked.

"Isn't that John over there?" Annie asked as she pointed to a man sitting in the corner of the café. At that point John looked over and reluctantly waved. Mark paid for the shopping as Annie stormed over to the café, with Matt in hot pursuit.

"What you doing here?" Annie demanded.

"Hello to you too Annie," John said. "I have been to Knaresborough and called in here for some shopping."

"How convenient!" Annie replied starting to be very suspicious of her colleague. She couldn't resist asking, "Why have you told Elspeth about Mark and me?"

He smiled wryly. "I am sorry Annie but I don't know what you're talking about. Is that why I am covering your lecture on Monday morning? I just assumed you wouldn't be gracing us with your presence again."

Annie was red in the face when Mark came over.

"What's going on?" he said as he looked at both parties.

Annie's fury subsided. "Nothing Mark, it's fine. Let's go to our home."

Annie watched John's reaction. He was furious. He hadn't found out that she'd moved in with Mark. Annie hadn't told anyone but her boys. John watched the three of them walk across to the car.

"Shall I go back in and confront him?" Mark asked.

"NO! You're not Rambo remember?" Annie smiled and buried her head in Mark's chest. He was happy to oblige, lifted her chin up and kissed her tenderly on the lips.

"All right you two, I'll put all the shopping in the car while you two play at being lovesick teenagers," Matt said as he lifted the last bag in the car.

Mark replied, "What do you mean play?"

This made Annie laugh out loud probably more than it was worth but knowing John was still staring, she wanted him to see it. When Mark pulled out of the car parking space Annie deliberately waved to a seething John.

"Mark?" Annie turned to him, "I didn't want to say anything in there but I am seriously considering John may be our tormentor. He has known from the start when we started seeing each other. Lucy told him." She paused for a minute to watch Mark's reaction, he did nothing. She continued, "He knew I was off and he didn't know I'd moved in with you... Oh God he knows all about your past." Panic started to appear in her voice.

Mark soothingly put his hand on Annie's knee. "But love, do you really think he is capable of doing this?" She shook her head.

Matt interjected, "Yeah but do any of us really know who would be capable of this? I have to admit it does feel a bit of a coincidence that he is there when we are there. Doesn't he live in Otley, Mum?"

"Yes he does," Annie replied. "I suppose it's not far away from here."

The conversation halted as they pulled into the driveway.

"I could really get used to coming here Mark, it's great coming up this driveway." Matt looked up at the beautifully lit house on the hill.

"You can come and live here whenever you like," Mark said, "and the same goes for Ed."

They unloaded the car and put all the shopping away. Annie couldn't believe how much they had bought just to impress her mum and dad. Mark got the beers and wine and they all went into the living room.

Mark sighed, "Argh the perfect evening. I have my beautiful sexy lady, a superstar in the making, beer, Wigan v Saints on the box and err... Monopoly."

Annie threw the cushion at him. "Stop moaning. You can moan when I have fleeced you of all your money." Annie realised what she had said. "I mean at Monopoly!"

Mark jumped across the floor and grabbed Annie. "You can have everything I have."

Matt tutted, "For God's sake get a room! Anyway, rugby's on and you come second to rugby where Mum is concerned."

Annie laughed. "Sorry Matt but I'd make an exception for Mark." She kissed Mark again. Matt frowned and put the cushion over his head. They both laughed at him. Annie got up and gave Matt a big hug then returned to the floor next to Mark. They both set the game up and Annie said, "Let battle commence."

The childish behaviour continued between Mark and Annie much to Matt's dismay. He kept telling them to grow up which made them much, much worse. There was no surprise that Annie won but then as the boys were distracted by the rugby, she slipped herself some money from the bank. It served them right, she thought for not concentrating.

Annie was over the moon with Mark and Matt's relationship. They got on really well considering they had only just met. It was great that Matt had someone to talk to. With Annie splitting from his dad early in Matt's life, Annie was worried that it would affect Matt massively. He was lucky he had a fabulous relationship with his grandpa. They wound each other up but in a good way. Matt had never really seen eye to eye with Paul but had tolerated him for his mum's sake. Annie had read the situation wrong and thought Matt loved Paul. It wasn't until she confided in Matt about leaving Paul that she had found out her son's true feelings. Annie hoped she and Mark would make it through all this because Matt was so at home with Mark. They were mates already.

"Well, I don't know about you two but I am off my feet and going to bed," Mark said as he got up and cleared the beer bottles away.

"Yep I agree," said Matt. "Ed's big day tomorrow and I want to be on top form to give back the abuse he has given me."

Annie laughed. "You two! Remember he is your little brother and you are a professional now, you need to set an example."

Matt kissed his mum goodnight. "You spoil all my fun Mother."

Mark re-entered the room. "Annie you go up, I'll show Matt the alarm system just in case he's up before us and wants to use the gym." Annie left the room and rubbed Matt's arm. As she walked upstairs she could hear them chatting away. It was so nice for Matt to have a laugh with another man without him being criticised or being dragged down.

When Mark joined Annie in the bedroom she was already in bed. Mark climbed under the covers with her and drew her into him.

He whispered, "Matt's in the room at the other end of the hall. He won't hear us." His breath felt so warm on Annie's neck.

She whispered back, "Good 'cos if you keep whispering in my ear, I don't think I could help myself."

Mark kissed the back of her neck making her knees go weak. He whispered, "So if I keep breathing and talking in your ear I can make you explode?"

She nodded and replied, "I was hoping for more than that."

He squeezed her and breathed heavily in her ear. His arms were around her breasts. He reached for her nipples and started massaging them. She closed her eyes, it was bliss. She could feel him growing behind her. She nestled her back further into him, which made him breathe even harder.

"I love you Annie," Mark whispered as he moved his hand down her stomach to between her legs. He turned her towards him and looked in her eyes. "You are so beautiful and sexy. I want you to be with me forever."

She shuffled up the bed and kissed his lips. Her tongue melted in his mouth. He slipped inside her and they slowly moved around the bed continuing to kiss. She felt every ounce of his body and love. She knew it was as deep as her love for him. Whatever happened she loved being lost in his embrace and he loved being lost inside her. They both reached their peak together. This time Annie couldn't help it but a tear ran down her cheek. Mark laid half on her and half on the side of the bed. He rested his head on his arm and leant over and kissed the tear from her cheek.

"I felt it too Annie," he said. She grabbed his head and held it close to hers. She whispered, "Please let it always be like this between us. I love you Mark, with all my heart, I love you."

14

"Annie?" Mark tried to move Annie without waking her but he had pins and needles in the arm that was under her. Annie opened her eyes and saw Mark wincing at the side of her.

She sat up. "What's up?"

"I have pins and needles in my arm."

Annie whacked Mark. "I thought there was something really wrong with you," she said as she lay back down, tucking her legs around his.

"No really Annie I did," he said laughing at her. He repositioned himself at her side and stroked her hair. She closed her eyes once more and lay there enjoying his tender touch. Without opening her eyes she said, "What time is it?"

He leant over to the cabinet and told her it was 9.15 a.m. He squashed himself against her naked body. She let out a pleasurable moan. He ducked under the covers and kissed her breasts. She stretched her body out and submitted to his advances. Mark had a gentle touch; he instinctively knew what drove her wild. He worked his way down her body kissing each contour. She lifted her legs over his torso and around his neck. He loved it and immediately was turned on. He played with her and she writhed with pleasure. Annie slipped her hand under the cover and gestured for Mark to come to her. He complied like an obedient puppy. As he came to her heel, she pushed him flat on the bed. It was her turn to play with him. He watched her every move as she worked her magic on his body. She sat astride him and massaged his chest. He could feel her thighs gripping his sides as she slipped him in. He was in ecstasy and lay there and let her do it to him. As he came he grabbed her hips and sat up, kissing her on the lips so hard Annie couldn't breathe. She broke free from his embrace and held him in her arms resting her head on his shoulder.

Mark lay down. "Jeez you are fit for your age lass." Annie slapped him then turned over onto her side facing Mark.

"So how old do you think I am then?"

Mark knew he was on very dangerous ground. "Oh no I love you too much, if I get it wrong, you will kill me."

"No I won't," Annie said. "You guess my age and I'll guess yours."

"No Annie, I have a better idea. You tell me yours and then you guess mine." Annie laughed and leapt onto Mark. She sat astride him again and held his hands over his head.

"Guess now Mark or you will live to regret it." Mark laughed at her and pulled a face.

He replied, "I am really regretting you sitting on me restraining my hands aren't I?" The sarcasm made Annie let go of his hands and she started tickling his waist.

Mark was squirming round the bed. "All right, all right you are thirty-nine," he conceded.

She stopped and kissed him. "Yes I love you but you're such a liar. I am forty seven."

Mark was shocked. "You never are, you're lying. Annie you look fantastic and in spite of everything that you have gone through, you look great." He sat up and said to her, "I am forty-nine, it's my big five-oh next year."

"You're nearer to retirement than me then." Annie dug her hands into his ribs. Mark yelped, "I am but I really can't get over that you're forty-seven. You never cease to amaze me. Come here you beautiful geriatric." They rolled around the bed together laughing their heads off.

After showering and dressing they came downstairs to find Matt hard at work in the gym.

"Morning," he shouted puffing and panting. Annie and Mark shouted morning. Annie went to put the coffee on whilst Mark stood chatting to Matt.

"I could get used to this," Matt admitted. "I didn't have to get dressed before hitting the gym," he smiled. Mark sat down on the weights bench to the right of Matt.

"Matt I meant what I said last night. Now your mum has moved in, we would love you and Ed to treat it as your home."

"It's very kind of you Mark but we'll see. I think you and Mum deserve some time alone to really get to know each other and do what you need to do. We, I'm sure I can speak for Ed too, would love you two to stay together. You are made for each other. Don't get me wrong once you are sorted, I will be moving in." Matt stood up and placed his towel over his shoulders. He patted Mark on his back before leaving to shower.

Mark stayed sitting in the same position pondering his life. He could not believe how lucky he was. He was going to do everything he could to resolve the issue hanging over their heads so that they could get to know each other properly.

Mind you, Mark thought, I think we pretty much know each other's bodies by now. He left with a smirk on his face and joined Annie in the kitchen.

They had a cooked breakfast. Matt and Mark couldn't resist a game of FIFA, without Ed this time, whilst Annie prepared dinner. She decided they would make use of the dining room and opened the doors into the room to find it was incredibly dusty and had a musty, not used smell. She opened the curtains and unlocked the patio door. It was cold but fresh. She took the cover off the table to reveal a wonderful Italian hand carved mahogany table. She walked out of the dining room and popped her head round the living room door.

"Mark, do you need to use any special polish on the dining room table?"

Mark paused the game and followed her into the dining room.

He kissed her neck. "No sweetheart, furniture polish will be fine." He rubbed his hand over the table. "It's such a beautiful table. I have never actually used it."

Annie tucked herself under his arm and looked up to him. "Well baby I have a feeling it's going to get plenty of use from now on."

He kissed her and left her to it.

*

They left the house at half past twelve to travel to York. They were meeting Charles and Andrea in the car park at the York City Knights then agreed to walk across to Monks Cross for a drink. It was a wonderfully crisp day and the sun was shining for Ed's debut.

Charles and Andrea were already standing next to Splash world. Andrea was waving like mad when she saw them pulling in.

Matt mumbled, "God love her."

Annie ran over the car park and embraced her parents. Mark put his jacket on and nervously approached her parents.

Annie took him by the hand and said, "Dad this is Mark. Mark this is my dad, Charles." Both men shook hands and nervously surveyed each other. Charles was satisfied he was okay for his daughter. Both men chatted to each other as they walked over to the shopping complex. Matt walked with them and every now and then he would push his grandpa or scuff his head with his hand. Mark thought it a bit strange but remembered what Annie had said about their special relationship.

Mark did not feel an outsider at all. In fact, he very much felt a member of the family. Mark paid the bill and they strolled back to the stadium just in time to see the London coach arrive. Ed copped his grandparents and jumped off the coach giving them both huge hugs, much to the delight of his team-mates. As they alighted each one of them ruffled his hair and said hello to Annie and Matt.

Annie gripped Ed's arm. "I am so proud of you Ed. Make sure you enjoy every bit of it. What position you playing?"

Ed couldn't contain his excitement. "Number twenty-seven Mum, but scrum-half." His beam was wider than the Mersey tunnel.

Annie jumped in delight. "Aww Ed I am so, so, so proud of you." She kissed him.

Annie's face changed from a smile to a frown within seconds. Mark looked in the direction she was looking to find Paul stomping across the car park with two older people in tow.

The party joined Annie's family and Annie spoke first. "Hi Julian and Mary, how are you both?" She smiled at them only to get a frosty reception.

Paul moaned, "Good job I found out from someone at work that Ed was playing today, you lot weren't gonna tell me."

Matt jumped in to Annie's defence. "Not up to Mum to tell you Paul. Julian, Mary, hello." Matt shook Julian's hand and kissed Mary on the cheek.

"Time to go inside," Charles said. Both parties reluctantly walked in together. Mark could definitely sense the tension and surmised that Julian and Mary must be Ed's other grandparents. They certainly weren't as warm as Annie's parents.

Thankfully they were sitting apart from each other. Mark and Annie walked hand in hand. Mark also smiled at Andrea and Charles doing the same.

Matt tutted, "Feel like a right gooseberry with you olds!"

Andrea slapped him then tried to cuddle him but he was having none of it.

"Right. Who's for a beer?" Matt asked. Charles, Mark and Matt headed for the bar. Andrea and Annie sat together. Andrea had no interest in rugby save her grandsons.

Andrea looked at Annie. "Well that was a bit awkward out there." Annie nodded as she flicked through the match day programme to see her son's name.

She looked up. "It was, wasn't it? Silly old git! He will never change. Ed didn't want him here!"

"Annie?" Andrea looked straight at her daughter. "Your dad and I are really pleased you have met someone. Mark seems a really nice person and Matt and Ed seem to like him too. Whenever I ring them they are always Mark this and Mark that."

Annie smiled. "Mum," she confessed, "I have never been this happy. I have got to forty-seven and finally feel I have someone really special. Someone who isn't insecure or miserable but loving and funny. It's a real bonus the kids like him too."

The boys returned from the bar. Matt sat between his mum and grandma. Mark whispered to Annie, "Your dad is great. We have had a right chat at the bar. I can see where you get all your traits. I am so lucky to be with you." He snuggled up to her and they both went through the programme again to see Ed's name in there.

It was really hard for Annie to shout for London being a fervent Leeds supporter but she always knew she might have to support another team. She was just thankful it was not Bradford!

The teams came out and Ed was on the bench. He waved to them as he warmed up on the touchlines. Just before half-time he got his chance. The party learnt afterwards he heard them all carrying on when he stepped out onto the field. Annie had tears running down her face, which Mark wiped away. Matt scorned her but when they looked round Andrea was crying too. Mark and Matt shrugged and laughed.

Mark griped, "That's girls for you Matt." Annie dug him in his ribs and made him squirm again.

At half-time London were in a commanding lead. Ed had supplied the ball really well to his team-mates. It earned him a pat on the back from his coach as he left the field at half-time.

The second half was awesome. Ed scored his first try. Annie nearly fell over the man in front of her. After apologising, she explained to the man that Ed was her son. He was really pleased for her. He then realised Matt was sat behind him and shook his hand. Andrea and Charles looked on with pride.

When the final whistle blew, Annie leapt out of her seat and ran down the stairs. She jumped up and down like a crazed fan and Ed jumped into her arms when he left the pitch. She couldn't speak for the tears, tears of joy and pride. Ed shook Mark's hand and kissed his grandpa on his forehead. He saved his biggest celebration for Matt. They hugged each other for a minute or so. This made Andrea and Annie cry again, giving the boys something else to laugh about.

The celebrations continued in the bar. Annie and Matt jumped up and down singing Ed's name much to the amusement of everyone in the bar. Billy and Marcus had been at the game. They shook Mark and Matts' hands and hugged Annie.

Billy spoke first. "Wow Annie, I think you should take my job. You've done a great job with both your boys."

"Thanks Billy but they are the ones that have done all the hard work." Ed joined the party and was pleased to see Billy and Marcus. He shook their hands.

Marcus held onto Ed's hand. "Come and speak to us next week with your mum. We need to talk."

Mark and Matt looked at each other. Matt was longing to play alongside his younger brother and hoped one day it would happen.

Ed was tapped on the shoulder, he turned around and his dad hugged him. "Well played son. Great game today."

"Err thanks Dad," Ed said. "Thought we might go out after with your gran and granddad?"

"I am so sorry Dad but I'm going to Mark's with Mum, Matt and Grannie and Grandpa. If I'd have known I would have done." Paul's face was turning purple.

He snarled, "Fine you lot, go and play happy families. It will all go wrong then you can come running back to me." With that he left.

As Paul turned away, Matt put his arm around Ed's shoulders. "Forget him Ed. He always manages to turn our days into his! Don't let him upset you." Paul turned around to signal he had heard what he said. Matt continued, "Besides, our new dad is going to get beat at FIFA tonight!"

Annie intervened, "That'll do Matt. Mark doesn't need to be involved in the silly games."

Mark interrupted, "It's okay Annie, I'd be proud to be their dad. But they are wrong about me getting beat – sorry boys but who holds the winning record..." Mark cupped his hand around his ear. "Sorry... I didn't hear you... Yes that's right ME!"

Annie shook her head and slapped Mark on the stomach. "You're as bad as them."

"Come on then drink up, it's time to go home," Mark said. Andrea had been looking forward to seeing Mark's house. The boys had given her a brief outline that it was small and humble. They did love to wind people up.

*

Ed and Matt decided to travel with their grandparents. They could direct them to Mark's house. They also wanted to see their grannie's face when she saw the house for the first time.

The daylight was fading but it was a beautiful clear evening. Mark and Annie pulled out of the car park.

Mark spoke first. "Annie you are amazing. Your kids are amazing, both of them. In my wildest dreams I could not have wanted two more gifted boys than you have and I hope you will let me share them with you. Your mum and dad are great too. In fact you have a great core family around you and I am envious."

Annie smiled and was so matter of fact. "They are your family too."

Mark smiled. There was not much conversation for the rest of the journey. They listened to the music and were both lost in their own little worlds.

Mark and Annie arrived home first. They went in and started organising the food. When they heard the car pull up they both ran to the front door. Andrea's face was as much fun as the boys' were when they arrived for the first time.

Charles got out of the car. "Jesus Annie, is this big enough for you?"

Mark laughed and cuddled Annie. This was perfect. Mark and the boys collectively showed Annie's parents around the house. She retreated to the kitchen to prepare the dinner.

Mark crept up behind her and kissed her. "What have you done with them all?" Annie enquired.

Mark pinching a piece of carrot from the side replied, "They are all in the living room. Ed and Matt have challenged them to a game of Monopoly. Your mum is more competitive than you!" Annie smiled, it was very true!

As Mark and Annie worked together in the kitchen, they could hear muffled laughs and taunts from their guests. Mark waited on them and now and then stood at the living room door just watching Annie's family interacting with each other. The special relationship Annie had with her boys was not mutually exclusive. Mark was impressed with Annie's parents' attitudes towards their grandsons. There was a respect for them being grown men but yet a childlike handling that was so endearing. The boys reciprocated and adored their grandparents.

Mark returned to the kitchen smiling from ear to ear. The house was alive at last, something he had longed for so long but resigned himself to never achieving.

Dinner was great. The conversation flowed as much as the wine. After dessert, Mark tapped his glass and cleared his throat. Everyone stopped and listened. "I just want to say today has been very special for all of us. Congratulations and well done to Ed." He addressed Andrea and Charles directly. "Annie and I would like to announce that Annie has moved in here with me and I feel so privileged and honoured to have met such a wonderful and lovely lady." His voice broke slightly and he raised his glass in Annie's direction.

"Whoop! Whoop!" Ed shouted making everyone laugh. Annie looked directly at her father to gauge his reaction. For the first time in her life she actually felt that he approved of this one. She was a little surprised when he jumped to his feet and walked towards Mark.

Charles shook Mark's hand. "Please make sure you look after our Annie, she is a treasure." Mark reassured him he was going to do everything to make her happy.

"Oh enough of this lovey-dovey stuff, who wants to play on FIFA?" Ed asked standing up.

Andrea turned to Mark. "He's never been into all this mushy stuff, gets it from his father. I pity the girl who meets him. I on the other hand can't resist a mushy story and I am really, really happy for Annie. I can't remember ever seeing her so radiant." Andrea hugged her daughter.

Annie smiled. "It's so nice of you all to speak about me as if I'm not here!"

Charles defended his wife. "Annie you are our little girl and always will be."

Andrea and Charles left the house at 9.30 p.m. Whilst Mark filled the dishwasher, Annie opened her laptop to prepare lessons for tomorrow and notes for the dreaded meeting with her Dean.

"I have texted Lucy to say we will have to arrange another time for her to come here. It's Sophie's recital tomorrow night and we promised her." Mark had forgotten all about his promise.

Just as they discussed the detail, Ed popped his head around the door. "Come on Mark we are waiting to thrash you again. What's this about Manchester?" Ed had always had an inquisitive mind.

Annie explained about Sophie's recital and Ed invited himself along, as he was curious to meet Sophie. Annie knew that would be an interesting meeting! Annie's phone bleeped. It was a reply from Lucy: *okay no problem, what about next weekend?* Annie replied advising she was being taken to London next weekend but the weekend after was free.

Walking into the living room she announced, "I forgot to tell you Ed we are coming down to London next weekend to watch you play. Mark has booked a hotel for us in London so we can spend some time on our own Saturday night. Mark, I've told Lucy we will organise something for the weekend after next."

The boys just nodded, they were too enthralled in playing their games. Annie tutted and left the room.

15

The morning was drizzly and overcast. Matt had left early to call for his training bag. Annie left Ed and Mark fast asleep. She was fully prepared for the morning particularly the meeting with Elspeth. She had lived it in her head a dozen times but opted to play it cool and see what the Dean had to say first. She felt sure they couldn't take action against her. She'd done nothing wrong.

She arrived at the college at 8.30 a.m. and headed straight for the café. She wanted to go over her lecture notes for after the meeting and grab a coffee to chill out. Lucy had already got her coffee and was sitting with John at their usual table. Annie walked in and was in the process of an about turn, when Lucy saw her and signalled for her to join them. This was not what Annie needed at all this morning.

"Morning. Good weekend?" Lucy asked. Annie nodded and sat down. She did not even acknowledge John's presence. She was still angry at bumping into him on Saturday and did not buy into his story that it was a coincidental meet.

John tried to speak to her. "It was nice to see you on Saturday. It was a lovely surprise."

Annie glared at him as if her eyes were lasers cutting through his body. How dare you, she thought.

Lucy tried to break the awkwardness. "What time are you going over to Manchester today?" Annie looked at her, why was she asking? Her paranoia was rising. Stop it, she thought.

"The recital is at six, so whenever we are ready really. Ed is coming over, think he is eager to meet Mark's daughter."

Lucy laughed. "Well knowing Ed he will have her eating out of his hands in no time."

"Probably," Annie said. "Listen, I'm sorry I need to go and prepare for my meeting this morning with Elspeth. She has asked to see me and I don't know why but I can probably guess." She glared again at John who did not make eye contact with her. He was shuffling uncomfortably in his chair.

"Lucy, I'll come and find you after the meeting." She left. She stomped over to her office furious that she had not had it out with John but that would have only played into his hands.

The couple of hours dragged so much for Annie. She spent most of the time staring out of the window thinking of the weekend and how wonderful it had been, how wonderful Mark had been. She sent him a text saying that she loved him and missed him and she'd be home around oneish.

She received a text message from Matt asking if she was available tomorrow at 5.30 p.m. to meet Billy and Marcus for contract talks. She replied she was. She rang Billy and Marcus to confirm her attendance and agreed that Ed would also attend to start his discussions after Matt's meeting. She advised Mark would be accompanying them but would not be party to the contract negotiations. It was all agreed. She forwarded the messages to Matt, Mark and Ed so everyone knew the score.

Finally at 9.55 a.m. Annie locked her office door and headed over to the Dean's office. She was really nervous even though she had done nothing wrong. She knocked on the door and entered. Annie was surprised to see it was only Elspeth, her PA and Annie in the meeting. She expected a full committee of senior managers. She felt strangely reassured that this could be just a chat.

"Morning Annie, glad to see you are feeling better." Elspeth signalled for Annie to take a seat.

"I am, thank you," Annie replied.

"I will get straight to the point. It has been brought to our attention that you currently have a," there was a pause, "a problem, shall we say."

"I don't know what you mean, I have no problems, and in fact life is wonderful at the moment."

"Oh that's not the impression we got."

"Where from?"

Ignoring Annie's question, Elspeth continued, "We were advised that you were seeing Mark Smith, the former rugby player, and that there could potentially be a problem that could put the college is an 'awkward' position."

"Well I am sorry Elspeth but you have been misinformed. Mark and I do not have any problems and to be honest I am not sure whether it would be any business of the college's in any case."

"Fair enough Annie, that's all I needed to hear."

As Annie stood up to leave Elspeth issued words of warning. "Annie we really value you as a member of our family but we will have to take any evasive action necessary for incidents that jeopardise the health, safety and welfare of staff or students. If there is anything we should know, you have a duty to come and talk to me." Annie nodded and then left the room.

Walking back to her office, she felt mildly pleased with herself that she had kept her cool and the college could not do anything. She was also mighty pissed off that someone had gone to the trouble of stirring it, which could have resulted in her suspension. Annie located Lucy and told her what had happened. She made a point of giving all the details in the hope that Lucy would go back and tell John. Annie felt she had scored a minor victory against him as she was convinced it was he who had given the information to Elspeth.

The remainder of the morning was light relief. It was soon lunchtime and Annie skipped out of the college knowing she was going home to her boys. Matt would probably still be at training. Ed was more than likely still in bed!

There was another note on the windscreen of her car that flapped in the morning wind. Her heart sank as she plucked it from under the windscreen wiper. With trepidation, she opened it and it read: 'so you think you can get away with loving him. You'll learn and pay for it the hard way.'

Looking around the car park, there was no one in sight. She ran over to the security guard and he admitted he had not seen anyone approach the car. Annie was beyond upset now. This was starting to really irritate her. There was no need for it. Strangely she wasn't fazed by this new note and couldn't decide whether it was because she was past caring or she thought she knew it was John. It was time for her to take control and get to the bottom of it.

She drove home determined now to live her life her way and to make the most of life with Mark. This idiot was not going to get the better of her or stop her and Mark from forging a life together.

She parked the car in the garage and entered the house through the utility room. Mark was waiting for her in the kitchen. He had been in the gym and his T-shirt was ringing wet. He kissed and hugged her, much to her dismay. He offered to shower her and she laughed. Ed, on hearing his mum's voice, bounded into the kitchen and gave her a hug. He'd been working out too.

Annie showed them the note and recounted the morning's events. "I was thinking," she said. "Why don't we get ready and take Ed up to Garry's pub on the way out to Manchester? We can have a bit of lunch."

"That's a great idea," Mark replied. "I'm going for a shower. I think we should drop that note into Harry on the way out."

Ed went to his room to get ready and Annie and Mark went to their bedroom. Mark closed the door and grabbed Annie. He gave Annie a long, lingering kiss, which made her go weak at the knees. She stumbled onto the bed and pulled Mark on top of her. She wrapped her legs around his body. He started to undress her and she obliged. She rubbed her hands along his sweat soaked back.

"Mark I love you," she whispered. He looked straight into her eyes and beamed like a Cheshire cat. She continued, "Nothing is going to stop us from having our life together." He rested his head on her chest and she ran her fingers through his hair.

"Annie, I love you too." He kissed her breast and squeezed her waist. Annie pulled his head up towards hers and whilst they kissed she wriggled out of her trousers. They made love there and then, neither said anything they just kept eye contact throughout. She watched his every expression and moves and loved how she pleasured him.

*

"About bloody time!" Ed said as they walked into the living room.

"Sorry we got waylaid," Annie and Mark laughed.

"Really guys I don't even want that picture in my head, thank you!" Ed walked to the door. "Come on I'm hungry," and he entered the garage to get in Mark's car.

Annie had opted for a pair of jeans, white camisole and long black cardigan. She also wore a silk scarf tied around her neck. Mark really admired how she had her own style and was not one of those women who followed what the fashion was – not that she was unfashionable; she was stylish and always looked stunning.

After dropping the note into the police station, Mark drove to Garry's place. "Wow, this is some pub," Ed said craning his head to survey the property and the land. It was true, from outside it was magnificent. The building was stone built and three storeys. There were annexes to the left and old sheds to the right. "Wait 'til you see the rugby memorabilia inside," Annie said.

Ed walked into the pub first closely followed by Mark and Annie, hand in hand. It was a quiet day with only two people propping up the bar, talking to Garry.

On seeing his old team-mate, Garry excused himself from the discussion and bounded over to the end of the bar.

He leaned over. "Good to you see you again Mark, Annie and this must be, be... Matt?"

Ed scoffed, "I'm far too good looking to be him. I'm Ed the more talented one." Ed held his hand out to shake hands.

"My apologies young man!" Garry said. Turning to Annie, "So you have managed to cope with Mark then." Annie found his manner and words really odd and if she was totally honest he gave her shivers down her spine, not in a good way. She did not have a clue why she felt this but he was Mark's friend and she didn't want to let Mark know how she truly felt.

Mark interrupted, "Garry behave yourself. This is Annie's youngest son Ed. He's currently playing for London but not for much longer, I think." Garry nodded and looked the party up and down. Mark continued, "Are you doing lunches today?"

Garry nodded his head. "Yes but only a limited menu – tatties, sandwiches, things like that."

The party ordered sandwiches and drinks. Annie took Ed to the room where she had had dinner with Mark and showed him the memorabilia. Annie looked at the images with Ed. She turned around to see Mark and Garry in full conversation, their heads almost touching – no guessing what they are talking about, she thought. Mark brought the drinks over to the table and Ed continued to look at the Rugby League artefacts.

Annie asked Mark, "What were you and Garry talking about?"

Mark put his drink down and leaned over to kiss Annie. "I was telling him about the problems we have – Garry was there the first time around. He is gutted it's happening again and he was warning me not to let you go, in his words 'don't be an idiot this time and lose her like you lost the last one'."

Annie was curious at this. "So Garry thinks you and Louisa split because you let her go."

Mark nodded. "Yes but he had a soft spot for her and she worked her manipulative magic on him. Garry and I fell out for a short time but I'd lost everything and when I needed him, he came up trumps." Annie squeezed Mark's hand and wrapped her leg around his ankle.

During lunch they chatted about Annie's work, the contract discussions that were to take place the following evening and the Grand Final. Every so often Annie would glance at Garry staring at them. Once she made eye contact he hurried off and tried to look busy behind the bar. It was a lovely, pleasant lunch. Annie texted Matt just to make sure he was safe. He was back at his home now and chilling with the boys before his personal appearance at an amateur club.

The journey over the M62 was slow but bearable. Annie had spent some of the journey in her own little world trying to piece together all the occurrences and who the possible culprit could be. She had an idea who it might be but had no proof and fearing that people would suggest she was losing the plot, she decided to keep her thoughts to herself until she had the proof she needed. She decided that as of tomorrow she would start to try and solve the mystery and put her planning and research skills to good use. This person was not going to get the better of her or stop her from being with the man of her dreams.

Annie snapped out of her action plan when the engine stopped. They had arrived at the University of Manchester. Sophie had texted her dad the postcode for his Sat-Nav. The auditorium was a lecture room, the walls covered with posters from the University's musical society. It was warm and inviting. The instruments lay on the floor at the bottom of the rows of seats. Sophie was sorting all her equipment out when she saw her dad arrive. She thought, 'oh he has brought HER with him'. Sophie ran across to greet them.

"Hi Dad and Annie." Sophie kissed her dad and looked at Annie. Annie knew not to expect too much of a greeting.

"Hi babe, this is Ed, Annie's youngest son," Mark said pointing to Ed.

Ed beamed and as Lucy had predicted, Sophie took an instant liking to him. Maybe it's not that bad Dad being with her, after all, she thought.

Mark caught a glimpse of his ex-wife out of the corner of his eye. Louisa was wearing a black tailored suit with a white blouse. She saw him and came over.

"Annie," Mark said holding his arm around her waist, "this is Louisa my ex-wife and Sophie's mother." Annie didn't know what to say or do.

"Pleased to meet you," Annie settled for. They shook hands. Louisa was nothing like she would have thought, in fact she wouldn't have even put her and Mark together. Louisa was greying more than Mark and she had a sour look on her face. Her eyes were wrinkled and her hair tightly held back in a ponytail.

"So you're his latest conquest then," Louisa said looking Annie up and down. Annie felt really uncomfortable and just wanted the ground to swallow her up.

Mark sensing Annie's unease gripped her side. She looked up at him and smiled. "Shall we take a seat love?" he said to her.

Unfortunately Louisa decided she had a right to join their party and sat at the other side of Mark. Mark held Annie's hand and now and then stroked his thumb along the palm of her hand just to let her know she was okay.

"You okay Mum?" Ed whispered.

"I am love," Annie said.

"She's a bit of a battle-axe," Ed said.

Annie put a finger to her mouth. "Shush, only a bit!"

Both Ed and Annie laughed; Ed leant over again and whispered, "But her daughter's a bit of all right."

Annie laughed and shook her head.

The recital was excellent. Mark was enthralled by his daughter's performance. The same could have not have been said for Louisa. She spent most of the recital tapping into her mobile phone. Annie could tell this annoyed Mark.

After the recital, the party met with Sophie in the student union bar. Louisa had one drink, made her excuses and left.

"Well at least she came," Mark said to Sophie. Sophie shrugged her shoulders.

"Sophie, shall we go get some more drinks?" Ed asked. A little surprised at his forthrightness, Sophie agreed and off they went.

Mark smiled. "She will eat him for breakfast!"

Annie replied, "More than likely. It's been a really lovely night Mark. Thank you for letting me share it."

Mark looked at Annie. "I don't want to be with anyone else. Sophie will get used to us, she hasn't had the fabulous upbringing that your boys have had."

Annie gave Mark a kiss and whispered, "She has a wonderful dad."

The kids returned with more drinks. Sophie and Ed continued their discussions whilst Annie and Mark watched on. There was definitely a spark.

At 10.30 p.m. they gave Sophie a lift back to her halls of residence and said goodnight. They had got no further than one mile away, when Ed's phone bleeped. He read it, smiled and laughed out loud. Mark and Annie just looked at each other and smiled.

Part Two

Never Ending Hell?

16

At 7 a.m. Matt and Ed entered the cubicle with coffee for Mark and Annie. Annie was still asleep and Mark gestured for them to be quiet. He rose from the chair, stretched and ushered them out of the cubicle.

He said, "I am going to go for a walk and to freshen up. Can you two sit with your mum 'til I get back?" They nodded and disappeared behind the curtain.

It was 11.30 before the doctor returned to the ward. After much pleading from Annie and her crew, the doctor agreed to discharge her. Andrea and Charles agreed they would help as much as they could. They had already contacted the college and the boys' respective clubs to say they wouldn't be available today.

The journey home in Matt's car was very uncomfortable for all three of the victims. Ed sat in the front but was eagle-eyed the whole journey home. Annie laid across Mark on the back seat but she felt every bump in the road. Finally they pulled into the driveway and were home.

Andrea insisted on fussing over Annie. She organised a makeshift bed in the living room strategically placed so her daughter could see the breathtaking views from the window. Mark was going to make them all some lunch but Andrea insisted she and Charles would do it whilst he sat with Annie and the boys.

Matt asked, "Mark, you know you said I could move in if I wanted, would you mind if I do at least until Mum is back on her feet?"

Ed interrupted, "Both feet," and he smiled.

"There's no need, Matt. I am okay," Annie reassured him.

"But I'm not Mum." His admission took them all by surprise. "For my own peace of mind I would like to be here. I'll still go training, work, out with the lads but I think I need to come here every night to see you."

"Matt we can go get your stuff today while Andrea and Charles are here," Mark said.

"Listen, I need to say this to you all." Mark cleared his throat and held Annie's hand. "I love you all. I know we have not known each other for long but all that's happened has shown all your true characters and I love you all the more. You are so supportive of one another and that makes me so proud."

His head lowered to look at his feet, he continued, "I am so sorry this has happened and I know it is all my fault but I promise you it will all get sorted. I know it's a lot to ask for you all but I would love it if we could all stick together and get through this. It will be over someday and then I can promise you, you all will have the best life possible."

These were heartfelt words and Charles had listened to them from the hallway. Charles was convinced Mark was behind everything in a ploy to trap Annie but now he knew he had been so wrong.

Mark went on, "Matt, you and Ed can make this your home. We would love to have you here and we have the room."

Annie interrupted, her voice breaking with emotion. "Thank you all. Your help and support is great but I also want you all to have your own lives. These are worrying times for all of us and the more we spend together the better. I am relieved and happy you want to move in. I also want to say now in front of you all, I don't in anyway blame Mark for what has and is happening. I actually think this could be as much someone from my life as his. We will work it out. I love all of you very, very much."

Andrea came in with sandwiches, biscuits and snacks. Charles followed her with tea and coffee.

Charles said, "I listened to what you both said." He turned to Mark. "I am sorry Mark I doubted you, I thought you was somehow connected to what was happening to my daughter but I feel so guilty now. I have realised over the last twenty-four hours that you and Annie belong together and these two," pointing to his grandchildren, "think the world of you. I am very proud of how you all have handled yourselves."

Lunch was great. Annie hardly ate anything; she was suffering but did not want the boys to know or to worry.

After lunch, Mark cleared away the plates and was in the kitchen filling up the dishwasher when Andrea came in. She stood at his side looking down at him.

"Mark," she said. "Annie has had a really tough life. She deserves to be happy. I know that you want to make her happy. Charles and I will support you but our daughter and those two boys are our world. Please keep them safe."

Mark stood up and placed his hands on Andrea's shoulders. "I promise you Andrea I will do everything to keep them safe. I love your daughter very much. I have got to forty-nine and have finally found love. I would die for her."

Charles walked in. "That copper's 'ere. Andrea put the kettle on please."

Mark squeezed Andrea's shoulder then left to greet Harry in the hall.

"Hi Mark. How are you?"

"I'm okay Harry. I'm hoping you have made a breakthrough."

Harry shook his hand. "I need to take statements from the three of you. If possible it would be better to do the statements separately."

Mark agreed he could use the dining room but would have to speak to Annie in the living room as she was resting. Mark walked in to the living room to see the boys whispering on the sofa and Annie with her eyes closed. Mark walked over to her and pulled the covers up. They all left her to sleep.

Ed gave his statement first, then Mark. Annie was still asleep when Harry had finished so he agreed to come back later.

"Shall we go get your stuff Matt?" Mark asked.

Andrea suggested, "Why don't you go too Charles, you can load two cars then. Ed you can go give them a hand. I'll stay with Annie."

The boys left in two cars. Mark really was unsure whether to leave the girls alone but the security on the grounds of the house was very good.

Annie slept for four hours. The boys returned after two hours. They had box after box. Andrea laughed at the amount of clothes Matt had. Matt was given the room down the corridor from theirs. It was tastefully decorated in black and white and had a plasma television mounted on the wall.

Andrea fussed over him, hanging his clothes up and putting things away in the closet.

"How did your mates take it when you told them you were moving out?" Andrea enquired.

"They were okay Grannie. They're getting a nice house to live in without anyone laying the ground rules down. They're good lads though." He sat on the bed and looked at his grandma. "What if she'd have died?" He put his head in his hands.

Andrea sat next to him on the bed and put her arm around her grandson. "But she didn't Matt. You can't think like that. You have to stay positive and stick together. There are people out there that will do their best to split you all up. They will also try and manipulate you. Don't let them. Your mum has been through so much in her life. She is a brilliant person and she may have made mistakes in the past and misjudged people, but we can't all be wrong about Mark, can we?" Matt shook his head.

"Grandma, I don't blame Mark at all. I think he is a good man. I just want Mum to be happy and safe. I can't bear the thought of anyone hurting her." Tears rained down his cheeks. They hugged and then carried on unpacking his stuff.

Ed bounced into the room. "I've spoken to the coach and he has given me compassionate leave this week. I have to report back on Friday. I know it's the wrong time to think about this but what about the meeting with Marcus and Billy?"

Matt confirmed, "I have spoken to them and explained what has happened. I have to report to training on Friday. Marcus asked if Mum could ring him once she's feeling better and they can arrange another meeting."

Andrea left the boys to talk in the bedroom and went into the living room. Charles was watching television and Mark was watching Annie. She stirred and opened her eyes. She beamed at Mark.

"What time is it?" she asked sleepily.

"It's six o'clock," Charlie replied.

"Shit!" Annie exclaimed, trying to get up, "I have the meeting at Leeds."

"Annie it's fine you have to ring Marcus when you are up and about to rearrange it. Matt's just been talking about it upstairs," Andrea said. She then turned to Charles. "Shall we leave these to it now and go home. It's been a long couple of days."

"Thank you," Annie shouted as Andrea and Charles left the front door. Mark closed the door and rested his head on the doorframe. He was worn out and his head was banging. When he returned to the room, Annie was on the telephone. "I know Marcus it was truly terrifying but we are all okay thank God… Thanks Marcus and thanks for giving Matt a couple of days off… Yeah it shook us all up… why don't you come here? To Mark's place… we don't mind, no honestly if you don't mind making the trip… we can discuss the deal here… No I am fine and no you won't get an easy ride 'cos I'm in pain. See you tomorrow then… yeah… why don't you bring Alicia with you, we can have some dinner… well a takeaway then. Okay… thanks… see you tomorrow… I will."

She hung up.

"Honestly I turn my back for two seconds and you're on the phone. Annie you need rest," Mark said smiling. He lifted her legs up and sat down, resting them on his knees. His arm stretched along her side. "You okay sweetheart?" he said.

She nodded. "Are you?"

"Yes I am, I have a bad headache but nothing compared to you."

She told Mark, Marcus and Billy would be coming to the house at 4 p.m. tomorrow to discuss Matt's contract and Ed. Marcus was bringing his wife Alicia so they could stay on and have some tea. Mark laid his head back and closed his eyes. Annie shuffled a little. He lifted his head. "Are you comfortable?"

She nodded. "Where are the boys?"

Right on cue they entered the living room. Annie told them about the meeting tomorrow.

"Put the PS3 on if you want to boys," Annie said. They didn't need telling twice. Mark opted to watch them with Annie instead of playing. Annie asked him to sit with her. She shuffled down and he relocated. As he sat down she kissed his lips and mouthed I love you. Mark wrapped his arms around her breasts and gently held her. He was so afraid of hurting her.

Two hours later, Matt gently tapped Mark on the shoulder. "Mark why don't you take Mum upstairs? Ed and I will sort out down here." Mark looked around and realised they had both nodded off to sleep. He carried Annie upstairs much to her disgust. She was more than happy to walk to bed. He helped her get undressed and put her to bed. Annie lay there laughing uncontrollably. Mark was totally oblivious to the reason.

She explained, "I just had visions of you doing this in twenty years' time." Trying to gain her composure. "Sorry I know it's probably not that funny but it really tickled me."

Mark lay next to her, getting as close to her body as possible without hurting her and whispered, "I will gladly do it for the next forty years if it means we are together."

Annie rubbed Mark's arm. "We will be, we will be."

They fell asleep in each other's arms.

17

Mark and Annie awoke to the smell of cooking bacon and the sound of the smoke alarm! Mark was laid up to her back. She tried to turn over to face him but the pain was unbearable. Mark helped her to turn over.

"Thank you," she said. "Am I dreaming or can I smell bacon?"

"Well I'm dreaming too," he laughed. "Do you think they will bring it up to us?"

"Knowing them, they've probably made their own and we'll have to make ours," Annie joked but she knew that wasn't really true.

She laid on Mark's chest rubbing her hands across it longing for him to make love to her but there was no way she could function her whole body especially her leg. There was a knock on the bedroom door.

Mark shouted, "Come in."

Matt walked in with a tray of two cooked breakfasts, fresh juice and Ed followed with coffee. Mark was so impressed.

"Thought you both might need this," Matt said.

Ed pinching some toast said, "But if you tell anyone about this, we will deny it."

Mark laughed. "Thank you, both of you. We are touched."

Annie tried in vain to sit up but the pain was excruciating. Her whole body felt battered. The boys helped her sit up and put the tray on her knee. Mark put the television on and the boys left them to enjoy their breakfast.

Mark spoke whilst eating a slice of toast. "Sophie would never have thought to do anything like that."

Annie confessed, "It's not just down to me. My mum and dad, especially my dad, have been wonderful role models. I am so proud of them Mark."

The breakfast was delicious and not burnt! Annie was taking a sip of the coffee when Sky Sports News delivered the headline 'Ex rugby star and junior star in motorway crash!' She spat the coffee all over the bed and looked at Mark. Mark turned up the volume. The reporter said, "There are reports coming in that last night the car crash on the M62 involved the former rugby player, Mark Smith, who was driving and his passengers included Ed Swift, sixteen-year-old rising rugby player with London and brother of Leeds star Matthew Swift. The other passenger was their mother Annie Swift. Police declined to comment but witnesses stated one of the passengers was seriously injured. The rugby clubs declined to confirm or deny these reports."

Suddenly the house came alive with all the phones ringing. Matt and Ed stormed into the bedroom. They hadn't seen the report but their team-mates were on the telephone.

Annie sat up and said, "Right boys. We'll have to switch all the phones off for now. Ed ring your grandma and your dad on the landline and tell them there might be reporters and not to speak to them. Tell them we are turning the mobile phones off in fifteen minutes until we work all this out. Mark, ring Harry ask him to come over. Matt ring Ben at the house and tell them not to speak to anyone about us or to let anyone in the house. Shit! Really need this on the day we are negotiating your contracts."

Mark was so impressed with how professional Annie was even in a crisis.

She continued, "Mark, ring Sophie and tell her everything. Pass me my phone please."

As the others carried out their tasks, Annie rang Marcus. "Hi Marcus it's Annie. Have you seen the news this morning?"

Marcus answered, "No but Leon did and he is with me now."

Annie carried on, "Can I borrow Leon. I need someone who can advise us on publicity and damage limitation. There are things happening that we need to keep a lid on for the time being especially with the Grand Final looming."

"Yes Annie of course. I'll send him over. What's going on?" Marcus asked.

"Can we talk tonight Marcus? I don't want to discuss it over the phone. It's nothing to do with the boys," she reassured him.

Marcus replied, "I never thought it would be. Is it to do with Mark?"

"Sort of."

"We'll talk tonight. Leon will be there in about an hour. Take care," Marcus said.

Mark came back in and Annie explained, "Marcus is sending his best media guy over to help us draft a statement. Did you get in touch with Harry and Sophie?"

"I did. Sophie took it well, NOT! She said she'd ring later tonight. Harry is on his way over to see us," Mark said.

"Help me get up and dressed please Mark." Annie sat up on the side of the bed. She had a splitting headache. She tried to stand but the room spun. Mark grabbed her and eased her back on the bed.

"Annie it's too early for you to be doing all this," Mark said.

"I know Mark but we need to minimise the impact on the boys' careers." Annie said, "I promise I will get you or the boys to do things but I need to be downstairs for Leon and Harry. I also need my laptop." She shouted, "Are all the mobile phones switched off now?" Muffled yeses came from the distant rooms.

"I will help you get dressed if you promise that as soon as you are downstairs, you will lay on the sofa. We will fetch and carry as long as you take it easy," Mark declared.

Annie reluctantly agreed although she didn't have much choice. She really wasn't physically well enough to run around at her usual pace. As Mark dressed her she caught a glimpse of her face in the wardrobe mirror. Her nose was swollen with a deep red gash across the bridge and two blackened patches under her eyes. Her left eye was swollen and blood shot. There were scratch marks all over her face.

Matt and Ed had made a makeshift bed up again and had brought the table closer to her seating position. Her laptop was on and ready for her.

Annie smiled at her boys and said, "Right, do not speak to anyone about what's been happening. No one other than the close people we have around. Matt, Ed be wary of telling your team-mates anything for the time being. We need to keep a lid on it all. It won't help the police if it's leaked and it won't help your careers. You all know what the press are like. Nothing will be turned into something. Leon is coming over shortly to draft a statement. We'll get Harry to check it over as well. Someone has leaked this to the press."

Mark was in awe of Annie again. He had gone to pieces this morning at the story being leaked but she was calm and methodical. The gate intercom sounded. Mark went to investigate – it was Andrea and Charles.

Annie filled them in with the latest instalment whilst Mark made tea. They were going to need a lot of tea today he thought. Harry arrived and shortly after Leon.

It took them two hours to draft a statement that they all agreed upon. Leon left with the statement and agreed to circulate it. Annie gave her full statement to Harry.

Harry concluded, "Thanks Annie. We are still looking for the driver of the vehicle. We have found traces of blood from the driver so it's only a matter of time before we find matching DNA. My Super has agreed to increase the number of bodies dealing with this now."

Annie asked, "Can we talk tomorrow in detail? I am a little tired now and have Matt's boss coming over soon."

"Annie that's perfectly okay. I'll come about eleven and we can have a good chat." Mark showed Harry out. Annie took some painkillers and drifted off to sleep.

Annie woke up in good spirits. There was an hour or so before Marcus and everyone would be arriving. The boys were playing on FIFA and she just lay there watching them.

She suddenly sat up and said, "Right boys I need to ask you what you want from these contracts before the heavy mob get here?"

Ed said flippantly, "Err two hundred and fifty K a week, sports car, big mansion." Annie frowned. "Okay, okay I'll settle for a full time professional contract," Ed added.

Annie said, "They might not go for it, you're still very young. They may offer you twelve months then see how you go."

Ed pulled a face. "I suppose I'll live with that. What about you Matt?"

Matt shrugged his shoulders. "I'll be happy renewing on the same terms but see what they offer. There are more important things than money."

Andrea said, "Don't sell yourself short Matt. You are brilliant but then I'm slightly biased."

Charles agreed. "Yes lad you're the best. We will keep our fingers crossed and hope you get everything you deserve. Now come on Andrea let's go home. We'll call tomorrow, if that's okay?" Charles looked at Annie.

"Of course it is Dad. We will have more time tomorrow. Harry is coming at eleven but come over whenever you're ready."

"Is he Dirty Harry?" Charles laughed.

Andrea laughed. "Make my DAY!"

Everyone laughed and said goodbye.

"Jesus, Annie, look at your face. How are you?" Marcus said as he walked into the room and leant over to kiss her cheek. He handed her a bouquet of flowers.

Annie replied, "I am on the mend Marcus. Thank you, these are beautiful. Hi Alicia and Billy, please all come in and sit down. You'll have to forgive me but it takes a while for me to stand up." Her guests reassured her it was not necessary for her to get up.

Annie and Mark explained the current situation being as vague as possible. They really didn't want any details to be leaked, unintentional or otherwise. Marcus, Alicia and Billy listened intently and nodded from time to time as if acknowledging they understood but Annie knew it was impossible for anyone to really understand.

Mark got the drinks and the boys made a brief appearance together but it was soon down to business. Mark left the room with Alicia and the boys. Matt returned when it was time to discuss his contract. The club provided a very attractive package and it did not take long for them to agree the deal. The contract would see Matt staying at the club for a further five years. Annie explained St George had wanted to speak to Matt but he'd declined declaring his loyalty to Leeds. Marcus appreciated his honesty and integrity. The only stipulation Matt made was that the club gave Ed a chance too. The club complied without hesitation. They agreed to give him a two-year contract with an extension clause after twelve months. Matt left the room and Ed came in. Ed tried his best to contain his excitement when Marcus explained the club's offer. He sat opposite his mum and just stared at her.

"So what do you think?" Marcus looked directly at Ed.

Ed smiled, took a deep breath and replied, "I am delighted and accept the contract. Thank you Billy and Marcus, I won't let you down and will work incredibly hard."

Billy responded, "We know you will. We have high hopes for you and your brother."

Matt and Mark re-entered the room. Alicia had opted to stay in the kitchen as she had no interest in rugby at all in fact she was sick of hearing it 24/7 at home.

"Well I think that's that," Marcus said. "Annie, you have two great young men that you should be incredibly proud of. I am delighted they will both be with us. I would like you all to keep it within these walls until we organise a press release. If we get to the Grand Final."

"When," Billy said. Marcus glared at him. "When we get to the Grand Final," Billy continued.

Marcus smiled. "Sorry when we get to the Final, my thought is we announce Matt and Ed the week running up to it – give us a boost and the fans something else to celebrate."

All parties agreed, although it was going to be difficult. This was massive news and at last the brothers were at the same club.

Mark said, "Well if that's the business taken care of, time for celebrating, champagne anyone?"

"If it's okay with you all, I am going to get off. I promised my boys I would not be too late tonight," Billy asked.

Marcus nodded as if to provide approval for his departure. This time Annie tried to stand up with Mark's support.

She thanked Billy and hugged him. Alicia joined the others in the room. Marcus told her what had been agreed. She nodded but Annie was sure if anyone would have asked Alicia to repeat it, she wouldn't have known what he had said.

The boys were bursting to tell their grannie and grandpa but agreed to tell them when they called in the morning.

The evening was really enjoyable. Mark had not seen a relaxed side of Marcus before. A man in his late fifties, he had always appeared aloof and patronising but he was not like that at all. He had a sarcastic sense of humour and adored his wife. He was like a lap dog, pandering to her every whim. Mark was amused at Matt and Ed. They knew they had to behave but found it incredibly hard not to be relaxed and wind each other up. Marcus enjoyed their banter. He had never had children and it was clear he genuinely liked the boys and Annie.

Mark and Marcus went into the kitchen to order the food.

Alicia turned to Annie. "Mark's nice Annie, seems to really love you and the boys."

Annie smiled. She had always found Alicia a bit standoffish. "He does. I am very lucky to have found him."

Alicia continued, "You are very lucky. Annie I am glad you are okay. I know we haven't really become close friends but I would have hated for anything to happen to you. Marcus was devastated to hear what happened. Mind you he was probably more devastated that one of the boys was in the car." She half smirked, "I am only kidding."

Annie was used to Alicia having a go at Marcus. Their relationship seemed to thrive on them not getting on. Alicia hated rugby but enjoyed the lavish lifestyle. She was at home all day and whatever she wanted, Marcus would give her except what she really wanted and that was for him to sell the club and retire. The club was in his blood and although he cursed about the hard work, he thrived on the business. The best part of the job for Marcus was giving the contracts to young men and seeing them grow within the sport. He was a very rare breed and was fair but firm when it came to negotiating.

Marcus turned to Mark. "It was a lucky escape, the accident?"

Mark nodded. "It was, very scary. Just wish I'd have been hurt not Annie. She is such a strong lady. I would have been in bed for weeks if it'd been me."

Marcus laughed. "She is one tough cookie! I have to admit I really admire her and the way she has brought the boys up." Marcus stared into his glass. "Today's contract talks were probably the easiest decision I have ever made. Matt and Ed are great kids and really reflect what we are looking for at the club. If I'd have had kids I would have been really proud of them turning out like Matt and Ed."

Mark agreed. "Yep they are a chip off the old block. Annie is an incredible woman."

Marcus smiled. "Look after her Mark and make her happy. I adore Alicia but if I hadn't have been married and been a bit younger I would have loved to have been with Annie. She's vibrant and clever." Marcus almost forgot who he was speaking to and had said far too much. Mark was taken aback by his candid remarks but was not surprised. He had suspected Marcus held a torch for Annie but Mark knew the feelings were not mutual.

"I will do everything to make her happy Marcus. I love her and want to spend the rest of my life with her."

The men ordered the food, which Marcus insisted on paying for.

It wasn't long before the food arrived. Mark had set the dining room table with help from the boys. Matt and Ed were buoyant and continued their banter at the table. Marcus started to relax more and joined in the banter with the boys. After dinner they retired to the lounge.

Marcus realised Annie was flagging. "Alicia I think we should make a move now."

Alicia nodded. "Right I'll just finish my drink, if that's okay with you." The sarcasm in her voice did not go unnoticed by everyone.

After lingering kisses, cuddles and shaking hands, the guests left.

Annie let out a huge sigh and said, "Well that was a great night and congratulations to my beautiful boys. It's just a great shame Great Granddad wasn't here to celebrate with us." Tears welled up in her eyes at the thought of her granddad. He would have been so proud. Matt and Ed sat either side of their mother.

Matt placed his arm around her and said, "He would have been more proud of you and how you handled the negotiations."

"I was really proud of you sticking up and looking out for your brother," Annie said.

Ed looked puzzled until Annie explained how Matt had negotiated Ed's contract as part of his package. Annie was worried that Ed would see it as Matt pulling in favours but Ed knew better than that.

He said, "Thanks mate. I don't know what to say but it would have been hilarious if they'd have said no. What would you have done then?"

Matt laughed. "I would have had to come to London with you or gone to Aus!"

Mark said, "Well I have to say I am impressed with you all. What a brilliant day, under the circumstances. It is just what we all needed. Harry is coming at eleven so I am taking your mother to bed. We shall see you two professional rugby players in the morning."

Annie kissed her precious boys goodnight. She walked up the stairs this time but found it really hard work. She lay in bed watching Mark get undressed. She loved the contours of his body. As soon as he climbed into bed she was stuck to him like a limpet. He stroked her face and kissed her nose tenderly. She wrapped her arms around his warm, inviting body. He kissed her lips and she winced but kissed him back harder. Mark moved even closer to her body. She could feel his manhood pressing against her leg. She was turned on.

"Shall we try?" she whispered. "You'll have to do most of it," she laughed. Mark mounted her gently ensuring none of his weight rested on her broken leg.

Annie was in pain but wanted his pleasure. His body felt warm and sexy, the smell of him overpowered her. She wanted it no matter how much pain she was in. Mark gently rode her every now and then checking she was okay.

She whispered in his ear, "I am more than okay Mark, give it to me, I want you to come inside me."

He moved faster and harder, his heavy breathing in her ear, turning her on even more. Before she knew it they were both ecstatic. Mark slipped over to the side and she clung on to him.

She kissed his chest and declared, "I love you Mark." He squeezed her even tighter.

18

Annie was wide-awake at 8 a.m. and desperate for the toilet. She rolled onto her side and managed to sit up. Mark stirred but did not wake up. Annie managed to go to the toilet by herself, which she thought was an amazing feat. She really wanted to jump in the bath with Mark but that was not possible with the cast on her leg.

As she came out of the bathroom, Mark was standing in the bedroom doorway. "Good morning sexy," Annie said hobbling towards him. "Will you help me get a shower please?"

Mark smiled. "Erm I can think of a few things we can do."

They were interrupted by the gate intercom ringing constantly. Mark ran down.

"Dad, it's me. Let me in now," Sophie bellowed down the intercom.

By the time Mark unlocked the front door, Sophie's car had screeched to a halt. Her face was full of thunder and her cheeks were blushed.

"It's good to see you Sophie," Mark said as he opened his arms to hug his daughter but she walked through to the hall.

"What the hell is going on Dad? Where is SHE?" Sophie fumed.

Mark was taken aback. "You mean Annie?"

"Yes. She could have got you killed!" Sophie was beside herself. She went from kitchen to lounge when Mark halted her, grabbing her shoulder.

He softly said, "Calm down Sophie. Please calm down."

"Dad, whoever she is, she's bad news for you."

Mark declared, "Now Sophie, calm down. It is not Annie, this is my past. I want you to sit down. I will explain everything if you just calm down."

The commotion had woken Matt and Ed who came downstairs in their bed shorts.

Sophie fumed, "Oh so they've all moved in now! Great, not only has she got her claws into you, they have too!"

"No one has their claws into your dad Sophie," Annie said from the top of the stairs.

Sophie stood open-mouthed at the sight of Annie. The bruising and swelling on her face was much worse than she had imagined but Sophie continued her tantrum. "Thank God you didn't get hurt like her, Dad, she deserves it!"

Matt and Ed were furious.

Ed shouted, "How dare you!"

Mark shouted, "Sophie, THAT'S enough!"

Mark had had enough, daughter or no daughter she was not going to be allowed to treat Annie with vile disrespect. He continued, "I am not having you speaking about or to Annie like that!"

Sophie stamped her feet like a petulant child.

Mark continued chastising his daughter. "The incident wasn't Annie's fault, and she is a victim, as we all are." Sophie rolled her eyes in indignation. Mark continued, "You sit down and let us explain or you leave now."

There was a very awkward silence as Matt and Ed glared at Sophie and in turn she threw looks like daggers at Annie. Everyone seemed to wait for Sophie's next move. It seemed an eternity before she moved towards the lounge. She slumped down on the sofa sulking. Not to miss a confrontation, Matt and Ed followed her in. Mark helped Annie down the stairs and into the room.

Mark explained it all to Sophie but her reaction convinced the others she thought Mark was making excuses for Annie. Sophie didn't want Annie in Mark's life; any excuse will do to get her out.

When Mark had finished, the room was silent. He was still furious with his daughter and asked her, "So what have you got to say for yourself now?"

Sophie shrugged her shoulders like a five-year-old.

Annie spoke for the first time. "Sophie, I know you don't want me to be with your dad but I am. We love each other and no one is going to split us up. I understand how you feel but…"

Sophie stood up, tears rolling down her cheeks. "No you don't, you stupid cow, you have no idea how I feel. I could have lost my dad!"

She stormed out of the house, slamming the doors as she left.

Ed mumbled, "Awkward!" He and Matt decided it was time to make their exits to the gym. Annie walked over to Mark and hugged him. Mark was angry and annoyed with this daughter.

He whispered to Annie, "Told you she wasn't like your boys!"

Annie didn't know what to say. What could she say? She had never been in this position before, never would one of her boys speak to someone like that.

As Annie hugged Mark, she glanced out of the window to see Sophie climbing into the tree house.

Annie said, "Mark, she's in the tree house. Go speak to her."

"No," Mark insisted. "I need time to calm down and she can stew in her own anger, the little madam. She has her mother's temperament. Time I didn't give in to her histrionics."

*

"I have the previous case notes Harry," Charlie said, walking into the incident room.

"Excellent," Harry responded. "Can you spend today going through them, get as much information as you can out of them? I am going to look at her past and current friends, colleagues and family members."

Harry walked across to the board that displayed photographs of Mark and Annie and Susan Chadwick was Lawrence, their number one suspect and said, "I am not sure the past case has any relevance at this stage. All the threats have been made to Mrs Swift."

Harry stared at the photographs then looked across at the photographs of the crash scene. He couldn't help but feel sorry for his victims, two middle-aged people just looking for love. He knew how that felt. He was married to the job.

He snapped out of his thoughts when Phillipa walked in the room. Phillipa was an excellent detective, never left anything to chance and worked day and night on any case she was assigned to. She was carrying a brown envelope in her left hand and balancing two cups of coffee in the other.

"White no sugar," she said as she passed one of the cups to Harry. Harry smiled and leant against the conference table. He really admired Phillipa. She managed to do her job so well and still have a husband and two children.

"Sir, the forensics from NW68 STH. Nothing, absolutely nothing!" Phillipa was disappointed that there were no leads for her to follow.

Harry opened the envelope and read the report as Phillipa looked on. "When do we get the results from the car in the RTA?" Harry said without looking up from the paperwork.

Phillipa shrugged her shoulders. "A day or two. I've tried to hurry it up but now the lab numbers have been cut, it's hard to get them to move fast. I even tried Gabby but she was snowed under too."

"Err… thanks Phillipa. Can you let the team know there will be a briefing in ten minutes? The Super will be here – potential high profile case now and all that crap." He gave her a warm smile and watched her leave the room. Without doubt he was attracted to her and that brief encounter at the Christmas party two years ago only made his feelings stronger.

Determined to remain focused on the task in hand, he studied the boards. What was he missing? His gut feeling took him away from the obvious 'schizo' girl. He had a feeling this was someone closer to the couple.

The team filed into the room. The chatter started as a whisper but soon reached a crescendo. In an instant, silence descended on the room as the Superintendent walked in, she smiled. "Good morning all. I am going to sit in and listen. Harry will be in charge of the investigation. I am sure I don't need to remind you all that this case has the potential to be very high profile. Any parts of this investigation should remain confidential and anything we feel should be released must have my authorisation via our press office. Harry can you begin please?" The Superintendent sat at the front, which made some of the younger officers feel very uncomfortable and self-conscious.

Harry recounted the events and facts of the case for almost an hour setting down character details for Mark and Annie and recounting the previous case involving Mark. He explained all the recent incidents culminating in the accident on the M62.

The Superintendent interjected, "Are we sure the accident is definitely linked to the other incidents?"

Harry nodded. "We are waiting for the forensics report and until that arrives I can't categorically say yes but I was on the mobile phone to Mrs Swift during the incident. I heard it all and eye-witness statements corroborate there was a car taunting Mr Smith."

Sarcastically the Super said, "So the answer is no at this stage! It could have been just a one off?"

Harry could feel his blood boiling. Why was she questioning his professional judgement in front of the team? She continued, "Until the forensics are back I cannot authorise the manpower you have requested. I can give you two teams of four and will increase it if more evidence comes to light."

Harry was furious; he could feel his cheeks reddening. How dare she sit there and question his judgement after all she was only there 'cos this could be a high profile case, he thought. He decided not to question her authority, as it would have been fruitless. Instead he addressed the team calmly.

"Okay then we work with what we have. Phillipa and Charlie are going to work on the previous case and look through all witness statements and locate the suspect." He pointed to the board. "Alpha team, I would like you to look into Annie's past and present. We know a lot of Mark because of our previous dealings but very little about her. We know she is forty-seven, married once, one long-term partner and two children who are both rising stars in Rugby League. It's not premiership football but nevertheless they are still in the limelight. Find all you can about her, her ex-husband and ex-partner and all her friends, colleagues, etc. Beta

Team I would like you to look at Mark's family and friends, ex-wife and he has one daughter," Harry looked down at his notes, "Sophie – she is studying at Manc's Uni and that's where they had been before the RTA." He paused and continued, "Whoever did this, if it wasn't just an RTA," he glared at his Super, "knew who they were and possibly where they had been. We have witness statements from Ed Swift, the son and passenger in the car and from Mark and Annie. I am going to go back over the statements with them over the next twenty-four hours. Let me know as soon as you all find anything. Thank you." He dismissed the group and the Superintendent left leaving Charlie, Phillipa and Harry alone staring at one another.

Phillipa spoke first. "If it's any consolation sir I think you are right, the accident wasn't an accident at all."

Charlie nodded in agreement.

"Well we're just gonna have to prove it," Harry said as he sat down at the conference table. Phillipa sat opposite him; she could see he was troubled by something.

"Charlie, do you want to grab the coffees and we'll sit in here and go through the old case notes?" Charlie took the hint and scuttled out of the office.

"Harry I have known you a long time, more than most. What's going on?"

Harry looked at Phillipa. "I'm okay. Maybe I should have done more about the threats, I just thought it was a mischief-maker until I saw the wreckage on the motorway. You should have seen the state of Annie Swift when they brought her out of the car. It brought back some terrible memories."

Phillipa leant across the table and held Harry's hand. "Oh Harry it must have been awful for you." Phillipa was the only one in the office that knew Harry's seventeen-year-old daughter had been killed in an accident on the M1. He had heard of the incident in his patrol car and went to offer help. He had no inclination it was his daughter's car. She had hit black ice and spun into a bridge.

Harry withdrew his hand from Phillipa's and clasped hands around his face. After a couple of seconds he shook his head and replaced his hand on Phillipa's. "Sorry, this case is such a strange one. I have a gut feeling about it and it's not good. These two people seem level-headed, lovely people, victims because they want to be together. We have to solve this one."

He looked straight at Phillipa and she smiled warmly at him and said, "Of course we'll crack it, best team in Yorkshire."

They both laughed. Charlie re-joined them with the coffees.

"Sir we have found her."

"Who?"

"The suspect, a Susan Lawrence, now known as Susan Chadwick."

They all knew this was a breakthrough. Susan Lawrence could be the key.

"Where is she?" Harry asked.

"She lives in a small village near York, Kirkbridge."

"Come on then what we waiting for." Harry collected his keys and mobile phone.

"Are you coming too?" Harry asked Phillipa.

She shook her head. "No you two go, we don't want to go in heavy-handed at this stage. I will start reading all the notes. I will ring you if I find anything significant."

Harry's mobile phone rang.

"Hello Mr Smith, it's Harry." Harry stared at his colleagues.

"I will be round in ten minutes."

As he hung up, he advised his colleagues, "Accident just an accident eh? Mark and Annie have received an envelope today with photographs of the crash scene, graphic photographs. We need to go round there now."

"I thought we couldn't have any more manpower?"

"If it was an accident," he mocked. "This proves it wasn't. You go to the Super and fill her in. Charlie and I are going to the Smith's house now and then we'll go see the Lawrence woman."

Phillipa thought, bloody typical, he puts me in the firing line again!

*

The photographs were very graphic, showing Annie unconscious in the mangled car and the anguish on Mark and Eds' faces. Unfortunately they had been sent to Annie at Mark's address so he had not been the one to open them. He couldn't spare her from even more pain.

When Harry and Charlie arrived, it was clear to them that Annie had been crying and there was a lot of tension in the house. The boys were sat either side of their mother as Mark led the officers into the living room. Sophie was stood at the window staring out at the garden.

Harry thought Annie, despite her red eyes and bruising on her face, looked much better than the last time he saw her. The officers sat down. They studied the photographs very carefully. Harry spoke first. "We will take these to the lab. Was there a note or anything with them?"

Annie and Mark both shook their heads.

Mark said in a broken voice, trying to hold his emotions in check, "This is getting worse. We are all scared to death and don't even want to leave the house. We all have very busy lives and I want to know what you can do to protect my family. What you can do to stop all this." Annie placed her hand on his knee.

"Mark, they are trying. We need to remain strong and need to go through everyone we know who may do this."

Harry nodded. "Annie is right. I need a list from you all of all the people you have crossed paths with, past and present. It's not to accuse them all but to eliminate them and help us find the loony that's doing this to you." Harry paused, should he tell them? "We have located Susan Lawrence."

Mark sat bolt upright. Annie assumed this was the lunatic that had caused Mark so much misery in the past.

"I, we are going to see her but I don't want you to get your hopes up, you still have to be vigilant." Harry didn't want to share his theories at this stage nor did he want them to know his stalker was living less than ten miles away. "If you could make a start on that list for us and I'll call back this afternoon to get it. The sooner we start working on it the better. We still have the forensics report too which I am confident will provide us with another lead."

After Harry and Charlie left, Annie turned to Mark. "Why is it they don't fill me with confidence?"

Mark nodded. "Erm, I know but at least they've found that mad cow. Right we have a few things we need to sort out today. Ed and Matt go back to work Friday and I need a car. Do you fancy going to look at some new cars with me? If Matt doesn't mind he could drive us. Only if you're up to it. Tomorrow I thought we could laze around the house."

"Oh my God I thought you were never going to ask – get me out of here," Annie said laughing.

"Don't you get a courtesy car?" Matt asked.

Mark nodded. "Yes I do and that will be delivered tonight but I'm going to need a car once all the insurance is sorted. I fancy something a bit bigger now I have your mum and you boys."

Ed interjected, "And a slower car so you do less damage." Ed smiled cheekily.

"Funny man," Mark said smiling, "I better get a Corsa then!"

Annie joined in, "You've no need to bother! I'd like something with style and elegance, a bit like the driver." Mark hugged and kissed her.

"Are you coming?" Mark asked Sophie.

"No. I'm going back to Manchester. You don't need me, you have your new family now!"

Annie tried to speak but Sophie cut through her. "Don't bother. I'm not needed here," and she stormed out.

The four stood in disbelief. Annie went to move and Mark held her back shaking his head.

It was quite an ordeal, getting Annie into the car. She and Mark sat in the back whilst the boys were in charge. They travelled around four dealerships. The boys played around choosing their own cars for when they made it big! Ed opted for a top of the range Mercedes SLK whilst Matt wanted the M six series limited edition BMW.

Annie sat in the showrooms watching Mark and the boys. They were all so excited and happy. Annie on the other hand, was feeling sick and tired. She kept seeing the graphic images and could not help but think she had put her boys in danger by wanting to be with Mark.

Mark settled for a Range Rover Vogue limited edition. Annie's practical dream car. Her ultimate dream car was a Ferrari but Mark knew he couldn't deliver that. After leaving the showroom, they headed into York for some lunch. Annie had her eyes closed and was resting on Mark's shoulder.

He whispered, "Annie you okay? You have been quiet all afternoon. If you don't feel right we can go home."

She shook her head. "No I'm just a bit tired. I am fine honestly." He squeezed her but Annie knew she was far from fine. The boys had had a really happy day and she didn't want to spoil things.

The boys talked over lunch non-stop. Annie picked at her food but only so she could take more painkillers. She was now wishing she had taken Mark up on his offer to go home. She rose to go the ladies. Mark tried to help her but she didn't want assistance.

"Ed, Matt I need to ask you something," Mark whispered watching Annie hobble across the pub. "I've had to cancel the trip to London because your mum is not up to it but when her leg is better I want to take her away for a weekend, just her and me. Somewhere really special, where she has never been but always wanted to go." Mark paused and looked round making sure Annie was not on her way back.

"Mark she likes the Lake District, Scotland, London, Edinburgh, anywhere really," Matt said.

Mark leant further over. "No I mean abroad, somewhere really special."

Ed and Matt looked at each other and simultaneously shouted, "New York in the fall!"

"Shush!" Mark said laughing. "She's coming back."

All three boys were laughing when Annie sat down. "What you lot laughing at?"

"Nothing baby," Mark said and gave her a huge kiss.

Annie wasn't fooled. "I know you three are up to something."

Mark admitted, "Okay I wasn't going to tell you but." The boys looked at him and thought he was going to spill the beans about the break, Mark continued, "I wasn't going to tell you but the boys told me what car you have always wanted."

Annie nodded, "A Ferrari?" She laughed.

Mark nodded, "I wish! We decided on a Range Rover."

Annie screeched with delight. "Well that's cheered me up." She held out her hand to Mark but looked at all three of them in turn. "I'm sorry I have been narky, it's the pain and I'm tired now."

"It's okay Mum we're used to it," Ed said with a smile.

Annie smiled, "Let's go home boys."

Matt stuck to the country roads between York and Wetherby. As they pulled up at a junction they saw Harry and Charlie at the same junction turning into their path.

Annie looked at Mark and thought for a moment. "Weren't they going to see that Susan woman?" Mark nodded.

Annie sat upright. "You know what this means don't you?" All eyes turned to Annie. "She must live around here!"

Mark said, "Hopefully now it will all stop."

Annie's eyes lit up. "Yeah and we can get back to getting to know each other again." Mark threw his arms around Annie and kissed her lips.

Ed said, "Urgh! At least wait 'til we get home!"

Four photographers were standing outside the house gates when they arrived home. They tapped on the windows of the car and flashed their cameras but once the gate was opened the car pulled into the safe haven.

The mood had somehow lifted when they got back home. They were having a game of family Monopoly, Ed cheating as usual, when the gate intercom sounded. Harry and Charlie pulled up the drive and were greeted by Mark at the door.

"Good evening, we won't keep you long," Harry said entering into the living room.

"Hi Annie, you're looking brighter." Harry smiled.

"Thanks."

"Have you done that list for us?"

Annie lied. "We started it but it's not finished. I'll email it over to you later when we've done it all." In reality they had not even thought about it. They were convinced it was a waste of time.

"How did you get on with the nutter?" Ed asked.

Harry smiled. "Susan Chadwick was strangely cooperative. She answered all our questions and has alibis for the car incidents. Obviously we need to check into these but we need that list from you."

Mark and Annie promised to do the list and email it to the station.

Annie said, "We saw you today." Harry looked surprised. She continued, "Yes we were coming back from York and you were on the Wetherby Road, just at the time you were going to see her."

Harry was really surprised and laughed it off. "You should be the detective Annie, we never saw you."

Annie continued, "So she lives close to here then?"

Harry replied in a defensive tone, "You know I can't give you any details Annie. We have located her, spoken to her and now will look into her alibis."

Harry and Charlie left.

Matt turned to his mum. "Boy he is one arrogant…" Annie put a finger over her mouth to stop Matt.

"He might hear you," she said laughing. "But you're right, he is an arrogant, you know what! Right come on, I want to win this game."

Mark came in. "After this Annie, we need to do that list. We can't have him thinking we're not bothered, even though I think we are wasting our time."

They finished their game of Monopoly just in time for the gate intercom to go again. This time it was Mark's replacement hire car. The boys went outside to see it and came back in, hysterical with laughter. Ed could not speak he was laughing that much.

Matt stammered to Annie, "They've sent him a Mini Cooper!" Matt burst out laughing again.

Mark came in red faced and furious. "I'm glad you two are amused! How can I get your mum around in that?" He looked at all three of them laughing and could not control his laughter any longer.

Annie said, "Oh it hurts when I laugh! Oh well I'll stick my leg out of the window!"

That made them laugh even more.

"Well as much as I love being here, I suppose I better get packed and ready to go back to London, not for much longer though thanks to my fantastic manager," Ed announced cuddling Annie.

They were all sad to see him go and would miss his sense of humour but he would be finished in London by the end of next week. Matt took him to the train station and had agreed to call in on Mick and Ben and make sure they had not trashed the house.

Mark and Annie were alone at last. Mark poured a small glass of red wine and a beer out. He returned to the lounge to find Annie with her notebook on her lap. Mark took the notebook under his arm and signalled to the door. "Mrs Swift, let's go to bed!"

Annie smiled. "It's only seven o'clock!"

"Never stopped us before. Get up those stairs now you wench," Mark said laughing.

Annie hobbled upstairs and welcomed the warm covers. Mark propped up her pillows and when she was comfy he handed her the notebook. She re-opened it. Mark climbed into bed with both drinks and handed Annie the wine. She shouldn't really but it was only a very small one.

"To us!" Mark announced as he chimed the two glasses together. He kissed Annie and whispered, "I am so looking forward to getting back to normal!"

Annie laughed. "There's no such thing as normal where me and the boys are concerned!"

They both laughed. Mark placed the glasses on the table and they started to make their list. Mark started first. He listed close friends, relatives and work colleagues. It was a substantial list of over 250 names. Annie's list was much smaller but still 120 names long. Both felt they had betrayed their best friends by placing their names on the list but they agreed they would ring them in the morning and let them know.

Annie emailed the list to Harry and shut the notebook down. Mark placed it on the floor and took Annie into his arms. She laid on his warm, bare chest and felt safe not just because she was in Mark's arms but because the police had found this crazed woman. It was not long before they both drifted off to sleep.

Mark awoke when Matt came home. He looked at the clock and it was 2.15 a.m. He shuffled around so not to wake Annie and got out of bed. Matt met him on the landing.

"Hi Mark, sorry did I wake you?"

"No Matt it was okay. Your mum is fast asleep. I need a drink. Fancy a night cap?"

"Yeah why not," Matt turned back down the stairs, "I'm not due at training until eleven."

They both sat in the kitchen at the table with bottles of beer.

"Did Ed get off okay?" Mark asked.

"He did but he didn't want to go, you could tell. It's been great being back together again and I can't wait 'til he comes home for good."

Mark nodded.

Matt continued, "You know we've been thinking, Ed and I. If we are in the way here, when he gets home we can move back into Mum's house."

Mark was taken aback. "Why?"

"No reason, just you and Mum deserve time with each other not with us mooching around."

"Matt, you and Ed are welcome here. You lift the place and your mum would be devastated if you both moved out. No we both need you and want you here," Mark said.

"Okay, you all right Mark?" Matt looked at Mark's ashen face.

Mark looked into his beer bottle and then at Matt. "Yeah I am I suppose. It's just been a really tough time and your poor mum has had to bear the brunt of it all. I love her Matt, I really do. I don't want to lose her and I'm scared if this does not stop now she will get fed up and leave."

Matt looked at Mark. "You have a lot to learn about my mum. She is no quitter and extremely loyal. I can see how much you mean to each other and I hope when I finally meet someone we have a fraction of the chemistry you two have. You will both get through this. I know how tough my mum is. Just remember she loves you." He paused then continued, "She has had a really tough life but she won't let it get her down. She has worked incredibly hard and kept going when anyone else would have quit. Stick with her Mark, she is a remarkable lady."

Mark smiled. "Oh I know she is and I am blessed to have met her. I'm okay the strain is getting to me a bit. I am hoping now they've tracked HER down all this will be over."

"I'll drink to that," Matt said holding a bottle aloft.

The two men changed the subject and sat and talked about the play-offs and the Grand Final. At half three they called it a night and went to bed. Mark spent half an hour watching Annie sleeping peacefully until he drifted to sleep.

19

"Have you seen this list from Annie and Mark?" Phillipa announced as she walked into Harry's office throwing the email onto his very untidy desk.

"How many?" he said without looking up.

"Three hundred and fifty," Phillipa replied. Harry looked up at her and took hold of the email.

He perused the list and replied, "Jeez, it's the who's who of Rugby League!"

"I wouldn't know Harry, I'm a football girl," Phillipa replied.

"Poncy game then!" Harry smiled at her. "Rugby League is a tough game and the best game in the world."

"Okay you win! I'm not going to argue with you." She pointed to the email. "I have been through the lists and highlighted the names of those people that were around when the first case was heard."

"Thanks but I don't think that will help that much," Harry said not meaning to sound patronising. He continued, "The first case was such a high profile case that anyone could find out the details of it even now, especially over the internet but we'll start with those you have highlighted and Mark's daughter, Sophie. She was at the house yesterday and there was definitely tension."

Phillipa was used to Harry's idiosyncrasies. She had worked closely with him in the past so was not easily offended by his brash chauvinistic ways. She thought so many other people would have taken offence and ironically he would have, if someone else had said it to him. Phillipa knew the tension between him and the Super was because he had been turned down for the post and in all honesty, she thought, it would be hard to imagine him as the Super; diplomacy was not his strongest point.

Harry pondered over the names. He was convinced the culprit was on that list.

Charlie rushed into the office, red-faced and out of breath. "I've been checking Chadwick's alibis and something does not add up. On the day of the accident she said she was home by ten, before the accident but her elderly neighbour said a taxi dropped her off at half one in the morning."

Harry interrupted, "The taxi firm?"

Charlie nodded. "Yep I've checked it out. They dropped a Chadwick off at her address at just after half one."

"Where had she been?" Phillipa asked.

Charlie could not contain his excitement. "They picked her up from Huddersfield."

Harry picked up the handset of his phone. "Hi Ma'am, it's Harry. Do you have a moment please? I think we have a breakthrough in the Swift, Smith case… okay… I am here now with Charlie and Phillipa."

As Harry returned the receiver, the door burst open and the Superintendent imposed herself on the room. Harry stood up but she gestured for them all to sit and perched herself on the end of the desk. Harry explained the latest events and she agreed to a search warrant and for Chadwick to be brought in for questioning.

The Superintendent left the room and Harry spoke first. "Right you and I," he pointed to Charlie, "will go to Chadwick's house. I have to say I think this blows my theory out of the water."

Phillipa did not share Harry's optimism and continued to work on matching the original case with the current events.

*

Matt left for training before Annie woke. Mark grabbed a towel from the bathroom, a bottle of water and switched the wall-mounted television to Sky Sports News. He needed something to keep him entertained whilst he trained.

Annie could vaguely hear voices in the distance but realised it was the television. She could not believe she had slept until after twelve. She got up and tied her hair back. After last night and making the list of possible suspects, she had decided to have a dig around herself, after all she was a qualified researcher and maybe she could unravel the bits the police weren't bothering with. She decided her starting place was Mark's office. She leant on the bed so she could crouch down and pick her notebook up and hobbled down the corridor to the office. The window faced the rear of the house so she knew no one at the front gate could see her.

She looked around the office and powered up her notebook and considered whether she should speak to Mark first but she knew he would stop her and tell her to return to convalescence.

She hadn't heard Mark walking up the stairs and jumped when he stood in the doorway of the office.

"What you doing?" he asked.

"I thought I would spend the day researching the last case and this. See if I can unravel all of this."

Mark shook his head. "There is no point Annie."

"Mark there is. The police are no nearer to stopping this. I want an end to this. I want us to have a normal, happy life together, all of us."

"No Annie there is no point because it's just been on the news that the police have arrested HER!"

Annie looked at Mark, he was happy and relaxed.

"Come on," he said. "It's on Sky Sports News. The lads have been on returning to their training grounds and then it cut to her place and they've arrested her. Come on quick it will be on again."

Mark ran ahead and put the news on. Annie reached for the remote and increased the volume. She sat with bated breath waiting for the Rugby League news to come around again. Sure enough, there was Ed and Matt at London and Leeds respectively, both dodging questions and the cameras, like true professionals. Then, for the first time Annie caught a glimpse of HER.

"Oh my God is that her?" Annie said.

Mark shuddered and held Annie's hand. "Yep that's HER! God I hate her more now than I did before; I thought that wasn't possible." He tightened his grip on Annie's hand and it hurt.

She pulled it away. "Ouch that hurt."

She looked at Mark and could see the rage in his eyes. The stare was broken when her mobile rang, it was Ed.

"Yeah we have seen it," she said. "It's great news... yep... I know... no we are still coming to your game on Saturday... we'll be in the Mini... Yep deffo... okay love you too, bye."

Annie turned to Mark. "I am still going to Ed's game on Saturday. Ed said you told him we weren't. Matt plays tonight then all three of us can go to London."

"Annie," Mark interrupted her, "you can't go love like this. It will kill you to sit in a car for four hours."

"I AM GOING!" she shouted. Mark stopped in his tracks. It was the first time he had seen her lose her temper.

Annie realised she was losing control and took a deep breath. "I have never missed my boys play a rugby match and I am not missing one now. I know what you're saying but what about the train? A hire car or better still a car with a driver?"

She sat on the end of the bed and wept. "Sorry Mark I can't miss Ed play, I just can't."

Mark sat with her and consoled her. She was in pain but also very angry. How dare anyone think she would miss her baby's match? How dare they all assume it?

"I'm sorry Annie I was only thinking of you," Mark said.

"But Mark you made the decision without asking me. That's what's upset me. If you don't want to go to London, fine, I'll go with Matt."

"That's not what I said Annie. I am sorry I didn't ask you but I was thinking about how tiring it would be. Come on, we'll organise the trip now in the office." He kissed her forehead and led her back to the office. Annie sat in the office chair and Mark knelt beside her. He rested his head on her shoulder and looked up at her.

"I'm sorry Annie, I truly am."

She looked down at his gorgeous blue eyes and tried her best to maintain a stern look but it was no good. She kissed him on his head and said, "Don't ever do it again. We make decisions together especially where the boys are concerned."

He replied, "Was that our first argument?"

She nodded.

He continued, "Good that means we have to make up then."

She laughed and squirmed as he grabbed her waist.

They booked the intercity train from Leeds and decided to get a taxi to the hotel. Luckily there were two rooms available at the Premier Inn in Twickenham. It was two minutes from Whitton train station, which was twenty minutes from central London and only fifteen minutes from the Stoop. Taxis would not be that expensive, Annie thought.

Mark rang Ed and told him of the change of plan. He was ecstatic and told them he would book a restaurant for Sunday lunch, as their train back to Leeds wasn't until eight o'clock Sunday night.

Annie felt much calmer and shut the notebook down. She wandered into the bedroom to find Mark laid out on the bed, looking at her.

"Come here please," he said holding out his arms to welcome her. Annie scrambled onto the bed and fell into Mark's arms. He placed his hand under her chin and kissed her tenderly. She kissed him back and slowly rubbed her hands under his T-shirt up his back. Still kissing her, he slipped his T-shirt off. Annie lay in his arms. He kissed her and played with her breasts making sure he was not too rough this time. She slipped his manhood out of his shorts and slowly rubbed it. He gasped in her ear and whispered I love you as she continued to pleasure him. His hands moved further down her body until he reached her inner thighs. They couldn't resist each other any longer and he gingerly climbed into her. He was gentle and she was in heaven. His chest rubbing against her breasts, she could feel every part of him so warm and inviting.

As they reached their peak he slipped off her to her side to avoid any unnecessary pressure on her leg and ribs. They pulled the covers over them and just lay there. Annie rolled on to her side and looked at Mark.

"That will do for starters," she said.

He looked at her. "What do you mean?"

"That will do as a start to you making it up to me."

"You cheeky…" Mark grabbed hold of Annie's waist and started to tickle her. It wasn't long before she was begging for him to let go.

"I'll let go but you are still cheeky."

Annie cupped her arm around Mark's neck and pulled him towards her and whispered, "I know I'm cheeky but you wait 'til this cast comes off, I'll show you what cheeky is."

Mark kissed her passionately. "Ooh I can't wait," he said and kissed her again.

"Right," Mark said decisively. "I am going to run the bath, you and I can get in and then I am making you some lunch. Kick-off is at eight tonight so we have loads of time to get you into that Mini." He started to laugh.

Annie slapped him across his chest and laughed too. She lay in bed whilst Mark ran the bath and got a black bag to wrap around her cast.

Mark walked in naked, apart from the black bag wrapped around him like a loincloth.

"The new fashion!" he announced as he entered the bedroom.

"You silly sod!" Annie laughed. "Good job the boys aren't home, that would take some explaining." They both laughed.

Mark helped Annie get undressed and now and then they would stop to kiss each other. Eventually they both stepped into the hot tub. Annie sat at the edge with her broken leg aloft on the side. It felt a little uncomfortable but the hot water and bubbles were fabulous. Mark tenderly washed Annie and vice versa.

They had just changed and were downstairs when Matt walked in from training. He kissed his mother and said, "I've seen the news. It's great isn't it?"

They both nodded. Annie was sitting at the kitchen table watching Mark cook lunch.

"Oh that smells good," Matt said smiling.

Mark replied, "Well I've made enough for the three of us."

"Sound," Matt replied. "Training was good this morning. Can you believe one more game and we might be at Old Trafford? What's more amazing is London are in the same position. It's just a shame that if we both win this weekend we will play against each other in the final."

Mark said, "We'll have to wear both club scarves if that happens."

Annie joined in, "Stuff that, Leeds through and through. That's what Ed would say anyway."

Matt agreed. "He would, Mum, but it won't matter next season, you have your dream – both of us at Leeds."

Annie admitted, "Yes but not just my dream."

Matt agreed he couldn't wait to play on the same team as is brother.

Mark interrupted and explained to Matt what he and Annie had booked for the weekend. Matt offered to pay his way but as usual Mark and Annie wouldn't have any of it.

"I feel like a gooseberry," Matt admitted.

Annie and Mark laughed. "Don't be silly," Annie said. "We have separate rooms!"

They all laughed. Lunch was fabulous and after he had eaten Matt excused himself to begin his pre-match ritual, which included music and a nap.

*

"What's the delay in interviewing Chadwick?" the Superintendent asked as she popped her head into Harry's office.

"She's asked for a duty solicitor, Ma'am."

"Where is the solicitor?"

"Leeds Courts. Should be here about six Ma'am, if the case does not run on."

With that the Superintendent left Harry to his thoughts. He wanted to plan the questioning, to be absolutely sure Chadwick was the culprit.

"Phillipa, can you come in here please?" Harry asked. Less than a minute later, Phillipa appeared with the files from the previous case as if she knew what he was going to ask.

She said, "I have been through the previous case files although some of the acts are similar i.e. the notes, text messages there was no sinister life threatening incidents."

She sat down opposite Harry and continued without giving him the opportunity to question her. "That could be because she was caught in time or maybe she has been festering in the hospital waiting to exact her revenge."

Harry digested what was being said but longed for her to throw her arms around him. It had been a couple years since their kiss but he wanted her, he wanted physical contact. His own marriage had broken down just after his daughter died. Since then his work consumed him. He was lucky not to have turned to the dreaded bottle like some of his colleagues but still he understood why they had taken that path.

"Harry?" Phillipa broke his thoughts.

"Sorry, I was miles away. What were you saying?"

"I said, what are your thoughts on whether Chadwick is responsible for these latest events?"

"Not sure. We'll find out when we interview her. I want you in with me. I'll tell Charlie to continue digging whilst we conduct the interview." Harry's tone was very decisive. Charlie would not be happy at being usurped but it was my decision, Harry thought.

"Any more on her whereabouts on the night of the RTA?" Harry asked.

"Nope. We are still trawling through CCTV footage but nothing yet."

"Shit. Could have done with something else. Forensics?"

"Due back early tomorrow, maybe late tonight at a push. I've explained to the lab that we have the suspect in custody and could really do with it within the arrest deadline. Whether we get them or not, well we'll see."

"Thanks Phillipa. Your efforts have been brilliant as always."

Phillipa smiled. "It's my job and I like working with you."

"You must be the only one," Harry replied.

"I'll ring Mark Smith and let him know what's happened," Harry declared.

Phillipa's reply shocked him. "I wouldn't bother it's been on the news about Chadwick's arrest."

Harry stood up. "How did it get out?"

Phillipa shrugged. "I have no idea."

"Oh Phillipa they're going to think I'm a right idiot for not letting them know first."

Phillipa said, "Harry what is wrong with you? The Harry I know and love wouldn't care what they thought. What has gotten into you?"

He slumped back into his chair. "This case has got to me. I think it's seeing Mark and Annie so happy and seeing it torn apart by jealousy or worse. From the moment I met them, there is something about them, well her mainly. She has this aura around her. I've never met anyone like her."

Phillipa went red. "You fancy her?"

Harry shook his head violently. "No, no Phillipa, no. It's not like that at all. I can't explain it but she is an incredibly strong and clever woman. The true backbone of the family. My grandmother would have called her a 'trooper'. She is very modern but yet has remarkable retro qualities."

Phillipa did not understand what he was going on about and asked, "If you feel this way, maybe you should have the case reassigned."

Harry looked Phillipa straight in the eyes. "No way! I may not be Superintendent 'material' but there is no way my hard work on this is going to someone else. I don't think there is anything wrong with showing that you care. This couple have worked hard all their lives, both have earned their money the hard way, both but particularly her have spent all their lives instilling outstanding qualities into their children. I think they deserve us to catch the person who is doing this and when we do, I am going to throw the book at them!"

Enough said, thought Phillipa. She had never seen Harry so passionate and although she tried to ignore it, she was turned on by it. She blushed.

Charlie interrupted the awkward moments that followed. "Duty Solicitor's here sir."

"Thanks Charlie," Harry said as Charlie left the doorway.

"CHARLIE!" Harry shouted. Charlie, like a yoyo appeared once more and Harry continued, "Phillipa is going to conduct the interview with me."

Before Charlie could respond, Harry stood up, grabbed his jacket and walked out the door.

*

Mark helped Annie into the car. It was a tight squeeze and they laughed as they tried to find the most comfortable position for her. Mark suggested she lay across the back seat but she managed to sit in the front. They set off for Matt's game at 6.30 p.m. It was a strange feeling for them both to be back in the car but Annie sensed Mark's anxiety behind the wheel.

"Are you okay?" she asked.

Mark nodded and smiled. "A bit nervous, first time since the..."

Annie agreed. "I know love but you're doing great. We only have a short journey to do and we'll be fine. I love you Mark."

"I love you too. Well if Matt wins tonight he'll be in the final. Not bad for such a young lad eh?"

Annie beamed with pride. "Not bad at all. I am really nervous tonight for him. He seemed relaxed though when he left for the game."

Mark replied, "That's because he is level-headed and confident."

The rest of the short journey was in silence. Annie's mind wandered between Ed and Matt and how proud she was of them. She thought about what she had missed at work and whether she would still have a job when she was better.

She turned to Mark. "I've been thinking, I think I might go back to work on Tuesday."

Mark frowned but she continued, "Only a couple of hours a day. I will email Elspeth when I get home and ask her if I can do a phased return. We need to get our lives back on track especially now with the police getting her."

Mark smiled. "Okay I have a couple of meetings lined up next week. I think I'll go to them if that's okay with you. Mind you I think I'll have a bad back by the time our new car comes." They both laughed.

Mark pulled into the car park. The steward walked across to the car. It was Keith. He opened the passenger door. "Hi Annie oh my God I heard about your accident. How are you?"

Annie smiled. "I am on the mend Keith. How are you and Penny?"

"We are great thanks. Penny asked me to give you this. It's a get well soon card."

"Aww thanks Keith, it means a lot. Tell Penny when I'm back on both feet I will ring her and meet up for lunch."

"Will do. Do you need a hand to your seat?"

Mark interrupted, "We should be okay thanks Keith."

Keith smiled. "Glad to see you're okay too Mark. Damned business, hope they lock 'em up and throw away the key. Listen I'll get them to let you in here rather than you walking all the way up to the next gates."

"That's really kind of you Keith, thank you," Annie said as Mark helped her out of the car. She stumbled a little on the crutches but used the car door to steady herself.

They made their way across the car park. Random people started saying hello to Annie and wished her and her boys well. One little boy ran across the car park to her, he must have been five or six. "Please Mrs Swift can you get me your Matt and Ed's autographs please. I love them both."

Annie smiled and lowered herself on her crutches. "Where are your mum and dad?"

The little boy pointed behind him to see a small group of adults congregated near the turnstile. Annie took the little boy by the hand over to his parents. Mark followed intrigued.

"I'm sorry he bothered you Mrs Swift. He is mad on your two sons," his father said apologetically.

"It is no bother. Can you write your name and address on a piece of paper? I will get the boys to send him their autographs. It's a bit hard for me to write and balance on these stupid things," Annie said pointing to the crutches.

Annie addressed the boy. "You know Matt was a bit younger than you when I brought him here for the first time. He fell in love with this place at that point and Ed was only six weeks old when he went to his first game. I promise you they will send you an autograph. Please write your address down, it is no trouble."

The boy's father looked at her and mouthed thank you. He then caught Mark at her side and shook his hand and said, "I watched you when you played for Great Britain. You were fantastic."

Mark smiled. "Thanks."

Annie got the little boy's name and address. She also got a big hug from him too, which was a bonus.

"You were great Annie. That little boy felt really special," Mark said.

"That is what growing up is all about; those special moments they will remember for the rest of their lives. When Matt and Ed were growing up I always wanted to make sure they had loads of special moments. That is what makes them appreciate life," Annie said.

She had to stop talking as walking on crutches, coupled with her ribs hurting, was really hard work. After what seemed a 10k walk, they finally reached their seats.

Annie and Mark smiled at everyone who wished them well. Annie was very embarrassed at all the unwanted attention. She was so used to being in the background and being suitably invisible.

"Would you like a drink Annie?" Mark asked as she sat down in her seat.

"Can I have a coffee please and a bottle of diet coke? It's thirsty work on these things."

Annie was already uncomfortable but there was no way she was going to let Mark know.

Mark stood up and kissed her forehead. "You can have anything you like," he said.

Annie sat alone just watching the children running along the rows of empty seats. She thought back to her children doing the same and then before that when she used to watch the game with her grandpa. He would have been so proud of his great grandchildren. Both now with new contracts for his home club. A tear fell from her eye. She wasn't sad but the reminiscing brought back such powerful memories and emotions.

"Annie," a voice shouted and she attempted to turn around.

"Oh Annie. I am so glad you are all right. We have all been so worried about you," John said as he leant down to hug her. Annie's first reaction was to tell him where to go but there was no point holding a grudge.

"There is no need John I am on the mend. In fact, I'm thinking of coming back next week, need my routine back."

"That'll be great. I hope we can put all this behind us now and carry on how we were before you met him."

Annie could feel her impatience growing again. "You mean Mark?"

"Yes whatever," John replied. "Well I have to go find the others. See you next week at work then."

He left her but she was seething. She didn't want to hold a grudge but he wound her up. Him! she thought. How dare he refer to Mark as 'him'.

Mark returned and Annie told him of her visitor. Mark laughed at her as she was getting wound up again. He put his arm around her shoulders and drew himself close to her. "Don't worry about him. I'm here and with you and tonight is a massive night for us."

*

Harry and Phillipa walked into the interview room. Susan Chadwick and the duty solicitor were huddled together at one side of the table deep in conversation.

Harry announced, "Do you need more time with your client?"

The solicitor shook his head. He was tall, dark short hair and Harry thought he looked about fifteen years old.

Susan had tied back long bedraggled brown hair. She was about five feet tall and slim build but not toned. Her face was gaunt and her eyes deep set giving her an unfortunate scary look. She was wearing black leggings and a grey oversized jumper.

Harry read out the usual blurb of the interview being taped and each person announced his or her presence in the room.

The solicitor spoke first after the formalities. "My client would like to cooperate fully with you; she has nothing to hide."

Harry thought it did not bode well when she had already lied about her alibi.

"That is good to hear," Harry said. "Miss Chadwick you said in your first statement that you were at home at the time of the accident involving Mrs Swift and Mr Smith."

"Yeah that's right I wa'," she said. Her tone was very cocky and arrogant.

"Can you explain then how your neighbour saw you return home at one thirty a.m. in a taxi?"

"He's lying, he hates me!" Chadwick shouted.

"Then the taxi company must be lying too," Harry interrupted. "They confirm they picked you up and took you home. Where did they pick you up from Miss Chadwick?"

All three of the room occupants had their eyes focused on Susan. She could feel them burning through her skin.

"Where did they pick you up from?" demanded Harry.

Susan snapped, "'uddersfield, I was in 'uddersfield."

"So why did you lie?"

"'Cos I knew if I told 'u where I'd bin yous would accuse me of this." She looked down. "I saw it on the news the day after. I would never hurt Mark, never!"

"You see this is my dilemma. You have form with this man. Why would I believe you have nothing to do with this?"

"'Cos I'd never hurt him, I love HIM!" she shouted.

The solicitor sat back in his chair.

"Okay on the night of the accident, what were you doing in Huddersfield?"

"I went for a drink with some friends from work," Susan replied. "You can ask them, I was with them all night. They work with me at the Community College, we are cleaners. It was Ivan's leaving do. It was the first time I'd let me' self go out since… all that!" Susan slumped back in her chair.

"DS Phillipa Davies left the room," Harry said and continued. "We will check your alibi. Susan, look at me." She reluctantly lifted her head. "Is there anything you are not telling me? Have you had any contact at all with Mr Smith since you were convicted?"

There was silence. "Susan, it's really important you are honest with me. If you have nothing to hide you can tell me the truth."

She lifted her head to speak but then put her head back down. Harry sensed there was something but for now he suspended the interview.

"Are you letting my client go?" the solicitor asked.

"Not yet," Harry explained. "We will have a break. We'll look into her alibi and then come back to you. I suggest you explain to your client the importance of not lying to us."

"With all due respect, please don't tell me how to do my job," the solicitor barked.

Harry left the solicitor and suspect alone again.

*

Matt blew his mum a kiss at full time. She hobbled her way down the stairs in time to grab a quick hug from him before the media interviews started.

"That was a close call," Mark said as he hugged Matt.

Matt smiled. "It was but we're going to Old Trafford, Baby!" Matt jumped up and down and kissed the badge on his shirt.

"Yep. We'll see you up in the bar," Mark said patting Matt on the back. "I need to get this invalid upstairs."

Matt laughed but Annie slapped Mark across his arm and said, "There's a lift!" and started walking away.

By the time Matt joined them, Annie was exhausted. The painkillers had started to wear off. Mark could see the pain and exhaustion in her eyes and crouched down to speak to her. "Shall we go home?"

Annie nodded. "I'll just see Matt then we'll go. We can wait up for him at home."

Matt gave his speech and received his Man of the Match award.

"Matt, I'm going to take your mum home, she's exhausted," Mark said.

"I won't be far behind you. I'm knackered too. It's been a long week. What time is the train tomorrow?"

"Taxi is coming at half nine and train leaves at twenty past ten," Annie said as she walked towards the pair. "If it's okay with you Mark, I'll let you go and get the car. I'll wait here, I can't walk down there now." Mark kissed her and went off.

Matt was concerned for his mother, for the first time she looked frail and vulnerable. He put his arm around her shoulder. "Thanks Mum, for coming tonight. You are one in a million. Come on I'll walk you down to the entrance. I'm coming home now too. Shall I call at the takeaway?"

"You and Mark can have something, I feel a bit sick, and I think it will wear off once I've had some painkillers. It's my own fault I should have brought some with me."

Walking out of the bar, Annie literally bumped into Marcus. He gave her a kiss and a hug. "It's great to see you out and about. You look much better than the last time I saw you."

"Thanks Marcus. I am mending."

"You're a tough cookie Annie and that's why we all love you." He placed his hands on her shoulders and whispered in her ear. "Looking forward to next season. You know if you need anything, anything at all you only need to pick up the phone."

"Thank you I know and yes I'm looking forward to next season too. Ed is playing on Saturday."

"Yes I will be watching with interest. If they win, it's a final against us. Interesting... Especially for you."

Annie kissed Marcus good night and could see Mark pulling into the car park. Mark gave his order for the takeaway to Matt and they left.

*

"Sir, the Chadwick woman," Harry looked up to see Charlie at the door again, "her alibi adds up. We've spoken to her work mates and they've confirmed she was with them."

"Are we absolutely sure?" Harry asked.

"Ninety-nine per cent sure, sir," Charlie confirmed. "One of them even confirmed the time she got into the taxi. The alibi is watertight so it looks like back to square one."

Harry walked along the corridor and up one flight of stairs to the Superintendent's office. He knocked and entered. He explained the recent events to the Superintendent who concurred their only course of action was to release her.

As Harry turned to leave, the Superintendent asked, "Do you think she did it Harry?"

Harry sighed. "I am not sure. I think she is hiding something but I don't know what. I have a gut feeling she knows more than she's letting on."

"In that case get someone to keep an eye on her. Nothing too heavy but if it isn't her and you are right she knows more, she might just lead us to the real culprit."

Harry was mildly satisfied with the outcome. The Superintendent actually trusted his professional judgement for once.

Harry entered the interview room and announced, "You are free to go."

Susan was surprised to say the least. "What? That's it?"

"Yep for now."

With that Susan left the room.

She buttoned up her coat in the entrance and entered the night air. It was chilly now and she needed to get back home. She lifted her mobile phone out of her pocket and saw fifteen missed calls. No guessing who they are from, she thought.

She dialled the number. "Hi it's me. Yep I'm free, they let me go. Silly wankers, they don't have a clue. I think we should cool off for a bit, let it die down. No I disagree… what… yeah I know I owe you… yeah … But… All right, all right but we can't meet up. We'll have to find another way. Yeah but nothing we've done so far has split 'em up. Okay this last one thing and then it's over… I don't owe you any more, right? Good I'll ring you soon."

She hung up and flagged a taxi down.

*

The mobile phone made Annie jump as it vibrated in her handbag.

She looked at the screen. "It's Harry," she announced.

"Hello."

"Okay Harry... It's okay. We are just coming back from the match. I see... Okay... Right I'll tell Mark... no problem." She ditched the call and looked at Mark. He could see the disappointment on her face.

"They've let her go, haven't they?" Mark said.

Annie nodded and recounted the full conversation.

"Back to square one," Mark said, the hurt clearly evident in his voice. Annie placed her hand on his thigh.

"We'll get through it and first thing tomorrow I am going to have a look at it all. Maybe a fresh pair of eyes will help them."

When they arrived home, Annie went to bed. Matt and Mark sat up half the night discussing the game and the police's inept actions. Mark had been here before and it was exactly what he expected. She was good at dodging the police; she proved that all those years ago.

20

"Can you get me all your newspaper clippings that you saved please?" Annie asked Mark as she sat on the edge of the bed putting the last touches to her make-up.

"You want them now?" he said.

"Yes I am going to take them with us. We can have a look at them on the train."

"Okay but if you are sure."

Mark opened the office door. Did he really want his past being dragged up on a public train? he thought. No but then he didn't want to upset Annie either. She might have thought he had something to hide if he had resisted. He grabbed the box file from the top shelf and blew the dust off it. The first thing he saw when he opened the box, was her face. A scrawny looking kid with deep inset, scary eyes. He loathed her.

"Are you ready? Taxi's here," Matt shouted up the stairs to the couple.

Mark collected the suitcases from the bedroom and Annie hobbled down the stairs. It was going to be a challenging weekend for her but she was not missing Ed's game.

The train left the station on time and they were settled in a comfortable table seat. Matt sat opposite Annie doing his best not to knock his mum's leg under the table.

"This takes me back," Annie said. "I used to get the train to work every day. I used to love the coffee first thing and relaxing for the journey. Your dad and I had a car but he used to take the car to work. I should have known then what it was going to be like."

"You're quiet this morning Mark, is everything okay?" Matt asked looking at Mark.

"Just chilling Matt. It's nice to sit down and do nothing."

By the time they reached Doncaster, Annie had itchy feet. She was never any good at sitting doing nothing. She asked Mark to get the papers out of her bag and her laptop.

"Are you sure you want to do this?" Mark asked again.

"Why wouldn't I?" she asked.

"Nothing. It may upset you though."

"Maybe but I want to, we both want all this to stop and the only way is to find out who is doing it."

Mark sat in silence as Annie started flicking through the newspapers.

"Is that Garry?" she asked Mark pushing the image towards him.

He screwed his eyes up. "It is yes, when he had hair. He helped me so much during that time. Louisa was distant and I was convinced she was seeing someone else. She couldn't bear the press and she accused me of leading Lawrence on and went as far as telling my friends I *had* slept with her. That's how it ended up in the papers."

Matt asked, "Who is Lawrence?"

Annie replied, "That was her name at the time but she must have changed her name to Chadwick."

Annie asked, "Doesn't it seem strange to you that she would go to the lengths of changing her name but live only a few miles away from you. She must know where you live."

Mark shrugged. "Maybe. We moved in after she had been caught. She was already in custody."

Annie started making notes. Her research would start with Mark's playing days, Garry's friendship, Louisa and her life, the divorce and the court case. She had a gut feeling the truth was hidden amongst it all.

The newspaper clippings were very graphic and Mark could sense Annie's repulsion.

Matt said, "I take it from the look on your face, these stories are awful."

Annie nodded and looked up. "Typical press! Most of this I imagine is at best over inflated, at worst completely fabricated. You know how much respect I have for the press... NOT."

Mark hugged Annie. "I am so glad you understand. Lots of my so-called friends and family read this trash and believed every word. I was hung, drawn and quartered and I was the victim."

Annie held Mark's hand. "I am not that gullible. In the nineteen eighties I helped out in the miners' strike kitchens. The reporting of rioting and trouble by the strikers was completely untrue. I was a teenager then and disgusted with the press. My relationship and feelings towards them haven't changed. Then there was Hillsborough!"

The announcement interrupted their conversation that they would be arriving at King's Cross in ten minutes. They packed up all the clippings and the notebook. Annie was pleased with the progress they had made but not as pleased as Mark. All his fears were allayed when he realised Annie was not going to believe all the lies. He was panicking inside that she would be angry with him and mistrust would replace their closeness. He couldn't have been further from the truth. They were stronger than ever.

*

Ed was waiting for them in the hotel reception. He gave his mum a huge hug.

"I have missed you," he said.

Matt scoffed. "You soppy sod, you only left two days ago."

Ed glared at him. "So! I love my Mummy." He hugged her again.

Mark checked them into their rooms and along with Matt, took the luggage up. Ed and Annie headed for the bar. She fancied a glass of wine and Ed, although couldn't drink, wanted some time with his mum.

"There you go," Annie said. They sat opposite each other. Annie felt Ed had something to say.

"What's up baby? I know you have something on your mind," she asked.

"Nowt really. It's just I can't wait to come home now. After what happened last week I don't like being down here anymore. Today could be my last game or I may be in the final." He paused. "Mum, am I being selfish if I say I hope tonight is my last game?"

Annie smiled. "No love, you're not but you have a wonderful opportunity at your age to get to the Grand Final. Ignore everything that is going on and enjoy your moment. There are not many kids your age that get this opportunity and your hard work has got you where you are."

Ed sat with his head down. Annie reached over and cupped her hands around his chin. "Listen to me Ed. Enjoy your life and take every opportunity that comes your way. You know I have always told you and your brother, hard work opens doors and gives you choices. The choices you have made have led to your new deal with Leeds. The new chapter starts when you finish down here. If you go out tonight then so be it but you play to win."

Ed smiled. "We will win, Mum. I'm just nervous and the thought of possibly having to play against Matt in the final."

"I'd have thought you would have relished that."

"Yes Mum, I know, but he is so much better than me."

"No he is not. Look at me Ed." Annie looked straight into Ed's eyes. "He is not better than you at all. You think he is and he is not. You are both brilliant. Now stop all this."

Ed looked at his mum. "There is something else."

"What?"

"Dad will be at the game tonight and I haven't told him about the move to Leeds. Please don't say anything tonight; I need to pick my moment."

"Oh Ed, you have to tell him. He moved down here to be with you."

"I know but he has his own life down here now."

Annie looked a bit taken aback by his last comment and asked, "What do you mean?"

"He has found someone. She is all right, a bit of a battle-axe. I'm glad I'm not sticking around but she will be at the game tonight."

"Who's a battle-axe?" Matt asked joining them with a pint in his hand.

"Dad's got a new girlfriend," Ed said.

"Oh my God! At last, maybe she can stop him from being a miserable git!" Matt scoffed.

Ed replied, "I doubt that." They laughed.

Mark took a drink of his pint of lager as he walked to join the group with four menus.

"I think it's time for a snack," he said handing out the menus. Ed declined to eat; it was too close to kick off for him.

During the meal, Matt's phone bleeped. He smiled as he read the message. Sharing its details with the group, he announced, "Apparently it is on Twitter that I have been seen in Twickenham today and could it be that I am going to sign for London!"

They all laughed. The rumour mill was rife.

"Oh whilst we are all together, I need to ask you both something," Annie announced.

"Last night at the game I met a little boy who wanted your autographs. He was a little star and was so polite. I have his address for you."

The boys looked at each other and smiled.

"Ed, I think we can do better than just a signature." Matt looked at his brother.

Ed nodded. "Yeah, Leeds shirt signed by both of us."

Matt interrupted. "Yeah hand-delivered too!"

Annie smiled. Mark knew where they got their big hearts from.

Ed looked at his watch. "Sorry but I am going to have to make a move. I need to get my stuff then get to the stadium."

Matt stood up. "I'll come with you if that's okay? If it breaks your routine just tell me. I wouldn't mind just hanging around the club for a bit."

Annie laughed. "Ooh give fuel to the rumour mill!"

"Haha that's true," Matt said as he leaned over to kiss his mum and hug Mark.

Ed passed his mum her tickets and kissed her goodbye. Annie watched the boys walk across the car park, pushing and shoving each other until they were out of sight.

Mark moved his chair closer to Annie. "They are brilliant kids Annie. Do you fancy taking these drinks up to our room? I don't know about you but I could do with a rest before we go to the ground. We can order room service."

Annie raised her eyebrows and Mark laughed at her; she knew exactly what he meant.

The room was a standard double room with a separate bathroom and a flat screen television. It was plainly decorated apart from a print above the bed of an enlarged crocus in purple to match the room's colour scheme. Annie climbed onto the bed whilst Mark looked for the television remote. He booked a taxi for five o'clock and set his alarm on the mobile phone just in case they did fall asleep but sleep wasn't really on his mind.

Mark turned to the bed to find Annie had fallen asleep. She was curled up in a ball with her broken leg sticking out. He smiled. He gently climbed onto the bed, kissed her cheek and lay at her side.

*

Harry was perplexed. Why did he get the feeling Chadwick was lying to him yet the alibi was so clear. He knew his instincts were right. He wandered to the canteen and ordered a bowl of pasta with a coke. Lunch, then back to work he thought. The canteen was deserted. There was a big football match on and most of the shift was drafted in to help out. He was glad he no longer had to get involved in all that shit. He hated football. He hated the hooligans and he hated being cold.

He sat eating his lunch staring into space. His life had come to this he thought. Saturday afternoon, sat alone eating boring, tasteless pasta. His mood lightened when he saw Phillipa approaching him with a tray of sandwich, crisps and tea.

"Can I join you?" Phillipa said smiling as she sat down. "That doesn't look very appetising."

"It isn't," Harry said pushing the bowl away. "Why are you working on a Saturday?"

"Overtime. Liam has lost his job again so I have to work extra hours," Phillipa said with a hint of resentment in her voice. "Still I suppose all I would be doing is reffing the kids' fights and listening to him moaning at them."

"Married bliss then," Harry said sarcastically.

"Something like that." She opened her sandwich and offered Harry half but he declined. She continued, "So what you doing this afternoon?"

"I am spending today going through the case. There is something missing, I'm missing something. Then on Monday I am going to get everyone together."

Phillipa nodded. "I agree. Chadwick was hiding something yesterday. She knew something."

"You saw it too?" Harry asked.

"Sure. The problem we have now is finding out what. I'll bring my notes to your office. I have gone through the court transcripts and the press releases again."

"Great. We'll use the incident room. We can go through all the facts and add things to it."

They finished eating and met up again in the incident room. Harry was perched on the end of the table facing the main wall looking at the images. Phillipa threw her papers on to the desk and made Harry jump. He frowned at her.

"Sorry," she said. "Right where do we start? The last trial?"

"I think we start when the first contact was made with Annie Swift. You see I find it really hard to understand why she is the one that is being targeted and not Mark Smith. He was the centre of the first case."

"Well jealousy could lead to hatred of the person he has met," Phillipa suggested.

"Perhaps but her mobile phone number? Text messages, just after they start seeing each other? Notes to her house? This couple only started seeing each other on the Thursday and by the following Tuesday the messages start. A bit soon isn't it?"

"Maybe but if you are watching someone's every move you would know," Phillipa added.

"Or you are close to the couple and feeding information out?"

"Erm, you think this is someone else?" Phillipa asked.

"Or her colluding with someone close to them?" Harry suggested.

They both looked at each other.

Harry continued, "My feeling is Chadwick is involved in some way but with an accomplice, or she is the accomplice. Maybe the scapegoat? Supposing it is someone who hates Mark as much as Chadwick loves him? Well love, it's not love. I think we need to look at everyone who was involved in the first case and then tie him or her in with the second. His ex-wife? Ex-team-mates? His daughter? She was acting strangely when I visited the house. Still doesn't answer my feeling of why Annie and not Mark."

"It's a starting point," Phillipa smiled and added, "I'll get on to the phone companies on Monday and get details of any mobile phones registered to Chadwick."

They wandered back to the incident room. Harry started dismantling the evidence board.

"What you doing?" Phillipa asked.

"We are starting from scratch. Right, Annie Swift at this end." He moved Annie's image to the far right of the board and placed Mark's at the far left top.

"There has to be something we are missing." Harry perused the evidence.

"Contacts with the two?" Harry asked.

Phillipa read out the list. "Postcard to Ms Swift's address, note on Mr Smith's car, text message to Ms Swift, note on her car, a car following them, incident involving the black car in Salford, car accident! Photos sent to the house!"

"Erm in my experience, this has escalated pretty damn quickly into something very sinister. That's what gets me. The previous case involved Chadwick's contact and obsession over eighteen months. This is less than a month!"

"Yes, but she has been inside and if the obsession is still there, it could…"

"No, I believe someone else is fuelling this. Someone who hates the couple being together more than she does. Have you got the list of contacts the couple provided?"

Phillipa nodded and shuffled through her papers until she passed it to him.

He admitted, "I think your first assumption of someone who knew Mark during the first case could be the source of these incidents." He paused and smiled. "You don't have to look so smug."

"I'm saying nothing sir." Phillipa shrugged her shoulders and smiled. "Okay then so who was around in the first case?"

"We'll make a list of them and then go through each one. What time are you finishing work?" Harry asked.

"I'm not due off 'til ten but I can work all night if you want me to."

"Let's see how long it takes us to get through this list. I'd love to spend the night with you," Harry paused. "Working of course."

Phillipa blushed and swung her arm across his chest.

*

Annie awoke to find Mark looking at her and stroking her face. He said softly, "We need to get ready. The taxi will be here in forty minutes."

She smiled. The journey had taken its toll on her. She felt tired and sore but needed to move, albeit very slowly.

After a refreshing wash and change she was ready for the match.

It was a chilly evening at the Stoop. The taxi pulled up into the car park, which was starting to fill with fans filing in from the local pubs. Once inside the ground, they headed for the shop. It was a pokey little shop but very friendly. She decided to break with tradition and wear Ed's colours in the hope it would boost his confidence after their little chat earlier.

Matt had been watching for them to arrive and walked into the shop, sneaked behind Annie and placed his hands over her eyes.

"Hi Matt you had a good afternoon?" she said laughing.

"How did you know?"

"I heard you laugh. You always did give yourself away. Ah well." Annie held out a London scarf for Matt.

He scorned, "What do I want one of them for?"

"Your brother." Annie stared at him.

"Fair enough." He leant over and whispered, "We won't need it soon."

Annie smiled.

Mark, Annie and Matt took their seats, which were located near to the London's dugout. Ed was starting on the bench and beamed when he came out with the team. Annie was pleased he seemed to have got over his earlier insecurities.

Just before kick off the television camera panned around the crowd and to Annie's dismay focused on her, Mark and Matt sitting together. Matt smiled at the camera and the crowd cheered.

Matt turned to his mum. "I have had a day full of people asking me if I'm signing here. I can't wait to tell them about the new contract."

Annie put her finger over her mouth to signal for Matt to be quiet. The last thing they needed was an eagle-eyed lip reader letting the cat out of the bag.

It was twenty minutes into the game when Ed finally got onto the pitch. Just like his brother, his introduction reaped immediate rewards. Mark shouted Ed's name constantly and seemed to be thoroughly enjoying the game. At half-time, Mark leant over to Matt. "Shall we get a beer?"

At the bar, some young lads came up to Matt and patted him on the back. One of them shook his hand and said, "Think your brother has outplayed you today. He's looking good out there." Matt laughed and agreed.

Annie was fed up of not being able to wander around freely. She had at least another four to five weeks of being incarcerated by the damned cast on her leg. The only saving grace was the hospital appointment on Monday when she would learn the true extent of the damage.

The boys returned to recount the conversation in the bar.

Annie laughed. "Do me a favour? Tell your brother Matt. He was feeling a bit down before the game. He thinks he will never live up to you."

Matt tutted, "He doesn't have to live up to me. He's his own person."

"I know but he does look up to you," Mark agreed.

Ed's game continued to impress everyone. He scored a seventy-metre interception try, which looked pretty spectacular.

The television camera panned around again to show Annie, Mark and Matt celebrating the try in style.

In spite of Ed's fabulous game, Wigan was just too strong for London and with ten minutes to go, they ripped open London's defence three times.

After the game Ed was gutted but picked up the club's Man of the Match award. He knew it was the last time he would play with this group of players.

Mark was the first to shake his hand. "Well played mate. You were brilliant today, really good and lively. Just a shame about the result."

"You couldn't have done any more mate," Matt said patting his little brother on the back.

Ed hugged his mum. "Thanks Mum. I needed the chat earlier."

Annie smiled. "I knew you would play well. You are brilliant and now believe it."

He nodded and turned to Matt. "Some of the lads want to go out for a drink. You fancy coming with me, I need someone to buy me drinks?"

Matt laughed. "Yeah why not but it's orange juice for you."

"Look after each other," Annie warned. "Don't forget lunch at one o'clock at the hotel tomorrow."

The boys left in high spirits. Annie and Mark left shortly after and arrived back at the hotel at 9.30 p.m. They ordered room service and settled in for the night.

Annie sloped off to the bathroom and changed into a see-through red chemise. Mark could not contain his excitement and delight. His face gave it all away.

"You like?" Annie said posing in front of him. Mark did not speak he pulled Annie towards him and buried his face in her breasts. She placed her hands on his back and rubbed them under his shirt. She kissed his cheek moving down to nibbling his ear. Mark started taking his clothes off whilst Annie had him in her grasp. She rested on one leg but the pain was not going to stop her making Mark happy.

Annie unbuttoned his shirt and slipped it off. Once his trousers were removed, she slipped onto his knees and perched herself over him. As she passionately kissed him, she pushed him backwards and he complied by falling onto the bed. Annie crawled further on to him. She slowly kissed his chest rubbing her hands down his sides, making him squirm with delight. Her right hand kept moving until she felt his piece in her fingers. Mark moaned with pleasure. He gently moved around and moved Annie onto her side. His hands were now free to consume her body. Annie turned on her side so her back was facing Mark. She

173

signalled for him to move closer to her and he complied. His torso pushing against her back, Mark worked his hands over her body from behind.

"Oh Mark," Annie whispered as his hands moved into her inner thighs. He slipped himself inside and she let out a pleasing moan.

This was a new experience for Mark and he found it hard to control himself. He was in heaven so much pleasure. They both loved the intimacy but also the fun.

"Annie I love you," Mark sighed as he reached his peak.

They lay in each other's arms, neither having any energy left to move. Annie rested her arms across his arms on her breasts.

*

"Good work," Phillipa said as she and Harry surveyed the new evidence board. They had narrowed down Mark and Annie's lists to just a handful of people.

"On Monday we will need to start compiling details of these people. Where they were? What sort of relationship they have with Annie or Mark. I feel a bit happier now. I feel sure our culprit is in this list." Harry tapped his pen on the board. "Joined up with her," he pointed to Chadwick's photograph.

"Harry, do you fancy a drink?" Phillipa asked.

"Yep why not?"

The pair left the station and walked the short distance to the local pub, the Swan. It was a quaint, rustic pub that had lots of nooks and crannies.

Once they had their drinks, Harry and Phillipa chose a quiet corner spot. They both sat on the same bench rather than opting for separate chairs.

There was an awkward silence between the pair until Phillipa spoke. "It must be nice to find someone that you fall for and that falls for you almost instantly like Mark and Annie." She looked down into her drink.

"Yes it must. Neither of them had easy lives before they met, so I'm told."

"But it sounded like a fairy-tale ending for them both until all this started."

"Yeah," Harry laughed. "If you believe in fairy tales."

"I'd like to," Phillipa admitted. "Let's face it, none of us are really where we want to be. Not like this pair are."

Harry looked at Phillipa and could see her eyes welling up.

"Eh," Harry said reaching out for Phillipa's hand. "What's all this? It's not like you to be so soppy and unhappy."

"Like you said Harry, this case makes you think about what you have, or what you don't have."

Harry stroked her hand and whispered, "I wish it had been different between us. I wish we'd have had the bottle to go with our feelings instead of thinking of others and what others would have thought."

Phillipa smiled. "Me too but too many people would have been hurt. My kids were too young and you wanted promotion."

Harry scoffed, "That didn't happen anyway did it?"

Phillipa shook her head. She turned her body towards Harry and put her hand on his chest. She leant forward and kissed him. His first reaction was to pull away but he looked at her again and kissed her back.

"I'm sorry," Phillipa said. "I should have had the courage to leave Liam when I had the chance. I shouldn't have hurt you."

Harry replied, "Well you did hurt me. Let's just enjoy the moment today." He kissed her again.

Phillipa's mobile phone rang.

"I'm sorry Harry I have to go. The kids want to see me before they go to bed."

Harry replied, "Come on then let's go."

In the car park he pulled her towards him and kissed her. They walked hand in hand back to the station. They said goodbye and went back to their own lives.

*

At 4.30 a.m. Annie's mobile phone bleeped signalling a message. She reached over to the cabinet thinking it would have been the boys telling her they were home. There were three unread messages, one from her mum congratulating Ed on his performance, one from Matt saying he and Ed were back in the hotel room and the final one made her heart race. No name just a number.

She drew a deep breath and opened the message. It read:

'Enjoy ur weekend playing happy families? The job will be finished off next time. By the way, nice house. You won't have the fairy-tale ending.'

Annie shook Mark until he woke. He was dazed but came round quickly when Annie read the message out to him. Annie forwarded the text message to Harry's mobile phone. Within a few minutes, her phone rang.

"Harry," Annie announced to Mark as she answered it.

"Hi Harry," Annie said.

"There was only my mum and dad that knew we were coming down here. We changed plans at the last minute."

Annie listened to Harry for what seemed an eternity to Mark. He wanted to know what was being said.

"Okay. We are back tomorrow on the eight o'clock train, so will be home about eleven thirty-ish."

"Taxi, why? Okay if you want to but there's no need. Okay fine. See you then."

Annie hung up and said, "He wanted to know who knew we were here. Did you tell anyone?"

Mark shook his head. "No not one person."

"Harry is picking us up from the station tomorrow. He is going to send a car to the house tonight to check it over. Oh God!" Annie exclaimed and re-dialled Harry.

"Harry, it's me. We didn't tell anyone else but we were on the television tonight. The camera caught us in the crowd."

"Yeah sure, see you tomorrow." She hung up and said, "That's how they knew we were here. They were watching the game!"

"Well the good thing is they don't know where we are staying or what train we are going back on," Mark said.

Both of them couldn't sleep. They laid watching television for a while, and then Annie turned to Mark, "So much for it ending here."

Mark nodded. "We'll sort it but not tonight. Come here."

Annie lay across Mark's chest.

21

Annie cringed when her phone bleeped another text message. It was 9.30 and as she tried to focus her tired eyes, she realised it was from Matt.

'Ed's coming home with us. I've got him a ticket. We are going to get some of his stuff. We'll explain when we get back. Luv u xx.'

She dialled his number but it went straight to the answering machine.

Mark asked, "What's going on?"

Annie shrugged and showed him the text message.

By the time the boys reappeared, Annie and Mark were sitting in the bar drinking coffee. The meal was booked for one o'clock. Both boys looked worse for wear and Annie guessed it had been a heavy night.

"So what's going on boys?" Mark asked.

Both boys looked at each other and started laughing.

Their laughs were infectious and raised a few eyebrows from other guests in the bar.

Matt explained, "Well you know that theory of keeping our contracts quiet..."

Annie interrupted, "Oh lads what have you done? You could lose..."

"Hang on Mum, it wasn't us. Apparently Marcus told the London Chief Exec last night at the game. He was not happy things had been signed. He asked if Ed could come back on loan and Marcus said no. According to the coach it got quite heated," Matt laughed.

Ed took over the tale. "So when we went to the pub last night, Matt and I were playing pool when Rob came in and told me I wasn't welcome at his club any more. So I am coming home."

He took a drink and continued, "Oh yeah and to top it all off, Dad was in the pub with his new bit and he overheard it all. He went for me Mum. He tried to push me out of the door but Matt and the other lads helped get rid of him."

What a mess Annie thought. "Bloody men and their egos! Wait 'til I speak to that Marcus!"

"I rang him, Mum," Matt said.

"Oh my God you didn't?"

Matt nodded. "I did! He said Ed could come in with me next week to training and spend time around the club. I think he felt embarrassed about his actions."

"Okay what about your dad?" Annie asked Ed.

Ed, straight faced said, "I don't think Marcus will let him come training."

Mark, Matt and Ed burst out laughing.

Mark got a slap from Annie. "Don't you encourage them," she said laughing.

"Seriously, I don't know. No doubt he'll ring when he's calmed down," Ed added.

"Well I for one am glad you're coming home with us," Mark said.

"Me too," Annie said.

"Yep." Mark stood up to go to the bar. "I can smash you both at FIFA now instead of just Matt." Rapturous laughter followed again. Annie felt she was fighting a losing battle.

"What's so funny? You all laughing at my expense?" shouted a familiar voice as the red-faced Paul stormed through the door closely followed by a woman with short black hair and a ruddy complexion.

Matt and Mark stood side by side in front of Ed.

"Come on Paul please don't make a scene," Mark said.

"And when was you going to tell me about HIS new contract?" Paul pointed at Annie.

Annie very calmly, "Shush Paul. It's not public knowledge yet."

Matt interrupted, "You know now Paul. It was Ed's decision to come back home."

"Yeah right. She manipulated him again just so she can have him to herself."

Ed stood up. "No Dad I want to move back home. I have loved being in London but I want to play with my brother and I want to be near Mum."

"'alf brother!" Paul said spitefully.

Annie was beginning to lose her patience and cool. Up to now Mark had kept out of it but he turned to Paul. "The boys are free to do what they want to do. It is their choice."

Paul, furious with Mark speaking, snapped, "What would you know? You have known her for less than a month and suddenly you're an expert on her and my boys. And all you have done so far is put them in danger."

Paul's new girlfriend tugged his arm and said, "Paul, don't get wound up. We can travel up to Leeds as much as you like."

Ed commented, "Yes you can if you are going to be civil. Dad I love you but you are an arse at times."

Annie was surprised, Ed had never stood up to his dad before. He lowered his voice and continued, "I have made the decision to move back home. I want to be near Mum and Mark. Get used to it."

Paul raised his voice again. "So you want to be near a man that seems determined to get you lot killed! Great. I think you have turned out to be as selfish as your mother."

That was it, Annie lost control. She was not having him slagging her son off. "You despicable man! How dare you, how dare you speak to our son in that way. If you actually put your own selfish feelings and self-pity to one side, you would see that both our children have grown up into fine, considerate, clever young men."

"Obviously traits they have got from you Annie," Mark said.

"I suggest," Annie drew a deep breath and continued, "you say goodbye to your sons. Try with dignity for once, and make arrangements to come and see your sons soon. Now if you don't mind, we are having our family time together."

Paul turned and stormed off with his woman in tow.

The afternoon was a little sombre and Annie sensed Ed was upset – he hated confrontation. Before they knew it they were on the eight o'clock train. Annie slept most of the journey; the weekend had really taken its toll on her. The boys played cards and soon the train was pulling into Leeds Station.

*

As promised, Harry was waiting for the party. Luckily he was alone. Harry explained what had happened with Chadwick.

"I'm not convinced she is not involved in some way," Mark said.

Harry tried to act surprised and asked, "What makes you think that?"

"I know her, I know how she works and this has her written all over it. Why would you set up home close by? I have this feeling she is involved."

Harry didn't want to share his own thoughts even though he was tempted to.

"Harry," Annie said. "I have been going over the papers from the last case. Could we sit down over the next couple of days and go through it all."

"Annie, I am happy to sit with you but you have to let me do my job. There are things I need to ask you and Mark separately. I was thinking, why don't you come down to the station tomorrow?"

"I can make it in the afternoon but I have a hospital appointment in the morning."

Mark added, "I am back at work tomorrow. I am over in Salford in the afternoon."

Ed asked, "So who's taking you to the hospital, Mum?"

Annie replied, "Grannie. Okay Harry I can be at the station about twoish depending how long it takes at the hospital."

*

The noise of the siren was deafening. Ed and Matt came running out of their bedrooms and met Mark and Annie on the landing.

"What the hell?" Matt asked.

Mark shouted, "It's the intruder alarm. Ed you stay here with your mum. Matt you come with me." Walking away, he looked back and requested, "Annie phone Harry."

Mark and Matt flew down the stairs. Mark stamped the alarm code into the panel and the sound stopped. The panel indicated the viper on the patio door in the dining room had been tampered with. Mark could hear some noise from the dining room. He slowly turned the door handle with Matt closely by his left shoulder. Mark's heart was pounding so hard he felt as though it was going to give him away to the intruder before he opened the door.

Mark and Matt burst into the dining room to find the door lock had been jemmied. The door was wide open the curtain blowing in the wind. Nothing, as far as he could see, had been taken.

Both of them raced outside but no one was there. Mark turned to Matt. "Go tell Mum and Ed they can come down. I'll ring the CCTV company for the footage."

"We are here," Annie announced, surveying the damage from the top end of the room. "Come on let's leave the room as it is. Harry will be here in a minute."

Harry arrived. He explained, "We'll have to wait for the CCTV footage. The alarm company are going to bring a DVD around tomorrow and the scene of crime officers have been informed. They will be round between eight and nine. I have arranged for glaziers to come and they will be here within the hour."

Annie was making coffee in the kitchen when the boys joined her.

"Harry and his cronies have left. I can wait up if you want to go to bed," Mark said as he hugged Annie.

"It's okay, I am awake now," Annie replied.

"So who is this then?" Ed asked.

"Well if we knew that…" Matt replied.

"I know what you mean but this is staring us in the face."

All three stared at Ed who continued, "We can work this out if we look at it logically. I think we should all spend some time tomorrow going through all this. Whoever is doing it is not going to be smarter than us."

Matt scoffed, "You always did want to be part of the Scooby gang, solving crimes."

Mark smiled.

Ed replied, "Very funny Matt! I mean it."

Annie nodded. "I agree, this is someone who knows one of us or all of us. Did they think we were in or did they think we were still in London?"

Mark agreed. "Our original plan was to stay down Sunday night too but we didn't discuss it with anybody, did we?"

Annie said, "I told Lucy but this isn't down to her."

Ed interrupted, "No but I bet she told John!"

Everyone stared at Ed.

"Do you really think he is capable of this?" Mark asked Annie. She shook her head but was not a hundred per cent convinced.

The glazier arrived to interrupt the discussion. As the boys left the kitchen with coffee cups in their hands, Annie shouted, "We'll carry this on tomorrow." The boys grunted.

It was 4.30 a.m. when they finally got back to bed but all of them struggled to get some sleep. Annie felt she was keeping one ear alive to listen for any further problems.

At 6.30 a.m. she struggled out of bed and hobbled downstairs. Matt was watching the news laid on the sofa.

Annie asked, "How long have you been up?"

Matt yawned. "I haven't been to bed. Couldn't sleep. Would you like a coffee and some toast?"

"That would be great Matt, thanks."

Annie sat watching the television until Matt returned with their drinks and toast. They sat together on one sofa. Matt asked, "This is really serious now Mum, isn't it?"

Annie nodded and looked straight into her son's eyes. "It is and it's really scaring me. All my life I have protected you and Ed and now I feel I've led you straight into danger."

"You wasn't to know," Matt said.

Annie knew that was true. She didn't know enough about Mark. She should have slowed down but she was impulsive and let her attraction to him rule her head.

Matt stood up. "I'm going to spend some time in the gym. You could join me."

Annie smiled. "Funny man! I'll wait 'til the cast is off thanks!"

Instead Annie hobbled to get her laptop. She sat at the kitchen table and opened her emails, all fifty-eight of them! She waded through the emails and came across one sent last night from Lucy. She missed her chats with Lucy and was excited to open it. She started reading the message and laughed out loud on occasions. Lucy had met someone, at last. He had been on campus to discuss a course when he approached her for a coffee. She was due to go on a date with him and was very excited. Lucy advised Annie John was still bad mouthing Mark. Annie thought that would never change.

Annie replied to Lucy wishing her luck on her date but also to let her know she would be returning to work on Wednesday. She thought it was best to go for two days for the time being and the Dean had approved a phased return. Annie wasn't sure it was the right thing to do but she needed some normality back in her life. The pain from her leg was exacerbated by the lack of sleep. She felt old and exhausted. She pushed the laptop away from her and cupped her hands around her face. With her eyes closed she tried to imagine how life had been just a few weeks ago when she was working hard and the boys were forging their own way in life. Now it was a mess. She was a mess. With a deep sigh, Annie pulled herself together. She made some fresh coffee and poured herself a drink.

Matt shouted, "Mum, the police are here!"

Annie hobbled out to the hallway to greet the police, holding her cup with both hands.

"Morning Mrs Swift," Harry smiled as he directed the forensic team into the dining room.

Annie signalled to her cup and Harry nodded whispering thanks as he followed her into the kitchen. Matt followed the scene of crime officer, as he was intrigued by what they would do.

"How are you this morning Annie?" Harry said nodding acknowledgement of the coffee.

Annie sat at the table. "I'm okay, tired and feeling it this morning."

"I bet you are," Harry continued, "we are doing our best to find the culprit and we are confident this will not last much longer."

Annie did not share his optimism this morning. She shook her head and said, "I have a strong feeling this is someone Mark knows well, that was part of, or witnessed the last case."

Harry was a little taken aback that she shared his sentiment, he asked, "so who do you suspect?" Harry decided to ask the direct question. He had his own suspicions but was interested in her thoughts.

Annie shook her head again. "I am not sure, and it's just a gut feeling. There is someone who knows our moves, our lives, I just don't know who yet."

Mark joined the party in the kitchen, after collecting the post and as he said good morning, he leant over and kissed Annie on the lips. Annie watched him shake Harry's hand and pour himself a coffee and offer them all a refill. He handed Harry the CCTV footage from the intruder alarm company.

"I was just telling Harry how I think this is down to someone connected or at least was close to the last case with Chadwick."

Mark, staring into his coffee cup, did not look up at this revelation. It was no surprise to him.

Annie continued, "I just can't work out who, maybe that will give us clues." She pointed to the DVD in Harry's hand.

Harry suggested, "May I play this on your laptop?" He pointed to Annie's laptop on the table. Annie nodded and moved the laptop around the table to open the disk drawer.

Mark looked up. "Take your pick, there's plenty of people who don't like me!" He returned his look to the bottom of his cup.

Harry asked, "Can you think back, both of you, to who knew your whereabouts, particularly the night of the accident? Who knew about the recital?"

Mark and Annie looked at each other. Annie spoke first. "Well I told Lucy at work because she was going to visit us that afternoon and I'd forgotten we were going out." She paused. "Then Ed and Matt and Mum and Dad, I think. I don't think I told anyone else."

Mark interrupted, "Well I didn't tell anyone other than Garry. He was at the pub when we called for lunch. Obviously Sophie knew and Louisa knew, although I'm not sure whether she knew until she saw us there."

"What if?" Annie paused. "Ignore me sorry."

Mark replied, "No Annie say it."

"Well," Annie continued, "Lucy could have told John at work."

Mark and Harry exchanged blank looks. Annie went on, "I have had my suspicions that John, one of our lecturers could be behind this. Err, his wife died and I was a shoulder to cry on before Mark came into my life. Anyway, my colleagues ribbed me that he wanted more than friendship but I didn't believe it. Since meeting Mark, his attitude has changed towards me. He went to great lengths to show me old newspaper clippings. He even turned up in Harrogate one day when we went out. He lives in Otley. He has been horrible when I've seen him and something about him was starting to scare me."

Once Annie shared her suspicions they seemed even more credible.

Harry joined in, "But you said you felt it was someone connected to the previous case?"

"Yes, but what if it is someone who wants us to think it's someone from the previous case. I also had feelings of being watched from home," Annie sighed. "I might be wide of the mark but you asked for any information."

Harry said, "Well let's see if this gives us any clues."

He pressed play on the player and an image appeared of four small squares each displaying different images. The top left hand corner showed the gate and there was no movement. The top right showed the front door entrance. The bottom left showed the outside patio around the entrance to the dining room and the final square showed inside the dining room. Harry clicked on the bottom left and the screen changed to show the outside of the dining room. Within three or four seconds a dark shadow appeared in front of the doors. The screen showed the culprit dressed in all black with a dark baseball cap covering part of their face. The party watched the person use a blunt instrument, although it was hard to see clearly what it was, to prise open the patio doors. The screen blanked out once the culprit entered the property.

Harry sighed and returned to the main menu. He clicked on the bottom right, which led straight into watching the culprit opening and closing the drawers in the dining room.

Harry whispered, "What are they looking for?"

Mark and Annie shrugged their shoulders; their eyes were transfixed on the screen.

Mark screwed his eyes up. "Who is it? Is it a woman or a man?"

They watched the shadow move around the room. It was then clear the alarm must have activated as the shadow became startled and agitated. At that point they fled.

Harry closed the laptop and retrieved the disk. "Interesting! I'll take this back to the office and ask my colleagues to enhance the images. I am confident they will find some characteristic in there."

"It's very hard to see who or what it is. I think it looks like a woman – the head is small in the baseball cap and the hands looked small when prising the door open," Annie said out loud.

Harry nodded and was about to reply when the forensics officer gestured for him to join her in the dining room. They shut the door behind them.

Matt joined his mum and Mark in the kitchen. He said, "Well she has found something but wouldn't give anything away. If Ed had been up, he would have charmed the information out of her."

Annie and Mark smiled.

"Why the tension?" Matt asked.

Annie shrugged. She didn't know why the dark cloud had descended on them. Mark seemed to have got up in a similar foul mood as hers, she thought. Mark put his cup down and moved over to Annie. He knelt on the floor in front of her and put his hands on the chair arms. He looked her in the eyes and said in a soft voice,

"I'm sorry Annie." He laid his head on her lap. She stroked his hair and looked at Matt.

Annie said, "It's okay Mark. Come on, neither of us have had much sleep. I'm sorry too for not being very positive this morning but I'd be lying if I said it wasn't getting to me. I just want it to be over." She squeezed Mark's scalp as her lay in her lap.

Matt joined in, "Come on, both be strong. It can't be much longer now before they are stopped. The scumbags will be caught. You two need time to sort your heads out. I'm heading off to the club shortly and I'll take Ed with me. You two can go back to bed when the police have finished. You've both cancelled your appointments today?"

Mark nodded and Annie added, "Mine wasn't today, it's tomorrow, got the days wrong."

Mark lifted his head up. "You don't have to Matt. I mean leave the house. We will be fine."

Matt placed his hand on Mark's shoulder. "Mark I need to go anyway for a meeting. Ed can come in too. You and Mum can relax today. We'll call you when we are coming back and I'll cook tea tonight, Ed can help me."

"Help you with what?" Ed asked as he walked over to the coffee pot. He poured himself a drink and turned round to find three pairs of eyes staring at him.

Matt spoke first. "You're helping me make tea tonight. These two need a rest."

Ed nodded, "Yeah no problem. The olds need a rest!"

Mark and Annie smiled.

Ed continued, "You going training Matt?" Matt nodded. Ed continued, "Good I'm coming with you."

The party laughed. Matt and Ed said their goodbyes and headed off to training. Harry re-joined Mark and Annie in the kitchen. Both were now chatting away sitting around the table.

Mark and Annie looked directly at Harry waiting for his information. Harry responded, "Well, the SOCO can't find any fingerprints but has found a footprint. The gait of a person is unique and this could be a breakthrough. In addition it appears to go with your theory Annie that this is a woman, size four to five."

Annie nodded. "That's good news, isn't it?"

Harry continued, "It is if we can find a match. I have to head back to the office now. I'm sorry the dining room is in a bit of a mess with fingerprint powders, but you should be able to clean it with washing up liquid. I think you should forget about coming to the station today. We'll talk later."

Mark showed Harry and the forensic officer out. As he closed the door, he rested his forehead on the door frame. He knew it was going to be a long day.

Annie was putting the pots into the dishwasher when he returned to the kitchen. He couldn't help but think how sexy she looked and stood in the doorway admiring her. In spite of all the problems they were having, Mark loved her. She was strong and positive and very, very sexy. His heart felt as if it would burst.

Annie, sensing Mark was present, looked up and smiled. Once she closed the dishwasher, she stood leant against the cupboard and stared back at Mark with a big beaming smile. Mark advanced towards her and consumed her into his body. He was warm and inviting. He squeezed Annie tight and rested his head on hers. Mark released his grip a little and guided Annie's face towards him with his hand on her chin. Mark kissed her tenderly, holding her head and running his fingers through her hair. Annie pulled at his T-shirt to loosen it. She ran her fingers under his shirt across his smooth skin. Mark's kisses intensified as Annie pulled his T-shirt over his head and it fell to the floor. She guided Mark around and led him into the lounge. The television was talking to itself but they were both unaware of it. Annie pushed Mark against the door. She completely ignored the searing pain from her leg and she stood before him unzipping his jeans. Mark wriggled out of them and leant back with his eyes closed. Annie rubbed her hands across his bare thighs which made Mark wince in pleasure. Annie gasped as she leant forward and kissed his inner thighs. She immediately saw the pleasure she gave Mark. She continued to kiss his legs whilst she took him in her right hand. He was hard and inviting. He was in ecstasy. He ran his fingers through her hair as her head moved tenderly from one thigh to the other. Without warning and to Mark's amazement she slipped him into her mouth. Mark was uncontrollable. She was fabulous and he loved her warm mouth. She released him and looked up to see her lover standing with his eyes closed. She gestured for him to sit on the edge of the sofa and Annie slipped over him, he was inside her. She moved him forward so she could balance without hurting her leg. He complied like an obedient pup.

Mark undressed Annie as she writhed around on him. She rode him hard, he could feel her warm body making slow contact with his inner thighs. He grabbed her waist and screamed with pleasure as they reached their limits. Annie slumped onto Mark's chest. A shooting pain in her leg overtook her pleasure, she felt sick.

"Shit, I have to move NOW," she shouted as she tried to manoeuvre off Mark's legs.

"Oh God Annie you okay? You have gone grey."

Annie caught her breath and sat down next to Mark. She couldn't speak. She felt sick and light-headed.

"Annie speak to me. You okay?" Mark was starting to show signs of panic in his voice.

Annie looked at him and laughed out loud. "Yes I'm fine."

They both laughed. "You frightened me then," Mark said as he placed his arm around her.

They both fell backwards onto the cushions. "Sorry. I thought I was going to pass out. I got this shooting pain up my leg. Serves me right," she said laughing.

They laid there for what seemed to be an eternity. In each other's arms, they felt safe and loved. Every now and then Annie would squeeze Mark, just to let him know she was there. Mark would kiss her head to acknowledge the extra show of affection.

"Oh well, shall I run the bath?" Mark asked as he kissed her head.

"Yeah why not. Let's go have a chill. I'll bring us some drinks up," Annie said.

"Oh no you won't. I will run the bath, and then come back down for drinks. You've done quite enough already." He paused and rose from his seat. He leant over Annie, kissed her lips and whispered, "You are amazing, I love you so much."

"I love you too," Annie said.

Annie lay in the same position. She was afraid to move just in case the pain returned. She couldn't wait to go back to the hospital. She needed to find out how long she would be in this cast. She was hoping for good news tomorrow. Annie closed her eyes. She could still smell Mark, which made her tingle once more.

"The bath's ready," Mark whispered as he kissed her head. He continued, "Can you get up?"

Annie opened her eyes and smiled. "Erm that's a big question. I don't know yet."

Mark held his arm out to help Annie. She complied but as she leant forward to raise herself, the shooting pain returned. She let out a shriek and sat back down.

"This may take a while," she said laughing.

Mark sat next to her perched on the end of the cushion. "Take your time, we have all day." Annie looked at him and placed her hand on his arm. She edged forward and managed to stand through the pain. Mark helped her walk to the door and back upstairs. Annie lay in the hot water whilst Mark disappeared for the drinks.

When Mark returned with a tray of goodies, Annie was asleep. She looked so angelic. Mark smiled to himself at such a beautiful face, sleeping and a leg stuck out of the water with a cast on it. How on earth had she managed to fall asleep in that position, he thought? He joined her in the hot, soothing water. Annie opened her eyes and splashed Mark in the face. They laughed and he reciprocated. Before they knew it they were in the middle of a water fight. Water and bubbles flew everywhere.

"Behave yourself," Annie laughed. "You big kid!"

"You started it," Mark said as he placed some bubbles on her nose.

"We have toast and croissants, with coffee."

"Nice," Annie said as she leant over to take a croissant. "I could get used to this treatment."

Mark, knelt in front of Annie, placed his hand on the top of her thighs. "You better get used to it. I am going to spend the rest of my life waiting on you hand and foot."

*

Ed was practising kicking his goals when Matt joined him after the meeting. One by one the first team piled out onto the training field. It felt weird for Ed to be there with them. They had been his opposition for the last twelve months and now he was part of them. Each one of them acknowledged him.

Matt shouted, "Come on then soft lad, let's see what you got."

Ed set the ball up on the kicking tee just from the 20 metres line near the touchline. He was showing off, Matt thought.

"You'll never get it from there you muppet!" Matt shouted.

Ed was not going to be put off. He focused on the ball and prayed in his head that for once let the gods help him through and prove his brother wrong. He lined it up and struck it just underneath the point of the ball. It was a sweet touch and the ball sailed through the middle of the sticks. Ed felt twenty feet tall. Matt's team-mates laughed.

Ed just smiled as Matt approached him carrying the ball. "My turn," he said as he snatched the kicking tee from Ed's hands. Matt just had to prove he was the elder of the two and could not be out done by his younger brother. Ed watched on, smiling inside. He loved his brother dearly but felt sometimes he behaved like a spoilt brat and this was one of the occasions.

Matt lined the ball up and just as he went to strike it, the ball limped off the kicking tee. Everyone, including Matt fell about laughing. Matt tackled Ed to the ground and they wrestled on the floor until a wolf whistle stopped their antics. It was the head coach. Billy approached the team. "Right let's get set up for some back to basic defensive line work." The players moaned. Billy ignored them and continued, "Defence wins games! Come on set yourselves up into two teams. Ed you can join in too."

Ed's smile beamed from ear to ear. After forty minutes he found the pace was tough going and much faster than he was used to but he was not going to give up or stop for a breather. He was smiling inside and out. Life was sweet, he was training with his brother in the team he loved as a boy. This was it, he thought. It doesn't get much better than this.

Matt patted Ed on the back as they stopped for a drink. "Well done our kid," he said breathlessly. Ed nodded.

Billy shouted, "Right that'll do for today. Any aches and pains, the doc's available. Ed, you stay back for me please. Matt you better practise your kicks and try to keep the ball on the tee!"

The team filed out laughing at Matt. He made a number of hand gestures and then returned to concentrating on the task in hand.

"Now then Ed," Billy said, bending down to fasten his laces. "That was pretty good for your first session." He stood up and continued, "We have high hopes for you especially if you're half as good as your brother." Billy smiled.

"Thanks. I can't wait to get started," Ed said.

"Well, you may get your chance sooner than next season," Billy said.

"What?" Ed sat surprised at the revelation.

"You may, not sure yet but keep yourself fit." Billy walked off.

Ed's thoughts were spinning too fast for him to catch them. He ran over to Matt and said, "Billy reckons I might play before end of season!"

Matt nodded, "Well you never know Ed. Stranger things have happened." Matt struck the ball really well and it glided between the posts. Ed followed the line of the ball and as it hit the floor he saw a shadow of a man standing at the side of the trees. He recognised his silhouette.

Matt asked, "What's wrong with you?" Matt had seen Ed screwing up his eyes to see if he could get a clearer focus.

Ed answered, without breaking his stare. "You see that man over there, and I swear I know him. I can't think where from but he is very familiar."

Matt shrugged his shoulders. "Come on it's time to hit the supermarket. I want to make Mark and Mum one of my great meals."

Ed warned, "I'm not being your assistant, you always want me to clear up your mess."

Matt replied, "That's what dogsbodies do!"

Ed shook his head and walked into the changing rooms.

*

Harry picked his phone up from his desk to check the new message. Phillipa was going to be late, family trouble. Harry threw his phone on the desk. Great! He thought. He needed her in today and she wasn't here.

"Sir." Charlie was lurking at the door entrance. "Everyone has assembled in the incident room." Harry nodded in acknowledgement but did not move. He was not really sure what he was going to say to the troops. There was a gaping hole in his enquiry, bigger than the hole in his personal life and he was at pains to find a solution to either.

He entered the room full of his colleagues except the one he needed this morning.

"Right, I've just come from Mark Swift's home. In the early hours of the morning, someone broke into the house, accessed via the patio doors in the dining room, at the back of the house. This," he lifted his hand holding up the disk, "is the DVD from the security company. I have looked at it briefly with Mr Smith and Ms Swift. Neither immediately identified the culprit but the images are grainy. I suggest we get the tech guys to enhance the images and see if we can get any clues to the identity of this person."

Charlie interrupted, "But how do we know this is not just a coincidence?"

Harry nodded. "Fair point but when you see the DVD they are looking for something. We need to find out what. They may have just been burglars but from the brief look, it looks like a woman of slight build. Let's keep an open mind at this stage."

Harry took a sip of water. "In addition to the footage, SOCO found a footprint. It would appear to corroborate that it could be a woman. The shoe size is four to five. Photographs are here. We need to try and match the gait of the foot and the pattern of the shoe. Can you two get onto that please today?" He passed the photographs to two police officers sitting to his left.

The door opened and Phillipa sneaked in smiling at Harry and mouthing 'sorry'. He smiled at her but didn't want to make it obvious that he was really pleased to see her. He retained his composure and continued, "Right, DS Davies and I have reviewed the whole case so far." He glanced at Phillipa and gestured for her to make her way to the front of the room. A few of their colleagues raised their eyebrows.

He continued, "Although Chadwick claims she is not part of this, I believe she is but she is working with someone else."

"Who?" asked an officer sitting at the back of the room.

Phillipa interjected, "That's the million dollar question." Harry motioned for her to take centre stage. He sat back and admired her confidence.

"The main suspect remains Chadwick." She pointed to the photograph of the woman. "However, we believe one of these people could possibly be working with her." Next to Chadwick's photographs, there were four other photographs and one blank page with a question mark on. Phillipa explained. "John Boyd," she pointed to his photograph, "senior lecturer at Leeds College. He is Annie Swift's senior colleague. According to colleagues, he appears to be shit stirring at the college."

PC Fowler, a budding detective and very bright officer asked, "Is that all we have on him? It seems circumstantial to me?"

Phillipa nodded, "Yep I agree but if that's the case we will eliminate him."

Harry interrupted. "It's interesting but I found out this morning that he has a bit of a crush on Annie Swift but she doesn't have the same feelings. His wife died and Annie helped him through it."

PC Fowler interrupted again. "But she didn't believe it?"

Harry shook his head. "According to Annie, since she met Mark he has been rude and acting very strangely towards her. He turned up in Harrogate on the day she was out with her family and he went to great lengths to discredit Mark Smith to her at the start of their relationship. Like you say PC Fowler, some of it is circumstantial but I want you two to dig around."

Phillipa passed them a file with John's details in.

"Next," Phillipa continued, "Sophie Smith, the daughter. We need to check her alibis. There is definitely tension between her and the family."

Harry passed the files to another set of officers. "Check her and her contacts out. Find out if she knew of the previous case and find out about her relationship with her mother but particularly with her father. I'll also give you this," he pointed to another file on the table, "this is Louisa Smith."

Phillipa gave details of her. "Mother to Sophie, Mark Smith's ex-wife. She has cast iron alibis yet the car involved in the incident in Salford was hired in her name using her passport. This file contains copies of the passport and signatures etc. You need to speak to her again. She claims her passport went missing. How? When? Speak to the hire company and if possible chase any CCTV. We know she left Mr Smith as a result of the first case, dig around to find out what she has been doing since she left. Who has she lived with?"

"Garry Pearce!" Phillipa tapped her pen on his photograph. "Ex player, bit of a ladies' man. Mr Smith's best friend. According to Mr Smith he helped him through the first case. He seems genuinely helpful. We need to look at his involvement in the first case, his relationships and more importantly his movements and relationships recently."

Harry commented, "Annie Swift and Mark Smith both confirmed he knew of their whereabouts when some, if not all, of the incidents occurred."

Harry took control of the meeting once more and Phillipa sat down. "Charlie and DC Fowler will be looking into Chadwick. We need to know who visited her in the secured unit, who she has been in contact with and what her life has been since leaving custody. The rest of you will be chasing the forensic evidence in respect of all the incidents. DS Davies will be coordinating it all. Crucial evidence relates to the car accident. Was it hired or stolen? Who was driving? Were they hospitalised? Witness statements? CCTV from the motorway and local roads. We need someone to look at the text messages and call logs. I will leave DS Davies to organise you all. Annie Swift and Mark Smith are due to come into the station tomorrow. Any pressing questions or enquiries to them, let me have them today. They may be the victims but I will be looking into their pasts too. Let's crack this case; we have lots of information, which holds the answers. Good luck everyone."

The crowd filed out of the room apart from those officers allocated to the forensics. Phillipa sat with them and allocated tasks and work. Harry stayed in the room to listen to her instructions. She was very good at her job but there was also a warmth in the room when she was present. She wasn't patronising but managed to get people to connect with her and got the best results out of people. She was senior management material, for sure, but had never put herself forward for promotion. Harry had once asked her why and she had told him Liam would not allow her to. She was playing a key part in this investigation and he was going to ensure she received the praise she deserved and was long overdue.

Once the team had been dismissed, Phillipa let out a huge sigh and raised her arms above her head. She smiled at Harry and spoke. "I'm sorry I was late this morning. Liam left unexpectedly at six this morning so I had to get the kids to school."

Harry smiled back. "You don't have to explain."

"You're my superior officer. I hate letting anyone down."

"You haven't. We all have lives outside this place. Well you lot do! Are you okay?"

Harry sat opposite Phillipa and couldn't help but notice the pain in her face. With her head down she whispered, "Yes. I am fine." She lifted her head and looked into his eyes. "I am fine. I need to concentrate on this case right now. My mum has agreed to come up from Cambridge for the month. She is going to live with us and help with the kids. I told Liam last night and he went ballistic. He doesn't want her here but I can't rely on him to be there for the kids. I know my mum speaks her mind but she will be reliable and put the kids first. They are really excited about it. Anyway Liam said if she comes, he's moving out. This morning I got up and he'd already gone. Left this." She handed Harry a scruffy note which explained Liam was moving out and would be in touch when he'd got something sorted.

Harry reached over and put his hand on hers. "I'm sorry Phillipa but I'm sure it will all work out."

She smiled, folding the paper and placing it back in her pocket. "Don't be nice to me Harry, it will make me cry."

"Come on then let's crack this case. We've loads of work to do but first I need a coffee. Join me?" Harry stood up. Phillipa nodded and they left for the canteen. Harry thought the day had got brighter now Liam was out of the picture.

The day was spent working hard bringing all the evidence together. Harry and Phillipa chatted about work which distracted Phillipa from her problems at home. Harry stayed on later than Phillipa but got very little done once she had left the office.

*

22

Annie and Mark woke early, after being spoilt rotten by the boys the night before. They had a wonderful meal and the atmosphere had been very light-hearted. It was the first evening they had been a 'normal' family with not a care in the world. They played family games and finally retired about elevenish. This is what family life was about, Mark had thought. He had not experienced it before and he had loved it.

They lay in each other's arms listening to the rain pounding on the windows. Beginning of October usually meant cold, bright days but the morning felt more like November with thick grey clouds making the day dark and dreary.

"Oh well I suppose we better move," Annie said moving gingerly out of bed. She asked, "What are your plans today?"

Mark yawned. "I am coming to the hospital with you this morning then I have an interview with Yorkshire Radio at three. What are you doing?"

Annie smiled. "After the hospital I am going to see Harry at the station. You can drop me off if you will. I'll ring Mum and tell her you're taking me to the hospital. I'll ask them round for tea I think. It dawned on me last night I'd not told them about the boys' contracts."

*

"Good morning." Phillipa beamed at Harry as he entered the office. She followed him in and closed the door.

"Good morning, how are you this morning and what time did you get in?" he asked.

Sitting down she answered, "I was in at six. Mum came last night and the house is so different already. The kids are laughing and joking and my mum is in her element."

"Good," Harry said as he read a letter on his desk. He looked up. "Sorry. That is good news and you seem a lot happier, the worry has lifted from your face."

Phillipa blushed and laughed. "You always could tell my moods by just looking at me."

"Do you fancy a drink tonight?" Harry blurted it out quickly and whilst the mood was good.

"Yes okay but not too late. Don't want to piss my mum off on her first day." Phillipa smiled. Harry's heart melted. The effect of her on him was ridiculous. He wasn't sure whether she felt the same way. He spoke again. "So what's the latest news on the forensics?"

"Well, we know the car in the accident was stolen from a home in Holmfirth. The owner reported it missing two hours prior to the accident. The blood found in the car is not a match to Chadwick, so someone else was driving. We are currently in touch with doctors and hospitals to trace any admittance that evening and the next day. The car in Salford is proving trickier. Definitely hired in Louisa's name. She says she lost her passport but it would be a hell of a coincidence if someone just found it. She is either involved or covering something up. She is coming in for an interview when she arrives back in the country."

"So is Annie Swift," Harry interrupted.

Phillipa continued, "The phone used in the text messages is a pay as you go so it's virtually impossible to trace unless we find the phone. We rang the number during a search of Chadwick's house and it wasn't there."

Harry interjected, "Or it was on silent or switched off! She had a phone with her when we released her. Did we check it?"

Phillipa pulled a face. "Not sure, will check it with the duty Sarg'." She made a note on her notepad. "The handwriting is definitely not Chadwick's so your theory of someone else involved is correct, as always." The sarcasm in her voice made Harry smile.

She continued, "We are asking for a sample of handwriting from all the witnesses and suspects. Chadwick is a size five shoe but the enhancements so far are not clear enough to ID her. Charlie and Fowler are going to see her today. They've taken another search warrant that the Super reluctantly sanctioned with a warning that we have to be careful not to make this into a harassment complaint!"

Harry fumed, "We either carry out a thorough investigation or not! Maybe if we could have held her longer we would have got more out of her. Ask the searching officers to look for mobile phones, phone bills etc. We need to know who she had contact with."

Phillipa half ignored his comment as she had confidence in her colleagues to carry out the search thoroughly. She said, "I think that's it so far." She glanced through her notes.

"Good," Harry said, "I have a really good feeling about this case now. We are so close to finding out who it is, I can feel it."

Harry and Phillipa spent the remainder of the morning discussing the previous case and the public profiles of Annie Swift and Mark Smith. Harry felt a real connection with the couple but more so with Annie. He felt Annie and Phillipa were very similar – strong and determined women but loving and caring. Both were great mothers and very loyal, perhaps misplaced loyalties at times.

*

"Hi," the portly man said as he approached the young woman in the café.

Lucy looked up from her book and smiled.

"May I sit here?" he asked.

Lucy was very suspicious. "Why?"

"Well, I couldn't help but notice you. I am visiting here and just wondered if you could help me," he explained.

Lucy dropped her guard and warmed to him. What's the harm? she thought.

"Please sit down," she gestured for him to join her. "How can I help you?"

"I am looking to enrol on a course and I can't find the old cottage," he said.

Lucy smiled. "No problems it's quite easy to miss if you don't know it's there. It is out of this café, turn left, follow the signs to the sports hall and two buildings along is the old cottage. You can't miss it." She let out a playful giggle.

He charmed her. "Thank you I'm Simon by the way."

"Nice to meet you Simon, I'm Lucy."

"Well I better get off," he said. He started to walk away then turned back. "I know this sounds crazy but would you like to come for a drink with me tonight?"

Lucy was not sure. He sensed her anxiety and added, "We can stay in the campus bar if you like. I'd just like to get to know you."

Lucy beamed with excitement. "I'd love to."

They exchanged mobile phone numbers and set a time for 5.30 p.m. when Lucy finished work.

He left her, walked in the direction she advised and as soon as was out of sight, he detoured to his car and left. He had a plan and Lucy featured in it.

*

The hospital gave Annie the all clear to return to work but with a warning not to overdo it. Mark was a little disappointed as he felt Annie had browbeaten the doctor. Her cast was replaced with a weighted boot, which improved her mobility.

Scans to her face showed the fractures were healing at an unusually fast pace. Leaving the hospital they felt relieved and happy. Annie clung onto Mark, not for physical support but to show how much she needed him.

"I may as well come to the station with you. I don't have to be at the radio station 'til later. It's going to be busy in the run up to the Grand Final."

"I'm going to go back to work tomorrow. The most challenging part will be how to get there and home."

"Well if we look at my schedule I will try and arrange stuff around dropping you off and picking you up. I'm sure your mum and dad and Matt will help where they can. Don't rush back though Annie. How many days you going to work?" Mark asked.

"I thought I would try Wednesday and Thursday until my leg heals. They're the two days I have second and third year students. Monday is first year and can be covered. Friday is my usual day off. I need to get back into a routine. My brain is going to mush."

Mark suggested, "After the Grand Final, I think we should go away, spend some time together. The boys can have the run of the house and we'll just go and relax somewhere. What do you think?"

"Yeah it sounds a great idea. Not sure whether leaving the boys in your house is a good idea," she laughed. "Only joking they'll be fine. Anyway I wouldn't be surprised if they book somewhere before pre-season training."

They pulled into the police station car park. Mark smiled to himself, as he knew exactly what holiday he had planned.

The reception area in the police station consisted of a small six feet squared area with three walls and a glass counter facing the entrance. Mark rang the bell and a portly officer came scurrying to the other side of the glass.

"Can I help you?" he said in a deep voice.

"We are here to see Harry, DCI Fisher?" Mark announced.

Harry appeared from behind the closed fire doors.

"Oh hello Mark, I was only expecting Annie," Harry said.

Mark explained, "I know but I don't have to be at work until later."

"Okay good. My colleague will be out to see you shortly Mark. This way Annie," Harry smiled.

"Hi, Mark Smith?" Charlie Dunne appeared from behind the door.

"Hello again," Mark said and held his hand out which the officer reluctantly shook.

"Please follow me."

"This is PC Fowler Mr Smith," DC Dunne announced.

Mark replied, "Please call me Mark."

"Please sit down. We are going to ask you a few questions about the recent events and the previous case."

Mark nodded. He felt guilty and intimidated even though he had done nothing.

*

Annie sat with her arms on the table, leaning slightly forward towards Phillipa and Harry. Annie was brilliant with body language and she knew she had nothing to hide.

"Mrs Swift, we are going to ask you a few questions, nothing too taxing," Harry said.

Phillipa was taken aback by his attempt at flirting with the witness. She was amused by this but could understand what Harry had been talking about. Annie had a demeanour that made it very hard for anyone not to like her. Her honesty and warmth was almost tangible.

Annie was keen to get started. She surveyed the room and in particular its occupants, Harry and Phillipa.

Harry said, "Please bear with us. The equipment is older than me and that's OLD!"

Phillipa let out a playful giggle more suited to a six-year-old girl being chased in a playground. Annie felt the chemistry between the pair. She smiled to herself.

"Okay I think we are ready to begin," Phillipa announced.

"Annie, thank you for coming in today. You understand why we are taping this interview?"

The routine questions of where did they meet, how long had they known each other and how well did Annie know Mark, were all expected by Annie. The next question threw Annie for six and was put to her by Phillipa. "Do you think Mark is in some way involved in this plot against you?"

Annie was lost for words. Her mind was travelling faster than the space station. She surveyed the accuser and after taking a minute to compose herself, launched her counter-attack.

"No absolutely NOT! I would have left by now if I thought that. He is a victim in this like I am and my boys."

Phillipa suggested, "But he did make a tidy sum of money from the first case."

Annie glared at Phillipa with complete disdain.

Annie hit back, "He made money? No he successfully sued a newspaper for libel."

Phillipa blushed a little.

Annie paused again before she outpoured her rage. "Is that the best you can come up with? After all the investigations and forensic evidence which I'm assuming you have from, at least the accident, that's the best you can do?"

Harry sensed her offence to Phillipa's direct question. "No Annie my colleague was just asking your opinion."

"There's a different way you could have asked who I thought was behind it!" Annie replied sarcastically.

"Well do you?" Phillipa asked.

Annie's response was curt. "Do I what?"

Phillipa was uncharacteristically losing her patience. "Know who is behind this?"

Annie paused and tempted to give a sarcastic, evasive answer but she wanted an end to all this more than she wanted to score points against a meaningless detective.

"I think there are a number of potential suspects but I'm not a professional detective." Annie glared at Phillipa, then continued, "I have my doubts about his ex-wife and... err... Sophie, his daughter."

"What makes you think that?" Harry asked leaning further towards Annie as if she was about to spill some MI5 secret.

"Well, the split with Mark was acrimonious, to say the least. Louisa was convinced he had had an affair with Chadwick."

Harry interrupted, "But she's got a great job and a good life now."

"Not to mention cast iron alibis!" Phillipa added.

"But the hire car was in her name," Annie argued. "I don't buy into the theory that she lost her passport. She strikes me as a highly organised meticulous woman."

Annie sat back in her chair. She'd had enough now. They had asked her opinion but she felt she had been shot down in flames. She resigned to letting them solve the crime; they get paid to do it. In reality she didn't know enough of Mark's past to have a definitive answer for them.

Phillipa asked, "Have you met Garry... Err," she looked down at her notes, "Pearce."

"Yes I have met him," Annie replied not divulging that he made her skin crawl and there was something she did not like about him.

"When did you meet him?" Phillipa asked.

"I was introduced to him on our third date and then we went to his pub for lunch on the day of the accident," Annie replied, the cogs started to turn in her head but she resisted from saying anything.

Again Annie felt a sickly feeling knowing she did not really know enough of his and Mark's past relationship to answer anything with clarity and certainty. A wave of exhaustion hit her and slouched back into the chair.

"You okay Annie?" Harry asked.

She nodded and leant forward. "There is one thing that struck me as odd and I keep going over it in my head. When I met Garry for the first time he referred to me as Mark's 'latest conquest'. On the night of the accident, at the recital, Louisa called me exactly the same thing. It just seemed an odd thing for two different people to say."

There was a long pause in the room whilst each of them digested the information.

Phillipa broke the silence. "I assume, Annie, you believe these incidents are linked to Mr Smith's past then and not yours?"

"Yes I do. I have never had any problems up to now, apart from a divorce and a split from a long-term partnership. Neither was pleasant but they weren't nasty. Having said that I can't imagine anyone wanting to do this to someone. People do have a tendency to shock you even when you think you know them."

Harry smiled at Annie. He really admired her. Her magnetic personality mesmerised him. She was academically very clever but was also very warm and amiable. He couldn't help but agree with her it was unlikely anyone would want to hurt her or hold a grudge against her.

Phillipa continued with the questioning. "I suppose it's hard when you hardly know Mr Smith's past. What about John Boyd?"

Annie was furious at the cheap swipe and Harry shared her sentiment. He glared at his colleague. Phillipa knew she had riled them both but that was part of the plan; well to rile Annie to see if she would bite.

Annie remained dignified. "John is a colleague of mine at the University."

Phillipa interrupted, "We know that but according to your colleagues you are very close?"

Annie smiled and shook her head. "Close as in we talk yes, close as in anything else no!"

Phillipa continued, "That's not the impression your colleagues have?"

Annie tried to refrain from retaliating but could not help herself. "No we are not close. I helped him when his wife died by talking to him. We see each other at work and not on a social level… except when he turns up in places I am in." She drew a deep breath and continued, "If you are implying anything other than friendship, you will be very disappointed to hear I have no interest in him at all!"

Phillipa smiled at Annie. "Your colleagues have the impression that he has feelings for you to the point of being in love with you."

Harry abruptly ended this line of questioning before Annie returned her thoughts. "Annie, you can't possibly answer on his behalf. I think we have everything we need from you today. Thank you for your time and thank you for being so open with us. We will be in touch."

Harry stood up and held his hand out to shake Annie's. As she shook his hand, Harry squeezed hers slightly as if to apologise for his partner's abrasiveness. Annie smiled, let go and offered her hand to Phillipa and said, "It was nice to meet you." Annie was a good liar!

Annie had been in the interview room for a couple of hours. Mark was waiting in the reception area when Annie returned.

Harry was surprised to see him. "Sorry Mark are you still waiting?"

"No," replied Mark, "I have seen your colleague and finished about twenty minutes ago."

Harry was eager to hear the outcome of the interview. He shook Mark and Annie's hand and departed.

*

"So would you mind telling me what that was all about?" Harry demanded as he slammed the papers on his desk.

Phillipa glared back at him. She hesitated before beginning her explanation. "I was interviewing Mrs Swift in connection with recent events."

Harry interrupted, "Don't get clever; remember who the senior officer is here." He could see that he had wounded her with that comment. "Mrs Swift is a victim not a suspect. You were very abrupt and curt with her."

Phillipa interrupted, "As opposed to you pussy footing around her! She may be a victim but we don't know whether she has any involvement or is withholding any information."

Harry's faced blushed with rage. "How dare you suggest I was not doing my job! Mrs Swift could have died in that motor accident."

Phillipa looked to the floor, she knew she had been unprofessional but her life was a mess. She and Liam were over and the one person she truly loved, had been smitten by a victim! She was hurt. She didn't have a valid defence at all and could feel herself reddening.

Harry looked at her. "Phillipa, I am the SIO in this case. You were unprofessional. However," his voice softened, "I know what strain you are under at the moment. Pray that Annie does not put in a complaint. Promise me that if it's all too much for you, you will take some leave or transfer from this case if it's too much for you to work with me."

Phillipa looked up. "No that's the last thing I want." She paused to gain her composure. "I am sorry sir. I will apologise to Mrs Swift. Please keep me on the case."

Harry nodded. "Let's get on with the work we have."

They both sat next to each other at the conference table. There was an awkward silence only briefly broken by Phillipa snuffling.

Harry broke the silence. "So what are your thoughts about the interview?"

Phillipa said without lifting her head from reading the papers, "I think Mrs Swift, Annie," Phillipa looked directly at Harry, "doesn't have anything to hide. This is linked to Mark Smith, for sure. Someone is working with Chadwick. She is a pawn in this and someone else is orchestrating it all."

Harry sat back. "What makes you think that?"

Phillipa responded, "We have found no forensic evidence so far to tie Chadwick to this. We haven't found the mobile phones, the handwriting doesn't match hers and neither does the footprint."

"But she was in Huddersfield on the night of the accident," Harry interrupted.

"True but she has not been linked to the car at all. Too easy to link her to Huddersfield don't you think? Also, how did she know the accident would happen at the particular stage of the motorway, if at all?" Phillipa sighed and continued, "We are looking at the wrong person. I think Chadwick is a distraction. Whoever is doing this is closer to Mr Smith."

"Who?" Harry asked. He had his suspicions but wanted to hear hers.

"Not sure yet. I think we can rule a member of Annie's family out although her colleague, John Boyd needs to be pursued. My instincts are leading towards Garry Pearce and somehow Louisa Smith. Both were heavily involved in the original case. As much as I try to use logic to discount them, my instincts bring them back in."

Phillipa paused and looked at Harry.

He nodded in agreement and then said, "I agree, these are three to focus on at the moment but I also want us to interview and dig around about Mark's daughter, Sophie. If she isn't involved, she may lead us to who is. I'll ask Charlie to come in and go through Mark's statement and then we'll bring the troops in to refocus the enquiry."

Phillipa smiled at Harry. As he stood up, he brushed his hand across hers. Phillipa knew she had redeemed herself and was forgiven.

Charlie gave a full account of Mark's statement, which did not amount to any new evidence. Charlie admitted, "This guy has no clue who could be doing this. It's also hard to believe he would have any enemies. When I asked him whether he thought Garry Pearce was involved, he just laughed in my face."

Harry thought for a moment. "Thanks Charlie. Can you call all the troops in? We need to discuss the next stage of the enquiries and see how far we have got with the forensic evidence."

*

"Hi Lucy. You look great." Simon kissed her cheek as she arrived at his side. "What would you like to drink?"

"White wine please," Lucy replied.

"Go grab that sofa and I'll bring the drinks over," he said as he brushed his hand over her back.

When he returned to the table, there were a few awkward moments. He was much older than her and her immaturity showed at times but he wasn't interested in intellectual conversation. His goal was simple, use her to get to his bastard 'friend' who had stolen his girl, his professional career and whom he spent all of his life in his shadows. Death was too good for him; he was going to take his new love of his life away from him and use her best friend to do it.

"Simon have you been married before?" Lucy asked.

He nearly asked who Simon was but remembered he had given her a false name.

"No I haven't, never had the time and never met the right person, until now."

He knew his flattery was working. She was putty in his hands.

He continued, "You are very beautiful, why are you still single?"

Lucy answered, "I can't find anyone I can trust or that I am attracted to, until now." They both laughed.

This was going to be easier than he thought. He bought another round of drinks and placed them on the table. As Lucy leant forward to the glass, he slipped his hand across the table to touch hers. She smiled and bowed her head. Her heart fluttered. She was enjoying this attention. He got up and joined her on the two-seater sofa. He placed his arm across the back of the sofa and leant forward to kiss her. She complied and kissed back. He was gentle with her, he needed to gain her trust and at least pretend he was enjoying it. He placed his hand on her thigh and whispered in her ear, "Shall we go somewhere quieter?"

Lucy sighed. She knew she should not but she'd never had sex before and so wanted to. The opportunity presented itself in a kind, warm, albeit older man and she was not going to miss it. She whispered, "We can go to mine. It's a five-minute walk from here. It's only a one-bedroomed flat."

"Are you sure about this? I don't want to rush you," he said rubbing his hand along her thigh. She kissed his lips and nodded.

He grabbed her and dragged her into his arms. "Oh Lucy I can't wait to have you. I fancy you so much. He slipped his hand up her short skirt and rubbed her thigh.

She slapped his hand and giggled. "Wait 'til we get home cheeky."

She skipped like a schoolgirl all the way home. As they entered the communal area, he grabbed her from behind and started kissing her neck. She giggled and pulled him up the stairs and into the flat. He slammed the door shut and pinned her against it. She let out a cry of pleasure.

Lucy whispered, "Bedroom's in there." She pointed to the door but he ignored her and slipped her skirt from round her waist. He lifted up her blouse and took it over her shoulders to reveal a pink embroidered bra and matching knickers. He kissed her breasts and knelt before her with his hands on her waist. Lucy was breathless; she couldn't believe what was happening to her. She was scared but exhilarated at the same time. She wanted to slow it down but was also desperate for it to continue. He kissed her belly button and slowly moved his tongue down her body to the top of her pants. She moaned with pleasure and rested the palm of her hands on his head. She gently pushed him further down until his tongue was inside her. Oh my God, she thought, what was she doing? She'd never done it before! He came back up to stand in front of her and wrapped his arms around her body, picked her up and took her into the bedroom.

Lucy lay on the bed and watched him undress. She confessed, "I've never done this before."

He ignored her and continued to undress. When naked he joined her on the bed. He removed her underwear and slowly climbed into her.

"I know," he whispered as he lowered himself onto her. He wanted to just thrust it in and get it over with but knew he needed her for longer than one night. He was turned on more knowing she was making love and he was using her to get at him!

Lucy just lay there and let him do it all. She wasn't really sure what to do. She came first and her coming made him come. He laid there for a while, then slipped off her.

Lucy rolled onto her side and kissed him. His first reaction was to push her away but he played the game. He kissed her and held her close.

Lucy spoke first. "That was fantastic."

He smiled. "I'm glad I'm your first."

They fell asleep in each other's arms.

23

"It's so good to see you Annie," Lucy beamed with delight. She hugged her friend with great warmth. "How are you? Come, sit down." She gestured for Annie to sit in the chair and promptly joined her at the table.

"Lucy I've missed you," Annie said, taking her seat.

Lucy continued in her enthusiastic, childlike way. "So come on, what you been up to? You still lerrrved up?" she laughed.

Annie smiled and shuffled around in her seat. "More so now. I really love Mark, Lucy. It's been tough but I love him more each day and I miss him like I've only ever missed my boys."

Mark had dropped Annie at the college and neither of them wanted to say goodbye. It was the first time since the accident they had been apart and she had never felt this way before. Annie had always been fiercely independent but wondered now whether she had ever really loved Phil or Paul, at all. There was an aching and longing for Mark that she had never felt before and she could not wait for two o'clock when she would be reunited with him.

"It must be tough though knowing that it's your relationship with him that's causing all this and nearly cost you your life," Lucy said bluntly.

Annie wasn't offended by Lucy's naivety but calmly answered, "It's not our love that's causing this; it's the idiots that are doing this." She paused. "Lucy when the police catch who is responsible for this, Mark and I will still be together. We are determined not to let this spoil our lives."

Lucy could sense tension and quickly changed the subject. "I've also met someone. I think he's the one."

"That's great news Lucy. Who is he? Where did you meet?" Annie was genuinely happy for her young friend.

Lucy replied, wearing a wide beaming smile, "He's called Simon, I met him on campus and he owns his own business."

"Great, when do we get to meet him?" Annie asked. "Is he studying here?"

"No he was here for a meeting and not yet. He wants us to keep things quiet but I knew it would be okay to tell you."

Annie grew suspicious. "He's married then?"

Lucy shook her head whilst gulping down her coffee. "That's what John said. NO, he is NOT married. He is shy and wants to make sure we are right for each other."

"Fair enough," Annie said. She did not want to push the matter any further, besides it was time to prepare for her first tutorial. She gathered her belongings and hobbled off to Room 104. The faculty had kindly rescheduled her lessons to ground floor classrooms and theatres.

Her first lesson was uncompromisingly boring; the students were more interested in talking about Mark than Java programming.

Annie breathed a huge sigh of relief when the day was over without incident and was even more relieved when she was huddled in Mark's arms in the car park. She squeezed him tightly as he whispered, "Let's go home."

When they arrived back home, Matt and Ed were waiting on the doorstep, like they used to when Annie had had a rare day away from them.

Mark started to prepare dinner under the critical eyes of Matt and Ed. Matt handed an envelope containing five tickets to the Grand Final to his mother. Annie shrieked with delight and hugged her sons.

"I'll ring Grandma," she said.

"No need," Ed replied. "They've just pulled up on the drive."

Annie and Mark looked at each other. The boys had invited their grandparents round. Matt was the first to greet them with a hug, followed by Ed who playfully patted his grandpa on the head resulting in them wrestling in the hallway.

Andrea hugged her daughter. "How was your day darling?"

Annie nodded, still holding her mum and muttered, "It was okay. Glad to be home."

Andrea knew her daughter was struggling with the whole sordid affair and her brave face and stoic exterior was for the boys' benefit.

"Right then, don't keep us in suspense any longer Matt, why have you called us over?" Charles asked.

"To torment you," Ed replied.

Matt ushered them all into the kitchen where Mark had opened a bottle of champagne.

"Hi Andrea, Charles," Mark said as he shook Charles's hand and kissed Andrea.

Matt handed everyone a glass of champagne and cleared his throat. "Ladies and Gentlemen and Ed." Everyone laughed. "I would like to propose a toast. To Mum and Mark in finding love and happiness and being fabulous role models for my brother and me." Mark looked at Annie and squeezed her tight. Andrea had tears in her eyes as they all said, "Annie and Mark."

Matt continued, "And another toast to Ed and myself. It is going to be an honour and a privilege to play alongside my brother in a Leeds shirt next season."

Andrea screamed with delight.

"Oh Dad would have been so proud." She grabbed her two grandsons and kissed them, both of them squirming and trying to escape her clutches.

Charles hugged his daughter and proudly whispered, "Well done Annie. You worked so hard to bring them up and you have made two very clever, brilliant young men."

Annie burst into tears. Mark and Charles hugged her.

Charles continued, "I'm sorry, I didn't mean to upset you."

Annie sobbed and said, "You haven't. It means so much what you said."

Annie dried her eyes and said, "Can I say something please?" She cleared her throat. "I am bursting with pride and I am definitely the luckiest mum in the world."

Andrea interrupted, "One of the luckiest."

Mark smiled warmly at Andrea.

Annie continued, "Matt and Ed, you have worked so hard and made my job easy over the years."

Charles added, "Well Matt has!"

Ed playfully punched his grandpa.

"Really, I am very proud of you two. I also want to say thank you for accepting Mark within our family. I love Mark so much and I know all the pain and heartache we have been put through has led us to a long and happy life with Mark. Now, let's forget tea, let's go to the village pub."

No one disagreed. Mark ordered taxis and Annie spruced herself up.

The impromptu celebration was a fabulous, family evening. The whole family had found they were celebrities to the local villagers and were embraced with open arms in the pub. It was far from the quiet family affair Annie had anticipated but it was great. The kids had great fun with Matt and Ed and they even played a mini pool tournament.

Mark and Annie chatted with Andrea and Charles. Andrea and Charles accepted Mark's kind invitation of the guest room for the night. Annie was working 10 a.m. until 2 p.m. and would be driven to work by Charles, leaving Mark to catch up on his scheduling which he should have been doing instead of drinking. The evening was a far cry from the turmoil that had been forced upon them over the last few weeks.

At eleven o'clock the party left the pub. Annie and Andrea took the taxi home and the boys decided to walk the short journey home.

Andrea asked Annie, "You okay?"

Annie nodded and smiled. "I am Mum. My boys are growing up and finally I have found a kind, considerate and sexy man."

They both laughed.

*

"Okay team, bit of hush please," Harry shouted as he barged into the incident room. "We have a lot of work to get through."

Harry reshuffled the evidence boards. He tapped on the board at four photographs he had placed directly in front of the group.

"These are the people we will be concentrating on for the time being – John Boyd, Garry Pearce, Louisa Smith and Sophie Smith."

"What about Chadwick?" Charlie asked.

Phillipa joined the conversation. "We believe one or more of these are working with or using Chadwick as a decoy."

She gestured for Harry to continue.

"Thanks. Following interviews with Ms Swift and Mr Smith, we believe, whoever is doing this, is closer to them than we first thought."

Harry recalled the interviews in detail to the officers.

Charlie added, "Well the blood found in the abandoned car was not Chadwick's."

PC Duggan also confirmed the footprint at the house was not hers either.

Harry nodded. "Okay then. I want you two," Harry pointed to two uniformed officers, "to interview Louisa Smith and dig around, find everything there is to know about her. Bank details, friends, family, acquaintances, boyfriends, mobile phone records, as much information as you can."

Phillipa skimmed a brown file across the table towards the officers, which contained contact information and scant previous details of Louisa.

"I'm going to interview Sophie Smith with DS Simone Hathaway from Greater Manchester Police. She is Mr Smith's daughter. Very feisty young lady and has publicly condemned her father's new choice of partner. She and Louisa were at the recital on that Monday evening."

"Phillipa and P C Brookes, can you interview John Boyd and dig around."

He continued, "I and PC Blake will be working on Mark's friend and former team-mate Garry Pearce."

Harry glanced at Phillipa who was incensed she was not going to be interviewing Garry Pearce.

Phillipa knew it was impossible for her to change his mind, besides she knew why he'd done it. She had questioned his professionalism; this was his pathetic way of getting back at her. She would carry on with her job, she thought as she walked down the corridor. She slammed the door of the ladies' toilets and slumped over the sink. Why was it all falling apart? At home? At work? She looked at her own reflection in the mirror. She felt old and drained and she looked it too. She washed her face, dusted herself down and left.

"Phillipa," Harry shouted.

Phillipa was tempted to ignore him and carry on but he was the Senior Investigating Officer. She turned, smiled and said, "Yes!"

Harry caught up and was out of breath. "What time you finishing work?" he whispered.

"In about ten minutes," she replied.

"Drink?" Harry asked.

Curtly, she replied, "No sir. I have family commitments."

She walked off and did not look back. Harry stood transfixed by her until she was out of sight.

24

Annie woke first at 8.30 a.m. Ouch, she thought as she tried to move. For once the pain was from her head and not her leg. She was the only one working today and it had really lost its appeal. She watched Mark sleeping. His eyelids were moving slightly and Annie wondered what he was dreaming about. She shuffled sideways and laid her head next to his on the pillow. His breath warmed her face. She rubbed her hand across his face and gently kissed his lips. Unable to resist, Annie wrapped her arms around his torso. She kissed him again. He rolled onto her. His warm body enveloped Annie. Their lovemaking had become less frantic but no less passionate. They understood each other more. Their love was growing stronger and deeper by the day. The both climaxed together and just lay there, holding each other.

Mark whispered, "I've never made love like that before. It was amazing."

Annie agreed, they had always enjoyed great sex but this had been on a whole new level. She whispered, "It was beautiful," and buried her head in his chest.

"I really wish I didn't have to work today," Annie mumbled.

"I know," Mark replied. "But I have loads to catch up on too, even if I can do it in my slobby clothes. At this rate I will become unemployed."

"You're too good at your job," Annie said.

"I know," Mark laughed.

*

"Miss Smith?" Harry asked as he approached Sophie in the waiting room.

"Yes," she said. "This better not take long, I have tons of Uni work to do."

"I appreciate your time Miss Smith. I am DCI Harry Fisher and this is DS Simone Hathaway of Greater Manchester Police."

"Can we get on with it," Sophie interrupted impatiently.

"This way." DS Hathaway directed her into a small, pokey interview room. Whilst she set up the tape recording equipment, Harry explained why they were recording the interview. Harry's suspicion of Sophie being difficult was a huge understatement. She was uncooperative and brattish.

"Can you confirm, for the tape, you are Sophie Smith, resident at Linton Hall, Halls of Residence Manchester University?" Harry asked.

"Yes," Sophie said sighing loudly.

"Are you the daughter of Mark Smith?"

"I am." Sophie was growing impatient.

A series of mundane questions and answers resulted in Sophie becoming indignant. She asked, "Is there any point to this questioning?"

Harry sighed and avoided eye contact with the interviewee.

"How well do you know Annie Swift?"

"I don't," Sophie answered curtly.

"I get the impression you don't like her," Harry suggested.

"I don't know her!" Sophie replied. "And neither does my dad."

Harry continued, "You don't approve of your dad's relationship with Ms Swift?"

"NO!" Sophie said. "But he's stupid enough to think everything is so rosy when he doesn't even know her."

"But isn't that up to your dad?"

"Yes," Sophie became agitated. "It is but he's not the best judge of character. He and Mum split because he was an idiot then, and he's still an idiot now."

Harry surveyed Sophie. She was very beautiful and resembled her father particularly her eyes but the resemblance stopped there. Mark was meek, mild and softly spoken with a faint northwest England twang. Sophie had a strong Mancunian accent and displayed bitterness towards her father that perplexed Harry.

"Do you love your father Sophie?" he asked.

"Yes." Sophie shuffled around in her chair.

"Are you sure?" Harry pressed.

Sophie became agitated. "Of course I'm sure." She paused. "My dad is a great person, and he just makes poor choices when it comes to relationships. He had it all with Mum yet he still had an affair with a girl younger than I am now. And now, he's shacked up with a woman he doesn't even know."

Harry was getting the distinct impression that someone else, possibly her mother, had influenced this young woman's opinions of her father.

"Sophie," Harry continued in a softer tone, "your dad was a victim of a stalking campaign; he didn't have an affair when he was married to your mother."

Sophie sat for a short while looking at her hands. Harry pressed the issue. "Sophie, look at me." Sophie's eyes glared into his. "Your dad never had an affair Sophie."

Sophie shook her head. "You're wrong! Uncle Garry said he did he told me in their playing days they were wild and Mum suffered because of it!"

"Uncle Garry?" Harry asked.

"Garry Pearce, Dad's best friend, my godfather."

Harry was starting to get the full picture now. They both sat in silence for a couple of minutes while Harry's brain digested the information.

Sophie looked up. "Do you have any other questions, and I want to go?"

"Okay, just a few more questions," Harry said.

"Tell me about your relationship with Uncle Garry. Are you close? How often do you see him? How much time has he spent with you?"

Sophie looked confused. "Why?"

"Please Sophie, I would like to understand the dynamics of your relationship. You must be close and must trust him if you believe him over your father?"

"Uncle Garry has been around, like forever. He is my godfather and has been a constant part of my life. My mum and dad spent most of my childhood tearing lumps out of each other; he was there for me. I speak to him nearly every day. It was easier when we lived with him."

Harry interrupted, "You lived with him?"

So matter of fact, Sophie answered, "Yes we lived there for a couple of years. It was great, calm and he and Mum got on really well."

Harry asked, "How long did you live with him?"

"About two years. Mum and Uncle Garry started arguing over her new job and long hours." She paused. "I went to Uni and Mum moved on." She took a sip of water, then continued, "Mum's job really took off. It led her all over the world and Uncle Garry didn't want her to be away."

"What would it matter to him?" Harry asked.

"Dunno really. He said she should be here for me," Sophie replied.

"Sophie?" Harry asked, "Were your mum and Garry in a relationship?"

Sophie looked disgusted at the thought. "NO! Definitely NOT!" She continued, "They were close friends. They leant on each other, helped each other out. Dad really hurt Mum and Uncle Garry was there for her."

Harry said, "When did your mum leave Garry's?"

Sophie thought for a short while. "It was December last year. I moved to Uni in the August and she found a place in Cheadle Hulme in December."

"Thank you Sophie, I think that'll be all for now," Harry said.

As Sophie left, Harry's mind went into overdrive. He rang the office and advised the operator to assemble the team in one hour.

*

There was a low chatter in the incident room, which turned to silence when Harry entered.

"Right," Harry announced decisively. "I have just interviewed Sophie Smith, Mark Smith's daughter, and I think we may have a breakthrough." He paused, cleared his throat and continued, "Sophie and her mother, Louisa Smith, lived with Garry Pearce for a while." Harry pointed at Garry Pearce's picture on the evidence board. "I think he was having an affair with Louisa."

"Did Sophie Smith tell you so?" Phillipa asked.

"No," Harry admitted, "but I think they did. Sophie's words were 'they were close friends and leant on each other'. I think it was more than that. They split when Sophie went to Uni last year. Sophie still sees Garry who she refers to as Uncle Garry, who has been around all her life."

Phillipa interrupted, "Well that would explain why the first hire car was rented in Louisa's name."

The room was silent and all anticipated Phillipa's explanation. "Well if she was living there, Pearce would have had access to her passport and documents."

Harry nodded. "Yes, very true. Who spoke to the hire company?"

"I did sir," said Charlie, "they said it was booked online."

"Okay have we got an IP address?"

"Yes we do," Charlie said.

"Okay find out who it belongs to and where it is registered. I would bet it is Pearce's computer."

"It's a mobile laptop sir. If we could check Pearce's place we could see if he has one that matches the IP address."

"Did the hire company know who picked the car up?" Phillipa enquired.

Charlie looked down at his notes. He had to admit to the whole room he had not yet visited the hire company.

Harry's face reddened with rage. "Charlie go see them today. Let's hope the CCTV loop hasn't wiped any evidence we might have had. Go now please!"

Charlie left the room.

"Why? What motive would he have?" asked Phillipa.

"He was around in both cases. He has been the constant person in the Smith's family life during both incidents. Maybe he has a score to settle with Mark, or Louisa?" Harry sighed. "It's a hunch. I have believed all along someone has been colluding with Chadwick, maybe this is it. Maybe the motive is jealousy."

Harry paused again and turned to the evidence board. He faced the troops again. "We need to check who visited Chadwick whilst she was locked up. Look into Pearce's past, phone records, business, accounts, personal accounts, playing records. We don't have enough evidence for a search warrant but Phillipa and I will visit him today."

Every officer was allocated a specific task to work on and it was agreed the group would reconvene at nine the next morning. Any significant news would be relayed back to Harry immediately.

*

"I need to see you," Sophie said into her mobile phone. She listened intently to the response from the receiver.

"No Uncle Garry, I really need to see you today. The police have interviewed me and I want to ask you about Dad and his affair." Another pause as the recipient responded.

Disappointed, Sophie replied, "Okay fuck you! Mum was right you only want to help when there's something in it for you." She hung up, agitated as she'd not been able to tell Garry what had happened at the station. She rang her mum and received only the answering service. She thought about ringing her dad but after their last meeting, she stubbornly refused to make the first move even though she knew she had been a cow to him.

What if the copper had been right, she thought? What if her dad hadn't had an affair all those years ago? She had hated him for what he had done to her mum. All those years of hatred for nothing. Then she thought about Uncle Garry and her mum. They had been close and if she was completely honest with herself she knew there had been signs of an intimate relationship between him and her mum, she had just ignored them.

Sophie decided the best thing all round was if she returned to University and recommenced her hibernation.

*

"I thought Mick Duggan was going with you to interview Pearce?" Phillipa asked Harry as they left the incident room.

"He's been called onto another job. Would you prefer me to ask someone else?" Harry said.

"No." Both smiled as they walked to the car.

"So do you want to lead this interview?" Harry asked as Phillipa buckled into the passenger seat.

"It's up to you, you're the boss," Phillipa said wearing a wry smile.

"Well from what Annie Swift said, Pearce is a bit of charmer."

"A creep, you mean?"

Harry laughed, "Maybe he will react to you better."

"Female charm comes in handy then." Phillipa smiled.

"Flirting definitely does," Harry laughed.

After an uncomfortable couple of minutes' silence, Harry enquired, "How are you and Liam doing?"

Phillipa shrugged her shoulders. "Not great. He's moved back to his mother's and will only see the kids every other weekend. It will suit him though he can chat online and play on Mafia Wars all day long."

"How are you coping?" Harry asked out of genuine concern, knowing full well the job took its toll on single people let alone single parents.

Phillipa answered, "Thank God my mum could stay. Liam thinks I'll have to give up work if he doesn't have the kids but I won't do that."

"It must be tough," Harry acknowledged her words. He couldn't say he was absolutely gutted for Phillipa; on the contrary he desperately wanted a happy ending between the two of them.

Ever since the Christmas party encounter, he had suppressed very strong feelings for her and these had been stirred further by Annie and Mark's story.

Breaking Harry's train of thought, Phillipa shouted, "Harry, turn left in here." He would have missed the pub completely. "Jesus, Harry you were miles away."

Harry apologised.

Phillipa responded, "You need to concentrate on one thing at once."

Harry laughed, "If only! My head is going a hundred miles per hour and my adrenaline is pumping. We are getting somewhere Phillipa. If this Garry Pearce isn't involved in some way I'll run around Millennium Square on Saturday afternoon starkers!"

"You'll get arrested," Phillipa declared.

Yeah hopefully by you, Harry thought.

They both laughed but had to quickly compose themselves for what could be a crucial visit. Harry didn't want to spook Pearce, not yet anyway and he felt had he have asked him to come into the station, he might have done just that.

"Good morning," Harry said. "We are here to see Garry Pearce," Harry announced to the middle-aged woman standing behind the bar.

"Who shall I say wants 'im?" she replied.

"DCI Harry Fisher and DS Phillipa Davies," Harry replied.

She blushed and replied in her best attempt at a posh accent, "I'll get him for you."

Phillipa contained her laughter, now was certainly not the time. They could hear the woman shouting up the stairs to Garry, then a thudding sound of what presumably was Garry thumping down the stairs.

"Hi there," Garry said as he bounced into the room.

Harry surveyed him closely. He was stockier than Mark Smith and had a rugged, almost thug like look to him. He had a sinister face. Harry took an instant disliking to him, the exact opposite reaction to when he had met Mark Smith.

"DCI Harry Fisher and DS Phillipa Davies. We'd like to ask you some questions," Harry announced.

Garry flippantly remarked, "My licence is up to date," and laughed at his own joke.

Harry knew this was going to be a challenge.

"Can we sit down please, somewhere private if possible?" Phillipa said.

"Sure we'll go in the conservatory." He led them through the back into the lounge area. "This is where my best friend brought his lovely new partner; they sat here." He pulled the chair out at a table close to the window. In any other circumstance, Phillipa and Harry would have both loved to have sat having a drink or two overlooking the river.

Phillipa began the inquisition. "We are here today to speak to you about the attempted murder of Mark Smith, Annie Swift and Edward Swift-Brown. We understand Mark is one of your closest friends?"

Garry interrupted, "He*is* my best friend!"

Harry watched Garry's reactions very closely. He was so cocky and arrogant.

Phillipa continued unperturbed, "How long have you known Mr Smith?"

Garry replied, "Since we were kids in the under 8s at Waterhead."

"Have you always been close friends during that time?" Phillipa asked.

"Pretty much," Garry answered.

"What does that mean?" asked Phillipa.

"We've had a few fallouts throughout the years but thirty years is a long time for any friendship."

"What did you fall out over?"

"Does it matter?" Garry asked.

"Please just answer the questions," Harry interjected.

"Stupid things really, usually girls but more often because he was more talented than me and got picked a lot more than I did," Garry admitted.

"Did that wind you up?" Phillipa asked.

"Sometimes. I was young and ambitious and arrogant." He paused. Harry thought, nothing changed there then! Garry continued, "But I'm over it now."

"Are you?" Phillipa pressed.

Garry smiled. "Yes I am."

Phillipa changed her tack. "Tell me about your relationship with Louisa Smith?"

The change of tack managed to serve its purpose and threw Garry off guard. "What about Louisa?" Garry asked, getting slightly agitated and shuffling in his seat.

"How well do you know her?" Phillipa asked.

"She was married to Mark Smith for a while," he replied slightly suspicious of where these questions were leading to.

"How long have you known her?"

"I was best man at their wedding, so I've known her as long as he has."

"How did they meet?" Phillipa asked.

"It was a Challenge Cup Final at Wembley. We were in the bar, she was with one of Wigan's corporate sponsors. I started chatting to her and then Mark joined us. From that point they were inseparable. They married in the following summer and had Sophie a year later."

"Why did it all go wrong?" Phillipa asked.

"You'll have to ask them that," Garry said defiantly.

"We are asking you," Harry said.

"It was all to do with that Lawrence woman. Louisa felt there was no smoke without fire. In the end she couldn't live with it all anymore and left." Garry stopped suddenly as if stopping himself from continuing.

"And where did she move to?" Phillipa asked.

"Her mum and dad's, I think. Then she got her own place in Manchester," Garry lied.

Harry knew he had him. He was without doubt hiding something. Harry wondered whether he should intervene or would Phillipa go in for the kill? He sat in silence.

Phillipa continued, "Are you sure about that?"

Garry said, "Absolutely. She moved to Manchester to be near Sophie at University."

"Okay," Phillipa said, "Mr Pearce, did Louisa ever live here with you?"

Garry's jaw dropped. He started back peddling and stuttering, "Err... err... err." He thought whether to lie more or call their bluff. Shit, I should have spoken to Sophie earlier, he thought. I bet she'd told them or maybe it was Louisa, she could be a bitch if she wanted to. She could have told him all sorts, he thought.

Harry and Phillipa knew they had him. They could see the cogs turning in his arrogant brain; he was panicking.

Phillipa pressed on. "Garry? Did Louisa Smith ever live here?"

Garry became aggressive. "Yeah, she fucking did, all right?"

"Calm down please. Why did you lie to us?"

Garry paused again. "Because I wanted to keep Louisa out of it. It's none of your business."

"Were you involved, an item?" Harry asked.

Garry's face was getting redder and redder. "None of your fucking business." Garry stood up. "This conversation is over."

"Sit down! No, it's NOT over!" Harry said standing nose to nose with Garry.

"I am not speaking to you any more, we are done," Garry shouted.

"You sit down and continue, or I will arrest you and continue this down at the station," Phillipa said in a calm, unflustered manner.

This incensed Garry further. "I've not done 'owt. This is ridiculous. My private life is PRI-VATE!"

"Not when it could be linked with an attempted murder case," Phillipa insisted.

"What the fuck 'as that gotta do wi' me?" Garry bellowed.

"You tell us?" Harry asked.

If it had been humanly possible, steam would have ejected out of Garry's ears. That was it; he flipped. He threw his chair over and lunged over the table towards Phillipa. Before he could grab hold of Phillipa, Harry sidestepped and intervened. Garry lost his balance and lay flat out on the table top. Harry grabbed his wrists and placed his elbows over the back of Garry's neck.

"Something to hide?" Harry whispered into Garry's ear whilst tightening his grip. Garry wriggled but he was going nowhere.

"You are under arrest!" Phillipa said, collecting her notes together and passing Harry her handcuffs. Whilst Garry was pressed against the table she read him his rights. It was doubtful he took any of it in as he was going berserk. It was a struggle but Harry and Phillipa managed between them to get Garry into the back of the Vectra hatchback.

By the time they reached the station, Garry had calmed down. They escorted him into the custody suite and gave his full details to the custody sergeant. He was processed and placed in a cell.

"We'll leave him to stew," Harry said, walking away with Phillipa. "Well that went well, NOT! I'm knackered; he was a strong bugger."

"I know," Phillipa agreed, "he shocked me how quickly he flipped."

Harry agreed. "Yes and if he's capable of that from one conversation…" Phillipa interrupted, "Then he's capable of much more!"

"This has changed the case. I'm going to see the Super. We can get a search warrant now," Harry declared.

The Superintendent listened intently to Harry's version of events.

"We don't have enough evidence to substantiate he's directly involved in this case, Harry. Interview him; then come back to me. We'll reassess a warrant then." The Super continued signing papers as if to dismiss Harry.

Harry was disappointed but knew there was no point in arguing. He shut the door to the Super's office and huffed a huge sigh as he walked back to his office. He passed the incident room and saw Phillipa deep in conversation with Charlie. He was about to enter but changed his mind and shut himself away in his office. This was a tough case, even by his standards. Harry felt he was battling internal as well as external elements. A search warrant might have led to the laptop that booked the hire care or the mobile phone used for the malicious texts. Instead, he would have to try and get a confession from an obnoxious, arrogant man. His train of thought was interrupted when Phillipa knocked and entered.

"When we interviewing Pearce?" she asked.

"You're not," the Superintendent entered the room.

Harry and Phillipa glared open-mouthed.

The Superintendent continued, "Pearce has made a complaint against you Harry, excessive force! He claims you were too aggressive."

"But that's absurd, Harry was not aggressive. Pearce went for me, he was defending me," Phillipa argued.

"Well, I'm sure it's all bull but Harry you can observe with me. DS Dunne and you can interview him," the Super pointed to Phillipa.

"Bollocks!" Harry said.

The Superintendent shot a 'if looks could kill' glare at Harry which led to an immediate apology.

When alone with Phillipa, Harry threw his pen across the room, Phillipa ducked.

Harry said, "I'm sorry but this is total bollocks."

"I know," Phillipa conceded. "I need to know what you want me to ask him. You have suspected someone else was involved. Give me all your thoughts and I will get it out of Pearce."

Harry was not in the mood to assist her but he knew he was close to a breakthrough. Reluctantly, he disclosed all his thoughts and opinions to Phillipa. Harry would not usually partake in bitterness and self-pity but this case was getting to him. Actually it was working with Phillipa that was getting to him. He had dropped enough hints of how he felt about her yet she had not shown any signs of interest at all. As Phillipa talked, all Harry wanted to do was lean over and kiss her. If it weren't for the fear of ruining their professional relationship, he would have done it there and then.

Charlie, knocking on the door, brought Harry back to reality. His face was redder than usual and he was out of breath. "Sir, I've been to the hire company. They have given me the CCTV footage which includes the day the first car was hired."

"Excellent, get uniformed officers to trawl through it," Harry ordered. "Any news on the second vehicle?"

"Working on it," Charlie replied. He turned and scuttled away.

"Come on then Phillipa, let's get this interview started," Harry declared.

*

"Morning all. Please come in and sit down," Annie welcomed her class. She was on a mission today after a fantastic night with the family.

"Pass these around please," Annie instructed passing a wad of papers to a front row student. "Today I want you to write a programme using Eclipse Net Beans in JavaScript language. This handout gives you a brief outline and some examples of script BUT I want you to be creative and extend it however you like. The most imaginative and innovative will win a prize."

"What prize Miss?" a student called out.

"A surprise," Annie replied. "Give me a shout if you are struggling or need some advice. It's important you develop your programming skills independently but don't suffer in silence."

A hum of chatter descended on the room but it was controlled and not annoying. Annie switched on her laptop but wasn't quite sure what she wanted or needed to do. She had been so distracted for the last few weeks, she felt removed and alienated from her work.

She was about to open her emails when John entered the room. "Sorry to disturb you Annie but there is someone to see you."

Annie was puzzled, who would want to see her now. "Can't it wait until after the lesson?"

"She is insisting on seeing you now. I can cover for you," John replied.

As Annie approached John, she pulled a face and shrugged her shoulders. John knew what she meant, shrugged back and mouthed, "I don't know."

Annie stepped outside the room to find a scrawny looking woman in jeans and a hoodie. When she revealed herself, Annie recognised her as Chadwick.

Annie started to panic, her breathing became deep and short, her face ashen and she froze to the spot. "What the hell are you doing here?"

"I need to speak to you," Chadwick whispered, constantly looking over her shoulder as if she was on the run or being followed.

"I have nothing to say to you," Annie said. As she turned to re-enter the classroom, Chadwick grabbed Annie's arm and twisted her body round. Annie slipped, lost her balance and fell onto her broken leg. She let out a scream. Three classroom doors burst open as staff came to her aide. John knelt beside her and glared up at Chadwick who panicked and ran.

"Call an ambulance and call security!" John barked. "Annie what happened, you okay?"

Tears rolled down Annie's face. "She grabbed me and I lost my balance. It's my leg; I felt something move. Shit, the pain!"

"Sit tight, we've called an ambulance. Who was she?" John said.

"It was…" Annie writhed in pain. "It was Chadwick, the woman who stalked Mark."

"Shit Annie, sorry. If I'd have known I wouldn't have brought her in."

"John, pass me my bag please," Annie asked.

Elspeth approached Annie wearing a very stern and concerned look on her face. She announced, "Get all the students off this floor. When clear, man the doors – last thing Annie needs is an audience."

Annie couldn't even manage a smile. She struggled to operate a mobile phone. Shock and pain had taken over her whole body and she was shaking uncontrollably.

Elspeth knelt down beside Annie. "What are you trying to do? Let me do it for you."

Annie replied, "I need to speak to Mark, tell him what's happened. He's at home."

"No problem," Elspeth said. "I will ring him for you." She took Annie's mobile phone and walked down to the far end of the corridor. John followed her once the paramedics arrived to care for Annie. John explained to Elspeth what had happened and she relayed the information to Mark. The paramedics were wheeling Annie down the corridor when Elspeth enquired which hospital she would be taken to. Again the information was relayed to Mark. Elspeth passed the phone to Annie.

Sobbing, Annie stammered, "I'm in a lot of pain. Please come to the hospital, I need you." After a pause, she said, "I love you too."

She hung up. After a hug from both John and Elspeth, Annie was loaded into the ambulance. The police had arrived just after the ambulance left, so Elspeth was left to brief the police on an incident in her college that she had not witnessed first-hand or had no real clues what it was all about.

From the back of the maintenance building, Chadwick watched the events unfolding. She was shaking with fear. I just wanted to speak to her, she thought. She tried contacting her accomplice again but it went straight to the answering machine.

"Oi you!" shouted a security guard. "You shouldn't be round 'ere!"

Chadwick ran off campus and collapsed in a heap in the adjoining woods. She knew she had to get out of there before the police started their search. She dumped her hoodie, dusted herself down and began jogging along the footpath. She knew only 250 yards would mean she was on the main bus route and home and dry.

*

Charlie and Phillipa walked into the interview room. Pearce and his solicitor were already in place, chatting. They fell silent when the officers joined them.

"Good afternoon," Charlie said, "I am DS Dunne and this is DC Davies. Can you confirm your name for the sake of the tape please?"

"Garry Pearce," Garry announced.

"Sean Millard, solicitor," the other gentleman announced.

Charlie began the interview. "Garry Pearce you were arrested this morning on suspicion of causing or conspiring to cause murder and assaulting a police officer. Do you understand?"

"Yes but I didn't do anything," Pearce insisted.

"When we visited your pub, my colleague and I asked you about your relationship with Louisa Smith. You became very aggressive and refused to answer our questions."

Pearce interrupted, "I am really sorry. After seeing what Mark and Annie are going through, I like to keep my private life, completely private. I don't want everyone knowing my business."

In the adjacent room, Harry and the Super listened to his every word. They were interrupted by the desk sergeant, barging into the room. "Ma'am, sir. I have just received a message from the CAD office. There has been an assault at the Technology College; Ms Swift was assaulted. She is on her way to the Leeds General Infirmary."

"Harry, have this interview suspended. You and Phillipa go to the hospital; I will go with Charlie to the college," the Superintendent announced.

Harry entered the interview room, whispered in Phillipa's ear. Phillipa announced, "Interview suspended."

"Why? How long do you anticipate holding my client?" Sean demanded.

"We will let you know in due course."

Phillipa and Charlie left the room.

*

"Ms Swift?" the doctor asked as he entered the cubicle.

222

Annie nodded.

The doctor placed the X-rays on the machine and switched on the light. He closely scrutinised the images. "Erm... well... it would appear the tibia has become displaced again. Clean break, no fragments."

Annie listened but the pain relief had not yet kicked in. Mark stormed through the curtain. He threw his arms around her. Annie began sobbing uncontrollably.

"You're safe now love," Mark tried soothing her. He looked up to see the doctor staring at them both.

"Sorry," Mark said.

"That's perfectly all right. The X-ray shows a clean break across the original fracture. We will reset it, put on a new cast and see how you go, but you are going to have to stop getting into these scrapes!" the doctor said as he disappeared out of the cubicle.

"What happened Annie?" Mark asked.

The curtain opened and Matt and Ed came running in.

"You're making a habit of this," Matt said.

Annie recounted the events of the day and then again when Harry and Phillipa arrived.

Harry questioned Annie, "Do you have any idea what she wanted to talk about?"

Annie confessed, "I don't know, it all happened so fast. Erm... Chadwick said she wanted to talk to me. I was scared so I turned away. She grabbed me and caught me off balance." Annie's voice broke.

"It's okay Mum," Ed said with tears in his eyes.

"We'll leave it for now. Get some rest," Harry said as he squeezed Annie's hand. Phillipa smiled at Annie. As Harry turned to leave, Annie declared, "Harry... I don't think she meant to hurt me."

Harry asked, "What makes you think that?"

"The look on her face when I fell. She was panic stricken; her face was sheet white and she ran."

Harry left the family to recover once more from another ordeal. Seeing Annie frail and frightened again, made him even more determined to solve this crime.

"Let's get back. We need to interview Pearce," Harry declared. "Correction, YOU need to interview Pearce," Harry added. "We need to bring Chadwick in too."

*

Shit! Chadwick thought as she turned the corner of her street and saw the police car parked opposite her house. What was she going to do? Where was she going to go? Everything she owned was in that house. I could hand myself in, she thought. She hadn't meant to hurt Annie; she was trying to warn her. Since the accident, things had got out of hand. She had never wanted that and the money she was paid, it was never enough to cover attempted murder. The trouble was, past form, would for sure lead the police to the wrong conclusions. Chadwick knew she would end up back in that nuthouse and that was NOT going to happen.

The only option for Chadwick was to try one of her work friends. She had to get her story straight. What was she going to say? She was innocent? Well, sort of.

*

"How you doing?" Matt asked Mark as he walked into the kitchen. Mark was in a world of his own.

"It's been another long day," Mark said stirring the hot chocolate for the thousandth time.

"Is that for Mum?" Matt enquired.

"Yes it is. I'd better take it to her before it gets cold."

"Or before you stir the pattern off the cup," Matt said. Mark cracked a very faint smile and disappeared out of the room.

He found Annie fast asleep with the television emitting a dull moan. He switched it off, turned the lights out. He kissed Annie, stroked her cheek and left.

*

"It's going to be a late one," Harry announced to Phillipa.

Phillipa agreed. "Mum's with the kids so I can stay all night if necessary."

"We'll interview Pearce first thing tomorrow. That gives us about ten hours to get as much information gathered as possible."

"Harry," the Super popped her head around the door. "We've interviewed the college staff and witnesses. It was Chadwick, we have her on CCTV entering and leaving the building. A warrant has been issued for her arrest. We've alerted all ports and airports. I have sanctioned the overtime for your team and the press officer will meet us shortly to work through a statement and an appeal for help in finding Chadwick. She must be close by. Everything, including her passport was found in her home."

"What about Pearce?" Harry asked. "Can we apply for a search warrant now?"

"We don't have any connection with him, other than him being a friend of the victim, which as far as I know hasn't yet been made a crime. Bring me a solid evidential connection and I will gladly sanction a search warrant. I will let you know when the press officer arrives." She left.

"Right then let's get to work. You concentrate on Chadwick with Charlie," Harry instructed. "I'll chase uniform on the CCTV at the car hire company. I'll check to see if we have Pearce's DNA and whether it can be matched with that in the car."

Phillipa asked, "What evidence was lifted from Chadwick's place?"

"Good question, that's your starting point. Let's hope there's a laptop and some mobile phones there," Harry said.

Charlie added, "Yes with Pearce's number called frequently."

"Yes quite," Harry added as he left the room.

"Oh just one more thing," Harry said re-emerging around the doorframe. "Has anyone checked with Internet Providers about the IP address? Get onto Computer Forensics, pick their brains please." Harry did actually leave this time.

Harry walked out into the night's air; he needed to think clearly and really wished he hadn't stopped smoking. He could walk to the petrol station at the top of the road. Resisting the temptation to break five years' hard work, Harry opted to pace up and down and passive smoke from a number of officers that had lined the route.

"Evening sir." Harry was acknowledged by a number of officers. He was a bit of a station celebrity and had served at this location for twenty-eight years. Not everyone liked him but he'd got the job done and been commended for it three times.

The night air was fresh, more like the beginning of February than October. Stars twinkled prominently in the deep blue sky. Harry couldn't decide whether he could see his breath in the cold or whether it was remnants of the smoke from his colleagues.

As he wandered back to the main entrance, he saw Phillipa's silhouette coming towards him. "Sir the search at Chadwick's flat found nothing. No mobile phones, laptops, nothing."

It was a blow especially for the interview with Pearce.

"Shit! Shit! Shit!" Harry jumped on the spot in frustration, which drew unwanted attention from a few passers-by.

Phillipa interrupted the mini tantrum. "And the press officer is waiting for you in the Super's office."

Two drunks were harassing the desk sergeant in the foyer. Harry sidestepped them and guided Phillipa through the open door.

"Well unless we can get a confession out of Pearce, I can see us having to let him go," Phillipa suggested.

"Don't you think I know that?" Harry snapped. "This case is driving me insane! We are missing something that's staring us in the face," Harry declared.

He stormed off to see the press officer. This part of the job he hated. Why was it necessary to have some jumped up little graduate reshuffle his words and use one hundred instead of twenty to say the same thing?

Harry took a deep breath and entered the Super's office. The press officer looked about twelve! He was in a double-breasted suit and looked like he'd walked straight out of a picture from Eton.

"Good evening DCI Fisher, I am Leo Francis." Oh my God Harry thought, a poncey name too!

"Evening," he replied sceptically.

They went through the events of the day. Harry suddenly had a bright idea, a flash of inspiration. He announced, "I would like the press release to appeal to Chadwick for her help."

The Super stared open-mouthed. "Explain please," she said.

"Ms Swift said she felt Chadwick was trying to warn her not harm her. If that is the case she is frightened about something or someone. If we issue a press statement advising she is not wanted but rather needed to help the police. If we can let her believe she is not in trouble but can help us, she may buckle and hand herself in."

"Okay run with it. Let's see what it will bring in," the Super agreed. "You need to speak to Mr Smith and Ms Swift and let them know what is happening. I don't want them thinking we've lost our senses!"

"No I'm sure Annie, Ms Swift will understand. She was the one who insisted Chadwick was not at the college to hurt her."

The press release was finalised and Harry left feeling fairly smug. He hoped Chadwick would come forward with evidence before he had to release Pearce but knew in all honestly, unless he got a confession, he would have to release him in the morning.

Harry rang Ms Swift but she had already retired. He explained to Mark what the press release would say and why. Harry got the impression that, whilst Mark agreed with his thoughts, he was not really listening.

Walking back into the incident room, Phillipa announced, "Well we don't have any of the things we hoped for tonight. Let's go for a drink and start afresh tomorrow morning."

"Aye go on then, you've twisted my arm," Harry replied.

*

"Thank you," Phillipa said to the waiter as he pulled the chair out for her. The restaurant was crisp white with a beige contrasting décor. It was lit very romantically.

Phillipa leant over the table. "This is lovely Harry. I feel under-dressed coming straight from work."

"Nonsense, you look great and fit in very well. Now before we argue I want to make it clear, this is my treat."

"No, No," Phillipa argued.

"Yes, yes," Harry said. "Phillipa," Harry put his hand on Phillipa's hand and she squeezed it a little, "please let me do this. You can always pay next time."

The evening was so free and happy. The case was forgotten and so were their sad, miserable home lives. Instead, they lived within the moment. They flirted and laughed so loud that it attracted frowns and disdain from other customers. They didn't care; they were relaxed and happy.

By 10.30 they had eaten as much as they could and shared two bottles of red wine. There was no way either of them could drive.

"Come on," Phillipa said as they left the restaurant entrance. She grabbed Harry's hand and staggered across the bridge to the taxi rank. They stumbled into a taxi and Phillipa recited Harry's address to the taxi driver. They sat in the back like lovesick teenagers. Phillipa rested her hand on the top of Harry's left thigh and looked him straight in the eyes. Harry stroked his hand across her face and brushed her hair away. She cupped her other hand around the back of his neck and moved forward slowly. She kissed him tenderly on the lips, stopped, hesitated and kissed him again with great intensity that took both their breaths away. Phillipa wanted to have him there and then.

Harry had wanted this for a while and certainly had no objections. He was so eager for the journey to be over; he wanted her in his bed. His heart had yearned for her even more so than his groin. He faced a huge dilemma – he wanted to make love to her so much but wanted it to be when she was sober rather than half cut on wine. He wanted her to want him without the influence of alcohol.

The taxi pulled up outside Harry's apartment in the centre of Harrogate. The swish apartment was part of a three storey converted Georgian house. Phillipa dragged him out of the taxi and kissed him again on the lips. Her silky tongue slipped between his teeth. Sod the moral high ground, he thought. He wrapped his arms around her and slipped his tongue between hers and kissed her. She gasped and rubbed her whole body against his.

Harry fumbled for the door keys in his trouser pocket.

"Let me help you," Phillipa whispered in his ear and she slipped her hand into his pocket. "Ooh that's not the keys," she laughed.

Harry had never seen Phillipa like this. She had always been reserved and dignified. Harry stretched his arms up to unlock the Yale. Phillipa slipped her arms around his waist and rested her head on his shoulder. "Come on sir I have something I want to show you," and she pressed her breasts against his back.

Harry felt he was going to explode before they had even got into the hallway. He threw his jacket on the chair in the hall and pulled Phillipa towards him. She yelped in delight and threw her arms around his neck.

Harry whispered, "Are you sure about this?" as he spun her round so she had her back resting on his chest. He kissed the back of her neck slowly and ran his hands along her shoulders.

Phillipa gasped and replied, "I have wanted this for so long Harry. I have wanted you since our Christmas kiss. Now stop talking and fuck me."

Harry directed her to walk slowly forward and opened the door to reveal an unmade king size bed. Phillipa gave a huge sigh and started to unbutton her blouse. Harry covered her hand with his and together they undressed her. Her body was perfect. When her blouse and bra hit the floor, Harry turned Phillipa around to face him. He ran his hands across her back and kissed her lips whilst she undid his shirt buttons to reveal a bronzed chest sporting a few grey hairs. She ran her fingers down his body until she reached his trousers. She ran her fingers along his waistline, which made him wince with delight. She slowly undid his trousers and disposed of them.

They walked together slowly and he placed her on the bed. He slowly climbed onto her. Their breathing was like two steam trains, neither of them could contain their excitement.

Phillipa wriggled free and grabbed Harry by the wrists and pinned him to the bed. She climbed astride him and leant over, pushing her breasts on his chest and whispered, "Well sir, I think it's my turn to be in charge tonight."

Harry winced, he was getting more excited by the minute. "Please Ma'am don't be gentle with me," he whispered.

Phillipa smiled. "I don't intend to be. Now where are your handcuffs?"

Harry nodded in excitement. He drew his handcuffs from the floor and handed them to Phillipa. "Please do whatever you want to me," he said.

Phillipa pulled him by the hair up to the top of the bed. He complied. She cuffed his hands to the steel frame of the bed. Harry was so excited, he tried to kiss her but she pushed him back to the bed. "Do as you're told," she ordered.

"Yes Ma'am but please Ma'am I want you."

"I know you do, in good time," she whispered as she bit his ear lobe.

Phillipa took the pillowcase and used it as a blindfold on Harry. Now Harry was at her mercy. There was no turning back, he had to trust her.

"Now you are ready," Phillipa said as she got off the bed. Harry could hear her and feel her close by but not touching him. He felt her hair brush past his bare legs and then let out a pleasurable cry as her mouth engulfed his hard piece. He had to concentrate really hard not to come immediately. This was fantastic, way beyond any sexual fantasies he had had in his office or in this very bed.

Phillipa crawled up the bed released one of Harry's hands from the handcuffs, and lay at the side of him. "Now use your fingers to pleasure me," she ordered. Harry obliged and could feel her wet body next to his. She positioned her mouth next to his ear and deep breathed into it increasing the intensity of his desire. As if to sense how close he was, Phillipa climbed onto his body and slipped him inside of her. She rode up and down screaming as he re-entered her. She slipped the blindfold off to reveal herself coming on top of Harry. Harry burst like a firework on New Year's Eve. After being released, he held her tight in place and savoured the moment.

After what seemed an eternity, Phillipa opened her eyes, looked down at Harry and smiled. She leant forward to release Harry's other hand from the handcuffs and whispered, "And that is just the start of what I want to give you, sir." She slid off him and laid half on, half off his body. Harry wrapped his arms around her after wrapping them both up in the sheet.

25

It was 5.15 a.m. when Harry looked at the clock. Phillipa was doing a fabulous impression of a starfish across the bed with absolutely no bed linen on her. He instantly went hard at the sight of her. He slipped out of bed and went to the bathroom. When he returned Phillipa had moved onto her side facing the window. Harry crept around the bed and climbed in behind her. He slipped his hands around her waist and started kissing the back of her neck. His hands wandered across her breasts and he squeezed. Phillipa let out a pleasurable moan, so he squeezed a little more. He moved one hand down her stomach and placed it between her legs. He could feel the warmth of her pubic hair and she complied by parting her legs slightly. Harry obliged and slipped his fingers inside. Phillipa's moans grew louder.

Harry whispered, "Good morning Ma'am, my turn to show you what I have," as he increased the movement of his fingers.

"Keep going sir," Phillipa turned her head slightly and kissed the side of his lips. Harry kissed her back. He moved his naked body closer to hers and rubbed his erection across her backside. Phillipa moved her body closer to him signalling her approval. Harry pushed himself inside Phillipa from behind. Her little cry demonstrated he had hit the spot.

"Oh yes," she moaned as Harry thrust it inside her.

The pair were frantic, both wanted it so badly. Harry thrust it harder to Phillipa's moans of more. They both climaxed together and Harry released himself from her.

"Boy I'm going to have a heart attack," Harry said, holding his pounding chest.

Phillipa, laid flat on her back recovering. "Ha no you're not. You're fitter than a twenty-year-old."

"Thanks," Harry laughed.

Phillipa, having regained her breath turned over and slipped her head under his arm. Harry cuddled her. For ten minutes, nothing was said.

"Well I suppose we better get up. Big day today," Harry announced.

"Urm," Phillipa replied.

"Do you want the shower first?" Harry asked.

"No," Phillipa replied, "We'll go in together." She smiled and closed her eyes again.

Harry shook Phillipa from him and turned the shower on. Phillipa crawled out of bed and joined Harry in the shower. They got dressed and ordered a taxi.

"We need to go past mine first. I need a change of clothes," Phillipa declared.

"Why?" Harry asked.

Phillipa glared at him smiling. He knew exactly why. If they turned up together in last night's clothes, the office jungle drums would beat faster than Lewis Hamilton's car.

Harry was curious and whispered, "So where does this leave us?"

"Hopefully at work, it's a taxi," Phillipa laughed.

Harry squeezed her hand. "You know what I mean."

Phillipa sighed, "Well last night was the best night I have ever had, ever! I want to be with you Harry."

Harry smiled. "I was hoping you would say that."

Phillipa replied, "We will have to keep it under wraps for now especially during this case. I don't want Liam getting wind of it 'cos he'll make trouble with the kids and we definitely have to be careful at work."

Harry nodded. "We'll take each day as it comes."

They both laughed. After changing at the house, Phillipa and Harry arrived at work in an optimistic mood. Today was going to be a good day, Harry thought.

*

Mark watched Annie sleep. She was so peaceful but he was going to have to leave soon for a day of interviews in Manchester. Should he take her with him or would she want to stay here? Annie opened one eye and beamed a smile at Mark.

Mark said, "Morning sleeping beauty."

Annie smiled. "What time is it?"

"Six, forty-five," Mark replied. "I have to set off to Manchester soon. Would you like to come with me?"

Annie shuffled herself up into a seated position and thought for a while and answered, "What are the boys' plans today?"

"They have both gone for a breakfast meeting then will be back about eleven," Mark replied.

Annie held Mark's hand. "I'm going to stay here if that's okay with you?" Mark frowned. Annie continued, "I'm still tired Mark. Yesterday came as a bolt out of the blue. I am going to stay here and rest today. I need to speak to the doctors and get a note for the college. I'm going to speak to Elspeth and ask for compassionate leave until the police have sorted all this out."

"I understand. Harry rang last night to say they are issuing a press release this morning about yesterday. He said I had to tell you they were appealing for Chadwick to come forward to help them rather than making her a suspect. Harry thinks you are right, someone else was using her."

Annie nodded. "Good, let's hope they can put a stop to all this. I've not had a day off sick since I started this job! You go to Manchester. I'm safe in the house. I have resigned myself to being here now until I can get this stupid cast off." Annie pointed to her leg. "Do you have time to help me get dressed before you go?"

Mark nodded. He helped Annie to get dressed and helped her downstairs. He set up her laptop in the dining room and even brought the wireless printer downstairs next to her.

After a small breakfast, Mark set off for Manchester. So apprehensive of leaving Annie behind, Mark rang Harry to let him know she was home alone. Harry was very chirpy and agreed to send a police car to sit in the street outside the house. Mark was so relieved and knew now he could get down to business.

*

"Get up Sue now!" James shouted. "You're on the telly."

Chadwick could barely focus. She had taken refuge in her work colleague's spare room and had been scant with the truth.

"What?" she barked as she climbed out of the makeshift bed.

"There's a picture of you on the telly," he repeated.

She stumbled into the kitchen diner and watched with disbelief the rubbish that was coming out of the copper's mouth.

"See, if you go to the police they can help you," James said naïvely.

"No Jim," Chadwick responded. "You don't know what they're like. They say that then when I go in; they'll lock me up again."

James shook his head. "Well you're not going to work today. Lie low here. No one saw you come in last night."

"Ta Jim," Chadwick said. "Just 'til I figure out what to do next."

Chadwick went back to the bedroom. Did she trust him not to say owt, she thought. What if he rang the cops? Her first instinct was to run again but she had nowhere to go. She was also safer in the flat than anywhere else. He might be looking for her. There were no messages on her mobile phone, which freaked her out even more. Why had he not returned her calls? It had all got out of hand. She didn't even know Mark and her, not really, but she did need the money she had been given over the years. She thought about how different it would have been had she left and spent the money on setting up elsewhere. She would give anything to turn back the clock. The choices she had made had led her to hiding out in this rat hole. What an idiot she had been!

*

"Well the release has gone out," Harry announced. "Let's see what Pearce has to say for himself."

The Super and Harry took position in the room adjacent to the interviewing room. Pearce and his solicitor were in place once more when Charlie and Phillipa entered the room.

"Good morning," Phillipa said.

A muffled response came back. The solicitor announced, "You better have some new evidence because my client has been detained overnight and as yet there has been nothing to substantiate your suspicions."

Phillipa nodded, "Let's get started shall we?"

"Can you tell me, have you had a sexual relationship with Louisa Smith?" Phillipa set off with the same question that Harry had ended with. Garry glanced at his solicitor who nodded at Garry.

Garry admitted, "Yes I did have a while ago."

Phillipa was taken aback by his forthrightness but her facial expression never changed.

"When did your relationship start?"

Garry paused and confirmed, "About ten years ago." He lied.

Again this shocked Phillipa, she looked at her notes. "So you were seeing Louisa before she divorced Mark Smith?"

"Yes," he admitted, "but their marriage was already over. He had been with someone else and Louisa had found out about it."

Phillipa asked, "Who was the affair with?"

"No idea," Garry lied.

"So you have an affair with your best friend's wife, while they are still married, and you are still best friends?" Phillipa asked.

Garry defended his friendship. "Mark was unaware of our relationship and still is."

"So you make a habit of lying then?"

"Good girl," Harry mumbled as he listened from the adjoining room.

"Are you still together?" Phillipa asked.

"You know we're not," Garry barked.

"Do I?" Phillipa asked.

"Yes. I told you when you and that boss of yours invaded my house."

Phillipa ignored his tone. "When did Louisa move in with you?"

"When she left Mark, she had nowhere to go. She brought Sophie to me."

"You lied to us, you told us she moved to Manchester. Why?"

Garry shrugged his shoulders. "Dunno," he said.

"We could add the charge of wasting police time or perverting the course of justice?"

"DC Phillipa Davies. My client is helping you with your enquiries," Millard scowled.

Phillipa unruffled replied, "Your client assaulted my senior officer."

Phillipa was taking no crap today. She continued, "Why did you lie?"

"Dunno."

"Why?" Phillipa pressed.

Garry stood up, throwing his chair to the floor. "'Cos it's none of your fucking business."

Phillipa didn't even flinch. Calmly she continued, "When did Louisa move out?"

Garry answered, "About five months ago. She said she was moving to Manchester. She got a new international job. She didn't need me anymore."

There was a notable bitterness in his voice.

"Did she take all her stuff with her?"

Garry replied, "As far as I know." He knew what she was getting at. He had used the passport to hire the car.

Phillipa changed tack. "Where were you on the night of Monday 30th September?"

Garry shrugged still seething. "I can't remember, probably at the pub."

"It's important for you to think very carefully where you were." Phillipa's tone never faltered. There was silence. Garry stared at Phillipa. Harry looked on in amusement knowing he would have lost his patience by now but Phillipa was calm and collected.

"Mr Pearce…" Phillipa leant towards her interviewee, "Garry, I just want to eliminate you from the enquiries, which I can't do if you won't allow me to." She paused. "Now where were you on the evening of the 30th September?"

"I was at home, at the pub, all night. My barmaid Maggie can confirm it. You met her when you came to the pub."

Harry left the side room and sent two uniformed officers over to Garry's pub to corroborate, or hopefully in Harry's eyes not corroborate his alibi.

"Thank you. We will check that," Phillipa announced matter of factly.

"Where were you on Thursday 26th September?"

Harry had returned to his spying position and noted an element of surprise on Garry's face when asked about this date. Either he is a brilliant actor or he was genuinely surprised.

"Dunno," Garry said, "maybe cash and carry – Bookers. I go there Thursday to stock up for the weekend."

"Thank you. Do you know a Susan Lawrence?" Phillipa asked.

"No." Harry felt he was lying as he was fidgeting in his seat.

"Do you know a Susan Chadwick?" Phillipa pressed on.

Again Garry lied.

"Do you know of either of these people even if you have not met them?"

Garry hesitated; he had no choice but to make it sound authentic. "Oh yeah. Isn't she the freak that stalked Mark?"

Phillipa smiled. She watched him closely and got the distinct impression he was hiding something. She pressed on, "You see something puzzles me. If she was such a freak, why did you let Sophie believe that her dad had an affair?"

Garry was dumbstruck. "No, no, no I didn't. In fact I told her exactly what happened from beginning to end."

Phillipa announced, "Interview suspended."

Garry's solicitor asked, "How long do you intend to keep my client? He has fully cooperated..."

Phillipa interrupted, "We will corroborate his alibis."

With that the officers left the room.

"Well done," the Super announced as Phillipa joined her and Harry in the separate room.

"Have we checked the alibis?" she asked.

"In the process," Harry replied. "Do you fancy some lunch?"

Phillipa blushed and nodded.

*

"Have we got hold of Louisa Smith?" Phillipa asked while playing with the chicken pasta in front of her.

Harry replied with his mouth full of sandwich, "No. Her PA said she was in Sweden for two weeks."

Phillipa rolled her eyes.

*

About one hour later, the Super called both Harry and Phillipa to her office. Phillipa's head was racing. She felt sure the Super knew about their night together and she was going to get a humiliating telling off.

They both entered her office. She was sitting behind her desk like a disapproving head teacher. Phillipa's heart was racing. The Superintendent looked over the top of her glasses and gestured for them to sit down. Here we go, Phillipa thought.

"Both alibis stand!" The Super delivered the blow. Before either could respond she continued, "We have no choice but to let him go."

Harry nodded, "I know but I know he definitely has something to do with this."

"That may be but unless we find concrete evidence, he is innocent until proven guilty."

No shit Sherlock, Harry thought but echoed a more diplomatic approach. "That's very true Ma'am."

As the custody sergeant provided Garry with his possessions, he couldn't help but smirk at the two onlookers. He turned and walked out of the building with his solicitor.

Phillipa turned to Harry and whispered, "It's only a matter of time before we nail him, sir." She rubbed her hand gently on his and turned away.

Outside, Garry's solicitor passed him a mobile phone. Garry switched it on to find forty-eight missed calls and twenty-nine text messages.

"Jeez I never knew I was so popular!"

Two messages caught his eye, both from Mark Smith.

One read:

> 'Hi Mate. Hope all's well. I'm putting a team into the Leeds Charity Golf Day. There's four in a team – Matt, Ed, me and you if you want to. Let me know.'

Second message read:

> 'Hey Bud, not heard from you. Let me know if you want to play golf on Sunday 3 October."

Shit that's this weekend, Garry thought. He immediately replied:

> 'Sorry been away on business. Yeah would love to join you. How's Annie after her car accident?'

There was an instant response from Mark:

> 'Glad you can make it. She's bearing up. Chadwick turned up at her work, knocked her over and broke her leg again!'

Shit! Garry thought. He knew Chadwick had been trying to get hold of him.

"It's me," he said after waiting for a connection to be made. "What the fuck have you been doing?"

There was silence.

"SUE! WHY did you go see her?"

Still silence.

Garry shouted down the phone, "I am coming to find you, you bitch! You could've blown it all."

Finally Chadwick stammered, "You can't. If you do I will go to the cops."

"You will, WILL YOU!" Garry's tone was menacing and skittish. "And tell them what exactly?" mockingly he continued in a girly voice, "Please sir, I was forced into screwing up Mark's life and made to send text messages and breaking Annie's leg." His rant became even more threatening. "And it wasn't my fault I hired a car that almost killed three people!"

Chadwick burst, "That was all your fucking idea and you did it! I weren't driving, you wanker!"

Chadwick hung up. Garry tried to redial but the phone had been switched off.

*

"Good morning, could I speak with Elspeth please?" Annie asked.

"Hi Annie of course you can. I hope you are okay after yesterday," Julia replied. Julia was Elspeth's PA and by the sound of her voice they were expecting her call.

"Hi Annie, how are you today?" Elspeth asked.

"I'm okay thank you. A bit sore," Annie confessed.

"I understand that. You had a very lucky escape. Thank goodness it didn't end any worse. How can I help you?"

"I would like to take some leave until this is sorted out," Annie asked. She was in no mood for flowering things up or for chitchat.

Elspeth fell silent. "I think we can accommodate that for you. Do you have any idea how long?"

Annie admitted, "I have no idea Elspeth but I can't put people at risk." Annie's voice broke into a controlled sob.

Elspeth was just about to advise her that the Board had already decided they were going to ask her to take leave in any case but when she heard the sob she changed to being sympathetic. "You have five weeks' leave in total. I can also authorise two weeks' compassionate leave. I will approve this immediately. After these two weeks, we'll look at your annual leave. Is that okay?"

Annie was disappointed in her response but agreed. "That would be great thank you. I could do any prep work at home."

Elspeth said, "That won't be necessary. Concentrate on getting well again. Could you email your session plans and timetables over to Julia please? Stay safe and we will see you again soon."

Annie felt deflated when she hung up. Why should she have to give up her beloved job, her freedom, and her life! She cupped her hands around her face and sobbed uncontrollably. When was this nightmare going to end?

*

"It's me. Let me in," Simon pleaded.

"No you stood me up!" Lucy bellowed.

"I can explain. Please let me in. I don't want to talk to you through this stupid machine."

After a few minutes' silence, the buzzer sounded and the door released.

Lucy was standing at the door in pink fleecy pyjamas and barefooted. She was furious with him.

Simon gave her a sheepish smile and knelt before her. "Please, please forgive me. I'm an idiot. I was called away on urgent business."

"You could've called me," Lucy barked.

"I got so stuck into my business, I forgot about our date. What can I say, I'm a jerk!"

"Yes you are," Lucy agreed. She walked into the flat leaving the door open for him to follow her in.

"Glass of wine?" Lucy asked.

"Beer if you have it," Simon requested.

Lucy bent down to reach into the fridge. She squealed as Simon grabbed her hips from behind.

Simon whispered, "Please forgive me," as he brushed his left hand across her breasts. Lucy's legs almost gave way. He continued, "Let's go to bed, I can make it up to you."

Lucy didn't need asking twice. Sexual action had been very limited and since her friend had a new playmate, she wanted one too.

Before Lucy knew it, sex was over. Wow, she thought. She was only just getting started. Simon held her in his arms, her head resting on his heaving chest.

After a while, Lucy asked, "So where did you go on business then?"

"Oh, err… Milton Keynes," Simon advised.

"They don't have phone there then?" Lucy smirked.

Simon snapped, "They do but like I said I was busy!"

Lucy lay in silence.

*

It was early evening when Mark arrived home. He skipped through the door to find Annie sitting at the dining room table with her laptop.

"Now then sexy, how was your day?" Annie asked.

Mark kicked his shoes off and loosened his tie before slipping it over his head and throwing it on the chair beside Annie. He stood behind her chair and draped his arms around her shoulders. Annie let out a sigh and wrapped her arms around his. She felt safe and secure and already felt the tingling sensation – the Mark effect she thought!

He kissed her head gently and whispered, "My day has had something missing 'til now."

Annie's heart melted. He continued, "How was your day Annie?" Mark tightened his grip on Annie.

"It's been fine. I spoke to Elspeth, she confirmed two weeks' compassionate leave then I have to take my annual leave."

Mark sensed Annie's disappointment. He sat on the chair next to her. He placed his hands on her knees and looked straight into her blue eyes. He smiled warmly and kissed her lips. Sympathetically, he whispered, "I'm so sorry Annie. I'll stop working if you like, we could go on holiday?"

Annie sobbed, "Don't be silly. It's coming to the end of your rugby season now and you have to cover the Grand Final, it's the pinnacle of your year. If you want me to I can always come with you and keep you company between shoots."

Mark took Annie's hands in his and kissed her forehead. "Annie I know how much your job means to you and I'm sorry you have to do this. It would be an honour and a real privilege to have you with me every day. I miss you so much when we are apart. All this trouble will come to an end and when it does I will have the most beautiful woman in the world with me. Please, Annie, please don't cry, I can't bear to see you so unhappy. You can be my security."

Annie smiled back. "Your bouncer! Fat chance of that with this!" Annie pointed to her leg. Mark leant forward and kissed the tears on her cheeks. Annie took a huge deep breath. She released her hands from his grip and wrapped her arms around his head. "I love you Mark Smith, with all of my heart. You are kind, gentle, clever and great in bed."

Annie giggled as Mark buried his head into her chest. She kissed the top of his head and slowly moved her fingers across the back of his neck. Mark let out a little sigh of approval. After a few minutes of savouring his position, he lifted his head and looked at Annie. "I have nothing scheduled in after the Grand Final. Would you like to go away on holiday with me?"

"With this on?" Annie pointed to her leg again.

"Yes, why not? We can go somewhere warm," Mark replied.

"I'll end up with one tanned leg and one white one!"

They both laughed.

Mark suggested, "Okay then. I'll take you away for a romantic long weekend. We don't even have to leave the hotel room if you don't want to."

Mark tightened his arms around Annie's shoulders. She could smell his aftershave and wanted him there at the table.

Mark asked, "Do you want to book it with me or can I surprise you?"

For a moment Annie was too busy with her carnal thoughts but realised Mark was expecting an answer. "You book it as a surprise please."

He smirked, "I was hoping you would say that. You're gonna love what I have in mind. Do you want to leave the day after the Grand Final?"

Annie thought for a while, cupped her hands around his cheeks, kissed him on the lips and replied, "We can't. If Matt's team wins, there'll be a parade of the trophy and we have to be there. We can leave in the afternoon after that though." Annie was desperate not to dampen Mark's spirits but Mark knew how important it was to her and the boys to celebrate together. Besides he wanted to be there too.

"No problem my little lady. I will sort it," Mark said.

Annie's mood lifted as Mark started to prepare dinner. She watched him parade around in the kitchen in his navy Armani trousers and a white double-cuffed shirt. His bare feet were a real turn on for her. He was in home mode now and the domestic god image really suited him.

"What are you smiling at?" Mark asked, whilst chopping the onions.

"I didn't know I was. You!" she said.

Mark smiled. "And what has amused you Ms Swift?"

"You in your expensive work clothes and that very sexy apron," Annie laughed.

Mark looked down at the apron in amusement. "This? Sexy? Wait 'til I wear it with nothing underneath." Mark walked slowly and provocatively over to Annie. Annie held out her arms and wrapped them around his waist. Her head rested on the side of his trousers. "Ooh while you're down there," Mark said and laughed.

Annie raised her head to look at Mark. "You wish," and laughed.

Mark wiggled his hips in her face and she brushed her hand across the front of his trousers. Annie used Mark's body to rise out of her seat. She stood in front of him with her hands around his waist and bit his ear. Mark winced and grabbed her tightly.

Annie whispered, "Oh I want you now! I have wanted you since you walked in that door!"

Annie pulled Mark's head towards her and kissed him passionately letting her tongue dance around inside his mouth. She was not letting him go and pushed her tongue deeper inside his mouth. Mark responded. He had never been kissed as passionately as this and he wanted Annie to know he felt the same way as she did. The deep desire and passion they shared for each other was immense.

"Oh my God, will you two get a room?" Ed interrupted as he walked into the kitchen.

Annie blushed.

"Ha, that serves you right for not helping me carry the shopping in," Matt said as he burst into the kitchen with half a dozen Sainsbury's bags.

"What have you been buying?" Mark asked trying to hide the bulge in his trousers and to subdue the passion that had been aroused by their mother.

Matt disappeared back out to the car before replying. In a flash he was back. "These! For you Mum." Matt presented his mum with a huge bouquet of flowers. "For you from Ed and me. Just to say how much we appreciate you and thank you." Matt kissed his mum on the forehead. Annie burst into tears.

"Thank you so much, they are beautiful."

Ed hugged his mum. "Not as beautiful as you."

"Mark just so you know, we appreciate you too. We got you this."

Matt handed Mark a bottle of twenty-five-year-old single malt whiskey. Mark was stunned. He had never known such acts of kindness and certainly had never been the recipient of them from Louisa or Sophie.

"I don't know what to say. Wow, thank you but you really didn't have to."

Ed remarked, "We know but we want you to know we think you are great and so glad Mum met you. You've accepted all of us into your home and we love it here."

Mark opened his mouth to speak but Ed continued, "Yes Mark, even with everything that is going on."

Matt added, "You can open it when I bring my Grand Final ring home."

Matt put out his hand for Mark to shake it. Mark pulled Matt towards him and whispered, "I will hold you to that."

He released Matt and walked towards Ed who instinctively sidestepped Mark. They all laughed as Mark caught Ed and hugged him.

"So what's for tea old man?" Ed asked as he peered into the fridge and came out with three bottles of beer.

"Chilli and rice," Mark announced.

The boys shared banter whilst Annie sat and listened. She was very, very happy. Maybe she had lost her independence, but this was what life should be about. Her boys had grown into fine young gentlemen; both were caring and considerate and more importantly both adored Mark, maybe not as much as she did.

"Sue, you have to go to the police," Jim said. Chadwick was hunched up on the floor of the flat with her knees to her chest and her arms wrapped around her legs.

"I can't, you don't understand," she said.

"It can't be that bad. The police said they would help you."

Chadwick sat in silence. Jim knew that she wouldn't listen to reason. He had promised not to intervene and left her to her own devices. Jim changed the subject. "Are you coming in to work tomorrow?"

"No," Chadwick barked, "they'll be there and if they're not, he will be!"

Jim was confused. "Who will be?"

"The police or HIM!" she replied.

"You're starting to scare me now. Who is HIM? You're in more trouble than you're letting on, aren't you?" Jim asked.

Chadwick didn't know what to tell him. If she told him anything, he could go to the police for sure. She couldn't risk them or HIM finding her.

"I'm off to bed," she announced. She stood up and left the room.

"Penny for them?" Phillipa asked placing her tray next to Harry's on the canteen table.

"Hi love, you okay?" Harry asked.

"I am but are you?" Phillipa replied.

Harry nodded, "I was just thinking about last night." He smiled and Phillipa smiled back, nudged his arm and leant towards his ear. "It was fantastic. You sir, are fantastic," she whispered.

Harry wriggled in his seat. Phillipa was amused. "Yes I've been feeling like that all day too," she said.

"Have you?" Harry asked, very surprised.

"Oh yes. I was really wet earlier. Kept thinking about your handcuffs."

Harry laughed nearly choking on his pie.

Phillipa continued, "I swear the Super knows, she could see it on my face."

Harry shook his head and whispered, "You are a very naughty girl."

Phillipa replied, "I know," and she reached under the table and placed her hand on his groin. She could feel how hard he was. Harry groaned.

"Behave otherwise I will have to punish you later," the corner of his mouth curled slightly.

Phillipa's response made Harry choke again. "Yes please sir!"

Phillipa began eating her salad and ignored how uncomfortable Harry found it to sit at the table. She found it highly amusing and was turned on by the effect she had on him.

"Kids are at their dad's this weekend," Phillipa announced.

"Are they now?" Harry replied.

"They are sir. Back Sunday, nine p.m."

"I'm off Sunday," Harry said.

"Me too. Funny that isn't it?" She leant towards him and placed her hand on his thigh. "I asked for my day off to be changed."

Harry smiled, "You did, did you? But I might have something planned."

Phillipa's heart sank. "Well I hope that your plan includes me." Phillipa brushed her hand over his groin again.

"Argh! You're a very bad girl. I will have to punish you on Sunday!"

"Not sure I can wait 'til then," Phillipa said.

"Me neither," Harry said.

"Your place or mine?" Phillipa enquired.

"Mine," Harry said, "I want you tied to my bed. You're coming tonight!"

"Yes please sir but I can't the kids don't go until tomorrow morning."

"Now behave yourself please. We have to get back to work." Harry's voice was authoritative.

"Yes sir." Phillipa smiled as she left the table.

*

Back at the incident room, Harry pondered their next move. They desperately needed to locate Chadwick and review all the forensic evidence.

Harry announced, "We have holes in this investigation where the forensic evidence is still awaited. First thing Monday we need to chase all these loose ends. The answers are definitely here. I am going to call and see Annie on Monday."

"Yes sir," Phillipa smiled.

Harry stood up and walked over to Phillipa. He checked that the window blinds were closed. He stood at the side of Phillipa's chair and tugged it in his direction. Standing astride her chair, Harry leant over and kissed Phillipa passionately pushing his tongue deep inside her mouth. She pulled his legs in between in her knees and squeezed tightly. She wanted him now, Sunday was too long to wait. He had woken her up from her mundane life and she was alive again.

"I'm looking forward to Sunday," Harry said, as he stood upright. He looked down on her and smiled. "Come home with me, just for an hour. Tell your mum you're working late, please I need you."

Phillipa sighed, "I can't the kids need me tonight."

"Sunday it is then," Harry whispered as he left the room.

*

Annie woke up to an empty bed. She could hear background music and voices downstairs.

Mark, Matt and Ed were working out. Mark puffed as he worked on the treadmill. He announced, "I'm going to book a couple of days in New York for your mum and me after the Grand Final."

Ed whooped, "Good on you!"

Matt added, "Great but you'll be here if I win won't you?"

"Of course we will. I'm booking flights for late Sunday and we'll be back Wednesday or Thursday."

"That's fantastic. Mum will love that," Matt said.

"That's not all," Mark announced, "I'm going to ask her to marry me."

Matt and Ed stopped exercising. Shit! They're not happy, thought Mark.

They both jumped off their machines, danced a very childish jig and hugged each other. Mark watched in amusement. When they had finished Ed stood in front of Matt, coughed and held out his hand.

"What?" asked Matt.

"You know," Ed replied. "Tenner?"

"Oh yeah," Matt laughed and turned to Mark. "Ed bet me a tenner you would ask Mum to marry you before the year was out."

Mark smiled. "So you're happy then?"

"Jeez Mark, we are over the moon!" Ed hugged Mark. Matt nodded, smiled and stuck two thumbs up in the air.

"Thank God for that," Mark said. "Not a word to anyone! Your mum doesn't even know where we are going."

"When will you tell her?" Ed asked.

"At the airport," Mark replied.

"Sound," Ed said.

Mark continued, "I'm going to propose on the Empire State Building – cheesy I know but your mum loves those old movies so I thought I'd make it cheesy and special!"

Matt laughed, "She will really love that Mark."

They heard Annie's hobbling footsteps coming down the hallway.

"Shush! Not a word," Mark whispered.

"What are you three plotting?" Annie asked entering the gym. She walked up to Mark and kissed him.

"Nothing!" all three of them said simultaneously.

"Now I'm worried," she laughed. "Breakfast anyone? I'm starving this morning. Must have worked up an appetite."

"MUM! Too much information," Ed said.

Mark laughed.

"I'll make breakfast," Matt said.

At the breakfast table, spirits were high. The boys discussed the golf day and Annie announced, "Lucy's coming over this afternoon. Why don't you boys go have a round of golf, you need the practice for tomorrow now I can't play in your team."

The boys scoffed and Ed replied, "Don't mind if we do!"

Mark was less enthusiastic. "Are you sure? I won't see much of you tomorrow, we'll be entertaining the guests. I was hoping to spend some quality time with you today."

"Honestly Mark we can have an early night," Annie smiled.

Ed and Matt tutted and shook their heads.

"Honestly, Lucy and I are going to open a bottle of wine and have a girlie chat."

"Okay if you are sure but you will come to the charity day tomorrow won't you? I need you to help me with the guests and you're brilliant at chatting with people."

Annie rolled her eyes, she really loved playing golf but was literally handicapped.

"Oh please Mum, please come. You can sit in the golf cart and score!" Ed pleaded.

Annie smiled. "Well how can I refuse but if it's cold or raining I'll be in the lounge getting drunk. I love Oulton Hall, it's a beautiful place."

Mark held his hand out across the table and Annie placed her hand in his. He said, "I love you Annie Swift."

Ed joked, "Come on Matt, that's our cue to leave."

Mark laughed, "No it's our cue to go upstairs." Mark pulled Annie's arm.

"Ergh! Too much information," Ed said scampering out of the room.

*

Annie lay in bed most of the morning, reading the papers while Mark did his best to distract her. At one o'clock the boys left as Lucy walked in.

"Hi guys," she said bouncing into the hall. "Jesus Annie, look at the size of this place," she added.

It was definitely the right time for the boys to exit. Matt found Lucy overbearingly enthusiastic about everything and very childlike. He could put up with her for his mum's sake but only in small doses. All three lined up to kiss and hug Annie. Once they had left, Annie poured the wine and sat on the opposite sofa to Lucy.

Taking a gulp of wine, Lucy spoke first. "How are you Annie? It was awful what happened and I miss you so much." Tears welled into her eyes.

Annie smiled. "I am okay Lucy. Honestly, I have my three fabulous boys and I have time off work to spend with them. I know it's hard to believe but I am really happy. Matt plays in the Grand Final on Saturday and both boys will be playing for Leeds next year AND I have a wonderful man."

"But?" Lucy interrupted.

"I just want all this trouble to stop," Annie said. She decided to tell Lucy everything. Lucy sat with her mouth wide open, only closing it to tut.

When Annie had finished, Lucy hugged Annie almost smothering her.

"Anyway enough about me, what have you been up to?" Annie asked.

Lucy beamed with excitement. "Oh Annie, Simon and I are getting on great. He stayed the night last night but he's got some sort of an event tomorrow. He's coming round after it though."

Annie suspiciously asked, "You been to his place yet?"

Lucy shook her head whilst taking a large gulp of wine. "Not yet, we haven't had time."

Lucy knew what Annie was getting at but she chose to ignore it although she was starting to have her own doubts about him.

Annie suggested, "Well, I have two spare tickets to the Grand Final this year if you and Simon are interested in coming."

Lucy hesitated. "Err I don't know, I'll have to ask him. He might not want to."

"Well the seats aren't with us and you could stay in a different hotel. We could just meet up for a drink."

Lucy thought for a minute. "Yes, why not. It can't do any harm can it? I'd really like to see Matt play."

Annie was looking forward to meeting the elusive Simon.

Changing the subject Annie announced, "Mark's taking me away for a couple of days after the Grand Final." She hesitated. "Don't say anything but I think he's going to propose."

Lucy let out an almighty shriek and jumped to her feet clapping her hands. "That's great news Annie, brilliant! Can I be bridesmaid?"

Annie laughed out loud. "He hasn't asked me yet."

The girls chatted away for hours. The girl talk was interrupted by a text on Lucy's phone.

"It's from Simon," she announced and blushed as she read the message. "He wants to know when I'll be home so he can come and see me." Lucy smiled. She wanted to stay with her friend but had the urge to run home to see her man.

"It's okay if you want to get off. Mark and the boys will be back soon," Annie nodded. "I'll call a taxi for you."

Lucy replied to her text. As they waited for the taxi, the boys returned home. Mark walked through everyone giddily towards Annie and gave her a long, loving kiss, which took her breath away.

He whispered, "I love you Annie." He sat on the arm of the chair beside her and held her hand.

He is so romantic, thought Lucy. She gave her kisses and left. Leaving the room, Lucy turned to Annie. "I," she paused, "we – shall see you next Saturday at the Grand Final."

Annie explained to a confused looking Mark. "I've given Lucy two complimentary tickets for the final. She and Simon are going to stay in a different hotel to us but meet up for a drink."

Mark replied, "That will be great. See you next week then Lucy."

When Lucy had left, the boys eagerly shared their round of golf with Annie, in great detail! Ed and Matt talked over each other, like excited children and like old times, and Mark joined in when he could. Mark watched Annie closely and loved the way her eyes illuminated when the boys spoke to her. He adored this incredible woman and loved the two boys dearly, it was really hard not to. Both had great, larger than life but very different personalities.

*

The taxi pulled up and Lucy's beaming smile could be seen between the droplets of rain on the car window. She could see Simon's silhouette by her front door and she waved to him.

She skipped up the path. "Sorry," Lucy shouted as she ran from the taxi to her front door. "Went to spend the day with my best friend, Annie."

He almost asked how she was but stopped himself just in time. "Who is Annie?" he opted to ask.

Lucy replied, unlocking the door, "She is my best friend from work. She's been having a really bad time of it. Some nutter tried to kill her and her new boyfriend."

"Ooh that sounds bad." He tried his best not to smirk.

"That's not the half of it," Lucy replied. "Beer?"

Simon nodded.

Lucy continued, "Anyway whatever this nutter is trying to do is not working."

"What do you mean?" Simon asked.

"Well if he's trying to split them up, it's doing the opposite. Mark is taking Annie away to propose to her soon."

Almost spitting beer everywhere he said, "Are they now?"

Lucy looked him up and down and wasn't quite sure what his change in attitude meant. "Yes, he is going to propose on holiday after the Grand Final at the weekend."

Lucy could see the news had distracted him. His portly face was red and he was staring into his bottle of beer.

"It's okay Simon, I won't be expecting a marriage proposal from you anytime soon."

Realising he was acting strangely, he smiled but it was really hard for him to remain focused on this woman when he had things to arrange.

"So you had a good time then?" Simon asked dragging her to sit on his lap.

"Yes," Lucy said kissing his lips, "I did but not as good as I am going to have with you."

Lucy rose from his lap and knelt in front of him. She had never done this before but always wanted to try it. She unzipped his trousers and he obligingly slid down the sofa. She pulled out his piece and played with it in her hands. Simon gasped and urged her to take him in her mouth. Hesitantly she complied and placed her lips around it. Simon grabbed her hair and forced her mouth onto him. She gagged and pulled away.

"Sorry," she said and steadied herself to try again.

His mind was on other things. How could they contemplate getting married, hadn't they got the message? What was it going to take to show Annie he was not worthy of having anyone? Pearce was furious with them and had to do something.

"Jeez Lucy," he shouted, "put a bit of effort into it!"

Lucy blushed. It was the first time she had done this and the last she thought. It was disgusting and did nothing for her. She couldn't understand why it was doing nothing for him; all her friends had described it as sexy and exciting. Losing his patience, Simon pulled her onto his knee, tore her pants off and slipped himself inside her. She cringed as it hurt. Impatiently he pushed her hips up and down. Lucy was really uncomfortable but dare not show it. She relaxed a little and was relieved when he had reached his pleasure. Lucy slipped off him and sat next to him in silence.

"I forgot to tell you! We've been invited to the Grand Final if you want to go," Lucy announced.

Simon smiled, "Have we? Who with?"

"Well no one. Our tickets are on our own but we can meet up with Mark and Annie for a drink, if you want to. If not, we can just book a different hotel and just us two go."

Simon thought for a while. Lucy was excited. "Come on we can spend the night in a hotel, please."

"Okay I will book the hotel for us," Simon agreed reluctantly.

Simon leant over and kissed her. He knew his next move. He whispered, "Let me take you to bed."

Lucy was so confused. He was very different this time. His hands wandered over her body, he caressed and kissed her tenderly. The lovemaking was soft and gentle. After reaching their peak, they lay in each other's arms and fell asleep.

*

"Did you enjoy your afternoon with Lucy?" Mark asked, getting undressed for bed. Annie was already in bed waiting for him.

"I did yes. She is so naïve and happy, blissfully happy. I wish I had her outlook on life," Annie replied.

"What do you mean?" Mark asked, noting sarcasm in her tone.

"She is blissfully ignorant to the bad things in life. She has no idea at all, bless her."

Mark climbed into bed beside her. Annie immediately snuggled into him and wrapped her good leg over his legs. Mark pulled her close and her head rested on his chest.

"I know what you mean love. She is very childlike for her age. How is she getting on with the new fella?"

Annie took a deep breath to take in Mark's aroma. She kissed his chest. "Okay I think. I can't help but think it's all a bit weird. He doesn't want to be seen with her. I get the feeling she is bigging him up!" Annie looked up at Mark and they both said together, "He's married!" They laughed.

Mark whispered, "Are you happy Annie? I mean really happy?"

Annie shuffled around so she was laid on her front, looking directly at Mark. She leant her chin on her hands, resting her elbows on the pillow. "Mr Smith I am more than happy – I feel at peace. I have found the perfect man and have two great kids. I love you more than I have ever loved anyone."

Mark leant down and kissed her. She obliged and sank her tongue deep into his mouth. Her heart skipped as it always did when he was close to her.

"Make love to me Mr Smith," Annie whispered.

26

The alarm woke Annie at 8.30 a.m. Mark stirred and moaned, "There should be a law against setting the alarm on a Sunday morning."

Annie replied, "It's your golf day."

Mark laughed, "So it is."

Mark pulled Annie towards him and wrapped his arms around her shoulders, leaning her head on his chest. "Are you coming with us?"

Annie replied, "I'm not letting you out of my sight Mr Smith."

Mark kissed her forehead. "I'll run the bath, and you can scrub my back."

"And the rest of your filthy body," Annie added.

"You love it!" Mark said, grabbing her bottom before leaving the bed.

"Oh I like the view!" Annie admired his naked body. Mark responded by flashing his body towards her.

The rest of the morning was manic. The three boys buzzed around the house, collecting the auction items and golf clubs. Annie was on strict instructions not to overdo it. It was going to be a very long day and the boys wanted her to enjoy every minute of it.

Mark declared, "I think we have everything and are ready to go."

Just as Mark was going to shout Annie, she appeared at the top of the stairs wearing black trousers and a white T-shirt. She had a pink scarf tied around her neck and a black cardigan draped over her arm. Mark and the boys stared at her.

Mark declared, "Annie, you look stunning."

Matt and Ed wolf whistled.

"Thank you," Annie said, descending the stairs. "I thought I would make an effort today."

She kissed Mark and the boys. "Now let's make lots of money for the kids today."

The hired minibus pulled up at the gate. Mark let them in and opened the front door to greet it.

Ed commented, "Can't wait 'til you get your Range Rover Mark."

Mark had forgotten about it and agreed, "Yes me too. It should be here next week, we will get it before the Grand Final."

*

The minibus pulled into the long drive up to Oulton Hall. The magnificent seventeenth century building was an impressive sight and Annie never grew tired of the look of it. Guests were already starting to arrive. Leon had volunteered to meet and greet people as they arrived. Marcus and Billy were standing in the entrance of the hotel, their smiles beamed as Annie walked from the minibus.

Marcus held out his arms. "Annie you look fantastic."

Annie smiled. "Thank you Marcus, I hope you're well. Billy." She nodded her head in acknowledgement. The boys joined her and Matt and Ed shook both Marcus and Billy's hands. Mark disappeared inside to see who had arrived.

Marcus teased the boys, "Right boys I hope you are looking forward to receiving a golf lesson from your bosses."

Ed scoffed, Matt just smiled. "We shall see," he said confidently.

"You may be outstanding rugby players but this is my patch now," Marcus added.

Ed couldn't resist the bait. "Okay then put your money where your mouth is."

Annie threw a disapproving glance at Ed. Marcus placed his hand on Annie's arm and said, "It's okay Annie I started this. Besides I like his cockiness."

"So what shall it be?" Ed asked Marcus.

"I bet you a hundred pounds we beat you today," Marcus suggested.

"You're on," Ed said and shoved his hand under Marcus's face.

Billy shook his head. "Marcus when will you learn? These kids run rings around us. It's coming out of your money."

They all laughed. The boys escorted Annie into the main hall. Standing with Mark, was Garry.

"Here she is," Garry shouted, "Mark's latest flame."

Annie blushed. She really did not like this vile man but he was Mark's best friend. Mark glared at Garry and hugged Annie. He was so embarrassed by his friend and it was not the first time. He had spent so many years being embarrassed; it was now like second nature to Mark to have these feelings in his company.

Mark ushered Annie away from him and whispered, "Sorry my love. I wish I hadn't asked him now."

Annie squeezed Mark's hand. "It's all right Mark just make sure you fleece him of his cash for the kids."

They both giggled.

Garry looked on. You won't be laughing with each other huddled in a corner by the time I have finished with you, he thought.

The teams were organised and the golf began. The golf course manager had kindly lent Annie a golf buggy and Leon offered to drive it for her. He was to spend the day writing for the club website and brochures but was looking forward to having Annie as company.

Mark caught up with Annie. "Are you going to be okay?"

Annie nodded, "Leon is going to keep me company. If we get bored we may just slip off to the bar."

Leon laughed.

"Don't worry Mark just enjoy a round of golf with the boys. Keep him in check!" She pointed to Garry who was staring at them. He gave a sarcastic little wave to Annie.

Matt and Ed ran over to the golf buggy. "Have fun Mum!" Ed said.

Ed and Mark headed back to the group.

Matt asked, "Who's the dickhead who thinks he's God's gift?"

"Oh I forgot you have not had the pleasure. That is Garry Pearce, Mark's best friend from his playing days."

"Charming idiot!" Matt said.

Annie smiled. "Play nice but if you get chance, knock him out with your five iron."

They laughed. He kissed his mum and walked away.

*

Harry busied himself tidying the flat, waiting for Phillipa to arrive. Where was she? Why was it taking so long? It was already eleven o'clock. The doorbell interrupted Harry's thoughts.

Standing at the door was Phillipa. She looked amazing. Uncharacteristically she was wearing make-up, a short navy blue skirt and three-inch high heels. Harry was gobsmacked.

He moved aside to let her in leering at her very sexy legs in the short skirt.

"I take it we are not going hill walking then!" Harry said, closing the door.

"Maybe later. I've brought a change of clothes and my toothbrush. Mum said she'll sort the kids out tomorrow." Phillipa walked towards Harry and took her hands in his. She kissed him slowly on the lips and he wanted more. He used his tongue to open her mouth and linked his hands behind her head. He had worked himself up to this but not quite expected her to make the entrance she did. Phillipa pulled slightly away from him and coaxed his arms from behind her head. She held both wrists and brushed his hands over the front of her skirt. "Suspenders, sir, just for you."

Harry winced. She had put a lot of thought into this. "I've also brought some toys with me sir."

Harry almost burst there and then. "Show me please," he said.

"All in good time," she teased. "Take me to your bedroom sir."

Harry picked up her bag and led her into his room. He sat on the end of the bed with Phillipa standing directly in front of him. She was so tall with her shoes on and towered over him.

She went to slip her shoes off. "No leave them on please," Harry begged.

Phillipa complied. She straddled his legs but wasn't sure what the next move was. She wanted him to take control. Harry sat with his hands on her waist and his head buried in her lap. Phillipa ran her fingers through his hair and down his back. He tensed as she moved further down, her breasts brushed his shoulder. Springing into life, Harry rubbed his hands up her legs and gathered her skirt and slipped it off, revealing the lace top of her stockings. He gently kissed the lace, making Phillipa's legs almost buckle under her. He kissed her inner thighs and moved his tongue along her legs. He rubbed his fingers along her knicker line and pulled them down. Phillipa stepped out of them. The anticipation of his next move was turning her on even more. Phillipa pulled his T-shirt over his head, revealing the greying hairs on his chest. She rested her hands on his shoulders as he continued to work his tongue between her legs. She leant further on his shoulders as he moved deeper inside. Her legs were about to give way when Harry pulled her on top of him on the bed. Sitting astride him, she eased him inside her and rode him frantically, she was not waiting any longer and it wasn't long before they both burst. Phillipa collapsed on his heaving chest.

Catching his breath Harry said, "What happened to all the toys?"

Sighing, Phillipa said, "They're for later. I wasn't waiting, I've waited long enough."

"You have, how long?" Harry asked.

"About two years," Phillipa replied.

Harry wrapped his legs around her waist and twisted over so he was on top. "You have not."

"I have. I have wanted you since the day I met you but there was Liam and the kids."

Harry was lost for words. He had spent so much time alone wishing he could pluck up the courage to ask her out and here she was now telling him how she had felt the same for all that time.

Harry squeezed her. "I have been wanting to ask you out for years but didn't 'cos you were married."

"Well I'm not now," Phillipa announced, kissing him slowly on his lips.

The love-making was less frantic this time but still as intense. Harry puffed, "You're gonna end up killing me at this rate."

Phillipa laughed, "What a way to go! But you are not going yet. I have all my toys with me."

"Yes I'm intrigued about all that," Harry said.

"You'll have to wait and see." Harry raised his eyebrows. She continued, "Now where are you taking me for lunch sir?"

"McDonalds?" he asked.

"Haha very funny. A small country pub please. Must be loads out here," Phillipa said.

"Oh I have somewhere perfect for us," Harry said.

*

"We are only on the third hole and I'm ready to punch him in the face," Matt fumed to his mum.

It wasn't like Matt to get wound up. "Why what's he done now?"

"We have two potential new sponsors for next season for both Ed and myself. All he can talk about is his rude antics when he was a player. He thinks he's impressing us. Mark is so embarrassed, I really feel for him!" Matt explained.

"Just let him dig his own grave. Mark looks so stressed," Annie said. She wanted to hug Mark and console him.

Ed joined his mum and brother. "He is a right nobhead!"

"Edward Swift-Brown, there is no need for that language."

"Sorry Mum but he is. He is making a right show of us, even more than I do!" Ed echoed Matt's disapproval.

"How are you doing?" asked Annie.

"We are okay as a team. These two sponsors play off good handicaps."

Leon disappeared whilst they were talking.

Matt asked, "Are you okay Mum? You're not too bored are you?"

"No love I am all right. A bit chilly but it has been quite entertaining watching all the different groups. Ben is doing well for his team."

Matt laughed, "Beginner's luck – he's only played Tiger Woods on the Xbox!"

Mark waved the boys back over; he said something to them then walked over to see Annie. Annie held out her hand and Mark placed his hand in hers. "How you doing baby?" she asked.

Mark rolled his eyes.

Annie smiled. "I know sweetheart. He's left an impression on the boys and it's not good!"

Leon returned with Marcus in tow along with Billy.

"Hi," Marcus said, "I understand from Leon that you are under unnecessary stress Mark?"

Mark smiled. "It's okay Marcus I can handle him. I am just concerned at John and Philip – they are great guys and I think they will sponsor the lads but their patience is wearing thin."

Marcus conceded, "Well Billy is going to join your team now and I'm going to take Garry into my team. Just tell the members of your team that the coach wants to spend some time with them."

Annie smiled and mouthed thank you to Marcus and Billy.

Mark was relieved to have Garry taken from his team. He was panicking at the prospect of losing potential sponsors. Garry, however, was furious but too much of a coward to confront Mark and Marcus. Leaving with Marcus he turned to Annie and mumbled, "This is your doing, I know you hate me, you bitch. Have fun while you can."

Annie was so shocked. She hadn't seen this side of Garry before. She didn't like him but he never struck her as being nasty.

"You okay Annie?" Leon asked looking at her ashen face.

Annie didn't want to add to Mark's woes and just nodded. She would speak to Mark another day and just prayed that he believed her over his so-called best friend.

Annie and Leon followed the boys around on the course. The mood was completely different and it was thoroughly enjoyable to watch and listen to the banter between the lads. The rest of the afternoon was hitch free and before long they were heading back to the great hall for the auction and afternoon tea.

Annie hobbled into the great hall, closely followed by a very red-faced Marcus. He put his arm around Annie's shoulder and smiled at her.

"How did your boys do?" he asked.

"I think you may have lost your money," Annie said.

"I did actually think I would. I know how competitive you Swifts are. Can I get you a drink?" Marcus asked.

"Yes please. I will have a red wine please," Annie replied.

"You find your table and I'll bring it over to you. You look a little tired now."

Annie confessed, "I am Marcus but I'm glad I came."

"Good," Marcus said. "Because this would not be the same without you."

Annie sat at the table waiting for the boys to return. Marcus brought the drinks to the table. He sneakily replaced his table nametag with Garry's and laughed like a naughty child as he did it. "Billy can put up with him for a bit. I'm coming to join you."

Annie smiled and was relieved. "He makes my skin crawl. He called me a bitch out there."

"He did what?" Marcus almost shouted but remembered where he was. He was loud enough though to draw some attention to himself.

"Marcus," Annie lowered her voice. "Don't not here. This is about Mark and the boys today. I will talk to Mark after but not now."

"I can ask him to leave?" Marcus stared at Annie.

She shook her head. "No Marcus please. It will ruin Mark's day."

Marcus circulated to all the tables, which were now filling up with people. It was an impressive sight. Over 200 people spread across ten tables. Mark had done really well and Annie was immensely proud of him. He showed the potential sponsors to the table and introduced them to Annie. She was an instant hit.

Philip shook Annie's hand and held it whilst talking. "You are Matt and Ed's mum?"

Annie nodded. He continued, "Well you should be very proud of them. They are two great lads and are real credits to you and themselves." Annie beamed with pride.

Mark, sitting down next to Annie and kissing her forehead said, "What a great success. Our two boys were absolutely brilliant."

Lunch was great only interrupted by Garry's bellowing laugh from the next table. Now and then Billy would shoot a glaring look at Marcus, which amused Matt and Ed immensely.

The auction raised over £30,000 for the Leeds Children's Hospital. Mark was overwhelmed by the generosity. During his final speech, he nearly broke down. Finally the guests started to leave. The potential sponsors had said goodbye but had agreed to sponsor both the boys for the next season. Billy joined the table and sat with Marcus. Annie rested her aching leg on the chair next to her. The boys were off with the other players having a drink at the bar.

"Has he gone?" Marcus asked Billy.

Billy nodded, "I 'gently' persuaded him to leave."

"Who?" Mark asked, returning to the table.

Marcus said, "Your mate!"

Mark rolled his eyes. "I don't know what got in to him today. He has never behaved like that before, ever! Especially when he knows sponsors are about."

Marcus said, "He is rude and an idiot. Thankfully you, Matt and Ed worked hard enough to secure the sponsors. He could have blown it. And he…" Annie glared at Marcus knowing what he was going to say but he continued regardless, "and he called Annie a bitch!"

Mark glared at Marcus and then looked at Annie. Tears were welling into her eyes.

"He did Mark, I heard him," Leon said sitting down at the table.

"Annie I am so sorry, I had no idea. Why didn't you tell me?" Mark asked.

"I would have at home. I don't think it's appropriate to discuss it here."

Mark smiled reassuringly at her. "Oh baby we'll discuss it at home."

Marcus called the team over to the table. He proposed a toast to Mark and Annie and thanked them for a fantastic day. He called Ed to the front of the group.

"Young man I understand from Mark that you wiped the floor with everyone else today at golf. Just remember I'm not giving you time off to play in the Open." Everyone laughed. "I think I owe you this," Marcus said, holding out £100.

Ed laughed. "Give it to Mark for the charity Marcus. It was a pleasure beating you," he winked.

After saying their goodbyes, Annie and her three boys were in the taxi on their way home. Mark was holding Annie in his arms. He closed his eyes; it had been a very long day.

Annie's phone beeped. She had a message from an unknown number. After a peaceful few days she wasn't sure she even wanted to look at it. The message was clear:

'You still haven't got the message you bitch. You will never be happy with him. Enjoy it whilst it lasts 'cos it won't be long now.'

Annie showed the phone to Mark. He shook his head. "Let's forward it to Harry and deal with it tomorrow."

Annie did just that, then laid back into Mark's chest.

*

Harry passed the phone over to Phillipa and said, "So it's started again!"

Phillipa studied the message.

"Funny how it's been quiet recently," Harry replied deep in thought.

"Pearce!" they both said together.

"You get the bill, I need the loo," Phillipa said. "Let's go back to the flat." Phillipa stood up, kissed his cheek and gave him the phone back.

They left the country pub in silence, deep in thought. Harry spoke first. He put his hand on Phillipa's knee. "Sorry. We are both thinking about the job in our time together."

"I'm sorry too. My mind has gone into overdrive. An advantage of two coppers together! We are going to nail him now!" Phillipa declared, adrenaline pumping through her body.

"It's what we both do," Harry said. "We better get used to it, being together will mean the job will get in the way from time to time but we'll be able to manage it."

Phillipa stared at Harry, wearing a huge grin.

"What?" Harry asked.

"You want to make a real go of it? As a family I mean?"

"Yes don't you?" Harry asked, the disappointment evident in his voice.

"Yes I do but I wasn't sure you did," Phillipa explained.

"Why?" he paused. "Phillipa, I have wasted too much of my life being cynical and talking myself out of things. It won't be easy – the job, the kids, Liam but I want us to work," Harry announced.

Phillipa rested her head on his arm. "There's a lot to sort out."

Harry placed his head on hers. "I know but we can sort it out after the case is closed. Right now we both know what we want and that's great. Now let's finish this job so we can be together. Mark and Annie don't deserve all this, they are good people. They shouldn't be put through this because they want to be together and you and I, sexy lady, are going to put a stop to all of this."

Phillipa really didn't know what to say. Harry Fisher a true romantic, who'd have thought it!

Harry announced, "We need to go back to work."

Phillipa nodded. Mrs Phillipa Fisher – erm, might have to work on that, she thought and smiled.

*

They worked in Harry's lounge until the early hours of the morning reviewing the evidence and the events over and over again.

"I think that's it," Phillipa suggested.

"Yes, we are done here," Harry announced.

The night wasn't really what they had in mind but both slept in each other's arms.

27

"Phone records!" Phillipa announced as she walked into the kitchen.

Harry handed her a cup of coffee and patted her on the behind as she walked past. "Pardon?" he asked.

"Phone records. We need to look at the records of the phone number used for the texting."

"We have," Harry conceded.

"But have we looked to see if there were other calls made on that phone? Who to? We need to look at patterns of calls. When were they made? Do they tie in to the other events or with things like, arrest times?"

"Brilliant," Harry declared. "I'll drop you off at the office. Can you look into this and chase the forensics? I'm going to see Annie and Mark. I'll come back and get you afterwards."

Phillipa looked confused. Harry continued, "We need to go to Chadwick's work. I want to interview her work colleagues – someone is hiding her and I need you to help me interview them. We need to find her."

Phillipa sat on Harry's knee and took his cup out of his hand. "Sir, thank you for yesterday. It was amazing. You are amazing."

They kissed.

Harry announced, "Let's get to work. The sooner this case is sorted, the sooner we can start planning for our future."

They kissed again.

*

"Good morning sweetheart," Mark said as Annie hobbled into the kitchen. "How are you this morning?"

"Good," she replied, kissing Mark on the lips. "I feel really stiff this morning and ache all over."

"I told you not to overdo it yesterday," he said pointing his finger at her.

She smiled.

"Sit down and I'll get you some breakfast. I was going to bring it up to you but you beat me to it."

Annie smiled again. "Thank you. I love you Mark Smith."

Mark moved towards Annie, wrapped his arms tightly around her and drew her into his chest. He was warm and smelt so good. He whispered, "Why don't you go back to bed and I'll bring it up to you. You can have a rest this morning?"

Muffled by his chest Annie said, "Only if you come back with me."

Disappointed Mark advised, "As much as that is the best offer, I can't. I am due at Radio Leeds at ten for a preview of the Grand Final. It's a busy week this week. I would ask you to come with me but you need to rest and I'll be back by one o'clock."

"I can't anyway, Harry is coming at ten to go over the recent events."

"Good he might have some answers for us," Mark said.

They broke away and Annie sat at the table drinking coffee, enjoying Mark fussing over her.

"Are the boys still in bed?" Annie asked.

Mark shook his head. "No they have gone to training."

"Ed is settling in really well, he wasn't supposed to join them until after this season," Annie observed.

"He loves it," Mark agreed, "and I think Marcus is enjoying having him at the club. He seems to love Ed's boldness and humour." He paused. "Mind you who doesn't?"

Annie smiled. They had breakfast together and chatted over their week. Annie agreed to travel to Manchester with Mark on Tuesday and Thursday.

Annie hesitated, "I think we should call on Sophie while we are there."

Mark fell silent. He didn't want any more confrontations with his daughter but knew Annie was right.

"Mark," Annie said. He looked up at her. "We need to do this love. You can't leave it. I know she was wrong but you're her dad."

"I know you're right but she's a right pain in the arse, like her mother," he smiled. "Not like your boys. I am such a crap dad. I should have been stronger when she was younger."

Annie shook her head and held out her hand. "You are not crap at anything Mark Smith. Sophie is stubborn and headstrong but we will get through this. We'll go see her and talk to her. If nothing changes, you haven't lost anything, have you?" Mark shook his head. He wished he had Annie's strength.

The gate intercom interrupted their conversation. Harry was waiting.

"Right," Mark announced. "I'll clean this place up, then I'm going to have to get off."

"Leave the kitchen Mark, I'll do it. It will give me something to do while you're out," Annie said.

Mark disagreed. "No! You, my dear will be resting today."

The argument was stopped by Harry's arrival at the door. Mark brought Harry through to the kitchen and shook his hand.

"Hi Annie," Harry said. "How are you?"

"I am good Harry. How are you?"

"Good thanks. In fact, I am very good. I have a good feeling about solving this mystery of ours," Harry announced.

"About time," Mark smiled.

"These things take time," Harry defended himself.

"I know Harry. I was only joking. Would you like a drink?"

Harry requested a coffee with milk no sugar. He sat at the table with Annie. There were some questions he wanted to ask without Mark being there. He fished, "You must be really busy this week with the build up to the big game on Saturday?"

Mark nodded, "Yes I am. I am off shortly to Radio Leeds for the first of many previews. It's always a really exciting, but exhausting week. If you would excuse me, I have to go."

Harry replied, "Have fun."

Mark bent down to kiss Annie and said, "Rest please." He turned to Harry. "Please be gentle. Annie is really tired this morning."

"I will," Harry said. He stood up and shook Mark's hand.

"So what is the big breakthrough?" Annie asked directly.

"Well, there isn't a big breakthrough but we think we are closing in on him," Harry announced.

"Him?" Annie asked.

"Yes, well," Harry cleared his throat. "We don't believe Chadwick is behind these incidents." Annie rolled her eyes, she knew that. Harry continued, "We believe she is being used by someone else. Someone who has a grudge against you or," he hesitated again, "Mark."

Annie replied, "I told you when Chadwick came to see me at work, I got the feeling she was trying to warn me about something. It's just a shame I lost my balance..."

Harry continued, "She has disappeared. We are looking for her but she has not been seen since your encounter with her. Everything went quiet until yesterday when you got that text message."

Annie added, "And if it was her, she could have carried on even in hiding. So why have they started again?"

Harry shrugged, "I'm not sure at this stage but I have a theory."

Annie listened intently. "Go on."

"How well do you know Mark's friend, Garry Pearce?"

"Not very well but he is an idiot. I really don't know what Mark sees in him." The penny finally dropped in Annie's brain. She raised her hand to her mouth and leant towards Harry. "You think he is involved in this?"

Harry fell silent.

"You do, don't you?" Annie said. Her mind was racing overtime. "Why haven't you arrested him?"

"We did," Harry conceded, "but we didn't have enough evidence to charge him."

Annie announced, "He was at our golf day yesterday. He was vile – loud, abusive and he…" she paused, "threatened me!"

Harry was taken aback by her last comment. "What?"

"Yes, he did. I didn't think anything of it. He is just a creep but he did, he threatened me."

"What did he say?" Harry asked.

Annie thought for a while. "He said, 'This is your doing, I know you hate me, you bitch. Have fun while you can'."

"This is your doing?" Harry asked.

"He was upsetting some potential sponsors, so the chief exec moved Garry off their team onto his."

Harry asked, "Had he left when the text message came through?"

"Yes," Annie answered. "We were on our way home in the taxi."

Annie continued, "What if," she paused. "What if it is him? Mark will find it really hard to believe."

Harry asked, "Will he though? Was Mark aware of the threat yesterday?"

Annie nodded.

"Do you know we arrested him?" Harry asked.

Annie shook her head. "When?"

"We released him Friday last. We held him overnight but had to release him." Harry pondered, "Why didn't he mention it to you? Or to Mark?"

"So what now?" Annie asked.

Harry thought for a moment. His mind wandered onto Phillipa back at the office. Snap out of it, Harry thought. "DC Davies is looking into patterns of calls and texts. Our priority now is to find Chadwick. I can assure you Annie the net is closing in."

Annie felt relieved that things seemed to be moving in the right direction. Harry suggested, "I know this is a big ask but I need you not to say anything to Mark about Pearce yet."

"That is a huge ask! You're asking me to lie to him and I can't do that."

"Please Annie." Harry explained, "I don't want Pearce to get wind of it. I know it's a lot to ask. Tell him about the arrest but not about the details. I want to nail Pearce."

Annie reluctantly agreed to keep quiet.

"Thank you for the coffee Annie. Take care of yourself. I will be in touch." Harry departed.

Annie locked the door. The house was so quiet, too quiet. What was she to do? Feeling exhausted, she grabbed the throw from the sofa, switched the television on and lay down to watch Sky Sports News.

*

"Morning Harry," the Super shouted, walking past him in the corridor. Harry returned the pleasantries but his focus was now on finding Chadwick and nailing Pearce. He had a real sense of purpose, which converted into his step. Solving this case would lead to him sorting his life out. The motivation was overwhelming.

Phillipa was at her desk on the telephone. She waved enthusiastically at him. Ending her conversation, she stood up to greet him and had to suppress the temptation to throw her arms around him.

"How was Annie?" Phillipa asked.

"Are you ready to go?" Harry asked.

Phillipa, surprised by his urgency and abruptness, nodded, grabbed her bag and coat, and practically jogged alongside Harry to keep up.

In the car, Harry answered her original question. "Annie is doing okay but the strain is evident, she looked drawn and tired today." He paused. "I spoke to her about Pearce. Told her he is a suspect."

Phillipa was really surprised. "What if…"

Harry interrupted her, "She won't. She thinks he's a vile man and she has promised not to tell Mark. Pearce threatened her yesterday!"

Phillipa smiled as Harry recalled his conversation with Annie. He concluded, "Worse-case scenario, Annie tells Mark who confronts Pearce. It might force Pearce into making a move, a stupid move and we'll be there ready!"

Changing the subject, Harry asked, "How did you get on with forensics and the phone company?"

Phillipa sighed, "Well the phone company are emailing the information this afternoon." She paused. "Forensics said Wednesday at the earliest."

Phillipa held her breath waiting for Harry to explode. Instead he shook his head. "They are really crap and slow these days."

Phillipa agreed, "Yep since they closed the labs at Wetherby, we just can't get a decent service."

"You expected me to lose it then didn't you?" Harry asked amused.

Phillipa giggled, "Yes I did. You surprised me sir."

"Oh I am full of surprises DS Davies."

"That you are sir," Phillipa agreed. Harry stroked Phillipa's right arm.

There was a pungent smell coming from the processing plant next door to the contract cleaning company.

"I'm glad I don't have to work here," Phillipa declared.

Harry smiled. Chadwick's Manager, Bev Wilson, greeted them in Reception. She explained Chadwick had not turned up for any of her weekend shifts. She had spoken to her probation officer, who had tried in vain to contact her.

"Was Chadwick close to any of her work mates?" Harry asked.

Bev nodded. "She was a bit of a loner at first but became friends with James Benson and Paula Bates. She had settled in really well and to be fair, was one of my best shift workers. Paula isn't in today but HR have confirmed hers and James's address is on here for you." She handed them a file.

She continued, "James is here collecting new stock. I'll get him for you. You can use my office."

"Thank you," Harry said.

Bev left the room. She returned shortly with a scrawny looking lad.

"James Benson," she announced.

"Hello Mr Benson, I am DCI Fisher and this is DS Davies. We would like to ask you a few questions."

James looked incredibly nervous and Phillipa noted his hands were shaking.

Phillipa spoke, "You're not in any trouble."

James gave a nervous smile.

"When was the last time you saw Susan Chadwick?" Harry got straight to the point.

"Err… err… last week some time," he lied.

"When and where exactly?" Harry pressed on.

"Here at work. Can't really remember, last Friday I think," he responded.

"How well do you know her?" Harry asked.

"Don't really." James was abrupt.

"If you do see her or she gets in touch, please ask her to contact me," Harry said. "You can leave now thank you."

Back in the car, Phillipa commented, "You let him off the hook easily didn't you?"

"So you think he knows something too then? He never asked what we wanted her for. Can you call in to the station and ask them to send a car to his home address? It's in that file." He pointed to the file on the back seat. "I don't want to spook her again, so we need to just watch the flat. We'll go back later."

Phillipa called into the station, gave Harry's instructions ahead of them returning to look through the phone records.

*

Mark found Annie fast asleep. He quietly closed the lounge door and crept away. He couldn't decide whether to work out in the gym or have some chill out time in the garden. The sun was shining although once the clouds covered it, it was very chilly. He opted for the latter and opened the patio doors in the dining room. He grabbed a coffee, the newspapers and settled on the patio sofa. To take the edge off the cold air, Mark lit the wood burner.

"When did you get back?" Annie asked, leaning on the doorframe.

"About an hour ago. You were fast asleep," Mark replied patting the seat next to him for Annie to join him.

"Would you like a drink?" Mark asked.

"Yes I would love a milky coffee please," Annie replied.

"Have you eaten?" Mark called out, walking into the kitchen.

Annie shouted, "No and I'm not hungry yet."

Mark returned with two hot coffees and sat beside Annie. Annie turned and placed her legs over his lap. Mark rested his arm across her legs and gently rubbed her feet.

Mark asked, "So what did Harry have to say?"

"Not much," she said. Testing the water she asked, "Did you know Garry had been arrested?"

Mark looked up. "No, when?"

Annie shrugged her shoulders. "They released him last Friday."

"That explains why it took him so long to answer my texts. Do they think he's involved?" Mark asked.

Annie panicked. She couldn't lie to Mark. She thought but had no real loyalty to Harry. "Yes they do."

"That is absolutely ridiculous. Is that the best they can do? Honestly, it's a joke!"

Phew, Annie thought, change the subject quick.

"How was the preview?" she asked.

"Yes it was great. I'm getting really excited now," Mark admitted. "Are you warm enough?"

Annie replied, "Not really."

"Come on, let's go inside. Do you fancy opening a bottle of wine, ordering a takeaway and watching last year's Grand Final?"

"Sounds like a plan to me," Annie said. "I'm going to change into my jamas, if you don't mind."

Mark laughed, "Why would I mind, although I'd rather you wore nothing."

"I'm sure the boys won't be happy about that," Annie laughed.

*

"Oh, Shit!" Chadwick said out loud reading the text from Jim. She had to leave. Packing her bags, she cursed his words begging her to go to the police. What had he told them? she thought. She tentatively left the flat scanning the area for police.

She darted into a garden, hiding from a police car approaching from the end of the street. Once passed, she ran in the opposite direction, looking back only once to see it stop outside the flat.

Chadwick stomped along with her head and shoulders down, wishing she was back in the unit. Life was less complicated there and she was safe. She had nowhere to go and very little money left. Hopefully she could sneak back into the flat once the police realised she wasn't there.

*

"Look at this," Phillipa said bursting into Harry's office. She joined him at his side of the desk and threw the phone records in front of him. She had already highlighted a number of key facts.

Phillipa began to explain. "This," pointing to a phone number, "is Chadwick's number. This next one is Louisa Smith's and this one is Mark Smith's."

She had a smug look on her face, which amused Harry. She went on, "And look at this," she could hardly contain her excitement, "this batch of calls and text messages were made immediately after Pearce was released."

Harry threw his arms behind his head. "BINGO!" he shouted.

"You were right all along," Phillipa declared. "Sexy and smart," she whispered. Harry sighed, "Right now we need to prove it was Pearce. We need that phone and we need Chadwick."

Phillipa suggested, "A visit to James Benson?"

Harry nodded.

"Can we get a search warrant for Pearce?" Phillipa asked.

"No we can't pick him up yet. Besides I don't want him slipping away again."

*

"Hi James, can we come in?" Harry asked.

James stepped aside. "I told you everything I knew earlier."

"We just want to ask you a few more questions," Harry said.

"Fire away," he said, sitting down on the couch. Phillipa was very suspicious of his change in attitude. He was like a rabbit in headlights earlier in the day and now he was cocky, full of attitude.

Harry continued, "Do you know if Chadwick has any other close friends or family?"

Phillipa took the opportunity to quickly scan the flat. There were two breakfast bowls and two mugs in the drainer.

Phillipa asked, "Sorry but may I use your toilet please?"

Harry scowled at her. He could not believe how unprofessional she was. Couldn't she have waited, he thought. James nodded.

Phillipa snooped around. She discovered female toiletries and spare bedding folded up on the end of one double bed.

Harry announced, "Come on we are going."

Phillipa asked, "Do you share the flat with anyone?"

James announced, "No."

"Who stayed here last night then?" Phillipa pressed.

"No one," he insisted.

"Then please explain why you have two bowls and cups on the drainer, ladies toiletries in the bathroom and spare bedding folded up on your bed?"

James blushed.

"The truth James please." Harry paused. "You are wasting police time. We need to find her. We think she is in danger."

"Danger?" James questioned. He conceded, "Yes she was here, okay. She stayed here."

"When did she leave?" Phillipa asked.

"This morning," James replied. "I asked her to contact you when we saw it on the television but she was scared."

"Of who?" Harry asked.

"You! She said you wouldn't believe her. She also kept talking about someone finding her."

"Who?" Phillipa asked.

"I don't know. She said 'HIM' or 'HE'. She wouldn't tell me who he was."

"We need to find her James. She could be in real danger," Harry explained. "If she gets in touch please ask her to ring me and me only. I will make sure she is safe and James," he smiled, "tell her we WILL believe her."

"I really don't know where she is. If I did I would tell you. I should have told you this morning."

"Yes you should have done," Harry agreed. "If she gets in touch, ring me." Harry handed James a business card.

They left.

"We need to put out another appeal," Harry suggested.

"Good idea," Phillipa agreed.

"I need to speak to Annie. I have an idea." He dialled on the loudspeaker.

"Hi Mark this is Harry Fisher. Is Annie available please?" There was a pause.

"Hi Annie. I wondered if you could do me a huge favour. Can I call and see you now?" He paused again listening to Annie's response. "Good we'll see you in twenty minutes."

*

Mark showed Phillipa and Harry into the living room. Matt and Ed were lounging on one sofa and Annie was sat upright on the other. She gestured for their guests to sit with her.

"Anyone fancy a brew?" Ed asked, jumping up from the sofa.

"Coffee would be great thanks. Milk no sugar for both of us," Harry replied.

Ed smirked and left the room. Matt followed him.

"What can we do for you Harry?" Mark asked.

"Do you still have the text message from last night?"

"Yes I do on my phone," Annie replied. She reached out for the phone on the coffee table and found the message.

"I'd like you to reply to it," Harry said.

Mark stuttered, "NO! Why would you want her to do that? She's already been put in danger and look at what the result was!"

"Mark, please it's okay," Annie pleaded, "what would you like me to say?"

"Anything, say anything. I just want to see if you get a response."

Mark suggested, "Write – leave me alone, I have a fantastic family. I've done nothing to you so stop trying to ruin my life, it won't work!"

"Okay." Annie typed it and pressed send.

Ed and Matt returned with the coffees. They drank their drinks and exchanged small talk until the phone bleeped.

Mark and Annie lurched forward but Annie got there first. The reply had clearly antagonised the sender. *'You arrogant bitch! You will pay, he is not worth loving, and you'll lose out.'*

Annie showed everyone the message. Harry immediately dialled a number on his mobile and spoke, "Yes, just now." Everyone fell silent, Harry then said, "I see okay, well that clears that up." Harry hung up.

Everyone was staring at him. He explained, "Thank you Annie. I'll keep you informed." Mark showed them out.

Matt whispered, "I still think Pearce is involved in some way!"

"Me too," Annie agreed, "but shush. Mark will hear. We'll talk later."

"They gone?" Ed asked when Mark returned to the room.

"Sure have," Mark said.

"He is so doing her!" Ed declared laughing.

"EDWARD!" Annie shouted.

"He's right though," Mark said laughing.

*

"What now?" Phillipa asked.

"Dunno," Harry said sulking. "I really thought it was him. Charlie said Pearce never moved from the bar."

"Me too," Phillipa added. "Harry I have to get home for the kids tonight."

"I know," Harry said.

"You could always come with me," she suggested.

Harry smiled. "Not tonight, another night."

Harry wanted to be alone with his thoughts and he was knackered.

They kissed goodnight and went their separate ways.

*

"I've locked up," Maggie announced, handing the keys to a very drunken Garry.

"Cheers my dear," he said raising another glass of whiskey. He slurred his words, "Thanks for sending that prank text earlier. My mate would have really appreciated it."

"That's okay, no problem. Anything for you," Maggie said. "I'm off home now. I'll see you in the morning."

"I'm going away for a couple of days," Garry declared. "I'm going tomorrow now, thought I'd go a bit earlier. You can cope 'til Sunday, can't you?"

Maggie replied, "Yeah course I can. Enjoy ye'sen."

"Thanks, I will," Garry said. "Night love."

He played with the mobile phone, dropping it through his fingers. He couldn't resist the temptation and typed:

'Well bitch – you think I'm not serious. I'm gonna show you how serious I am. Death serious enough for you?'

He finished his glass of whiskey in one gulp, switched off the lights and staggered up the stairs.

28

Putting the finishing touches to her make-up, Annie heard Mark bounding up the stairs.

"I'm nearly ready," Annie shouted.

Mark stood at the doorway admiring the view. "Wow Annie, you look beautiful."

"Thanks, is it time to go?" she asked.

"Not yet. Read this." Mark passed Annie her phone. She read the text message.

"This is what scares me," Mark explained. "Harry's tactics last night have now antagonised this idiot!" Mark was fuming.

Annie remained calm, walked over to Mark and put her arms around his waist. She kissed his lips and said, "Mark, I'm fine. We are all together today in Manchester. I'll forward this on to Harry. He can deal with it. To be honest we need to do something to get this idiot to make a mistake." She paused. "No one is going to spoil this week for us."

Downstairs, Annie was startled by the gate intercom. Who was she kidding, she thought? It would be a miracle if she didn't end up on valium by the end of the week.

"Mark," Ed shouted. "Your car's here!"

The boys were so excited, all three of them jostling to be the first out of the front door. Annie chose to make her exit out of the garage and met all three boys on the driveway.

The Range Rover Vogue in grey was lowered from the trailer. Matt and Ed jumped in the back like two excited puppies. Mark handed Annie the keys but she refused them. It was his moment, she thought.

"I'll drive when I have this off," Annie declared.

Mark announced, "Well, as much as I want to play, we need to be in Manchester in an hour. We need to get going."

Matt and Ed explored the car. The small DVD screens took Annie back to the days when the boys were small. They'd argue over which film to watch on long journeys.

"We'll have to buy a film in Manchester to try out," Ed suggested.

"I'm picking it," Matt said.

"No you're not! I am," Ed argued.

"No Ed you have no taste and I'm older than you," Matt declared.

"BOYS!" Annie shouted.

Matt, Ed and Annie all laughed.

Annie's phone rang.

"Hi Harry, how are you this morning?"

Annie listened, and then replied, "I'm sorry Harry. We are on our way to Manchester."

Mark wanted to know what Harry wanted. He was still mad with him over the antics the night before.

Annie spoke again. "We should be okay. We are in Mark's new car. No one else has seen it or knows about it. Will do, bye."

Mark looked at Annie. "Well?"

Annie smiled, "He just wanted to make sure we were all, all right."

When they arrived at the studios, the Producer asked if all four of them would be prepared to take part in the interview. Annie hesitated but Mark and the boys persuaded her to join in. The interview went really well. The four of them bounced off each other brilliantly. Their relationship with each other shone on screen. It worked so well, the producer asked Annie and Mark to provide an interview on game day at the stadium. They both agreed. Leaving the studio, they were looking forward to seeing the interview later on the BBC.

Annie checked her phone on returning to the car. Lucy had called her along with her mum. She also had another damned text message:

'Happy families, eh? Hope you like wearing black you bitch!'

"Oh I'm sick of these stupid games," Annie declared. She texted the number back saying 'Garry, leave us alone!'

She told the others the details of the message but didn't tell them she had replied.

Mark suggested, "Shall we drop off for a bite to eat at Garry's?"

Mark was bombarded with objections from all three of his passengers.

He laughed, "I'll take that as a no then?"

"Ha, funny man!" Ed commented.

The drive home was good humoured and the mood very light. The boys and Mark bounced off each other. Apart from the aching jaw from laughing so much, Annie was chilled and very, very happy.

"Shall we call and see your mum and dad?" Mark asked Annie.

Matt said, "You only want to show them your new toy.".

Mark laughed and nodded.

"You are such a child," Annie laughed, "but I love you."

Mark conceded, "I also need to make arrangements with them for when we go away, to look after you two scoundrels."

"You booked it?" Annie asked.

Mark nodded.

"Where are we going?" she asked sheepishly.

"Nice try Ms Swift but you'll not get a word out of me!" Mark said.

Annie turned around to see the boys wearing huge cheesy grins. "You two know don't you?" she quizzed them.

Both simultaneously said, "We know nothing!"

"Liars!" Annie smiled and sank back into the leather seat pretending to sulk.

"Can we go to Nandos before Grannie's please?" Matt asked. "I'm starving."

"Me too. Good call bro," Ed added.

Lunch was great. Annie recalled her and Mark's first meal at the restaurant. Mark wrapped his legs around Annie's. She responded by closing her eyes and squeezed his legs.

*

"Lunchtime sir?" Phillipa announced, popping her head around Harry's office door. He had been shut away all morning. He waved Phillipa in. "Close the door please."

Phillipa asked, "What have I done?"

Harry looked at Phillipa in surprise. He got up and moved to the front of his desk. He pulled her between his legs and perched on the end of the desk. Harry kissed her, listening intently to ensure no one caught them.

"You have done nothing wrong," Harry answered. "I'm pissed off it wasn't Pearce who sent that message." He kissed her again. They hugged tightly.

Phillipa suggested, "Just because he didn't send the message it doesn't mean he is not involved."

"True," Harry said.

The door handle turned and they quickly parted. Awkwardly Harry readjusted his trousers and sat back down. Phillipa tried to calmly sit in the chair opposite him. She pretended to read the contents of the file on his desk.

"Harry," the Super entered the room. "Hello Phillipa," she smiled. "I've read your email on the case update. I've given the forensics team a rocket up their arses. Let me know if you don't get the results by Wednesday lunchtime. I agree with you that there will be a sudden breakthrough but let's hope it's sooner rather than later."

"Okay thank you Ma'am," Harry said.

"My pleasure," and she left.

Harry and Phillipa glared at each other and laughed.

"Shall we go have some lunch?" Harry asked.

"Yes. Canteen?" Phillipa replied.

"No let's get out of here for a bit," Harry answered.

"A bit of what?"

"I wish! Steady on, my heart."

They both laughed.

"Your heart is stronger than mine," Phillipa admitted, pinching his bottom as he walked past her.

"Ooh nice," Harry whispered, so Phillipa did it again.

They walked to the local pub and found a quiet corner.

Lunch was interrupted by yet another text message from Annie. Phillipa and Harry discussed the escalation in threats and feared the case would turn even more sinister if they didn't put a stop to it soon. Harry decided that the time was right to press for surveillance on Pearce and put out another appeal for Chadwick.

*

Lucy had heard nothing from Simon since Sunday, in spite of her calling and texting him half a dozen times. She was getting more and more impatient. Was he losing interest? Or was he married like Annie thought. All sorts of scenarios were going around in her head. She really didn't know what to think.

She rang his number again and this time left a message. 'It's me, if you've lost interest, fine but I need to know if I'm booking my own room for the weekend. Call me or text me!'

Ten minutes later her phone buzzed, *I'll be over in ten minutes – warm the bed up Sx'.*

What a cheek! Lucy thought.

Her phone buzzed again, *'I have a surprise for you'.*

Lucy jumped for joy. She quickly tidied round, placed candles in the bedroom and bathroom and sorted her hair out.

The doorbell rang and Lucy skipped to the door and let Simon in. In one hand he was holding a bottle of wine and a takeaway and in the other he had a heavy holdall.

"Thank you," Lucy said, taking the wine and the takeaway.

Simon kissed her. "I hope you don't mind but I have cleared my schedule and have a few days off work. I thought I'd spend them here with you."

"I'm working," Lucy said.

"Throw sickies?" he asked.

She screwed her face up.

"Please, please Lucy. We can really spend some time together. And I've booked the hotel for tomorrow, Friday and Saturday night. We can make a full break of it."

Lucy was still unsure. "But Annie's not there and work need me."

Simon put his hands on her shoulders. "Please I need you."

Lucy's heart melted. "Okay but let's eat."

They sat with their meal on their laps in front of the television. He knew he only had one more day and they would be in Manchester and then he wouldn't be found.

*

"Hi Mum," Annie shouted getting out the car. Her mum was in the front garden looking after her precious flowers.

"Wow," Andrea shouted. "Wondered who it was coming here in such a flashy car."

"It's Mark's new toy Mum," Annie teased.

"Very nice it is too," Charles said. "I wouldn't let them two in it, they'll wreck it in two minutes – remember the chocolate on the back seat!"

"Gramps," Matt replied. "That was over fifteen years ago!"

"Yep and nothing has changed," Mark said.

Ed jumped out from behind the car and wrestled his grandpa who was too quick for him and put Ed in a headlock, rubbing his knuckles on the top of Ed's head.

"Good reflexes for an old timer," Ed squealed.

"Yes and don't you forget it!" Charles said releasing his grandson.

"Come on. I'll make us a drink," Andrea said linking arms with her daughter.

Mark held Charles back mouthing he wanted to speak to him alone.

"What's up?" Charles asked when they were alone.

"Nothing," Mark said. "Nothing at all. I just wanted to, well, talk to you about something."

"Come on then lad, spit it out," Charles said impatiently.

"I'm taking Annie to New York on Sunday," Mark said.

"That's great. She'll love that." Charles looked very confused.

Mark sighed and continued, "Annie doesn't know where we are going but while we are there, I'm going to ask her to marry me."

Charles didn't say anything; he just stared at Mark. Mark's heart was pounding. Shit, he thought!

Mark spoke nervously, "You think it's too soon?"

Charles shook his head. "No Mark I think it's the best news I've heard this year along with Matt and Ed's contracts and Matt playing on Saturday of course," Charles smiled.

Charles shook Mark's hand, pulled Mark towards him and hugged him. "Mum's the word," Charles said with tears in his eyes.

"What have you two been up to?" Andrea asked.

"Nothing," they both said together.

"Liars!" Andrea and Annie both said and laughed.

Mark admitted to Andrea he was taking Annie away but he hadn't told her where. The inquisition subsided when Charles started play fighting with his grandchildren.

Annie commented, "Dad thinks they are still five."

Andrea added, "Dad thinks *he* is still five!"

Mark asked, "Annie do you have that envelope I gave you please?"

She'd forgotten she was saving it and handed it to Mark. She'd not even asked what it was for. Mark passed it to Andrea and tentatively she opened it with a very confused look on her face, which soon changed to a big grin as she let out an almighty scream.

Mark smiled. "I thought you might like to join us!"

Andrea got up and kissed Mark and she passed the papers to her husband. He was close to tears as he read the information.

He said, "I don't know what to say Mark."

Mark explained to a bemused Annie, "Your mum and dad have hospitality tickets for the match on Saturday and a room at the hotel with us."

Matt said, "Thanks Mark. You have no idea what it means to me to have you all there on Saturday."

"Oh I really do Matt," Mark replied. "It's my way of thanking you all for accepting me into this brilliant family. Ed, you have one too. I asked Marcus on the golf day what the plans were. He'd like you to stay with the team at their hotel but said you can join us for the meal. He wants you to charm the hospitality guests and then join the team pitch side for the game. You've made a big impression on him!"

Ed high-fived Matt. "Get in there!" he said.

"Well I think we should go," Annie suggested. "The boys are leaving for training camp tomorrow and we need to get packed."

"One more thing," Mark remembered. "We will pick you two up at lunchtime Friday."

They all said their goodbyes. In the car, Mark noticed Matt had tears in his eyes. "You okay mate?"

Matt smiled. "I am. It just all seems so real now. God, I'm playing in the Grand Final!" He fisted the air.

29

Lucy had an interesting night. She enjoyed Simon's company and the sex was interesting but she always felt he was hiding or holding something back.

Lucy lay watching him sleep. He snored heavily and mumbled in his sleep. As Simon turned onto his back, she moved up close to him and tucked her head under his arm. She kissed his chest and he smiled. He drew her towards him and closed his eyes again. Simon was either full on like now when he wanted her to himself, or nowhere to be seen. Rather than worry about the latter, Lucy decided to make the most of the days she had with him.

Simon was awake but didn't want Lucy to know. He needed time to plan the next few days. Somehow he had to lie low but keep Lucy away from any news. He would have to preoccupy her but that wasn't really going to be a challenge for him. Silly cow thinks I love her, he thought. If I give her sex she'll be easy to keep in control. He smiled.

"You're awake then," Lucy said.

"I am," Simon declared, "I was just enjoying the peace and having you beside me."

"I'll be back shortly," Lucy announced.

Simon, listening intently for her movements, leant down to his trousers on the floor and took the mobile phone out of his pocket. There was one message it read: *'Garry leave us alone!'* He laughed out loud.

"What's up with you?" Lucy asked.

Simon recomposed himself. "Oh I'm fine just something at work," he smiled. "One of them for me?"

Lucy passed him a cup of coffee.

"Have you rung work?" Simon asked.

"I have," Lucy gulped her coffee. "Told them I won't be back until Monday so I'm all yours."

Simon put his cup down and took Lucy's and placed it next to his. He climbed on top of her. "So I have you to myself until Monday?"

"You do," Lucy said kissing his lips. Simon slipped Lucy's T-shirt above her head. He kissed her neck, chest and throat and onto her nipples. He suckled one whilst playing with the other. Lucy lay with her eyes closed thoroughly enjoying the attention.

Whilst his fingers stayed at one nipple, his mouth moved towards her stomach. She moaned in delight, running her fingers through his hair. He moved back up to her lips and kissed her. She gasped and wrapped her legs around him. Frantically he made love to her. Give her what she wants, he repeated to himself. He felt her buckle under him, mission accomplished! He collapsed at the side of her.

"Can I run the bath for us?" he asked.

She nodded, trying to catch her breath.

Simon headed for the bathroom. Once inside, he turned the taps on and took the mobile out of his pocket.

"It's me. Is everything okay?" He paused. "See you Sunday." He hung up.

"It's me, ring me." He hung up again.

He turned the phone off and turned the taps off. He was in the clear so far, he thought.

"Bath's ready," he shouted to Lucy.

He was already in the water, waiting for her. They laid together for over an hour, chatting uncomfortably about their childhoods.

After their bath, Simon laid on the bed watching Lucy pack her case.

"Would you like to go out for tea?" Lucy asked.

"I'd rather have tea in bed with you," Simon smiled. "Let's order pizza and watch a film in bed."

Lucy agreed.

*

It was an emotional morning for Annie. She rose early and made breakfast of eggs, smoked salmon, cereals and bagels. Mark knew Annie was struggling and helped in silence. He kept looking at her. When she caught a glimpse of him, she shook her head to signal for him not to say anything.

"Morning guys," Matt said, walking into the kitchen.

That was enough to set the tears off. Matt grabbed his Mum and pulled her into his chest. "It's okay, Mum. Today is a brilliant day that I wouldn't have got to without you."

Matt turned to Mark. "Mum has my nerves for me. She was like this on the day I went to the service area trials, my debut for the academy and my debut for the first team."

Ed walked in. "Hi Mum. Nerves have kicked in then!"

"I'm sorry," Annie apologised.

"Don't ever apologise Mum. You are one in a million," Ed said.

Mark added, "I have never met such a devoted mum."

He held out a chair for Annie. She sat down sniffling.

"What time do you have to be at the club?" Mark asked.

Matt replied, "Bus leaves at eleven. I want to be there about ten."

"We'll take you after breakfast," Mark suggested.

"That'll be great," Matt thanked him.

"Yeah we can show the lads your car," Ed laughed.

Annie calmed down during breakfast. There was the usual banter between the three men and Mark reminisced over his rugby days.

Time passed quickly and before Annie knew it, she was waving her boys off on the team coach. There was a great turn out of fans to wish them well.

"What would you like to do today?" Mark asked.

It was going to be a long day waiting for the weekend to arrive.

"I don't mind," Annie said, "but I think we should see what this baby can do." She patted the dashboard of the car.

"Annie, you read my mind," Mark said. "Any preferences?"

Annie smiled. "Well we better not go west, the boys will think we are following them! So, east, let's go to the coast. I love Bridlington in the autumn."

"Sit back and chill Ms Swift, you've earned a rest. I'm going to spoil you today."

"Like every day then," Annie smiled.

They headed to the A64.

*

"Morning sir," Phillipa said, walking into the incident room.

"Morning," Harry smiled. He liked his secret life. They had been texting each other since 5.30 a.m. He was looking forward to tonight. Both finished their shifts at six o'clock and the kids were having tea with their school friends.

An officer knocked on the door and entered with a sealed brown envelope.

"Is that what I think it is?" Harry asked.

"Let's hope so," Phillipa said.

Harry hurriedly opened the envelope. "Yes, get in!" he shouted.

He called everyone to the incident room and walked in with Phillipa at his side. "Right, can I have a bit of quiet please?" Harry shouted, entering the room.

"I have the forensics results here!" Harry held the envelope up. Scanning the results he announced, "Photographs from the street CCTV in Holmfirth show a middle-aged woman stealing the vehicle involved in the RTA and the same woman the week before collecting NW68 STH from the hire company." He threw the photographs across the table for everyone to see them.

He continued, "There is a ninety-five per cent chance this woman was the one who broke into the Smith's residence. Apparently her shoe size matches!"

He read on then shouted, "Shit! Blood samples are delayed until tomorrow. Ridiculous! Crucial evidence missing! Fuck!"

Phillipa studied the photographs. She held it up and declared, "Sir we know this woman."

Harry screwed his eyes up. "Do we?"

"Yes! In the pub when we interviewed Pearce?" Phillipa suggested.

"Shit it's his cleaner!" The penny dropped with Harry.

Harry's frown changed to delight. He ordered an arrest warrant and a search warrant for the pub and Maggie's flat.

He ordered, "Get uniform to run a background check on her."

Phillipa suggested, "I hope you don't mind but uniform are also running a financial check on Chadwick and Pearce. Pearce may have paid Chadwick?" She continued gauging whether Harry was annoyed with her rogue investigation. "Or Chadwick blackmailed him!"

Harry nodded. "Excellent thinking. I'm going to update the Super and see if she can get the DNA tests back. We are closing in people. Charlie, can you call in the CAD office and make sure they put out Chadwick's details again? We get her, we get the scrote responsible for this."

Everyone filtered out of the room.

Harry turned to Phillipa. "Good work. Once we have the search warrants, you and I will pay a visit to our friend Pearce."

Phillipa suggested, "That's why we didn't catch Pearce sending the text message…"

Harry finished her sentence. "…she sent it for him!"

The Super was pleased with the case's progress. She contacted the labs and after handing out a severe bollocking, they promised to supply the results by ten a.m. Thursday at the very latest. The Super sanctioned the search warrant and arrest warrant and arranged for them to be signed urgently.

Harry left the office feeling very pleased with himself. He even had the Super's approval if Pearce tried anything, he could be rearrested. Leaving for Pearce's place, Harry rang Annie to check in on her and Mark. He wanted to blurt all the recent developments to her but knew he couldn't at this stage. He enquired whether they had heard anything from Pearce but they hadn't. Harry was not sure whether this was a good or bad thing. If Pearce knew the net was closing in, would he go to ground or would he escalate his activities? The latter worried Harry. The case was moving faster than he had anticipated and if he could solve it over the next few days, he could start planning his new life with Phillipa. That was the biggest incentive of all, he thought.

There were two patrons sitting in the corner of the pub when the police arrived. Dunne was heading the search of Margaret Riley's flat but Harry and Phillipa wanted the pleasure of seeing Pearce's face when they searched the pub.

Maggie was working behind the bar. "He's not here!" she announced to the officers.

"It's you we have come to see," Phillipa announced.

"Margaret Riley I am arresting you on suspicion of causing serious injury by dangerous driving under the Road Traffic Act, on suspicion of sending malicious text messages under section forty-three of the Telecommunications Act nineteen eighty-four and harassment of persons under section one of the Harassment Act nineteen ninety-seven. You do not have to say anything but it may harm your defence if you do not mention when questioned something, which you later rely on in court. Anything you do say may be given in evidence. Do you understand?"

"I've done nowt!" Maggie protested as Harry administered handcuffs to her wrists. Phillipa had a wry smile at the thought of when they were last used.

"Where is Pearce?" Harry asked.

"Dunno. He's gone off for a couple of days. Piss up with the lads for the Grand Final I think. He's left me in charge," she said.

A uniformed officer asked the patrons to leave and they closed the pub. Eight officers searched the whole pub. Computer equipment, mobile phones were seized including a laptop.

"Sir," Phillipa said holding up a passport. "This is Louisa Smith's missing passport!"

Harry smiled and gave it to one of the officers to put in an evidence bag. Uniformed officers took Riley away along with the evidence retrieved. Dunne rang Harry and confirmed he'd found nothing at the flat where Riley lived with her mother.

Harry, driving back to the station announced to Phillipa, "I think we need to issue a statement to the press. We should announce Riley's arrest and the seizure of computer equipment and appeal for Chadwick to come forward." His mind was racing overtime and his head was spinning.

Phillipa asked, "What about Pearce?"

Harry replied, "He's going nowhere. Let's see what we get from the computers and mobile phones. We'll nail him. He won't be a happy man when he realises Riley is in custody. We need those blood results!"

When they arrived back at the station Harry announced, "I'd like you to lead the interview with Riley."

Phillipa was taken aback. "I thought you would have done it?"

Harry shook his head. "You and DC Dunne can do the interview. I want to concentrate on the press release and finding Chadwick."

They gave each other a broad smile and went their separate ways. Phillipa headed to the custody suite to wait for Riley's solicitor's arrival. Phillipa was ready for this.

Harry entered his office and closed the door. He looked over the forensics report, examining every minor detail. Harry wrote his press release and emailed it to the Super and the press office. He would have to wait until it had been approved before its release. Precious time was being wasted, he thought.

His phone bleeped. Annie had received another message:

'Celebrations this weekend will turn to sorrow. You two need to learn you'll never be happy together.'

Harry rang Annie; he placed the call on loudspeaker.

"Hi Harry," Annie shouted.

"Hi Annie," Harry replied. "Are you okay?"

"Yes thanks. Mark and I are off to blow the cobwebs off at the coast. Did you get my last message?"

"I did," he paused. "When did you receive this message?"

Annie thought and replied, "A couple of hours ago. Sorry just waved the lads off to the Grand Final and forgot about it. Why?"

"That's okay. We have made an arrest."

"Pearce?" Annie asked.

"Sadly no," Harry said, "Margaret Riley, Pearce's cleaner at the pub."

Annie fell silent, and then replied, "That's interesting. She was a bit weird. You could be right then?"

"I believe so," Harry said. "I will update you when I have more information."

"Bye," Annie said.

Harry decided to go and observe the interview.

"What's the delay?" Harry asked, joining Phillipa in the corridor with the custody sergeant.

"She's demanding a particular solicitor," the custody sergeant explained. "He's in court until six o'clock."

"Let me guess, Sean Millard?" Harry asked.

The custody sergeant nodded.

Harry conceded, "We'll have to wait then. Let her stew in custody. Coffee?" he asked turning to Phillipa.

Phillipa added, "We can check the computer equipment test results and the background check on Riley."

Harry answered, "We'll be in the canteen, then my office when he decides to turn up."

*

"Shit! Shit! Shit!" Simon said out loud.

"What's up?" Lucy asked, turning around from the stove.

"Oh, work," he said, "I need to make some calls. Can I use your bedroom please?"

"Of course you can," Lucy answered, returning her attention to the food.

He shut the bedroom door.

"It's me," he whispered. "What's going on?"

"I see. You know what to do. Go down and make sure she doesn't talk." He paused. "Great, let me know how it goes… No I'm away for a couple of days but keep me up to date. Better not use that other number now, use this number."

He emerged from the bedroom.

"All sorted?" Lucy asked.

Simon walked across and placed his arms around her waist.

"It is now," he declared, kissing the back of her neck.

They sat and ate in silence, which suited Simon perfectly. Lucy studied him closely. Something was on his mind; she knew that but assumed it was work. After lunch they settled down in bed to watch a DVD. Before long, Simon was asleep and snoring. Lucy lay bored to tears. She wriggled out of bed.

His phone was on the kitchen side. A message was flashing on the screen.

'It's sorted. I'll be there at 6 – making them wait, give you more time. She won't give anything away, Sean.'

What did it mean? She thought. She deleted the message. She couldn't explain to him why she'd looked at his phone apart from sheer boredom. She decided to finish her packing.

*

Mark pulled up in the harbour car park at Bridlington. They had a huge debate on where to park and what to do. Annie would have loved to have walked her usual route from the South Bay car park through to the North Bay. Annie recalled her family days out with the boys spending twelve hours on the beach playing rugby, badminton and volleyball, and then walking into town for tea. The boys hated the walk unless they had a rugby ball in their hands.

They strolled along the harbour in silence; Annie found it too hard to work the crutches and talk. By the time they arrived at the bar, Annie was exhausted. She collapsed in the chair. Mark laughed at how dramatic the fall was.

"Mark?" Annie asked. "Stop laughing and get me a wine!"

Mark laughed and retreated to the bar.

"I've been thinking," Annie said on his return to the table.

"That's dangerous!" Mark said taking a drink of his beer.

Annie pulled a face. "Are the boys going to be safe while we are away?"

Shit, Mark thought, I hadn't really thought of that!

"Yes, I've spoken to them about the trip and they are happy for us to go. They're probably in less danger if we are not here!"

Convinced he was not putting Annie at ease, he suggested, "I'll speak to Harry, let him know we are going away. He can keep an eye on them or you could ask your mum and dad to move into the house and look after them."

Annie thought for a while. "I'll see what Matt and Ed want. If I arrange for their grandparents to stay without asking them, they might never forgive me!"

Mark couldn't wait to get Annie to New York to make an honest woman of her or rather an honest man of him!

The walk back was even more difficult for Annie. Her joints had stiffened and after a good lunch and wine, her feet felt like lead weights. There was also a biting chill in the air as the sun disappeared west.

*

Phillipa was chomping at the bit! She was about to meet Riley's solicitor when Harry called her into his office.

"You okay?" she asked, half expecting him to say he wanted to do the interview.

"More than okay," he said waving the results of the forensics in front of her. "Fingerprints in the car match Riley's." He held the paper aloft.

"And the blood?" asked Phillipa.

"Pearce's," Harry said smugly.

"But he had no marks on him when we interviewed him?" Phillipa said.

"True but they could have been superficial or on his body."

"You knew it all along," Phillipa declared.

"I know. We'll get a warrant for his arrest now, won't be long before he is in custody. Will be a great week for Mark and Annie if we nail him before the Grand Final on Saturday. Do me a favour though?" he asked.

"Yes what?" Phillipa asked.

"Don't mention the blood results to Riley, not yet. I don't trust the solicitor. I'll speak to the Super and explain later."

Phillipa nodded and turned to leave. Harry whispered, "I love you."

Phillipa stopped in her tracks, looked back and saw Harry busily writing. She returned, "And I love you too, you clever, clever man."

*

Sean Millard was as smarmy as ever. He carried himself as a big shot lawyer yet he only covered legal aid cases for the scum of the earth. He smelt of cheap aftershave and stale tobacco.

"DS Davies, we meet again," he held his hand out for Phillipa. She obliged and resisted the temptation to wipe her hand down her jacket afterwards.

"Mr Millard, this way." She led him into the interview room and was joined shortly after by a uniformed officer and Riley. Phillipa looked her up and down. She looked tired.

Riley was in her late forties, early fifties. It was difficult to decide due to the nicotine-stained skin. She was five feet tall and about eight stone. Her clothes were stained and filthy.

"I'll leave you to talk," Phillipa announced. "Just tell the officer outside the door when you have finished your consultation."

Phillipa joined Harry and the Super in the next room. Time was pushing on and they really wanted to get the interview started.

"Patience is not a virtue of mine," Harry declared.

The Super commented, "Do you have any virtues?" She smiled but realised Harry had taken her comment the wrong way. "It was a joke Harry," she added, defending herself.

He managed a crooked smile and glanced at Phillipa. The silence was unnerving and the wait unbearable. Harry finally nodded his head to signal to Phillipa there was movement in the room. Millard left the room, which was shortly followed by an officer at the room door confirming they were ready to start the interview. Millard met Phillipa outside the interview room.

Looking very pleased with himself he asked, "Shall we get started?"

*

Simon picked up his mobile phone. There was one message from Sean. '*Spoken to Mags – she'll be fine in the interview. Going in now to see what police have to say. Expect bail by end of night. Keep you informed.*'

Simon checked the message details; it was received at 6.35 p.m. Nothing else had been received for three hours. Simon wasn't sure whether to be relieved or concerned.

"You hungry?" Lucy asked.

Simon nodded and put his phone on the kitchen side.

"A sandwich okay?" Lucy asked with her head in the fridge.

Lucy's phone beeped. It was a message from Annie. Lucy read it and smiled.

"Good news?" Simon fished.

"It's from Annie. The police have made an arrest in her case."

Simon feigned concern. "That's great. Has she said who?"

Lucy shook her head.

"Shall we take our snack to bed?" Simon asked kissing the back of her neck.

Lucy agreed, "Yes we can watch TV."

"A DVD. I'd like to watch a movie," Simon suggested. "You can choose."

The last thing he needed was watching television – what if they'd issued a press statement. They'd set off to Manchester tomorrow morning and he'd take her out for the day, away from any media – North Wales, away from the public. His thoughts were interrupted.

"Simon," Lucy shouted. She had been talking for five minutes but he had not heard a word of it.

"Sorry," he said. "It's hard for me to switch off from work."

She smiled and climbed into bed. Within ten minutes Lucy was fast asleep. Simon turned off the television and lay wide-awake staring at the ceiling. He wasn't really sure what his plan was for Lucy.

*

Phillipa read the arrest statement to Riley again and gave full details of the charges she was being accused of. DC Dunne observed Millard very closely during the interview. Riley confirmed her name and address.

"Do you understand the charge?" Phillipa asked.

Riley nodded.

"For the benefit of the tape the suspect nodded," Phillipa announced.

"'Cept I've done nowt!" Riley blurted out.

Millard frowned and Riley subsided back into her chair.

"Before we begin the questioning, I would like you Maggie, can I call you Maggie?" Phillipa asked trying to befriend the suspect. Riley nodded and grunted a faint yes.

"Good." Phillipa placed a pen and paper in front of Riley. "I'd like you to write your name and address on this piece of paper please."

"Why?" Millard asked. "This is highly irregular."

Phillipa stayed calm and explained, "The sooner we eliminate Maggie from our enquiries, the sooner we will be out of here."

Riley complied, much to Millard's annoyance. The officer, sat at the back of the room, took the note.

"Also," Phillipa continued, "please may we have your shoes?" Before Millard could object further, Phillipa went on, "We are going to take a print of them that's all. You will have them back in ten to fifteen minutes!"

Millard knew he had to be very careful not to cross the line of obstructing the police. Pearce wouldn't be happy but Millard would be disbarred if the police and the Law Society ever found out the full extent of his involvement. His actions and facial expressions had already caused alarm bells to ring in the other room. The Super picked up the receiver on the desk and chased up the financial records for all Pearce's accounts. She wanted to ascertain what Pearce was paying this weasel.

"Good girl," Harry said aloud. "She's rattled Millard!"

The Super smiled. Silence descended again as they observed their colleague.

The officer left the room with the battered trainers and note.

"Okay thank you," Phillipa said looking down at her notes. Her first task was to gain Riley's trust. Phillipa shared Harry's concerns that Millard and Pearce could be controlling her and Chadwick but Phillipa had no idea to what extent and why.

"So, Maggie, how long have you known Garry Pearce?" Phillipa looked straight into Riley's face and smiled.

Maggie opened her mouth to speak but Millard interrupted, "She's worked for the company for five years!"

"Please Mr Millard, you should know better. The suspect *must* answer her own questions," Phillipa demanded and threw a glare at Millard.

"Maggie. How long have you known Garry Pearce?"

Maggie looked at Millard for approval to speak. "Err, like he said, five years."

"Maggie, Mr Millard said you had worked for Garry Pearce for five years, I asked you how long you had known him?"

Millard went to speak again but Phillipa's glare prevented the words from coming out.

Maggie answered, "I've known him since High School. My mum took him in as a lodger when he got his first pro contract. Then, when he retired, he offered me a job at the pub."

Phillipa nodded. "Okay so what is your job at the pub?"

Riley glanced at Millard and he nodded. Riley answered, "I do a bit of everything, whatever is needed really."

"Including running errands?" Phillipa interrupted.

Taken aback, Riley nodded, "Yeah I suppose so."

"What sort of errands?" Phillipa asked.

"This and that," Riley replied.

"Do you own a mobile phone?" Phillipa asked.

"Yes your Sarg took it from me," Riley said.

"And what's the number?" Phillipa asked.

Millard shook his head but Riley ignored him. "It's 077771764159."

"Thank you Maggie," Phillipa said.

Harry, in the room opposite looked through the mobile phone records and sure enough the number appeared on the list of contacts. Again the Super telephoned the incident room and asked the officers to expedite Riley's phone records.

Millard was twitching in his seat. He was getting extremely nervous and knew Maggie was falling for the police bitch's acting. She didn't give a fuck about Maggie, only the result, he fumed.

"Thanks Maggie. Do you need a drink?" Phillipa asked.

Maggie replied, "No I'm okay."

"Okay," Phillipa continued, "so you run errands for Garry Pearce. Can you recall where you were on Wednesday the 25th September?"

Riley thought and replied, "Dunno at the pub."

"Are you sure?" Phillipa asked.

Millard intervened, "DS Davies my client has answered your question. If you have something, which I believe you could have, then just spit it out."

Phillipa very calmly replied, "Interview suspended at seven forty-five p.m. Mr Millard, could you please step outside."

DC Dunne was left in the room with Riley.

"Mr Millard, you are in this interview to advise your client on legal matters. If you continue to obstruct this interview, I will terminate it and have you removed."

Mr Millard looked down at his feet. He acknowledged her reprimand. "I was helping my client DS Davies. May I have a ten minute break?"

"Why?" Phillipa asked.

"I need the loo!" the first thing that came into his head.

The thought of slimy Millard and the toilet repulsed Phillipa and she granted the break. She retreated to the room with the Super and Harry.

Harry spoke first. "You're doing really well." He wanted to throw his arms around her and kiss her passionately.

"Millard is a wan…" Phillipa said.

The Super interrupted laughing, "He is but you are handling him perfectly."

"Can we have him removed?" Phillipa asked.

Harry replied, "Yes if we can establish either any involvement in the case or if he obstructs or perverts the course of justice. We are currently doing background checks and he is coming very close to being obstructive. Stay with him and keep doing what you are doing."

The Super echoed Harry's thoughts. "Riley is going nowhere tonight. We have her fingerprints. I suggest we ask her a few more questions, then adjourn for tonight. My hunch is Millard will contact Pearce when he leaves here."

Millard sat on the toilet and texted Pearce:

'Not going well. Police on to me I think. Riley falling for the false charms of the bitch. Could be a long night S.'

*

The interview reconvened at 8.30 p.m. Phillipa had had the opportunity to speak to her mum and explain she would not be home at all. The joys of being a working mother!

"So," Phillipa recommenced, "on Wednesday 25th September, we have CCTV footage confirming you hired a car from Enterprise in Leeds in Louisa Smith's name."

Phillipa laid the CCTV images on the desk in front of Riley and Millard; the latter twitched in his seat and was becoming even more uncomfortable.

Riley looked at the images.

"Is this you Maggie?" Phillipa asked lowering her voice.

"Yes," Riley admitted. "Garry asked me to pick a car up for Louisa 'cos she was really busy. He gave me her passport and I went to collect it."

Phillipa was excited by the admission. "You do know it's an offence to impersonate another person?"

"I wasn't," she shouted, "Garry told me he'd squared it with the hire company."

"So why not just sign your name?" Phillipa asked.

"Dunno, didn't think," Riley replied.

Phillipa placed another piece of paper in front of Riley. "I am showing the suspect the rental agreement for NW68 STH. Did you sign this form?"

Riley nodded.

Phillipa continued, "For the purpose of the tape the suspect nodded. Why did you sign it L Smith?"

Riley's face reddened as she realised the gravity of the crime. "Garry asked me to."

"What would you be prepared to do if Garry asked you to? Attempted murder?" Phillipa slipped the line in.

"NO!" Riley shouted. "I don't know what all this is about," Riley sobbed.

"Maggie. This car was hired using a stolen passport and used to follow and scare two members of the public."

Riley, visibly shocked, answered, "I had no idea. Garry asked me to get it for Louisa. When she lived with us I would do her running around for her. It wasn't unusual. I even helped to bring Sophie up."

"How well do you know Louisa Smith?" Phillipa changed direction.

"Really well. I was gutted when she and Garry broke up. She was good for him and he was good for her but they did have their arguments and boy they were loud. I once heard them…"

Riley stopped dead in her tracks, looked at Millard and then down at the table.

"What?" Phillipa asked.

"Nowt!"

"May I remind you, you are under caution," Phillipa threatened.

"I hoped they'd stay together for Sophie's sake," Maggie conceded.

Phillipa was surprised. "Why? Sophie is Mark Smith's daughter."

Riley raised her eyebrows.

"So is Sophie, Garry Pearce's daughter?" Phillipa tried not to act surprised but she was shocked.

Millard was red with fury. A bead of sweat ran down the side of his temple.

Riley nodded. "Garry and Louisa had an affair when he was still Mark's teammate. They thought they had kept it secret but I overheard them arguing. I also copped them in the bar one night after Mark had won the Challenge Cup with Wigan."

Phillipa trying to remain composed asked, "Does Sophie know?"

Riley shook her head. "Don't think so."

Phillipa tried to continue unruffled. "What did you do once you collected the car from Enterprise?" Silence.

"How do you explain stealing another car in Holmfirth?" Phillipa asked.

"I didn't," Riley protested her innocence.

Phillipa pressed, "We have street CCTV confirming you did!"

"I didn't steal it. Garry asked me to collect his friend's car for him. He gave me a key to get in," Riley confessed.

"Do you have any idea how serious all this is?" Phillipa asked.

Riley looked blankly at Phillipa, who almost felt sorry for this woman. She appeared to be blissfully ignorant to the crimes she'd been drafted into.

Riley answered, "I did what I was asked to do."

Phillipa continued, "Have you ever been asked to write notes or send text messages by Garry Pearce?"

Phillipa expected a disgruntled no but Riley was very candid in her response. "Yes he has but just wind up jokes to people. Garry is a practical joker and spends a lot of his time winding people up."

"What kind of messages?" Phillipa interrupted.

"I dunno, stupid stuff. Stuff that makes sense between him and his mates. Childish pranks!"

Phillipa could feel her mind wandering. She had to stay focused. This woman had no idea what she was involved in.

"Do you love Garry Pearce?" Phillipa asked frankly.

"As a younger brother yes," Riley admitted.

"I am going to terminate the interview for this evening," Phillipa announced.

"And my client?" Millard asked.

"Will remain in custody. We start again at ten prompt tomorrow morning. Interview terminated at nine thirty-five p.m."

Phillipa gathered her papers and left without another word.

"Wow! That was some interview," she declared, joining Harry.

"You were brilliant," Harry beamed with pride and spontaneously hugged and kissed her.

"I'm glad Charlie wasn't the one who came in here first," Phillipa joked.

Harry replied, "He'd have got the same greeting – equal opps and all that!"

They both laughed.

Phillipa declared, "My head is spinning I need a drink!"

"Dinner?" Harry asked.

"Yes great. Can we take something back to yours?"

Harry, astonished, asked, "What about the kids?"

"Mum has them," she explained, "wasn't sure how long we would be with the interview." She paused. "Food, drink and sex – not necessarily in that order!"

*

"Annie, love…" Mark gently rocked Annie, "we're home sweetheart."

Annie had slept the whole journey home. Before leaving the east coast, she had received a lively telephone call from the boys; they were having the time of their lives.

The phone call relaxed Annie and even though she knew it was the last time she'd speak to them until Saturday, she was relieved they were together and safe.

Mark opened the passenger door, unclipped her seatbelt and carried Annie into the house. She kissed him tenderly. He struggled to maintain his balance but delivered her into the house safely.

From the comfort of the sofa, Annie watched Mark close the curtains and switch the television on for her.

Handing her the remote and kissing her cheek he asked, "Wine?"

"Yes, please," she said, settling back to channel hop.

Mark returned with an opened bottle of red and two glasses. He pushed his way in to sit next to Annie. She shuffled down and rested back on his chest. Mark drank his wine whilst stroking Annie's hair.

Annie beamed with pride watching Sky Sports News report showing the boys leaving for Old Trafford. She almost spat her wine out at the next story:

'Staying with the Swift brothers for a moment, there is breaking news that police have arrested a 47-year-old woman in connection with the near fatal accident in September, which involved Ed Swift-Brown, his mum, and rugby veteran, Mark Smith. Police have also confirmed they would like to trace Susan Chadwick, was Lawrence. She has been missing for five days and police are concerned for her safety. It is believed it is the same person who was involved in the rape case nearly twenty years ago against Mark Smith.'

Mark spoke first. "Who is this woman? I wish they'd stop calling me a veteran!"

"Garry's cleaner," Annie answered then winced waiting for the outburst.

Mark looked puzzled. "How do you know?"

"Harry told me this morning. I wasn't going to tell you 'cos Garry is your friend."

Mark was hurt she hadn't said anything. "Can't believe you didn't tell me Annie."

Annie shuffled around and the hurt was so obvious in his eyes.

"I'm so sorry Mark," she kissed him. "I was going to tell you but we got sidetracked and you don't believe Garry could be involved."

Mark was silent. He drank his wine deep in thought.

"Annie," he said finally. "Don't ever keep anything from me again. Whatever it is, we must not keep things from each other, no secrets. Promise me!"

Annie conceded, "I'm sorry, I won't, I promise." She kissed him. "So where are we going on holiday then?"

"That's not the same," Mark chuckled, "and well you know it! Let's go to bed."

30

Harry reached over to turn the alarm off. Phillipa was fast asleep at his side. Even asleep she was beautiful. Her black, satin like hair was draped over the pillow. Usually it was tied back at work. Harry turned on his side, rested on one elbow and gently ran his fingers through her hair. Phillipa stirred and opened her eyes.

"Good morning," Harry whispered, planting a kiss on her cheek.

She smiled and yawned, "What time is it?"

"Six thirty." Harry couldn't resist her. He laid over her and kissed her, his left hand moved under the covers down her body to her inner thighs. Phillipa groaned playfully and parted her legs. Harry ran his fingers across her leg and placed them inside her. She gasped. She kissed him frantically and spun over to sit on top of him. Still his fingers played, toyed with her. She pulled at his arm and as she released it, she pinned both his arms to the bed. Slowly she held his hard shaft and it slipped inside her. Harry closed his eyes and enjoyed her movements as they increased in intensity. He tried to free his arms but she wouldn't let go. He was so turned on by her strength. Sliding up and down she reached down and bit his nipple. Harry moaned and could not hold his pleasure any longer. At the sight and sound of his release, Phillipa reached her peak too and slumped onto his chest.

She whispered, "Erm I know what turns you on now then?"

Harry kissed her lips. "You really don't know the half of it," he said and bit her ear.

"Maybe not but I'm going to enjoy finding out," she said.

They lay in each other's arms, both fantasising their next encounters. Finally, Harry spoke. "We better get ready. Big day today."

She nodded. "Let's hope so."

The drive into work was really pleasant, neither showed any nervousness or unease with each other. Today was a huge day for Phillipa; she had been entrusted with the biggest case their station had seen in the last ten years and she was going to do her best not just for Harry but also for herself. She was more than capable and was indebted to Harry for allowing her to do this.

The station was quiet for a morning echoing how quiet Wetherby was. Phillipa grabbed a coffee and sat quietly in the incident room, looking at the evidence clearly mounted on the white boards. She went through every event in detail in her head, preparing herself for the interview. Her thoughts were interrupted at 9.30 when an officer popped his head around the door to announce the arrival of Sean Millard.

She rose, took a deep breath and thought, well girl, it's time!

*

Lucy was awake first, woken by Simon's incessant snoring. She showered, dressed and was eating toast when Simon emerged from the bedroom, scratching his nether regions and yawning.

"What time is it?" he asked.

"Half ten," she announced.

"Okay I'll get dressed. Thought we could go to Wales today, lunch, walk on the beach?" he suggested.

"That will be great." Lucy let out a childlike scream.

Ten minutes later, Simon re-emerged fully dressed, carrying his holdall and Lucy's suitcase.

"Is this it?" he asked.

Lucy nodded finishing her coffee. She walked past him to finish getting ready and kissed him on the lips. "Thank you," she said.

Fifteen minutes later they were off, joining the M62 heading west. Lucy sat back and was determined to enjoy the weekend with her man. She texted Annie:

'How are you today? I'm going to Wales with Simon. See you Saturday. So happy, Love Lucy x.'

She was blissfully happy. Simon on the other hand was preoccupied. He knew today was a huge make or break day for him. Good news would mean he was in the clear and he could finish what he'd started. The worst-case scenario was he would have to leave the country. Manchester meant he could be at the airport within fifteen minutes and hopefully on a flight within a couple of hours. Alternatively, he could drive to Holyhead and get a ferry to Ireland.

"You okay?" Lucy asked.

Simon smiled, "I am, never better." He placed his hand on hers. "Thought we'd go to Llandudno and go up Great Orme's Head. We can see some amazing views from there and I used to go there when I was a kid." We are away from any media, he thought.

"Good morning," Phillipa announced her presence in the interview room. Riley managed her half smile but Millard maintained a stern sour-faced look. So he's in one of those intimidating moods, Phillipa thought. Good, he'll be easily riled then!

Phillipa finished all the usual formalities and began the questioning. She had a blind panic moment when her mind went completely blank. She closed her eyes, took a deep breath and glanced down at her notes. She decided to go for the jugular, no point messing if she got a confession out of her about the car, the rest would be easy pickings.

Phillipa started, "In the interview last night you said," Phillipa read from the transcript, "Garry asked me to pick up a car for Louisa 'cos she was really busy. He gave me her passport and I went to collect it." She stopped reading and looked Riley straight in the eye.

"You also admitted you forged Louisa Smith's signature on the rental agreement. In addition, you agreed you stole the car from Holmfirth."

Riley said, "I didn't steal it I had the key from Garry."

Phillipa carried on, "What did you do with the stolen car?"

Riley spoke frankly. "I took it to Garry's. He said his mate would pick it up at ten o'clock that night."

"Were you at the pub all night?" Phillipa asked.

Riley nodded. "Yes I was. Garry went out about ten, said he was taking the car to his mate and he would be back in time for closing."

"Did he?" Phillipa asked.

Riley didn't understand the question and looked blankly at Phillipa.

Phillipa asked again, "Did he get back for closing time?"

"Erm… yes I think he did," Riley thought. "Well it was about quarter to twelve when he got back."

"Did he bring the car back with him?" Phillipa asked.

Riley hesitated, shot a glance at Millard who frowned disapprovingly.

Riley continued, "I dunno."

Phillipa knew she was lying. "Are you sure? You hesitated?"

Riley looked down at the desk, fidgeted in her chair and replied, "I'm sure."

"I don't think you are sure," Phillipa pressed on.

"My client is cooperating DS Davies," Millard interjected.

Unfazed by the interference, Phillipa continued, "Maggie I know the car didn't return to the pub because the driver of it caused this accident on the M62! Look at the images please Maggie." The graphic images were placed on the table in front of her. Maggie couldn't bear to look at them. They were horrific. They showed the mangled wreck of a car that couldn't be identified. There was blood on the windscreen and parts of the car had been cut away. Maggie gasped in horror.

Phillipa ignored Riley's sentiment. "Do you know who the victims were?"

Riley shook her head. "No!"

"Mark Smith, Annie Swift and Ed Brown-Swift. Do you know them?"

Riley replied, "No I don't." She thought for a moment. "Only from what I've seen on the news!"

Phillipa was not fooled by her lies. "So you don't know Mark Smith?"

"Should I?" Riley asked.

"Well I'd have thought you would bearing in mind you talked about him yesterday. Louisa Smith's husband, Garry Pearce's so called best friend?"

Colour drained from Riley's face. "Of course I know Mark but it's a common name." Riley defended her ignorance. "I've known Mark for as long as I've known Garry."

"How close are they?" Phillipa asked.

"Surely you need to ask them that?" Millard interrupted.

"Oh Mr Millard, I will be," Phillipa said. "Maggie, in your opinion would you say Mr Smith and Mr Pearce are close friends?"

Millard gave a sly shake of the head to Riley but she ignored him. "They were very close, two peas in a pod. I was so surprised Mark was cool with Garry and Louisa's relationship; he didn't seem to mind. They have grown apart recently since Mark's new lass." She coughed. "A bit like when Mark married Louisa. Garry felt left out and alone. He'd never been alone before; he'd always had his team-mates or Mark. It hit him hard and he turned to drink."

Phillipa was about to ask another question but Riley continued her monologue. "Yep, Mark has used Garry and dropped him the minute he found a woman. Garry was too loyal to drop him. Mind you, other than Louisa there hasn't really been anyone else, except…" Riley stopped and shouted, "Ouch!" She glared at Millard who had kicked her shin under the table.

Phillipa had had enough of his meddling. "Mr Millard. I have asked you not to interfere with proceedings and you have just kicked the suspect which has resulted in the interview being impeded."

"I never, it was an accident. My foot slipped," Millard said.

"It bleeding well hurt!" Riley spat. "Can I have a new solicitor? Am I allowed?"

This was music to Phillipa's ears. She announced, "Interview suspended at eleven thirty-five to grant the suspect's wish of a new solicitor."

Phillipa left the room, very pleased with herself. She received a round of applause when she entered the incident room.

"You played a blinder." Harry smiled. "Come on its coffee time, I'm buying."

"I'm gutted he stopped Riley, she was in full flow and was about to blurt something out," Phillipa admitted.

"That's what he was frightened of!" the Super said. "I'm going to take great delight in writing a letter of complaint to his senior partner and the Law Society."

Harry and Phillipa, once alone, held hands under the table.

Phillipa admitted, "This morning could not have gone any better for us."

Harry nodded, "Your interviewing technique is so effective."

Phillipa smiled. "I wasn't aware I had one."

"That's what makes it so special," Harry admitted. "People trust you and once you've earned their trust, they reveal all to you. It's brilliant. Is Riley having a duty solicitor?"

Phillipa nodded. "Yes. They should be here by one o'clock. I can't wait to get started again, I'm buzzing."

*

Millard stormed out of the station after being bailed. Stupid bitches! He wasn't sure how he was going to explain it to Pearce. He tried his mobile numbers but both were switched off. Oh well, he thought. He typed a text message:

'Stupid bitch wouldn't shut up. Tried to shut her up but got kicked out. She's getting a new solicitor. If I were you, go to Plan B. S.'

*

The hour and a half wait was tortuous. Phillipa was relieved when the custody sergeant confirmed the arrival of the duty solicitor. She agreed a forty-five minute conference between him and the suspect. Hopefully this new solicitor wouldn't obstruct the case.

Finally the time came to resume the interview. "Good afternoon I am DS Phillipa Davies and this is DC Charlie Dunne."

The solicitor smiled. "I am Ian Wetherall." Phillipa smiled back. He looked about fourteen and straight from law school.

He announced, "I have reviewed the case with Ms Riley and she has agreed to cooperate fully with your enquiry. She has an elderly mother that requires round the clock care. If possible, we'd like to get through the interview and then post bail so she can take care of her."

Phillipa looked at the solicitor. "Bail will depend on the responses to the questions. I am sure you are aware Mr Wetherall that your client has committed a number of serious offences and possibly conspired to commit a few others. My colleague will notify social services who will ensure care is provided whilst your client is here." Phillipa nodded to the police officer at the door and he left to make the arrangements.

"Now it is good news that you will cooperate, Maggie, please remember you are still under caution. Let's get this completed today!" Phillipa said and smiled.

Riley smiled and nodded.

"Okay so before we had to stop the interview, you were telling me about Mr Pearce and about to tell me details of another relationship he had after Louisa Smith," Phillipa said.

"Before Louisa," Riley announced. "There was this barmaid he brought in before Mark and Louisa split. They'd met on a drunken night out and she'd attached to Garry like a limpet. Sue was her name."

"Sue?" Phillipa repeated.

"Susan," Riley confirmed.

"Surname?" Phillipa asked.

"Oh I can't remember that far back. Err… It was a boy's name," she recalled.

"Lawrence?" Phillipa asked.

Riley's eyes lit up. "Yep, yeah that's it!" she continued. "He said he felt sorry for her and they were never involved but they were always huddled up together in the corner whispering. I saw him slip her some cash a few times. Anyways, when Mark found out she was here he went ballistic – I mean proper shit hit the fan. Mark came into the bar and punched Garry; he nearly broke his jaw. He had a nerve dictating to Garry who he employed! He threatened Sue to stay away from him and his family. It was all a bit stupid. I had no idea what was going on… until the trial of course. Garry swore to me Sue had done nothing wrong and that Mark had led her on. That was why Garry and Louisa came close 'cos of what Mark and Sue were doing. Anyways after the trial Mark and Garry kissed and made up."

"Until Annie?" Phillipa asked.

"Yep I suppose. He's only seen Mark a couple of times since he met her and she's always been with him," Riley explained.

"I showed you the images of the accident." Phillipa laid the images on the desk again. "They were very lucky to be alive. Has Garry ever mentioned harming Mark?"

"Only when they've been scrapping. They are like two kids, two brothers. One wants what the other one has and vice versa. It's pathetic really. Garry wouldn't hurt a fly – I have to kill the mice and rats at the pub!" Riley smiled.

"Yesterday I asked you to provide a sample of your handwriting, which you did. For the purpose of the tape I am showing the suspect exhibit A2, a threatening note left on Mr Smith's windscreen on Sunday 22nd September. This note is your handwriting," Phillipa accused.

Riley looked down. There were a few minutes' silence then Riley looked at Phillipa. Tears had welled in her eyes and she sobbed, "Garry told me they were practical jokes. I had no idea they would be used in that way. I am really, really sorry." Riley sobbed uncontrollably.

"Sorry you did it or sorry we have caught you?" Phillipa said sarcastically.

Riley continued, "I really had no idea. The stuff he asked me to do had reasonable explanations."

Phillipa interrupted her, "Really? Nasty notes? Text messages? Forging Louisa Smith's signature?"

Riley added, "I know it looks bad."

"You think?" Phillipa replied sarcastically.

"But really I didn't know what was going on. I was told it was a bit of fun, bit of banter between ex-rugby mates."

"And breaking into Mark Smith's home?"

"I didn't!" Riley snarled.

"We have your footprint!" Phillipa declared.

"Rubbish," Riley said.

"The gait of your walk and thus your footprint is as unique as a finger print," Phillipa explained.

"Garry told me it was his place."

"Rubbish! I don't buy all this ignorance Maggie. No one is stupid enough to get involved in all this unknowingly. Breaking and entering, forging signatures, malicious notes, you know they are wrong, so wrong. Think very carefully, you are already in serious trouble and you are adding wasting police time and perverting the course of justice to your list of offences. We'll take a break. Speak to your client!"

Phillipa left the room seething and went straight through to see Harry.

"Well done," he announced.

"Do we have enough to arrest Pearce?" Phillipa asked. "How long do we have left to interview Riley?"

"The Super has gone to arrange the arrest warrant and to discuss an extension for Riley although we do have enough to charge her already. You don't think she's a naïve bimbo then?" Harry asked.

"Not a flaming chance! She's in on this and so is Millard, I'm sure of it. I have also just thought – we need to find out who represented Lawrence, Chadwick. I stake my house that it was Millard. I think Riley will do anything for Pearce but even the most besotted or stupid person knows breaking and entering is against the law. I don't buy she didn't know it was all wrong." She paused. "She really can't be that stupid."

Phillipa went to the restroom. She was going to nail her this time, without a doubt.

*

"Good morning gorgeous," Mark announced, walking into the bedroom with a tray of breakfast, enough to feed at least six people!

Annie sat up and pulled the covers back on Mark's side of the bed. Mark loved spoiling Annie, Louisa never allowed him to. It was bliss.

Mark asked, "I need some bits to take away with us, I thought we could go to Harrogate shopping this afternoon."

Annie nodded with a mouthful of toast.

When she had finished she lay back on the pillow and said, "Mark that was fantastic thank you. While we are on the subject of holidays, I need to know what to pack for Sunday and whether I need anything from Harrogate."

"You can fish all you want Ms Swift but I'm not telling you where I am taking you. You need a coat, jeans, maybe a jumper and an evening dress. The rest is up to you."

The drive to Harrogate was very pleasant, made even more so by the autumn sunshine. The Spa town was buzzing as usual with a long queue of chattering people waiting outside Bettys. They slowly wandered around the shops and passers-by occasionally stopped Annie to pass on their well wishes to Matt and Ed. She felt ten feet tall; her clever, beautiful boys were on the verge of fulfilling their boyhood dreams and a handsome, smart man by her side. Life was sweet!

"Annie, your phone's ringing," Mark said, snapping her out of her daydream. She fumbled around in her handbag, found it and hobbled to lean against the shop window.

"It's Harry," she announced.

"Hi Harry," she answered then listened.

"We aren't at home. We are in Harrogate, last minute shopping for next week. Yes we are going away for a mini break after the Grand Final... Don't know it's a surprise... I see, well that's great news... yes we'll make sure we are back for four o'clock. Bye."

Annie smiled. "Harry's calling at four. There's been a major development in the case and arrest warrants have been issued."

"Who?" Mark asked.

"He wouldn't say. Said he'll explain at four."

"Oooh the mystery of it all," Mark laughed. "It was the butler in the dining room with the candlestick."

Annie straight faced replied, "There's a problem with your theory, Inspector Cluesoe."

"What's that?" Mark asked.

"We don't have a butler!"

They both laughed and hugged. Their laughter attracted some very strange looks from passers-by.

*

One major setback with keeping Lucy away from any media was the distinct lack of mobile phone coverage. Lucy laughed as Simon walked around the car on the top of Great Orme with his mobile phone held aloft, cursing the lack of signal.

"Good you can't work," Lucy laughed patting the blanket at her side for him to join her.

"Fuck ME!!" Simon cursed.

"Yes please," Lucy smirked.

Simon threw his mobile phone onto the chequered blanket and jumped on top of Lucy. She squealed whilst he tickled her. He pinned her arms to the floor and sat on her. "So you want it here and now?"

Lucy nodded trying to catch her breath.

"I thought you was prim and proper?" he asked

"Me? Only 'cos I have never known anything else. You bring out my bad, wicked side!" Lucy whispered bringing her knees up to his groin.

Simon lay on top of her, still gripping her wrists and kissed her, or rather devoured her face. She couldn't catch her breath. He was rough and bit her lip but, whilst she wanted to scream out, she wanted him to continue. The intensity really turned her on.

"Let's go to the hotel," he whispered, "and I'll show you rough!"

Lucy was shocked and excited at the same time. She nodded nervously, her whole body tingling. The thought of the hotel room seemed to bring Simon to life. He chatted to Lucy about his work, albeit a pack of lies, but it passed the time back to Manchester.

As soon as they reached the M56 near Chester, Simon's phone beeped several times. He was dying to read them but couldn't ask Lucy to check them even though she was curious to what the contents were.

"Shall we stop at Cheshire Oaks?" he asked, giving him the opportunity to read the messages.

Lucy nodded.

Pulling up in the car park, he announced, "You go have a wander and I'll catch you up. I just need to reply to these queries. Here," he took £50 out of his wallet, "buy something special." He kissed her cheek.

"Thank you," Lucy said, "I'll get something for the hotel room." She scooted off to find a lingerie shop.

Simon read his messages. His crimson cheeks gave away his temperament. He was livid, more than livid!

He contacted Millard. "What the fuck is going on?"

Millard explained he was taken off the case, that he has been reported to the Law Society and his boss had forced him to take some annual leave.

"So you have no idea what they know now?" Simon fumed.

"Who's opening the pub?" Simon asked. Millard explained it was closed and forensics were still there.

"Fucking great! Why did I trust you two? If I go down for this I'm taking you too." He hung up.

He was so angry, he wanted to smack something hard! He hit the steering wheel with such intensity, the steering column shook. His hand throbbed with pain.

He looked up to see Lucy springing towards the car. She got in very excited, and gave him a very childish grin. "I got something sexy for you!" She attempted to kiss him but he pulled back.

Lucy was hurt. "What's wrong with you?"

"Work!" he said and reversed out of the car parking space. The mood had turned again. They drove to Manchester in silence. Lucy didn't like the mood swings but knew better than to confront him. She would speak to him when he had calmed down and relaxed again.

*

Phillipa walked into the interview room with a renewed determination. It was time she put an end to this defence of ignorance. No normal human being would carry out all these acts and not know they were wrong.

After going through the formalities again, it was Riley's solicitor who spoke first. "I have advised my client to fully cooperate with you and provide you with everything she knows."

"Very wise," Phillipa said. "Maggie did you know that Garry Pearce was sending malicious texts and communications to Mark Smith and Annie Swift?"

Riley sat in silence for a few minutes.

"This is your client cooperating?" Phillipa spoke to Riley's solicitor. He shrugged his shoulders.

"Do I take your silence as a positive response?" Phillipa asked.

Finally, Riley spoke. "Yes I did!"

"Did you send them?" Phillipa pressed on.

"Some of them," Riley admitted.

"Why?" Phillipa asked.

"Garry was really upset when Mark stole Louisa from him. He loved her with all his heart. He was infatuated and she led him on. She was supposed to be marrying Garry but when Mark got his professional contract with Wigan, she decided to marry Mark. But she kept coming back to Garry. She used them both but Garry wouldn't see any wrongdoing on her part. It was all Mark's fault and his obsession led to hatred; he became obsessed with Mark's life, more than actually living his own! I overheard him talking to Sue one night in the pub. He told her he would pay her good money to split Mark and Louisa up. He thought if Mark was out of the picture, she would stay with him."

"It worked?" Phillipa said.

"For a while but she was flighty and used Garry rather than loving him. She left and he was so convinced Mark was to blame again, he vowed Mark would never be happy again," Riley explained.

"Bit lame isn't it?" Phillipa asked.

"Not to Garry. He's a very passionate man," Riley explained.

"Passionate or obsessive?" Phillipa asked.

"Both I suppose. I thought it was all talk, drink talking, 'til I realised he was up to summat. The night I got the car, I realised Louisa wasn't even in the country. She'd texted him that night to say she was in Sweden on business. I read his text messages. I realised the car accident was Garry when I saw it on the news."

"Why didn't you come forward?" Phillipa asked.

Riley thought for a while. "I couldn't. I rely on the job to pay for Mum's treatment and care. Garry has helped us out, money wise and I couldn't afford to lose my job."

"You love him?" Phillipa observed.

"Yes I do. He's not a bad man, just been treated badly."

"He could have murdered the occupants of the other car," Phillipa stated.

Riley looked down. "He wouldn't have meant to."

"Have you heard from Susan Lawrence recently?" Phillipa changed the subject.

"She called at the pub about three weeks ago but Garry refused to see her," Riley said.

"Why?" Phillipa asked.

"He said she was in love with him and he didn't want her." Riley paused. "He told me he loved me and we were going to move away together. He was organising it all."

"When?" Phillipa asked.

"After this weekend," she announced. "He's gone on his annual piss up with his rugby mates. They go this time every year for the Grand Final."

"Where has he gone?" Phillipa asked.

"Dunno, probably Blackpool, they never make the game – always too pissed."

Phillipa announced, "Interview terminated four ten p.m."

"What happens now?" Riley asked looking at Phillipa then at her solicitor.

"You will be charged," Phillipa announced.

"But I've given you all you need," Riley stated.

"You have committed a series of offences," Phillipa replied.

"We will be applying for bail," Riley's solicitor advised.

Phillipa acknowledged his comment and left the room.

The room next door was deserted. Phillipa was disappointed Harry wasn't there. Upon returning to the incident room, Phillipa received a round of applause from her colleagues, orchestrated by Harry.

Phillipa blushed and asked, "Have we arrested Pearce?"

"Not yet," replied Harry, "he's disappeared. We've spoken to the police in Blackpool and have emailed his photo over to them. They are circulating it around the pub watch network. You and I are going to see Mark and Annie and we are late. I said we'd be there for four."

"We better get off then," Phillipa said. She would have liked ten minutes to collect her thoughts and have a cuppa but that wasn't going to happen.

Within ten minutes, Harry was pressing the intercom at the Smith's residence.

"They're here," Mark shouted up the stairs to Annie who was packing.

The guests were in the lounge drinking fresh coffee, the smell of which had wafted upstairs enticing Annie down to join them. Mark and the officers were discussing the Grand Final.

"How are you Annie?" Phillipa asked. Annie observed her usual frosty exterior had melted and she was almost human.

"I'm really good thanks DS Davies," Annie replied.

"Please, call me Phillipa."

Annie smiled and sipped her coffee.

Mark impatiently asked, "So what news do you have for us?"

Harry took a large gulp of the fresh coffee and glanced at Phillipa. He announced, "We have an arrest warrant out for Garry Pearce."

Mark laughed out loud. "Are you having a laugh?"

"No Mark," Phillipa added, "I only wish we were."

Mark was agitated and looked at Annie. Her look frustrated him. "You believe this too?"

Annie placed her hand on his knee. "Mark please listen to what they have to say. Please for me."

Mark's heart melted at the plea and he listened.

Harry went on, "I wouldn't normally divulge information about the case but I know how you feel about the suspect and how much you trust him. Over the past two days, Phillipa has interviewed Pearce's cleaner, Margaret Riley. We were led to her by CCTV images at the car hire company. She hired the car in Louisa's name and stole the car involved in the accident. Her handwriting also matches the notes and she's admitted sending some of the text messages." He took a drink. "She revealed that Pearce had orchestrated all this for revenge as you had taken Louisa from him."

Mark laughed. "Do you have any idea how ludicrous all this sounds? Maybe she is just trying to set Garry up. Louisa would never touch Garry with a barge pole! It's ridiculous."

Phillipa added, "Mark, it is Pearce's blood in the car involved in the accident! Did you know Garry and Louisa were seeing each other?"

Mark sat in stunned silence. He didn't know what to say next. He eventually spoke. "Louisa hated Garry."

Mark's head was spinning. Sophie had mentioned she'd spent some time with Garry but had no idea Louisa had been involved. Garry was Sophie's godfather so it just seemed natural to him.

Harry continued, "Did you know he pay-rolled Susan Chadwick?"

Mark interrupted, "He did yes. I confronted him one night in the pub and we had a fight. She was splitting my family up and my best mate gave her a job! His explanation was he felt sorry for her and thought he could influence her to leave me and Louisa alone."

Phillipa and Harry looked at each other.

"What?" Mark asked knowing their look meant something.

Phillipa explained, "Unfortunately it is alleged your friend was paying her to make your life a misery and split your family up. He made a number of large payments to her, way above the rate for a barmaid."

Mark couldn't believe it and didn't want to believe what he was hearing. This was his worst nightmare. He trusted Garry with his life, with his daughter's life. There must be some mistake, he thought. Annie grabbed Mark's hand and stroked his fingers. He looked Annie in the face, tears welled in his eyes and he mouthed, "Why?"

Annie whispered, "I don't know babe. Maybe jealousy."

"We need to find him Mark and ask him," Harry said.

Phillipa added, "He's left Leeds. Apparently he may have gone on a bender with his ex-rugby mates. Do you know who they are and how we can get hold of them?"

Mark nodded. "I'll get my phone and give you some numbers."

Annie interrupted and asked Mark, "Is he likely to turn up at the Grand Final?"

Mark's face filled with dread at the thought of their special family day being destroyed by his so-called best mate.

Harry intervened, "If he does, we'll be there." He continued, "We will be issuing a press release tomorrow asking for Chadwick to come forward and asking for public assistance in finding Pearce."

"The boys, what about the boys?" Annie panicked.

Mark squeezed her hand. "They have a media blackout Annie. I'll ring Marcus and let him know."

Mark fell silent, deep in thought. His best friend had caused a lifetime of misery. He'd done everything for Garry, leant him money for the pub, picked him up out of the gutter after his drinking binges and even let him share his family. He'd *tried* to kill Annie and Ed! What was he thinking? Why would he do this? Why? What if he was planning his final act of revenge at the Grand Final?

"MARK!" Annie shouted, bringing Mark back to reality. "It's going to be okay. Harry and Phillipa can put him away now. We are home and dry."

"Not quite," Harry said. "Once we have issued the press release, he may try something again; finish what he's started. You need to be extra vigilant. The Superintendent has agreed to provide protection for you. An officer will be assigned to you both. He'll be accompanying you to Manchester. I need to know your plans and which hotel you are staying in."

Mark gave the police a detailed itinerary of their weekend. Harry requested that they stick to it as much as possible. "Any major changes please contact me and let me know."

"What about our couple of days away next week?" Mark asked.

"Where are you going?" Phillipa asked.

Mark really didn't want to say. "It's a surprise for Annie. We are going abroad."

Phillipa reassured him, "It will be fine. A lot can happen between now and then. Funny as it sounds, you will probably be safer out of the country, just keep your plans under wraps."

When the police had left, Annie announced, "I can't go away on Sunday if that madman is still on the loose."

Mark hugged Annie and kissed the top of her head.

"They'll find him by then."

*

"I feel sorry for them," Phillipa announced in the car.

"Me too. Did you see his face? He was so shocked. He had no idea about Louisa and Pearce did he?"

Phillipa shook her head. "You think you know someone but it's so easy to be duped."

"Um it is. I can't believe he never had an inclination they were at it. I'd like to think if it happened to me I would know," Harry said.

"Yes but you're thinking of it as a trained investigator. My impression is that Mark trusts people, wears his heart on his sleeve and wouldn't look at anyone in a bad way," Phillipa said.

"Naïve then?" Harry asked.

"No not naïve, innocent. Not cynical like you and I," Phillipa smiled.

"Experienced not cynical!" Harry added. "When we get back, we need to formulate the press release. What are your plans for the weekend?"

Phillipa shrugged, "I haven't thought about it."

Harry smiled, "I think you and I need to go to Manchester, to the Grand Final. We need to be there; I have a feeling Pearce might turn up."

Phillipa made arrangements for the kids en route to the station. When they arrived, the station was buzzing. The single news crew that had been at the station over the last two days, had now swelled to half a dozen cameras. News was building on the arrest and with the final being two days away, the case had caught the attention of the press.

Harry stopped the car at the station entrance and announced to the press, "We'll be issuing a press release within the next couple of hours. Stick around." That'll keep them interested, he thought.

*

Who is this at this time, James thought sloping off the sofa to answer the door?

"Jeez," he said surprised. "What you doing here?"

"I had nowhere else to go," Sue said as she slumped on the sofa.

"You need to go to the police," he announced. "They want to help you."

Chadwick yawned. "I will in the morning. I've not eaten since yesterday morning and I'm starving. I also need a bath," she said frowning, smelling her own armpits.

"Promise me, you'll go first thing in the morning," James harassed her.

"I promise. It's one o'clock in the morning. Can I just stay here tonight please?"

James nodded. "I'll run the bath. There's some pizza in the fridge. I'll cook it."

Chadwick helped herself to a biscuit and smiled.

31

It was 2.30 a.m. when the press release was given the final approval. Harry was furious that it had taken the press office so long to approve his words but bureaucracy always interfered with his police work. At least it would make the early morning news, he thought. They left the office at 3.15 a.m.

*

Lucy was up and dressed by the time Simon awoke. She was sitting on the sofa, sipping hotel room cheap coffee near the window, watching the Manchester rush hour traffic crawl past.

Simon yawned, "What you doing?"

"Couldn't sleep," was Lucy's curt response.

Simon sat up. "What's wrong with you this morning?" He pulled a face.

"Nothing!" she barked returning her attention to the traffic outside.

Shit, had she heard the news, he thought. He got out of bed and joined her on the sofa. "Come on, something's wrong. What is it?" He stroked her leg.

Lucy exploded, tears rolled down her cheeks and she sobbed. "Well it could be you! Snapping my head off yesterday or the fact that I got all dressed up in new lingerie to find you already asleep on the bed."

Simon opened his mouth to defend himself but she cut him short. "Or it could be you was muttering Louisa in your sleep!"

"I'm sorry." Simon reached forward to hug her but she pulled away. He continued to grovel. "I am sorry for snapping at you. What can I say – I'm a short-tempered miserable old prick!" He offered a smile but Lucy was not at all amused. He continued, "And Louisa is my sister. I'll make it up to you. Let's go to the Trafford Centre. I'll treat you to lunch, buy you something nice and then you can try the fancy knickers on for me again tonight. What do you say?"

Simon looked straight into Lucy's eyes. Half smiling she agreed. "Okay but, I have not forgiven you. You have a lot of making up to do."

Simon kissed her. "And I will enjoy doing it too."

He left her in her window seat and went into the bathroom. He was pissed off with her and in fact he didn't have a clue what was happening back in Leeds. He felt sure it was safe enough to venture out this morning and besides he couldn't bear the thought of a full day trapped in the hotel room with her.

"I'm ready when you are," Simon declared.

They left the hotel room in better spirits. The five-mile journey took forty-five minutes in the traffic. Neither really spoke until Simon eventually broke the silence.

"Have you heard from your mate at all?"

Lucy answered, "Annie?"

Simon nodded.

"Ye, she texted me this morning. The police are going to arrest Mark's best friend but he's gone missing," she replied.

Shit! Shit! Shit! Simon thought. Maybe it's too risky to go out but then again it's much easier to hide in a large crowd.

"Oh that's good then," he said trying to hide his true feelings.

The Trafford Centre was really very busy even though it was mid-morning.

"I wonder if something's going on today. There's a lot of kids in rugby tops hanging about," Lucy observed.

Once inside, they realised there was a press conference and publicity for the Grand Final. It was too late for Simon to pull Lucy away; he couldn't think of a good enough excuse. Both teams were in the food hall and were attracting a rapturous reception.

Lucy shouted, "Come on, I'll introduce you to Matt and Ed, Annie's sons."

"NO!" Simon snapped. Lucy scowled at him. He justified his outburst. "There'll be loads of kids and press around 'em. We can meet them tomorrow or we'll arrange a night out when we get back. We can see them anytime, the kids here can't." He pulled Lucy towards him. "Please I'd like to meet them when we can talk to them properly and for now I want you to myself."

Lucy was disappointed but agreed.

Simon ordered coffees whilst Lucy watched the players encircled by a mass of children. The players seemed to be enjoying the experience as much, if not more than the children.

Simon joined her; she smiled and sipped the hot coffee.

Simon spoke first. "I'm sorry Lucy. It's not been much of a break for you. I am a miserable old sod."

Lucy smirked, "Yes you are!" She held out her hand and he held it. "But I love you just the way you are."

Simon laughed and began singing his own version of the song of the same name, embarrassing Lucy. She giggled and begged him to stop.

They finished their coffee and behaved like lovesick teenagers giggling and pushing into each other as they walked.

*

Matt and Ed played rugby with the makeshift rugby ball, made from a screwed up piece of paper, which incidentally was their instructions for the day's events. They pretended to play the ball and tackle each other much to the delight of the crowd of onlookers. Matt stood up to start signing autographs when in the distance he thought he saw his mum's friend Lucy. He stared at the woman who was fooling around with a man who had his back to Matt. Matt tapped Ed on the shoulder.

"Is that Lucy, Mum's friend?" Matt asked.

Ed screwed his nose up, strained his eyes and nodded. "It is. And look who she's with!"

"Oh my God! When did they get together?" Matt asked.

"It seems odd though don't you think?" Ed said.

"Erm very odd. Come on," Matt pulled Ed towards Marcus.

"Boss," Matt said, "We are just going to say hello to my mum's friend Lucy. She's here with that Garry Pearce which is weird!"

Marcus replied, "Matt you're needed for the press conference now. You can catch up with them after."

Ed said to Matt, "I'll go."

Before Marcus could step in, he skipped through the crowd and shouted, "Lucy."

Pearce turned around, looked at Ed and ushered Lucy away. Ed returned to watch his brother work his magic with the press. As usual he had them eating out of his hands. He threw a look at Ed but Ed just shrugged his shoulders.

Leaving the conference table, Matt asked Ed, "So what happened?"

"I called Lucy but he pulled her away. I've got a bad feeling about this. Why would he go in the opposite direction – he knows us!" Ed replied.

"Maybe it's because he knows we think he's a complete tosser!"

The boys laughed and continued to sign autographs until Marcus announced they were leaving.

*

Lucy pulled at Simon's arm. "Stop it, you are hurting me!"

Simon stopped. "Let's get out of here." He started walking off. Lucy stood her ground and refused to move.

"NO Simon. I'm not ready to go back to the hotel. I want to shop. Are you ashamed of me? Why don't you want us to be seen together? You married?" She almost burst into tears but held it back.

Simon's face reddened. He felt like he had a spoilt brat with him, aged two not in her mid-twenties. "We'll talk back at the hotel. I'm not discussing it here, in front of all these people."

He tugged her arm and she complied.

They stomped around the Trafford Centre. He wasn't in the mood for shopping now and she was too angry to even window shop. They decided it was a waste of time being there and left.

At the hotel, Lucy headed to the bar. Simon followed and ordered the drinks while Lucy sulked in the corner.

"It's a double," Simon barked and practically threw the glass at her. She picked it up and downed the drink in one, slamming the glass down on the table.

"Would you like another?" Simon asked.

"Yes," she barked.

Simon returned from the bar with two more doubles. She half smiled.

Simon said dryly, "Thought you might down these two as quick too. You'd put some of my rugby mates to shame."

"Dutch courage," Lucy said, taking another large drink out of the next glass. She was now determined to spend the afternoon paralytic.

*

"Hi Marcus, it's Mark Smith. Can you give me a call urgently please?"

No sooner had Mark left the message, Marcus was on the phone to him. Mark explained the situation with Pearce. In return, Marcus gave Mark a brief outline of the boy's encounter with Pearce and Annie's friend Lucy.

Mark replied, "Hang on Marcus. Annie is here now. I'll put you on loudspeaker."

"Hi Marcus," Annie said. "How are my boys?"

"Hi love. I'm looking after them," Marcus said. "I was just telling Mark, Matt and Ed were at the Trafford Centre with the team and they said they saw Pearce with your friend, Lucy. The lads were really confused and concerned."

Annie interrupted Marcus, "Are you sure?"

Marcus defended the boys. "Positive, well the boys were positive. They were both adamant it was the two of them together. I'll let the lads call you after the training session. It'll be about an hour."

"Okay thanks," Mark said. "We are setting off over shortly."

Annie advised, "I need to call the police NOW!"

Mark added, "We'll let you know what they say."

Marcus added, "Annie don't worry about the lads they are out of harm's way. I'll look after them as if they're my own."

Annie replied, "I know you will Marcus. See you tomorrow."

Marcus suggested, "I'll come over to your hotel tonight and have a drink with you both. Ring me later."

"That'll be great, see you then." Mark hung up.

*

Harry pressed speed dial for Phillipa and said out loud, "Pick up, pick up!" The call went to the answering machine, so Harry hung up and dialled again. At the fourth attempt, Phillipa answered.

"Jeez what's the emergency Harry?"

Harry laughed. "Good morning to you too. I'll be there in ten minutes. We've got Chadwick. I'll explain when I get there." He hung up.

Phillipa was waiting by the door when Harry pulled into the driveway. She waved the children goodbye and got into the car.

"Morning sexy," she said.

"Good morning," Harry smiled.

"Come on then, how did you find Chadwick?" Phillipa asked.

"I didn't," Harry replied. Phillipa gave him a confused look. He explained, "James Benson, her work colleague, rang me at six this morning to say Chadwick had turned up at his flat in the early hours. She said she'd turn herself in but he wasn't sure. He decided to give her a helping hand and called me. Uniform picked her up just before seven and now we get to interview her." His smile was as wide as the Mersey tunnel.

"Yippee! Breakthrough!" Phillipa knew this was the bonus they'd been waiting for.

"I'm going to do the interview," Harry announced, "but I'd like you to sit in it too."

Phillipa could hardly complain. She'd been given Riley and at least she was still involved.

Harry turned the radio up as his press release was finally being aired.

"Hopefully the public will help us trace Pearce," Harry declared.

Phillipa agreed. "It'll be nice to get him before the match tomorrow. Give Mark and Annie a peaceful break."

Harry laughed, "You scolded me for getting emotionally involved in this case."

Phillipa admitted, "I did but they kind of grow on you. You can't help but like them both."

There was a scrum of press now camped at the entrance of the police station. Some shouted questions to Harry but he ignored them.

The Super was waiting in the reception area, quietly observing the behaviour of the reporters and photographers. She walked up to Harry and announced, "She's here. In the cells. I'd like to sit in on the interview."

Harry was taken aback by her request but he could hardly refuse.

Phillipa spoke, "Okay Ma'am, I'll look on from the observation room."

Harry asked, "Did you hear the press release?"

The Super nodded. "Yes and it's been on Sky News, Sky Sports News, BBC and ITV. The images of Pearce and Chadwick were shown as well. The incident room phones have been going mad. Shall we?"

They headed for the incident room. After spending a couple of hours reviewing the possible sightings and information they had received, they agreed it was possibly time for Harry to gather his thoughts for the interview ahead.

Harry's phone rang. He stepped into his office to answer it, closely followed by Phillipa.

"Hi Mark. Phillipa is with me too," Harry announced.

"Hi. Marcus has contacted me to say Pearce was at the Trafford Centre about an hour ago."

There was silence as Phillipa and Harry took in the news.

Phillipa asked, "Who is Marcus?"

Mark explained, "He owns Leeds, the Rugby League team. The team were at the Trafford Centre for a public engagement including Matt and Ed. They spotted Pearce with Annie's friend Lucy but her phone is switched off. Harry, the boys need looking after. I'd never forgive myself if something happened to them."

"Where are the boys now?" Harry asked.

"Training, then back to the hotel. The club will keep them safe for now but Pearce has to be found. It's heartbreaking seeing Annie panicking like this, especially when this weekend should be a massive celebration." Mark was getting emotional and his voice was quivering.

Harry said, "I'll be round in fifteen minutes."

"No, we are leaving for Manchester now." Mark took a deep breath. "Annie wants to be over near the boys. We will both have our mobile phones on."

"We'll sort things out here. We have Chadwick in custody. We'll be over to speak to Matt and Ed later and to see you and Annie. I'll keep you up to date."

"Okay," Mark said, "bye."

"Oh and Mark. Anything strange at all, ring me on this number or call 999. Stay safe. We're closing in on him."

Harry hung up. He marched, with Phillipa by his side, into the incident room.

"Right, listen up," he shouted.

He gave everyone an account of Mark's conversation whilst Phillipa contacted Greater Manchester Police.

The Super suggested, "Harry, you and Phillipa head over to Manchester. I'll interview Chadwick with DC Dunne. Any developments, we can discuss."

Harry said, "We need CCTV from the Trafford Centre. We need someone to find out who this Lucy is. Start at the college and then go to her home address. Then find out if any hotels in the Trafford area have been booked in Lucy's name. Speak to her neighbours, find out her recent movements." Two detectives left the room.

Phillipa spoke. "Sir. GMP are getting CCTV images and circulating them to all hotels, bars, stations and taxi ranks."

The Super added, "Check the street CCTV where this Lucy lives and works. I'll speak to the Super at Greater Manchester Police and ask them to set up a mobile incident unit at Old Trafford. The police room, from what I can remember, is too small and pokey. Let's put this to bed before eighty thousand fans turn up tomorrow."

Harry and Phillipa left the building. Luckily they had both already pre-packed overnight bags in their lockers, kept there in case they were called away on an emergency.

"You drive," Harry said. "I want to make some phone calls."

"Hi Annie, it's Harry. We are on our way over to Manchester. We are going to set up a temporary incident room at the stadium. Can you let me have Marcus's contact number and I will need to speak to Matt and Ed." Harry paused to listen to Annie. "I am sure he will not try anything at the Grand Final. They'll be over eighty thousand witnesses." He paused again. "I understand that Annie but they are key witnesses. I promise I will keep the interviews short but I need their information to help trace Pearce and your colleague." Again he listened, "Thanks. I'll speak to Marcus and make arrangements. We'll see you at the hotel."

He hung up.

"Problems?" Phillipa asked.

"No not really. The club has a media blackout and Annie is reluctant for us to interview the boys. She's agreed to let Marcus decide whether we can although regardless of what he says, they are key witnesses."

Harry spoke to Marcus, who was very amenable. It was agreed they could go straight to the team hotel and see the boys. Harry also agreed to a uniformed officer being posted within the hotel reception.

The phone rang.

"It's the Super," Harry announced.

"Ma'am," he answered.

"Harry we have a positive ID on Lucy Tucker and Garry Pearce in the food hall and in Barton Square at the Trafford Centre between ten forty-five a.m. and twelve fifty p.m. Their photographs have been circulated to all public venues, pubs, rail stations, restaurants and hotels. I've agreed with Greater Manchester Police that two officers be stationed at Mr Smith's and Ms Swift's hotel at least until you get there. We've also agreed two rooms for you both. It was a nightmare but I managed to wing it," she laughed.

Phillipa smiled and gripped Harry's knee.

"Right," Harry said. "We are heading to the team's hotel to speak to Matthew Swift and Edward Swift-Brown."

"Any news on Chadwick Ma'am?" Phillipa asked.

"No. The duty solicitor has been delayed. What next after the team hotel?"

Harry replied, "We are meeting up with Mr Smith and Ms Swift. Ms Swift will give us the information on Lucy Tucker. I know she's frantically trying to get hold of her. I've given Lucy Tucker's mobile details to the incident room. They are trying to trace it and are trying to trace her bank account details – hopefully she booked the hotel room on her account."

"Good, good. I have spoken to Greater Manchester Police and they've reluctantly agreed an incident room at Old Trafford. Let's hope we catch this psycho before the fans descend on the stadium."

"We will," Harry said confidently, trying to stay focused on the conversation while Phillipa teased him by stroking his groin with her left hand.

He hung up.

"You are a very naughty girl, you're driving," Harry said laughing, his very feeble attempt at telling her off.

The remainder of the journey was chitchat. They arrived at the team hotel early afternoon. The car park was full of fans and the press. Security was not as tight as they would have hoped but at least they had to show their ID badges four times to get into the actual hotel.

"Impressive!" Phillipa whispered.

"Well thank you," Harry smiled.

Marcus was waiting in the bar for the officers. After greeting them, he took them to the manager's office. It was a pokey room, darkened by the closed blinds. Marcus explained, "You won't be disturbed in here. I'll send the boys in."

Shortly after Matt and Ed turned up. Harry could see Annie in both of them. They gave their account of the Trafford Centre sightings and Harry wished Matt good luck for the game. They left.

Phillipa commented, "What lovely young men. I hope my kids grow up to be as lovely as them."

"They will. They have a great mum," Harry declared.

Marcus returned, "You got everything you need?"

Harry replied, "I think we have. We are heading over to see Mr Smith and Ms Swift now. We will be at the Old Trafford stadium later to set up the incident room."

"I'm coming over to see Mark and Annie myself shortly. I may see you there." Marcus shook Harry's hand. "Annie is a dear friend of mine and I want her to be safe."

"So do I," Harry agreed. "Could you make sure Matt and Ed remain within the hotel, please?"

"They will until they leave with the whole team for training and the game but that will be on the team bus," Marcus explained. "I've given Annie my word I will look after her precious boys plus it's in my interests too."

*

"Hi Mum," Ed said. "How you doing?"

Annie wiped away a tear and sniffled, "Going out of my mind about Lucy and you two."

Ed tried to pacify his mum especially where he and Matt were concerned. They were safer where they were. He explained what had happened at the Trafford Centre.

"Okay love," Annie sighed, "I understand. Look you just enjoy tonight and we'll see you tomorrow. Love you loads. Tell Matt we're really proud of him too and we'll see him tomorrow."

Annie hung up and broke down into uncontrollable sobs. Andrea and Charles tried to console her whilst Mark had gone to get their bags out of the car.

"Matt couldn't come to the phone. He was with Marcus and Billy. Oh Mum, this should be the time of our lives and look at me, I'm a wreck," Annie sobbed.

Andrea spoke softly, "Annie, listen to me. You have been through so much in your life. You have always impressed us with your positive outlook and your strength and tenacity. Lucy is not your baby. You have to stay calm and be here for your boys. You have worked so hard and sacrificed so much to get your boys to where they are today. Without you Matt wouldn't be playing at Old Trafford for your granddad's team. Let the police resolve the other matter."

Annie wiped her eyes and nose on her sleeve. "I know. I just can't believe this weekend of all weekends."

"We know but the boys are safe and you deserve to have a fabulous weekend. You have done so well bringing Matt and Ed up on your own. It's time you enjoyed the results," Charles added.

Mark returned with the bags and announced, "Harry and Phillipa are downstairs in the bar. Baby, you have to stay calm and enjoy this weekend."

"That's what we've told her," Charles said.

Annie got up and launched herself at Mark. She clung onto him as if her life depended on it. He tried to reassure her. "Annie we are altogether and the boys are safe. Marcus won't let anything happen to his investment."

Annie managed a smile.

"What about Lucy?" Annie asked.

"Annie, she'll be okay. She's a grown adult and the police will find her. Now, I suggest we go downstairs to the bar, order your favourite wine, have some food and start relaxing."

Harry nudged Phillipa as Mark and Annie along with Annie's parents walked across the reception area into the hotel bar.

All six of them huddled into a corner of the bar. Harry could see the strain beginning to show on Annie's face.

He spoke first. "We've just seen Matt and Ed at their hotel."

Phillipa added, "They are fine Annie. No concerns at all."

Mark asked, "So what's the latest?"

Harry leant forward. "Chadwick is in custody. We have received CCTV images of Pearce and Miss Tucker, and these have been circulated at all pubs, hotels, shopping centres and other public places. Annie, we need to know when you last saw Lucy."

Annie replied, "Last Sunday, the golf day. She spent the day at mine. She was so excited, she'd met this fella; she thought he was called Simon. She was all loved up but we had our concerns." She pointed to Mark and herself.

"What concerns?" Harry asked.

Mark announced, "Well he didn't want to be seen. We thought he was married!"

"We now know why," Annie sniffled.

319

"Phillipa, go let the Super know Pearce could have booked the room in a different name."

"Excuse me," Phillipa said leaving the group.

"Anything else?" Harry asked Annie.

"They have tickets for the game – we've given them complimentary tickets! We've left them at the main ticket office, the one at the back of the North Stand. They are in Lucy's name. She texted me yesterday to say they were in Wales," Annie replied with panic in her voice.

"Wales?" Harry asked.

"Yeah, he took her out for the day. What's he playing at?" she asked, a single teardrop glistened on her cheek.

"I don't know Annie but we'll get him. I know we are close, it's only a matter of time 'til we do," Harry said.

"Annie!" Marcus called as he walked into the bar. He practically walked over the rest of the group to get to her. He hugged and whispered softly, "The boys are great and safe."

Annie nodded.

"Mark." Marcus held his hand out and Mark shook it.

"I'll get some drinks organised," Marcus announced and left with Charles to the bar. Charles had always hoped that Annie and Marcus would end up together but Marcus had too much respect for Annie to ever ask her.

Harry continued, "We are working with Greater Manchester Police on this and the public response has been outstanding."

Phillipa returned. "Sir, we need to get over to Old Trafford and brief the team."

Harry acknowledged her comment. "Yes I think we have covered everything here, unless you have any questions?"

Annie shook her head.

Mark spoke, "Please find Lucy."

"We will do everything we can, you have my word."

Harry and Phillipa said their goodbyes and left.

The story was the top headline now and had appeared on every news bulletin with live feeds from reporters at both the hotels into the newsrooms. The hotel reception was filling up with photographers and reporters.

Marcus returned with no drinks. "I think you should eat at our hotel tonight. The security is tighter. I've arranged for a private dining area."

Mark turned to Annie. "What do you think?"

Two press photographers flashed their cameras into Annie's face. The security rushed in manhandling them out of the bar.

Annie replied, "Yes let's go." Annie just wanted a bit of peace and besides she was hoping to catch a glimpse of Matt and Ed.

*

Lucy was true to her word. By the time she'd had eight double vodkas, Simon had to carry her to their room. Her speech was slurred and she was, well, clingy.

"I love you Simon. Why don't you love me?" Every word was slurred and just about coherent.

He ignored her. He was short of breath from carrying her and fed up with her childish behaviour. He was losing patience.

In the room, he threw her on the bed.

"Come, come and join me," Lucy slurred, holding her arms out to him, "please."

Simon shot a look of disgust and retreated to the bathroom. He locked the door and switched his mobile phone on. Twenty-two messages flashed up. He smiled, God I'm popular, he thought. The cat was out of the bag so to speak. The messages were from so called friends leaving verbal abuse. How could you? Seemed to be the general theme. Easily, he thought.

He loaded the internet up on his phone and searched Sky News. There it was, breaking news on the home page, a photo of him and Lucy walking through the Trafford Centre. Shit, he thought. Then, laughed out loud. He needed to leave but he was over the limit. He would draw attention to himself if he drove now. He had no choice but to wait until he had sobered up.

Lucy had passed out on the bed. Good, he thought. Two hours and eight cups of coffee later, Simon was ready to go. He started packing his clothes.

Lucy stirred. "What you doing?" she asked, wiping her eyes then holding her head.

"Leaving," he said.

"Why?" Lucy asked kneeling on the bed, crawling towards him. "Please Simon don't go. At least let's finish the weekend together."

Simon shrugged, "Why? So we can argue here?"

"No," Lucy said.

"You are too clingy. This was supposed to be fun. I'm not ready for a full on relationship," Simon declared.

Lucy begged, "Okay I know that now. Let's just have fun then. Please Simon, let's finish the weekend. Please..." she flashed her eyelashes at him, "please."

He smiled and jumped on her knocking her flying onto the bed. He kissed her. It was the first time he'd made love to her with passion and she loved it. After sex, they laid there. She was reliving his touch. He was rather pleased with himself. He'd managed to turn it around so she was the guilty party! The decision was made – he would leave in the morning!

*

The Super was looking forward to interviewing Chadwick. It had been a long time since she had actually done some hands-on police work. The duty solicitor was with his client and the Super was about to go in and start the interview.

"Ma'am," an officer caught her attention, "phone call for you." He pointed to the office. She took a detour and spoke to Phillipa. Her response was short. "I will let everyone know. Simon. Do we have a surname? I will have the information circulated."

After giving instructions to the incident room, the Super went straight to the interview room. She met DC Dunne in the corridor and announced, "Come on let's get this over with."

"Good afternoon," the Super announced, "I am Superintendent Jeannette Hallam and this is Detective Constable Charlie Dunne. Please could you state your names for the tape?"

"Susan Chadwick," Chadwick mumbled.

"Ian Thompson, solicitor for the defendant."

"Do you understand you are under caution Miss Chadwick?" The Super repeated the caution statement, read out a list of possible charges including breaking the terms of her probation order, assisting an offender, assault of Ms Swift and sending malicious communications.

"That's quite a list," the Super announced which raised a half smile from the young duty solicitor.

"We have a lot to get through Miss Chadwick. The first part I would like to ask you about is your visit to the Leeds Business College on Thursday 10th October. You assaulted Annie Swift," the Super accused.

"I never!" Chadwick blurted.

"Miss Chadwick, we have CCTV footage and eye-witness statements that positively ID you."

"I meant I never hit her. I was there but I went to warn her." Chadwick's face reddened.

"About what?" the Super asked.

"It's all got out of hand. It's been crazy and I didn't even want a part of it." Chadwick threw her face into her hands and rested her head on the table.

"Miss Chadwick. This is very important now. I need to understand what has happened. Who was going to hurt Ms Swift?"

Chadwick lifted her head from the desk and sat staring at the wall.

"You need to help me out here," the Super said. "If you are in trouble or any pressure has been put on you, we can help you." The Super paused. "Look at me Susan."

Susan turned to face the Super. "Why should I help you? You fucking put me away for summat I dint do!"

The Super smiled, "Susan, Mark Smith positively ID'd you and you were sectioned after a very thorough psychiatric assessment."

"I never stood a chance. I was set up and framed," Sue shouted.

"If that's the case, let's put it right now," the Super said. "Help me put away the right people."

Chadwick's expression and body language softened a little. She suspiciously looked the Super up and down, not knowing whether to really trust her.

"We can get this sorted. Please trust me. I can help you."

Chadwick sighed, "It's a right balls up. When I was younger I was a big Wigan fan. I loved it. Me and me mates would hang out at the club, go out in town where the players were and we got friendly with some of 'em. They loved the attention."

"Did you have relationships with any of them?" the Super asked.

She looked down. "Not relationships, quickies and a few fumbles but nowt until I met Garry."

"Garry?" Super asked.

"Garry Pearce," Sue said, "he was different. He'd take me out for meals, treated me nice and bought me nice things. After a couple of months, I moved into his flat." She paused and drank water. "It was great. He spent some of his money on a pub for his retirement. We moved in there and that's when it got fucked up." She paused again reliving the past in her head. "He wanted me to be 'nice' to his best friend – he wanted to share me. I didn't want to but he gave me ten grand to do it and you've gotta understand that's a hell of a lot of money for someone like me."

The Super thought, that's what he must have told her. The Super asked, "When you refer to 'he', who is he?"

"Garry of course," Chadwick said so matter of factly.

"Continue," the Super ordered.

"At first it seemed easy money," Chadwick said. "All I had to do was be nice to Mark and he was such a gentleman. I tried to seduce him as Garry asked me to but Mark wanted none of it. Garry got really impatient and started threatening me, telling me I was shit at everything. Anyhows he threatened to throw me out if I didn't help him split Mark and his Mrs up."

"Why?" the Super asked.

"'Cos he said I wasn't worth keeping anymore."

The Super interrupted, "No I meant, why did he want to split Mr and Mrs Smith up?"

Chadwick smiled. "I see. 'Cos he was in love with Louisa. I thought he'd forget about her when we moved in together but he didn't, he was obsessed with her. He would go to any length to split them up. I had to share Garry with her but at least I had a bit of him. He even wanted me to…" She stopped.

The Super looked straight into Chadwick's eyes. "What? Do what Susan?"

After another deep breath, Chadwick blurted, "Try and poison Mark. He wanted me to seduce him then poison him but Mark was too in love with his wife and daughter. He didn't want to know me. The more I pushed the more Mark pushed me away, the more Garry wanted me to try harder. When Mark found out Garry had hired me in the pub, he went mental, and I mean proper mental. He screamed, shouted and punched Garry laying him right out on the floor. It was proper scary. Anyhows, that's when Garry came up with the idea of the rape. Him and Millard took me to the local police station, helped me give a statement and even leaked the details to the press."

"You knew it was wrong Susan. Why didn't you stop it?" the Super asked.

Chadwick defended her actions. "Oh I tried, and I really tried. I even packed me bags and left but they found me. Told me, they owned me and brought me back. Told me if I went to the police, they'd hang me out to dry."

"They?" the Super asked.

"Garry and Millard," Chadwick replied.

"Millard? He was involved from the start?" The Super was not surprised but pleased she could nail the slimy toad.

"He drew up the agreement over the ten grand," Chadwick conceded. "He's more mental than Garry. He's an idiot and I hate him. She's just as bad, that Louisa, she got off on controlling Garry."

"So what happened when you were released? You could have gone away?" the Super enquired.

"I had nowhere to go. My social worker helped me get a flat, a job and I was happy 'til they found me. Millard came to the flat and told me we had unfinished business. He forced me into his car and took me to Garry's pub. I tried to run in the car park but he had hold of me. He slapped me and told me he could put me back inside with one call to my social worker. They'd put another ten grand in my account and said they would set me up for blackmail. They said they had a new job for me." She paused to take a sip of water. "I told 'em no but they said I was in no position to argue and one word from them and I'd be banged up again especially as they had me on CCTV turning up at the pub."

"I'm not sure I believe all this Susan. It clearly looks as though you just went back for more?" the Super stated.

"It's the truth. I had no choice. They asked me to hire a car but I flatly refused. Millard smacked me about until I told 'em I couldn't drive anyway. They gave up in the end."

"So why did you go to the college then?" the Super asked doing a full circle back to the original question.

"I told you, to warn her. They were planning something big but wouldn't tell me what. Said it was need to know basis only and they'd tell me when they needed me. Anyhows, I went to the college to tell her who was behind it all but she got scared and turned to walk away. I grabbed her and she fell. I never meant to hurt her," Chadwick confessed.

"What I don't understand is why this continued after Mr Smith left his wife. You all succeeded in splitting them up. Why start again?" the Super asked.

"Dunno," Chadwick shrugged her shoulders, "you have to ask those two that!"

"You say Pearce and Millard are planning something big. What?"

"Dunno. Maybe it was the car accident. I DON'T KNOW!" Chadwick answered.

"But the car accident had already happened." The Super was confused.

"Yep I know but I got scared. What if that wasn't what they had planned? What if what they had planned was worse? The wreck was bad enough. The scene was scary. Pearce would go to any length."

"Hang on," the Super said. "Were you at the scene of the accident?"

Chadwick's face and neck reddened.

"No I wasn't."

"How do you know it was scary?" the Super pressed. "You were there weren't you?"

Chadwick conceded, "He made me. He forced me to go. Said he was only gonna scare 'em and asked me to take photos."

The Super was shocked by the admission.

"Well yeah, he told me I had to," Chadwick said.

"You took photos of the scene of a near fatal car accident and then left?"

"Well yeah but he told me to," Chadwick repeated.

"Don't you have your own mind?" the Super was losing patience.

Chadwick nodded. "Yeah I do but he scares me," she admitted.

"Enough to break the law and be complicit in attempted murder?" the Super asked.

The look on Chadwick's face demonstrated that reality was hitting home.

She defended herself, "I dint know they would go to the lengths they had. Honestly, they threatened to kill me. I had no choice, no choice at all."

The Super couldn't decide whether Chadwick was incredibly clever or stupidly thick. She knew for the time being, no more information would be forthcoming.

"Interview suspended at twenty fifteen," the Super declared.

"My client has been cooperative. Can she be bailed?" the solicitor asked.

"No," the Super answered, "not yet. She will remain in custody for possible further questioning and her own protection."

"Will that be tonight?" the solicitor asked looking at his watch.

"No it won't be. If you can be here for ten in the morning please. We'll contact you if we need you before then."

The party left the interview room. The Super returned to her office and rang Harry to fill him in on the details. After a lengthy phone call, she arranged for an arrest warrant for Sean Millard. Arresting him would make her year!

32

Lucy was up first. Excitable as ever, she showered and ordered breakfast in the room. She found her mobile phone and switched it on. There was no response. That's strange, she thought. She fumbled in her bag for the charger, trying not to wake Simon up.

There was a loud knock on the door and Simon jumped out of bed. "Who's that?" he shouted as he leapt to his feet.

"Room service," Lucy replied smiling. She took the tray from the waiter and placed it on the table at the front of the room.

"Full English, toast, coffee and juice, sir," Lucy impersonated a waitress. "You must have been in a deep sleep for the waiter to scare you that way."

Simon nodded, stuffing his face with sausage and egg. He was starving. They ate in silence both savouring the food. When they finished Simon announced, "I'm having a bath."

Lucy smiled, "I'll join you in a bit. Just want to chill."

She lay on the bed stuffed. She'd eaten far too much for her small frame. She tried her phone again but it wasn't switching on at all. A little disappointed, she put it back on the table. She wanted to talk to Annie or at least leave her a message. She hadn't made arrangements of where they were meeting or anything.

She could hear Simon splashing around in the water and decided to watch a bit of the morning news, hoping to catch a glimpse of Matt and Ed preparing for the game.

The limited channels included Sky Sports News and Sky News. She opted for the latter as it repeated what was on the Sky Sports News items anyway. The first news item was the weather, which provided the excellent news of no rain during the Grand Final. Lucy looked through her bag for her make-up. The news reporter then announced:

"We now return to our top news story. Police are appealing for members of the public to help the police locate two people who are wanted in connection with the near fatal road traffic accident involving Mark Smith, Annie Swift and rising Rugby League star Ed Swift-Brown. The two suspects are Garry Pearce, former

Wigan Rugby League centre and Lucy Tucker, believed to be Annie Swift's work colleague at Leeds Business College."

Lucy turned to the screen. Did I hear that right, she thought? Sure enough, when she looked at the television, there was a picture of her and Simon at the Trafford Centre yesterday. Lucy listened in disbelief.

"Sky sources believe Garry Pearce, travelling under the name of Simon, is wanted for questioning whilst police are concerned with the whereabouts of Lucy Tucker, who was last seen with Pearce at her flat on Thursday. Anyone with any information are to contact Crime stoppers on 0800 555 111 or call 101. The numbers are displayed on the screen now."

The television switched off, startling Lucy. She turned around to see Simon, Garry switch it off and throw the remote on the bed.

Lucy had frozen with fear. She wanted to scream but stood staring at this man she thought she knew, loved even. Neither spoke, each waiting for the other to make the first move. Lucy's mind was running at a million miles per hour. Finally she moved towards her mobile phone. Pearce laughed out loud and flashed the battery at her.

"It won't work without this," he smirked.

Lucy lunged forward but he moved it at the last moment, she stumbled into him. Pearce grabbed her arm.

"Get off me or I'll scream," Lucy warned.

He laughed at her. "You really think I care about what you do!"

Pearce grabbed her arms. She whispered, "So what is the plan now?"

Pearce just stared at her, looking her up and down with piercing, menacing eyes. She found it hard to breathe regularly. She broke free and jumped to the back of the bed. Pearce took this that she wanted to play games. As he jumped to catch her, Lucy jumped off the bed and ran to the door. She managed to unlock it but Pearce was too strong. He slammed her up against the door, the force of which shut the door. He forced his arm over her mouth, pinned her between the door and wall; she was helpless.

Pearce whispered in her ear, "I've got you bitch, now what shall I do with you?"

His free arm wandered down Lucy's body and under her dressing gown. She tried to wriggle free but there was no room to move. He pressed his hand on her inner thigh and parted her legs. Tears rolled down Lucy's cheeks and her beautiful innocent eyes displayed sheer horror. In desperation she sank her teeth into his arm.

"Ouch you fucking bitch!" Pearce shouted releasing Lucy from the corner. Blood trickled down his arm. Lucy fell to the floor, breathless, weeping. So paralysed with shock and fear, she could not stop Pearce dragging her by her hair to the bed.

Pearce pulled her up the bed. Lucy found her inner strength and screamed. Pearce punched her in the face, grabbed a pillow and placed it over her head. She struggled but it was fruitless. He pulled her dressing gown off and climbed inside her. She tried to resist but he wasn't taking no for an answer. She wanted to be sick. For Lucy it was like a knife was cutting deep inside her. His body too strong for hers, she could hardly breathe not because of the pillow over her face but because of the weight of this beast. What had she been thinking of? She thought he was trustworthy and the one!

"Oh this is good," he bragged, "better than anything we've done so far. Even better with your head covered."

Lucy was struggling to breathe and becoming light-headed. The pillow had loosened but Pearce's sheer body weight was crushing her body. She just wanted it to be over.

Pearce satisfied himself and pulled himself up to sit across Lucy's hips. He took the pillow away and held her wrists above her head.

"Enjoy that?" he goaded.

Lucy refused to look at him. Tears poured down her cheeks. Pearce used his free hand to grab her chin. He pulled her face in line with his and kissed her. She resisted but he gripped harder. She sank her teeth into his lip. Pearce tried to pull away but she had hold of him. He let go of her arms and with all her might she fisted him in the groin. He released her and left the room to lick his wounds. She could not move, the pain was unbearable. In a bid for freedom, Lucy rolled off the bed, staggered to her feet and moved towards the door again. She was so light-headed and could barely see straight.

Pearce re-emerged from the bathroom. He struck Lucy across her face, the fierce force of which knocked her off her feet. She stumbled and cracked her head on the corner of the table. She was out cold!

Pearce took her dressing gown off and carried her into the bathroom. He wanted to drag her but it would have led to more mess. He deposited Lucy in the bath. Packing his stuff, he put the 'Do Not Disturb' sign on the door, knowing no one would come until they checked out on the Sunday morning.

Leaving the hotel room, he pulled the peak of his baseball cap over his face. The hire car was in the car park and was his ride to freedom.

*

"I still can't get hold of Lucy," Annie fretted. "Can we check with the ticket office to see if the tickets have been picked up?"

Mark wrapped his arms around Annie's shoulders. "The police will have it covered Annie. No news is good news!" He squeezed her. "Now your parents will be downstairs waiting for us to have breakfast."

Annie stood up. "I'm not very hungry."

"You need to eat. The meal isn't until tea time."

"Night-time kick-offs are a nightmare," Annie revealed, leaving the hotel room. There's too much time to kill during the day."

"I'm sure I can help you pass the time," Mark suggested, pressing his body up against Annie who slapped his chest and replied, "Maybe later sex god!"

"Ooh I love it when you talk dirty," he replied, smiling wryly at her.

Andrea and Charles were already seated in the dining room.

"Good morning, did you sleep well?" Annie asked, kissing her mum and dad on their cheeks.

"We did, more importantly did you?" Charles asked.

Mark shook his head. "She tossed and turned all night."

Mark pulled the chair out and Annie sat. The waiter took their orders and brought free coffee and teapots.

"Have you got hold of Lucy?" Andrea asked.

Annie shook her head. Andrea saw the tears well into her daughter's eyes. "No news is good news!"

Changing the subject, Charles pondered, "I wonder what our Matt is doing now and how he is feeling."

"Nervous and excited, that's how I felt," Mark admitted.

"It was good of Marcus to let us see them last night," Andrea said.

"It was," Annie agreed. "It was also good of him to pay for all our meals and drinks. I tried to argue with him but he doesn't listen."

Charles added, "He's very fond of you and the boys. He's always tried to look after you."

Mark admitted, "I tried to pay him but he was having none of it. As a pundit versus Chief Executive we haven't always seen eye to eye but now I know him, he's a top bloke with impeccable taste."

Mark leant over and kissed Annie on the lips. She held his hand. Breakfast had become light-hearted and about the boys, just has it should have been. Charles, Andrea and Annie recalled stories of the boys' younger years whilst Mark howled with laughter.

"I'm sorry to interrupt sir but you have a visitor." The waiter pointed to Harry who propped up the reception desk.

"Ask him to join us please," Mark instructed. The waiter added a place setting and chair to the round table and showed Harry through.

Mark stood up. "Good morning Harry," and gestured for Harry to sit in the spare chair. "Coffee?" Harry nodded.

As he sipped his coffee, Harry apologised, "I'm sorry to disturb you this morning but I thought you might like to know Chadwick has been interviewed. She has claimed Pearce and his solicitor, Millard, orchestrated this whole sordid affair and what happened to you previously Mark. Pearce is travelling under a false name, Simon – but we don't have a surname."

Annie asked, "Have you found Lucy?"

Harry shook his head. "No but Sky News are running the manhunt as their main story, with live cameras here, at the team hotel and at the stadium. It's only a matter of time."

"Have the tickets been collected?" Mark asked.

Again Harry shook his head. "As soon as they are, we will be there. We have officers in this hotel, the team hotel and at the ground. I will drive you to the stadium when you are ready to go. I'm also going to stick around for the full game."

Charles smiled. "There has to be some perks to working with the lowlifes you deal with."

Harry smiled, "Indeed, something like that," he leant over the table and whispered to Charles, "and I'm a big Rugby League fan. I used to love watching this man play every week," he pointed to Mark.

Mark asked, "You were a Wigan supporter?"

"Still am – all my life," Harry admitted.

"A pie eater," Charles and Annie said together. The party burst out laughing.

*

Matt was called down to the early morning press conference. He'd agreed to do it but after eleven he would be locked away with his team. The room was packed with reporters and cameras, far more than the usual press conference with some faces that were not recognisable sitting around the fringes. Billy sat to the left of Matt and Marcus to the right. Leon watched from the press floor. Marcus had fully briefed him and was under strict instructions to intervene, should non-rugby questions creep into the conference.

Marcus began, "Good morning ladies and gentlemen. We are here to discuss rugby today and I trust you will all respect that!"

Well I can live in hope, Marcus thought.

Once the conference was opened, it was a free for all until Marcus brought it under control. He shot a disapproving glance at his press officer. The first question labelled Leeds as the underdogs. Matt responded really well, he was used to the press and their accusations. He despised them intensely but he had a job to do. One freelance reporter could not resist the temptation and stood up.

"Matt. How is your mum and her new fella?" He paused to gauge Matt's reaction. Matt looked at Billy, Marcus then looked to Leon for guidance, who signalled for him not to answer it. Marcus diverted the questions to receive them from the other side of the room.

"Do you wish your brother was playing today?" one reported asked.

"He will have his opportunity."

The same obnoxious reported shouted, "Unless someone tries to kill him again." This unnerved Matt who twitched nervously in his seat until Marcus placed a reassuring hand on Matt's arm.

Leon stepped forward and asked the reporter to leave. Naturally he refused to. A scuffle broke out and he was ejected from the conference. Marcus drew the conference to a close and exited with his star player.

Leon came running through out of breath. "I'm sorry, I had no idea who he was."

Marcus was curt in his reply. "Well you should have done!"

"Any news on Lucy, Marcus?" Matt asked.

"Not yet but I'm sure they will sort it," Marcus replied. "Ring your mum and see how she is if you want to. If it will put your mind at rest – don't let the rest of the team know, I don't want them all pissing off to make phone calls, Billy will never get them to focus again!"

Marcus had displayed his soft, human side more in the past week than Matt had ever seen in the ten years they had known each other.

"Thanks. I will do I think," Matt replied.

Once he'd spoken to Annie, he refocused on the game and bringing the trophy home, leaving Marcus to wrestle with the swelling numbers of the press. He and Billy had agreed to issue a press statement in the hope they would leave the poor kids alone. Marcus drafted it and handed it to Leon. "Maybe you'll get this right," he said sarcastically.

*

"Coming up, a statement from the Chief Executive of Leeds Rugby League, stay here at your number one station," the music blasted out of the radio. Garry had to listen to what the idiot had to say although the DJ was starting to get on his nerves.

Pearce's plan had changed four times during his journey around the M60. He really couldn't decide what was best – chancing it at Holyhead for a ferry to Ireland or going south and trying to persuade some sucker to give him a ride to France, either by lorry or boat. He opted for the latter as it gave him more options.

Heading south on the M6, he waited until the Stafford South services to pull in and fill the car up with petrol. Trying not to act suspiciously, Pearce covered his face with a baseball cap and jacket. Returning to the car, he felt really pleased with himself. The phone rang, it was Sean.

"Now then," Pearce answered.

"Where are you?" Millard asked.

"Like I'm gonna tell you," Pearce replied.

"Cheers mate," Millard said sarcastically.

Pearce laughed, "Ha, so how are you me old mucka?"

"They've issued a warrant for my arrest too. That bitch Chadwick blabbed big style. I'm on my way to France, to the house."

"Jeez I never thought of that," Pearce said. "I'm heading down the M6 too heading to the south coast. Thought if I got to France, I'd be home and dry. I could hitch a ride with you," he suggested.

Millard fell silent. "Nah," he said eventually. "Sorry mate but I've terminated our contract. Too risky. Jean and the kids flew out to France last night. I spent twenty-four hours convincing her I wasn't involved in anything dodgy. If she thought I'd help you escape, I'd lose everything including my bits!"

"I'll pay you?" Pearce suggested.

Millard paused for a moment. "How much?"

"Ten grand," Pearce suggested.

"Nah no way. I could get three to ten years for assisting an offender. Not worth the risk and as a lawyer in prison, I'd get crucified. Nah, ta but I've done all I can for you," Millard stated.

"Twenty grand?" Pearce blurted.

"You 'aven't got that much," Millard pointed out.

"I have, I'll sell the pub and the flats. They're no good to me now," Pearce advised. "Please Sean. One last piece of help – I won't ask again, in fact you never have to see me again. Just get me to France and you'll be shot of me," Pearce pleaded.

Millard pondered the proposal. "Even if I agreed to do it, how on earth am I going to get you over there. You're public enemy number one today!"

"Yeah but old news tomorrow. Come on where's your sense of adventure? I'll go in the boot of your car. Anything, come on please – it's really easy money!" Pearce pleaded.

Millard fell silent again, this time for a couple of minutes. Pearce was about to plead his case again, when Millard spoke. "Okay meet me at the Premier Inn on Folkestone Road, A20. We'll discuss it then." Millard hung up.

Pearce was convinced Millard wouldn't refuse face to face; his love of money was far greater than his moral values. Smiling, Pearce set cruise control and headed for Dover.

*

"Room maintenance!" the cleaner shouted, knocking on the hotel room door.
"Shit!" she said out loud, only noticing the 'Do Not Disturb' sign after she had disturbed them.

"Leave it," the Supervisor whispered walking past. "Dirty weekend in more ways than one."

They giggled as they moved on.

Lucy's body lay in a freezing cold bath, no one but Pearce knew she was there. The blood had congealed on her face and around the wound. She had woken up briefly to find she had no energy to try and move. She desperately tried to call for help but no sound came out. She couldn't move her toes to let the plug out of the bath. Instead she fell to sleep wishing it was all over.

*

After a long morning of pottering around the hotel, Annie, Mark, Andrea and Charles were increasingly restless. They couldn't bear to be penned in but owed it to the boys to stay put and out of trouble.

Mark had spoken to Marcus and he'd suggested they went to the stadium for when it opened at one thirty. He agreed to speak to the Hospitality Manager who would look after them.

With a spring in her step, Annie quickly hobbled back to their room to change. She wanted to get to the stadium, to feel a part of her boy's special day.

"I'm really excited now," Annie said clapping her hands together. "Today is about my beautiful angels."

Mark smiled. "It is my sweet. It is."

Annie hugged Mark. "Whatever happens Mark, I'm glad we met and I love you more than I've loved anyone."

Mark kissed her head. "I love you too. Thank you for letting me be a part of your incredible family. Now come on, we have a match to go to."

Annie squealed with excitement.

"Do you think Annie will be strong enough to cope with all of this?" Charles asked, leading his wife back to their room.

Andrea laughed. "Oh my God of course she is. After everything life has thrown at her, she's always bounced back. She once said to me she felt like she was made of rubber. The harder she fell, the higher she bounced back."

Charles beamed with pride. "She has, hasn't she?"

Andrea nodded. "I'm so proud of her, I could burst. Through it all she managed to raise two talented, fine young boys. I'm not sure I could've done what she's done." Andrea's eyes welled with tears.

Charles put his arm around Andrea. "Now come on. Save your tears for your grandsons. We need to be happy and strong."

Andrea nodded, "I know. They're tears of pride and happiness, not sadness."

As they changed, Charles confessed, "I have to admit, I don't like what these idiots are doing to my family but I've warmed to Mark. Once this mess is cleared up I think our daughter will have the happy ending she's longed for."

"And deserves," Andrea added.

After an hour they reconvened in the hotel reception.

"Now before we go, I have something to give you all," Charles announced.

Everyone looked at him. Out of his pockets, he produced a packet of handkerchiefs for Annie and Andrea. "And one for you Mark too. I know you're soppier than these two."

Andrea, laughed and stated to Charles, "You better have your own packet too 'cos you're not sharing mine!"

Charles produced two ironed and folded handkerchiefs from his pocket. The whole party laughed including Harry.

Leaving the hotel was a challenge. Even though the security staff had tried in vain to keep photographers and reporters confined to the public footpath outside the grounds of the hotel, some had defied them and scaled the walls. The party were bombarded with questions and flashing cameras. The party jostled to get into Harry's car. Annie almost lost her footing but Mark unceremoniously bungled her into the back seat.

"Wow, anybody would think we were famous," Charles said trying to maintain the light-hearted mood.

Annie laughed, "Thank God we are nobody then."

Mark added, "But Ms Swift you can never be described as 'nobody'."

Harry piped up, "You're tomorrow's fish and chip wrapping," and laughed to himself.

"Oh my word, thanks for that Harry! You know how to boost someone's ego!" Mark said laughing.

"If you don't laugh, you'd cry. That was terrifying," Andrea concluded. Charles, already holding her hand, gripped it harder.

Mark asked, "Any updates since this morning Harry?"

Harry shook his head. "Not yet but I'll check in when we get to the stadium."

The rest of the journey was much more relaxed with everyone's focus returning to the Grand Final and Matt's appearance.

Marcus was outside the hospitality entrance at Old Trafford when Harry pulled up outside.

Mark whispered, "Perks of a police escort, we don't have to walk."

Harry smiled but Annie dug her elbow into Mark's ribs, causing a play fight to break out between them. As usual Annie had the final dig when she grabbed his little finger and twisted it. He submitted like a baby.

"Never fails," she said laughing.

"For a Leeds lass, this stadium holds so many happy memories for you Annie," Charles said looking up at the South Stand.

"Yep and it's always great to hear Leeds fans belting out *Marching on Together* at Man U's ground," Annie added.

Mark agreed. "Yep and it's always Rugby League fans, not footie fans," Charles replied.

Mark laughed, "Yeah once a blue moon, Leeds United play here and it's even rarer for them to win owt."

Charles quipped, "Blue moons are dirtier words here than Leeds United!"

"Very true," Mark agreed.

"Welcome to Old Trafford," the doorman said as they showed their hospitality passes to him, "this way."

"I'll take it from here," Marcus announced and shook the doorman's hand.

It was quite a squeeze with seven in the small lift but it beat walking up the winding staircase to the suite. The suite looked magnificent with the sun beaming through the massive windows, shining on the blue and amber decked tables.

"Wow," Andrea said, her mouth wide open.

"Close your mouth Mum," Annie smiled.

"Impressive, isn't it?" Marcus said to Andrea and turned to Mark, ushering him away from the main group. "Right I've put you on a table overlooking the pitch with me and Alicia. She'll be here in about an hour – doing her hair!" Marcus rolled his eyes. "I've organised a tab for the table so just get what you want."

Mark objected, "No way Marcus. This is my treat for Annie and her parents and you paid last night. Let me pay?"

"No honestly this is on me," Marcus said, "but these are my adopted family too. Besides it's on my business expenses." Marcus smiled. "If it makes you feel more comfortable, give a donation to the foundation."

Mark smiled. "I will do that and thanks Marcus."

Marcus replied, "Honestly Mark, it's my pleasure. Annie and the boys are like my family and I'm glad she's so happy in spite of what is going on. Besides there's a massive surprise for you all."

Mark looked at Marcus signalling for him to spill the beans but Marcus shook his head, smiling with a wait and see look. Mark smiled. Marcus left to greet other guests.

Mark re-joined the table. "What was all that about?" Annie asked.

Mark kissed her cheek. "He's only gone and opened a tab at the bar for us all."

Annie shook her head. "What's he like?"

"I know. I tried to argue but we've agreed you and I will send a donation to the foundation."

"We'll add to that too," Charles added. "Now ladies, wine?"

Both nodded. At the bar, Mark told Charles what Marcus had disclosed about a surprise.

"What do you think it is?" Charles asked.

"Honestly – I think he's made Matt captain," Mark suggested.

Charles beamed with pride.

"Not a word to Annie or Andrea," Mark warned.

"What are you grinning at?" Andrea asked Charles, who poured the wine into two glasses resembling goldfish bowls.

"Nowt. Just happy to be here," Charles blushed. "Where's Harry and Phillipa?"

"Gone to work," Annie said eyeing her dad up and down suspiciously.

Charles defended himself. "What?"

Annie smiled and shook her head.

*

"So far, we have no sightings of Pearce and Lucy Tucker since yesterday," Harry addressed a crowd of plain clothed and uniformed officers.

"The ticket office have confirmed they have not collected their tickets," Phillipa added. "Two colleagues are in the ticket office should they appear."

"Which seems very unlikely now," Harry continued. "You all have mug shots, watch for them although I suspect they are long gone out of Manchester now."

"Sir, Superintendent Hallam would like to speak to you," an officer spoke nervously across the filled room, in a very strong Mancunian accent.

"We'll leave it there for now. You all know what to do and where to go. Keep in touch." Harry dismissed everyone. He and Phillipa listened to the call from the Super.

"Ma'am, it's Harry. Phillipa is here too."

"Good afternoon to both of you. We have drawn a blank so far in all the hotels in the Salford area. We are expanding the search but whilst Miss Tucker's phone can't be traced, Pearce's was traced on the southbound Stafford services on the M6 about two and half hours ago. He received one call from Millard then we lost it again. Unless they're switched on we can't trace them," the Super explained.

Harry said, "Well we now know he's left Manchester, so Mark and Annie are safe. He's heading to the south coast."

"Have the ports been informed?" Phillipa asked.

"Yes and I've emailed his and Miss Tucker's images to all the forces on the south coast."

"Where was Millard?" Phillipa asked.

"Just north of Felixstowe on the M1," she answered.

Phillipa and Harry said, "Dover!"

The call was terminated.

"Well everyone is looking for the two scumbags and Miss Tucker. Our job is to look after Mark and Annie," he sighed deeply. "So I suppose we'll have to suffer some fine food and a rugby match!"

"Jeez it's a tough job but I think we'll cope," Phillipa smiled.

*

Charles and Andrea had never experienced anything like it in their lives. Neither was interested in sport other than encouraging their grandsons to do well. At 5.15 p.m. the party decided to leave the comfort of the suite and join the 80,000+ fans on the terraces. The noise was deafening and hit them when the doors were opened. The team appeared from the tunnel. Annie shouted, screamed and held her grandfather's scarf aloft. Ed waved enthusiastically from the side-lines. Andrea and Charles skipped down the stairs to hug their grandson, even though he'd only just left them. He squeezed his grandma and picked his grandpa off the floor. Mark and Annie joined them.

"We're here Mum, Matt playing in the final for our home club and me in this," he pointed to the tracksuit. "I could burst!"

"We are all really proud of you both." Mark patted Ed on his back.

"Cheers. You all okay?" Ed asked.

"We are mate," Mark said. "Savour today, it's your turn next season. Tell Matt we love him and whatever happens he's our superstar." Mark's voice broke.

Charles ribbed him, "Told you, you'd need the tissues first."

Annie cuddled Mark. "Two proud parents eh?"

Mark nodded.

"So are we," Charles said.

"Enough of this soppy talk, this is Rugby League!" Ed laughed singing *Marching on Together*, the crowd responded by joining in.

Matt was completely focused. He didn't want to speak to Annie because he knew she'd be emotional and would make him feel much more nervous. He'd go to pieces if he hugged her.

Ed went to join the team on the pitch and placed the kicking tee on the pitch for his brother to practise. Finally, the team disappeared into the tunnel for their last minute team preparations.

The match announcer gave full details of the teams, starting with Wigan. Annie screamed in delight when Matt was confirmed as the Leeds number 13 and captain.

Mark turned to Charles. "Told you."

"You knew?" Annie asked.

"Suspicion that's all," Mark admitted.

Harry and Phillipa took their seats. Mark leaned over Annie. "Any news?"

Harry whispered, "Pearce had been traced heading south. We are trying to track him but he's not here."

Mark nodded. Annie asked about Lucy.

"We think she must be with him," Phillipa added.

The teams emerged to fireworks and an almighty roar. After the anthems, Matt kicked off long and deep towards the western terrace. The first half was not classic Rugby League with a lot of spilled ball from both sides. At half-time, the score was an unbelievable 2–2.

Annie and Andrea remained in their seats at half-time. The boys disappeared to the bar. Annie was approached by fans, ex-players and players' wives all expressing their anger on hearing of the recent events. Without exception the support was overwhelming.

"Well Annie one good thing out of all this is people recognise how wonderful you are." Andrea hugged her daughter.

Annie admitted, "It's strange and nice but the recognition for my hard work is out there on that pitch."

Mark and Charles returned with drinks along with similar tales of support.

Whatever Billy said at half-time, it worked. Three unanswered, converted tries in fifteen minutes saw a commanding 20–2 lead to Leeds. Matt had set one try up, kicked a forty twenty and scored three goals and a penalty.

Annie had lost her voice. She and Andrea were going mental and to the fans' delight were caught on the big screen joining in the celebrations.

Wigan scored and the crowd's noise waned a little until Leeds got within ten metres of the Wigan try line again. At the play of the ball, the hooker passed the ball to Matt who slotted the ball over the crossbar for a one-point drop goal. The score was 21–8 and Leeds looked even fresher. Wigan on the other hand, had used their ten interchanges with ten minutes to go.

On Leeds' next set of six, Matt played the ball to the winger, who skipped past four defenders to score an easy try on the right wing. Matt converted to make the final score 27–8. The cup was coming home to Leeds. When the final hooter blew, the team and fans celebrated in style. Matt found Marcus on the pitch and hugged him, picking him up off the floor. Marcus pointed to the crowd and Matt approached the South Stand. He caught sight of his mum and family, kissed the badge on his shirt and blew them all a kiss, mouthing he loved them. He turned away wiping tears from his face. Annie and Andrea were sobbing their hearts out. Even Charles and Mark couldn't contain their emotions and when their images appeared on the big screen, the Leeds fans cheered.

Matt's speech, on collecting the trophy was even more emotional. Ed got permission to join his family for the speech and held his mum and grandma's hands. Matt nervously began to speak.

"Wow what a night." The crowd cheered. Matt waited until the noise subsided. "First of all, I'd like to thank Wigan and their fans, quality club and quality people." The few Wigan fans left cheered. Matt continued, "Thank you to all our sponsors, directors and staff. And you, our fans," the cheers erupted again, "you never let us down." The crowd chanted Matt's name, he buckled and his lip quivered. He held his hand in the air and the crowd stopped. "To Marcus and Billy for building such a great club and team and most of all to my beautiful, gorgeous mum," he pointed to her, "thank you for being there for me and Ed and for everything you have done. This is for you, Mark, Grandma and Gramps and most of all," Matt looked up to the sky and sobbed, "Great Gramps this is for you!" Ed squeezed his mum's hand. Andrea and Annie sobbed uncontrollably.

Harry turned to Phillipa and smiled. Tears rolled down her cheeks. "That was wonderful," she sobbed.

Mark hugged Annie. "I'm so proud to be a part of this family." He was crying too.

Ed tutted, "The water table in Manchester has increased by five metres tonight. I'm swimming down to the pitch." Ed could always make people laugh.

"Come on, I'll let you have a champagne with me," Charles said, putting his grandson in a headlock. The lingering fans laughed and took photographs on their phones.

*

"It's me. I'm using this number. Pick up the bleeding call." Pearce left a message on Millard's phone.

The phone rang. "I didn't know it was you," Millard said. "Whose phone you using?"

"Lucy's," Pearce replied.

"She's not with you is she?"

"Nah I dumped her. I'm about forty minutes away. Where are you?"

"Just got here but the place is swarming with police. We need to rethink this. Looks like they've sussed," Millard concluded.

"Ashford?" Pearce asked.

"Yep but no more phone contact. Get rid of 'em. Meet you in Ashford station. I've got that credit card we set up for Chadwick. I'll go online and book us two tickets return so it don't look suspicious." Millard had it all worked out. "I'll book us on a train about elevenish. In Paris we go our separate ways."

Pearce agreed. Switched off the phone and threw it out of the window. He thought about how he was going to escape. Providing he wasn't spotted his passport was in the name of Simon Thompson. He should get away with it, providing no one had found the silly bitch, he thought.

In the distance he could hear sirens. His heart began to beat fast. The police car was rapidly approaching from behind. Pearce could hardly breathe. Panic stricken, he maintained his speed at seventy mph and tried not to attract attention. His heart rate had reached fever pitch when the car sped past. He let out a huge breath and laughed out loud.

*

The executive suite erupted when Matt and the team walked in. Once the team had met all their sponsor requirements and posed for photographs, they were allowed to party in private with family and friends only.

By eleven o'clock, Annie and Andrea decided they really didn't want to see what the young men got up to once they were drunk.

"It's time to go," Annie shouted to Mark.

"Aww it's just started to get going," Mark moaned.

"That's what we're worried about," Andrea laughed.

"You stay if you want," Annie suggested, "I'm sure Marcus will give you a lift back to the hotel."

Mark smiled. "No chance, we stay together."

The four of them found Matt and Ed.

Ed put his arms around Charles. "Grandpa I love you so much. I love you all." He picked his mum up and kissed her goodnight.

Matt was more reserved than his team-mates and had only a couple of drinks. He never drank too much. "Night Mum, I love you," he hugged Annie, "thank you for everything. Will you be at Headingley tomorrow?"

"Of course, all four of us will be. Wouldn't miss it for the world. Marcus has told us to be there for ten, so we'll probably go from the hotel."

"Bye Gran. Hope you enjoyed today." Matt kissed her.

She replied, "The best day of my life since you were all born. You are a very clever young man." Matt smiled and turned to Charles.

"Thanks Gramps." Matt rubbed his grandpa's head.

"I've done nothing," he replied.

"You were here that's all you need to do. You're my hero." Matt squeezed him.

"Rubbish," Charles said all coy, "you're amazing Matt. Look after Ed tonight."

"I will." Matt shook Mark's hand and hugged him. "Thanks. I hope I did everyone justice."

Mark whispered in Matt's ear, "You were outstanding Matt, truly exceptional. I'll see you tomorrow. We'll be going about one o'clock to the airport."

Matt replied, "Yes. Can't wait to hear Mum's reaction."

It was a challenge to get the semi-drunken party back to the hotel.

"I can't believe I have to drive back to Leeds at eight in the morning," Mark said.

Charles suggested, "I can always drive!" slurring his words.

Mark laughed, "After the brandy you've had, you could fuel the car!"

*

Finally Mark and Annie were laid in each other's arms in bed, reliving the match and Matt's contribution.

Annie conceded, "I have always been really proud of the boys but tonight was out of this world. I thought my heart was going to explode."

"Mine too," Mark said.

Annie looked up at Mark and smiled. "I love you Mark Smith."

"I love you too Annie, so, so much. You are so amazing and an awesome mum."

Mark leant down and kissed Annie tenderly. She melted into his arms, kissing him, her tongue teasing his. Her hand played with the hairs on his chest. Mark slowly moved from under her and gently turned Annie so she was laid half under his body. He paused, looked at her, smiled and continued to kiss her. His mouth moved around her face and down her neck. Annie pulled her head back and gasped with pleasure. Mark's touch, sensual and slow moved down to her breasts. His mouth caressed her nipples. Annie moaned, enjoying every motion of his tongue. He rose and slipped inside her. Slowly he let her have every piece of him. He laid his body and soul to her. No frantic moves, only pure love. Annie reciprocated opening herself to take him. Both gave each other completely and their togetherness brought a deep orgasm to both, neither had experienced anything like it before.

They slept.

*

"Well, now I know how a taxi driver feels when they drop pissheads off," Harry said laughing.

"Oh they deserve to be merry. What a fabulous family," Phillipa said.

"That they are," Harry agreed. "The job makes you so cynical, you get used to only seeing the bad of society. It's not often we get close to see a truly great family with traditional values."

"I know," Phillipa said. "The strength within the whole unit is phenomenal. It makes you want to have it too."

Harry smiled, "You have. You're close to your mum and I'm looking forward to getting to know her. My room or yours?"

Phillipa laughed, "Yours, there's clothes all over mine! Something you'll have to get used to."

"Oh Phillipa you are funny," Harry smiled.

Once inside the lift, Phillipa pounced on Harry. She had shown incredible restraint whilst in everyone else's company. Now they were alone and no longer needed to pretend. Harry led Phillipa by the hand.

Entering Harry's room, Phillipa was undoing Harry's trousers. He negotiated the door and slammed it shut whilst fumbling with Phillipa's blouse buttons. They rotated around each other until they collapsed on the bed. Harry ended up over Phillipa. He kicked off his shoes then his trousers. Phillipa wriggled out of her clothes and pulled Harry up to the top of the bed. She bit his lip, turning Harry on even more.

"Steady on, I'll explode," he whispered.

"Yes please," Phillipa replied, gripping her hand around his erection. He was very close and tried to move her hand away.

"Not yet," he said.

Phillipa ignored him; she liked to tease him. "Make me!" she teased.

Harry knew she liked it rough although he was yet to discover her boundaries.

"Okay you asked for it," Harry said. He grabbed her arms and struggled but managed to clasp them above her head. She moaned with pleasure and tried to resist but he had a strong hold on her.

Harry couldn't wait any longer. Parting her legs with his knee, he pushed inside. Phillipa moaned loudly, making Harry push further.

"You dirty girl," he whispered.

Phillipa wrapped her legs around his waist and squeezed. "You love it!"

"I do, oh I do," Harry said breathlessly, trying not to come just yet.

"I have so much more to share with you," Phillipa gasped taking his full length.

"You do? Like what? Tell me please." Harry's breathing was deep and between each word.

"I like lots of things," she paused and bit his ear, "I like rough."

"I guessed that," Harry said trying to maintain his rhythm, "me too but how rough?" He was finding it increasingly hard not to reach his peak. Talking sex was a huge turn on for him.

"As far as you want to go," she teased, "love the handcuffs, being made to do things, being at your mercy."

"You're gonna make me come," he said.

She gyrated her hips and felt him swell. "That's the idea," she laughed. "You like me to talk about sex?" she teased, "I want you to tie me to the bed, blindfold me and play with my sex toys."

This final tease pushed both of them over the edge. They writhed together and climaxed, holding it in place for as long as possible. Harry collapsed in a heap.

"Jesus girl, you're gonna kill me!" he gasped.

"No," Phillipa hugged him, "but you're never gonna regret being with me."

"I don't and won't ever! My only regret is the time we've wasted."

Harry's mobile phone rang. It was the Super. Harry and Phillipa looked at each other and laughed. He decided to ignore the call, compose himself and then call her back. Phillipa crawled under the covers to wait for her man.

*

Taking the pay as you go phone from the glove box, he dialled the number.

"It's me," Pearce said. "I'm in Ashford now, parking up."

Millard confirmed, "Right, I'm waiting for you at the ticket sales. Hurry up, it's quiet here and I stand out like a sore thumb."

Pearce laughed, "Be there in ten max."

He hung up. Driving into the station car park, Pearce felt nervous but relieved. It had been an incredibly long day and wouldn't be long before he was free. He unloaded his bags, one of which had bloodstains on from the hotel. He double-checked the fake passport that Millard's 'friend' had provided.

Millard was waiting and they shook hands in silence. Pearce's heart was racing. The last thing he needed was being spotted or drawing attention to himself. There was a huge sigh of relief from both of them when they boarded the train. As it pulled away from Ashford, they looked at each other and smiled. Millard said sarcastically, "Au revoir, Angleterre!"

Pearce laughed out loud and ordered champagne.

*

"Good morning Ma'am," Harry said wearily.

"I'm sorry to wake you Harry but I thought you'd like to know Pearce has been spotted."

"Where?" Harry asked trying not to let on Phillipa was laid naked in the bed next to him.

"Ashford International Station, with Millard. They boarded the train at one ten a.m. We are liaising with the French police now. He boarded under the name of Simon Thompson. We've picked up the hire car, booked in that name."

"No Lucy Tucker then?" Harry asked.

"No but her phone was used near Dover. We are still checking for hotel reservations under Thompson for this weekend. I'll let you know if we find anything, but Harry." The Super paused. "SOCO found traces of blood in the boot of the car. We are waiting for confirmation of this. Will keep you informed." She hung up.

Harry recalled the news to Phillipa.

"How the hell was he allowed to leave the country?" Harry added.

"Someone's head will roll," Phillipa stated.

"Let's hope the French police cooperate. Bit embarrassing letting them make the arrest though!"

"Yep," Phillipa yawned.

At 3.45 a.m. Harry drifted off to sleep, listening to Phillipa's breathing.

33

"Oh my God, my head hurts," Andrea declared when Mark and Annie joined them for an early breakfast.

"I feel great," Annie announced.

"Good for you," Charles said, holding his head in his hands. "Why did you let me drink Andrea?"

Andrea replied, "You've only got yourself to blame. Have a fried breakfast."

"But no spewing at the table." Annie laughed.

"You all right Mark?" Andrea asked.

"Fantastic thanks." Mark pulled Annie's chair out for her. "Looking forward to flying out today."

"Morning," Harry said approaching the table.

Phillipa echoed his greeting but yawned.

"Join us please," Mark said.

"Everyone okay this morning?" Harry asked.

Annie smiled. "Yes mum and dad are hung-over. Setting such a bad example."

Charles threw a dirty look at Annie. "It's your fault, having such talented kids!"

Mark explained to Harry, "So far it's Andrea's fault for letting him drink and now Annie's for having great kids."

Harry laughed, "Well, you have to have a good excuse. Mine's the job!"

Phillipa sipped her coffee. "Annie what time is your flight?"

Annie finished the toast in her mouth. "I have no idea. It's a surprise."

Mark joined the conversation. "She hates surprises Phillipa. It's killing her not knowing."

"Okay don't rub it in," Annie smiled, "it better be worth it."

"Oh it is," Charles added. Andrea kicked him in his shins. "Ouch!"

"So you know too," Annie scowled. "Do you too?" she asked Andrea.

Andrea nodded. She couldn't lie to her daughter, Charles had blabbed.

Mark smiled, "Oh well Annie, you'll find out when you get to the airport. It's a shame we have to go to Leeds then come back to Manchester later."

"I know but I get the chance to drive your new toy," Charles added.

"If you've sobered up by then!" Andrea snapped.

"God, I didn't have that much!" Charles declared.

Annie told the party she'd received a text message from Matt advising her Ed had fallen asleep at half five on the floor of Marcus's hotel room. Marcus had decided to let him stay there.

Harry announced, "Well we, I mean, I had a phone call in the early hours from my Super confirming they'd had a positive sighting of Pearce and Millard in Ashford."

"Millard?" Andrea asked.

"Pearce's bent solicitor," Mark explained.

"We are liaising with the French police."

"You let him get out of the country?" accused Charles.

"It appears we did," Phillipa said.

Andrea tutted. Annie let the police off the ropes and spared them a lecture from Charles. "Was Lucy not with him?"

Phillipa shook her head and continued Harry's news. "Pearce is travelling as Simon Thompson. We are tracing to see if any rooms were booked in Manchester this weekend."

"We are optimistic we will find her today," Harry added.

Guilt overwhelmed Annie. She'd forgotten about her poor friend last night. How could she? She didn't know where she was and it was all her and Mark's fault. Tears welled in her eyes.

"Annie?" Mark asked tilting his head to one side.

"Sorry," she said using her napkin to wipe her eyes. "We can't go on holiday today, it's not right. What if…" she started crying again.

Harry spoke, "Annie we've got it in hand. Lucy's phone was used near Dover and we are tracing the hotel room where they stayed. We'll find her."

"But she might be," Mark said.

"Dead," Annie added.

Harry and Phillipa were silenced by her directness. Harry responded treading carefully, "It seems unlikely, we would have heard something by now. If you cancel your trip, Pearce has won. We'll keep in touch and let you know what's happening." He'd omitted to tell them about the traces of blood.

"Harry's right," Mark added, "we can't do anything here."

Annie reluctantly agreed to go away.

At 8.30 a.m. they loaded the car and set off back to Leeds. Harry and Phillipa followed them across the M62. It was a sunny morning with a light crisp breeze.

The journey back was uneventful, the peace only interrupted by the news reports of the sightings of Pearce and Leeds winning the Grand Final. The party agreed to call home and collect their bags and passports, so they could leave the celebrations as late as possible.

Things had changed since Mark played. After major finals, with the exception of the Challenge cup at Wembley, celebrations would have taken place on the bus home right after the match.

"What are you smiling at?" Annie whispered, not wanting to wake Charles up.

"I was just remembering how we'd celebrate wins on the bus travelling on the M62, going the other way of course."

Annie laughed, "How many of you pulled moonies at the passing cars and trucks?"

Mark howled with laughter, "All of us!"

Annie laughed and laid her head on his arm.

"So where are we going?" Annie asked.

"Home," Mark smiled, "you'll have to try harder than that!"

*

The train's motion combined with a whole bottle of champagne, made Pearce feel sick. Closing his eyes made it much worse.

Millard nudged him, "You see that guard over there?"

"Yeah, I'm not that pissed!" Pearce shouted, causing a few disapproving looks from parents who had sleeping children.

"Shush," Millard hissed. "He keeps giving us suspicious looks."

Pearce stared at the guard who looked away instantly.

"You see," Millard said.

Pearce closed his eyes. "You're paranoid. Chill out!"

Millard wasn't convinced and texted his wife then suspiciously kept watch. Something didn't feel right.

The train announcer advised in both French and English that there was a slight delay in alighting at the station due to an earlier broken down train.

"See? I've a bad feeling," Millard said anxiously.

"Shurrup, you big puff! You man or mouse? Nowt's wrong. It's typical – broken down train, it's like being in England!" Pearce mocked.

The train started slowing down and observed the ludicrously slow speed limits approaching Paris Nord station. Itching in his seat, Millard was growing even more agitated.

Pearce snapped, "For fuck's sake, you're gonna give us away. Now fucking relax. I'm glad we're going our separate ways in Paris. You're making me nervous."

"Where will you go?" Millard whispered.

"Dunno. Thought about hiring a car and travelling down to Spain. Can do some bar work."

"What about Sophie?" Millard asked.

"What about her?"

"Aren't you gonna miss her?"

"Yeah but when this has blown over she can come and visit me. Bring Louisa too."

The train ground to a halt.

"Well good luck," Millard said holding out his hand; Pearce shook it.

"Yeah you too. Give my love to Jean." Pearce laughed. Jean Millard saw right through Garry Pearce and detested him intensely. Millard gave a sarcastic smile and left the train.

The French Police aux Frontieres and the British Transport Police had all the exits covered. Millard was arrested trying to purchase a ticket to Toulouse where his wife would have collected him from the station.

Pearce alighted the train, bought cigarettes trying out his limited French with a strong North West England accent. Two French plain-clothed police drew up along each side of him and urged him to go with them. He tried to resist but they already had a good grip of both his upper arms. The game was over.

*

Harry and Phillipa were officially off duty at ten a.m. but Harry had agreed to stay with Mark and Annie. Phillipa had compromised between family duties and her beloved work and agreed with the Super she could take her kids to the homecoming party.

"Any news Ma'am?" Harry said walking into the Super's office. She was on the phone. Harry apologised for the intrusion but she gestured for him to come in and wait.

Once the phone call ended, the Super announced, "Finally the French aux Frontieres and British Transport Police have confirmed both Millard and Pearce are in custody. Honestly you'd think we were negotiating with terrorists with how long it's taken me to confirm it. They've been in custody for four hours. Four hours of wasted, bloody time! We need to find out which hotel he stayed in and where Lucy Tucker is."

Harry smiled. "You feel better now Ma'am?"

The Super softened. "I do actually Harry. Now, I've given strict instructions to the British Transport Police for interviewing the suspects but French law is blocking us. Apparently the police judiciaire are responsible for the arrest now. Once we have the go ahead, they will press for the information."

Harry was about to interrupt her but the Super put one hand in the air to prevent him. She continued, "The credit card used was in Thompson's name and was used to hire the two cars; Millard and Pearce used it to book the tickets to France. Card security is really shit in this country especially since they introduced chip and pin. No one bothers to check the signatures or names anymore."

Harry shuffled impatiently listening to another soapbox performance from the Super.

"Sorry, anyway, I suspect the hotel was booked using this too. We are in the process of checking all the transactions."

"How long is it gonna take?" Harry asked.

"Not long. I'm pressing for it."

"I know," Harry interrupted impatiently, "but we need to find Lucy Tucker especially if it is blood in the car."

The Super agreed.

Harry headed off to Headingley.

*

The celebrations at Leeds were very subdued in comparison to the night before. Matt, Annie, Mark and Ed were the only ones not nursing hangovers. Ed had still decided to wear dark glasses, even inside which resulted in an enormous amount of ridicule from his grandpa.

The players paraded onto the pitch in front of 7,500 adoring fans, most of whom probably felt the same way as the players. Matt and Billy were last out with the cup.

Matt spoke eloquently as usual and received a five-minute standing ovation.

Back in the bar, Marcus had arranged hot drinks and sandwiches. The coffee was a huge hit and any player drinking it, received copious amounts of ridicule from the rest of the team.

"We have to make a move," Mark whispered into Annie's ear.

She smiled, "Round up the boys please and I'll finish my drink."

Mark fetched Matt and Ed. They sat with their mum.

"Now boys," Annie warned. "Behave yourselves while we are away. I've left some money for food in the jar in the kitchen. Grandma and Grandpa will be checking up on you. Respect Mark's house please."

"Our house," Mark added.

"Respect our house," Annie repeated.

"I'll keep them in check!" Charles added.

"Bring it on Gramps!" Ed said.

"I mean it," Annie scolded.

Mark added, "Come on Annie. They're old enough to know if they have a party they have to clean up and replace anything that's broken."

The boys high-fived each other.

"You're fighting a losing battle, Annie," Andrea said. "The boys will be fine. Now come on, that plane to…" she stopped herself and put her hand over her mouth, "won't wait for you."

As they were leaving, Harry met them in the entrance hall.

"Good news," he said. "Pearce and Millard are in custody."

Annie and Mark hugged each other. "Lucy?" they asked.

"Not sure yet. We've traced the hotel where they were staying. I'm heading over there now. It's all good, enjoy your break."

"What a weekend," Annie sighed, sinking back into the passenger seat of the car.

"Yep and it's only the start," Charles said, taking hold of his wife's hand.

Mark looked through the rear-view mirror and smiled broadly at his future in-laws.

*

"Travelodge, Salford Quays," the Super announced to Harry as she joined him in the car. She continued, "Greater Manchester Police are on their way now. Let's hope we're not too late."

It was an arduous journey and in total would take less than forty minutes. A few times the Super held onto the door as if her life was in danger but she never commented on Harry's fast driving.

The Super's phone rang again. Harry tried to listen to the conversation but couldn't make out the news. The Super replied to the voice, "I see. We'll be with you shortly."

Announcing the news to Harry, the Super cleared her throat. "Staff found Lucy lying in the bath naked with a severe head wound. The ambulance has just arrived."

"Is she dead?" Harry asked.

"They wouldn't say – let's get there!" the Super said.

"Well do you have everything?" Andrea asked.

"Passports, tickets, Annie," Mark laughed. "I think I do!"

Andrea and Charles accompanied the couple into the check in area. Charles was getting quite emotional until his wife chastised him for nearly giving the secret away.

"Look after my baby," Charles said to Mark.

"I will. We'll ring when we land," Mark said.

Mark finally gave the tickets to Annie. Nervously she opened them; the first thing she saw was destination JFK. She screamed at the top of her voice and kissed Mark.

"You pleased then?"

Annie nodded jumping up and down on one leg. "Yes Mark, more than pleased. Excited! Happy! I love you!"

"Get gone," Andrea said, wiping a tear from her face. "Have a wonderful time. We are jealous."

They kissed and said their goodbyes. Annie hobbled through to the departure lounge hand in hand with Mark.

Back at the car, Charles complained profusely at the car parking charges even though Mark had paid them.

"Be careful," Andrea warned as he started reversing Mark's new car out of the bay. Charles shot a disapproving look at his wife who smiled back at him.

Andrea played around with the digital radio and found a local radio station. The news came on:

"Police have confirmed they have found a young woman's body in a hotel room in Manchester. Although it's too early to tell, eyewitnesses suggest it's the missing Leeds woman, Lucy Tucker."